ALISTAIR MACLEAN

Alistair MacLean, the son of [...] brought up in the Scottish Hig[...] age of eighteen, he joined the [...] war he read English at Glasgow University and became a school-master. The two and a half years he spent aboard a wartime cruiser were to give him the background for *HMS Ulysses*, his remarkably successful first novel, published in 1955. He is now recognized as one of the outstanding popular writers of the 20th century, the author of twenty-nine worldwide bestsellers, many of which have been filmed, including *The Guns of Navarone*, *Where Eagles Dare*, *Fear is the Key* and *Ice Station Zebra*. In 1983, he was awarded a D.Litt. from Glasgow University. Alistair MacLean died in 1987.

ALASTAIR MACNEILL

Alastair MacNeill was born in Greenock, Scotland in 1960. His family emigrated to South Africa when he was six, settling in the coastal city of East London. On finishing school he did a three year course in hotel management at the Hotel School in Johannesburg but, having nurtured a keen interest in writing since his teens, he returned to the United Kingdom in 1985 hoping to pursue a career as a writer. He submitted a manuscript to HarperCollins Publishers and, on the strength of it, was offered the chance to write a novel based on an outline by the late Alistair MacLean. He eventually wrote seven novels based on MacLean synopses and has also written five novels under his own name. He lives in Sheffield.

By Alastair MacNeill

ALASTAIR MACNEILL

Alistair MacLean's Rendezvous

HarperCollins*Publishers*

HarperCollins*Publishers*
1 London Bridge Street,
London SE1 9GF

www.harpercollins.co.uk

HarperCollins*Publishers*
1st Floor, Watermarque Building, Ringsend Road
Dublin 4, Ireland

This paperback edition 2021
1

Previously published in paperback by HarperCollins 2009

First published in Great Britain by
HarperCollins*Publishers* 1995

Copyright © HarperCollins*Publishers* 1995

Alastair MacNeill and the Estate of Alistair MacLean
have asserted their respective moral rights in this work

ISBN: 978-0-00-833667-7

Printed and bound in Great Britain by
CPI Group (UK) Ltd, Croydon CR0 4YY

MIX
Paper from
responsible sources
FSC
www.fsc.org
FSC™ C007454

This book is produced from independently certified FSC™ paper
to ensure responsible forest management.

For more information visit: www.harpercollins.co.uk/green

PROLOGUE

GLASGOW, 1995

'. . . Earth to earth, ashes to ashes, dust to dust; in the sure and certain hope of the Resurrection to eternal life, through our Lord Jesus Christ. Amen.'

The minister's eulogy was followed by a murmured 'Amen' from the small congregation of mourners who were huddled under an array of black umbrellas around the open grave on that cold, bleak Glaswegian morning. James McIndoe stepped out from under the protection of an umbrella and felt the light drizzle caressing his face as he reached down to scoop up a handful of soil which he tossed over the top of his father's casket. He stood motionless at the lip of the open grave, his head bowed respectfully in silent thought, his eyes lingering on the name which was embossed on the brass plaque on the coffin lid: *Samuel Donald McIndoe, 1914 – 1995.*

He stepped back and took the umbrella from his wife, Heather, who slipped her hand into his and squeezed it tightly. He watched as their two children each took it in turns to drop a handful of soil over their grandfather's coffin. Nineteen-year-old Isobel, who'd inherited her mother's beauty, was in her first year of a journalism degree at Glasgow University. The third generation of McIndoe to attend the prestigious university. And fifteen-year-old

1

James – or Jamie as he'd been known ever since he was a toddler – who wanted to follow in his father's footsteps and become a mathematics teacher once he'd finished school. James McIndoe was fiercely proud of both his children. And he knew that their grandfather had been as well.

A hand touched his arm, startling him, and when he looked round he found one of his father's friends standing behind him. The man gripped McIndoe's hand tightly, muttered his condolences, then moved off towards the row of cars which were parked outside the cemetery gate. The procession of mourners then dutifully filed past James and Heather McIndoe to offer their sympathies to the family on their recent bereavement.

'Who's that over there?' Jamie asked when the last of the mourners had left, pointing to an elderly man dressed in a raincoat and a trilby who was standing in a cluster of trees at the edge of the cemetery. 'He's been there for the past twenty minutes. Do you know who he is?'

James McIndoe shook his head. 'Can't say I do. He could have been someone your grandpa knew in the old days.'

'I don't recognize him,' Heather said, looking across at the man.

'I'll go and see what he wants,' McIndoe said.

Heather grabbed her husband's arm as he turned to go. 'Leave him. He's not doing any harm. If he wants to talk to us, he'll come over.'

'We'll see.' With that James McIndoe walked over to the man and introduced himself.

'My condolences to you and your family on your bereavement,' the man said in a clipped German accent.

'Thank you. Did you know my father?'

'Not personally, no,' came the reply. 'Samuel, that was his name?'

'Sam. Nobody called him Samuel,' McIndoe replied.

'I spoke with your father on the telephone last week,' the man told him. 'We had agreed to meet at his house today, but when I arrived I was told by a neighbour that he had died of a heart attack at the weekend.'

'What exactly was it that you wanted to see my father about?' McIndoe asked, removing his rain-spattered glasses and wiping them on his handkerchief. 'Perhaps I could be of help?'

'It was not so much me wanting to see your father as him wanting to see me,' the German replied. 'He has no doubt told you about the operations he carried out for the British SOE during the last war.'

'Yes, many times,' McIndoe replied with a wistful smile. 'I used to sit on his knee as a child and listen to his stories over and over again. I never tired of hearing them.'

'Then you will no doubt have heard about the covert operation in Sicily. February, 1942.'

'That was the one operation my father recounted to me more than any other,' McIndoe said in surprise. 'I heard it so many times that it got to a point where I almost felt as if I'd been there myself.'

'Then you will know there was always one elusive piece of the jigsaw which would have put the whole operation into perspective for him and, perhaps more importantly, also have put his mind at rest. And from what he told me when we spoke on the telephone, finding it had become something of an obsession for him since the end of the war.'

James McIndoe knew exactly what the German meant. He could still vividly remember as a young child overhearing the vitriolic arguments between his parents – before his father's successful career as a respected author of Roman military history could sustain what had ultimately become a fifty-year obsession – which were always centred on the same subject: his father wanting to dip into the precious family finances to pay some dubious informer who claimed to have the vital information he'd been searching for; and his mother yelling at him to start acting like a reliable parent and stop chasing after ghosts from his past. Her reasoning, however sound, never had any effect on him. It was an obsession he'd finally taken to the grave with him.

'And you have that last piece of the jigsaw?' James McIndoe asked suspiciously, recalling only too well those perfidious deals his father had struck with a succession of dubious con-men which had never brought him any closer to the truth.

The German nodded.

'Had he agreed to pay you for this information?'

The German's eyes narrowed angrily. 'How dare you suggest that I am in this for financial gain. I was a highly respected officer in the West German intelligence service for thirty-seven years. Your father insisted on paying for my plane ticket and for my accommodation while I was here in Glasgow. But any question of him paying me for this information . . .' He paused to wipe his hand across his mouth as if to remove the disgust he felt at such an accusation. '. . . I regard that as an insult.'

James McIndoe realized he'd touched a nerve and was quick to make reparations for his blunder. 'I'm very sorry, I didn't mean to infer anything by that. It's just that over the years there have been those who've tried, and in many cases succeeded in ripping off my father by giving him false and misleading information.'

'I am not one of them,' came the sharp retort.

'No, of course not.' McIndoe cast a despairing look up at the dark, overcast sky. 'We're getting soaked out here. Would you care to come back to the house? We can discuss this further there.'

'Thank you. I have a hired car parked nearby,' the German informed him. 'I will follow you to your house.'

McIndoe gestured towards the main gate. 'That's settled then. Shall we go?'

ONE

ITALY, 1942

He dispatched the German soldier with a single stroke of the finely sharpened steel blade across the throat. It wasn't his first kill; and he knew it wouldn't be his last. He slipped the fighting knife back into the sheath on his belt, then dragged the body into the thick undergrowth which bordered the deserted railway line. The moon ghosted out from behind the low clouds and, as he lowered the body silently to the ground, he caught sight of the soldier's face for the first time: a youth no older than twenty. It didn't bother him. Or rather, he didn't *let* it bother him. There was a difference. And it was that kind of disciplined professionalism which had made Lieutenant Sam McIndoe one of the most respected field operatives in the British SOE – Special Operations Executive – a clandestine organization which had been initially set up in 1938 to counter the threat of any German invasion of the United Kingdom by organizing subversive operations in enemy-occupied territory but which, with the appointment of Winston Churchill as Prime Minister two years later, had quickly had its brief changed to one of close collaboration with the various Resistance movements in occupied Europe.

A tall, athletically built Scot in his late twenties, Sam McIndoe had been one of the first operatives to be recruited under Churchill's broader proposals. His specialist arena was Italy. He spoke the language fluently; he was familiar with the customs; and he knew the lay of the land better than many Italians. He was a veteran of over a dozen successful sabotage missions against German military targets on the Italian mainland, which had already forced the commander-in-chief of the Axis forces in the Mediterranean, Field-Marshal Albert Kesselring, to increase the reward being offered for the capture of any SOE operative in Italy. The possibility of betrayal didn't deter McIndoe from his objectives, because he knew the higher the price being placed on their heads, the more damage the SOE – in collaboration with the Partisans – were doing to the Axis war movement in Italy. And being a persistent thorn in Kesselring's side only added to the satisfaction of that success . . .

He made his way back stealthily to the railway line, where he scanned the surrounding area. It was deserted. He cupped his hands over his mouth and blew into them to imitate the call of a night-owl. He'd never quite mastered the sound, he thought ruefully to himself as two shadowy figures emerged from the undergrowth on the opposite side of the track. Like McIndoe, they were dressed in black, with black balaclavas concealing their faces. They darted nimbly across the line and crouched down beside him. Both had been handpicked by the section leader of the Partisans in Naples to accompany him on the mission.

McIndoe looked at his watch. Eleven-seventeen P.M. The munitions train had been due to leave Naples at eleven. And if his calculations were right, it would pass that particular section of track in just under twenty minutes' time. He gestured to the rucksack one of the men was carrying on his back. The man handed it to McIndoe, who unfastened the straps and pulled it open. Inside was a 'fog signal' – a small, lightweight device containing a pressure plate fixed over three percussion caps and an amount of loose black powder, which could be clamped to the track by means of the two straps on either side of it. McIndoe attached the device to one of the tracks, then carefully connected a detonating cap to the spring snout which protruded from the side of the unit. Then, after securing a length of Primacord to the detonator cap, he removed a block of explosives from the rucksack and placed it in the small hole which one of the men had dug for him beside the track. He attached the other end of the Primacord to the explosives, then the hole was quickly filled in again and the loose soil smoothed over. The pressure plate would be activated when the wheel of the first locomotive passed over it. This would spark the percussion caps and ignite the loose black powder which, in turn, would activate the spring snout and set off the buried explosives. The size of the charge was large enough to derail the first locomotive and set off a deadly chain reaction which would hopefully destroy the highly volatile cargo of munitions which was being transported to a number of Axis bases in the south of the country.

'Let's get out of here,' McIndoe said as he straightened up and dusted his hands together. 'I don't want to be around when it goes off.'

They made for the jeep which had been parked out of sight on a dirt road fifty yards from the railway line. McIndoe got in beside the driver and the other man jumped into the back. The driver started up the engine and followed the winding contours of the road until they reached a stretch of coastline where the Partisans were to have left a dinghy for them to make their escape.

McIndoe was the first out of the jeep. He made his way cautiously down on to the isolated beach. He shivered as a cold, biting wind whipped in from the dark ocean. Satisfied that the area appeared to be safe, he moved towards the rocky enclave where the dinghy was to have been moored. The shredded remains of the boat were partially submerged in the water. It was obvious that it had been sabotaged. Realizing that they'd walked into an ambush, he turned to warn his colleagues, but found the two men standing on the rocks directly behind him, their submachine-guns now trained on him. They pulled off their balaclavas to reveal their faces. They weren't the same men he'd started out with from Naples. How had they managed to overpower the two Partisans and taken their places without his knowledge? The only time he'd been separated from the Partisans was when he'd had to deal with the German soldier who'd been standing guard beside the railway line. It must have happened then. It seemed the only logical explanation. And he'd walked straight into their trap.

'Drop the gun and kick it away from you,' one of the men ordered in German.

McIndoe reluctantly dropped his silenced Beretta submachine-gun on to the rocks at his feet and kicked it out of reach. 'What happened to the men who were with me?' he demanded.

'Dead,' came the disinterested reply. 'They weren't important. Not like you. We know that you're a member of the British SOE. Our colleagues at Gestapo headquarters in Naples are looking forward to meeting you.'

Gestapo, McIndoe thought disdainfully to himself. He should have guessed. And all the time his mind was racing as he desperately sought a way to extricate himself from what seemed to be an impossible situation. He knew he couldn't reach his own submachine-gun. And he couldn't spring either of the Germans – they had been careful to keep their distance. At that moment there seemed no way out . . .

'Who set me up?' McIndoe asked, now stalling for time.

The man shrugged. 'We're only following orders. Now, put your hands on your head and move towards us.'

McIndoe slowly clamped his hands on top of his head and was about to take a step forward when the man appeared to stumble off balance before managing to regain his footing again. For a moment he stared expressionlessly at McIndoe, then a trickle of blood seeped from the corner of his mouth and he fell forward lifelessly on to the rocks. The second German, seeing the bullet wound in his colleague's back, swung round and fired blindly into the thick foliage which lined the ridge overlooking the beach. McIndoe sensed his chance and made a desperate grab for his fallen weapon. The German noticed the movement and was already turning back towards McIndoe, his finger curled around the trigger, when a bullet struck him in the small of the back. He lost his footing on the slippery rocks and tumbled headlong into the water.

McIndoe retrieved his weapon and moved cautiously to where the man had disappeared. He drew back as a wave crashed against the foot of the rocks, showering him in a fine spray of water. Not surprisingly, there was no sign of the man in the dark, bubbling water below him.

'Lieutenant McIndoe?'

The voice startled McIndoe. He tightened his grip on his Beretta submachine-gun and swung round on the two men who'd emerged silently from the undergrowth. They were both wearing navy-blue roll-necked sweaters and matching trousers tucked into black Wellington boots. One of them was carrying a silenced Winchester rifle loosely in his right hand. 'Who are you?' McIndoe demanded suspiciously.

'Your fairy godmother,' the unarmed man replied with a grin. He was roughly the same age as McIndoe, and spoke with a distinctive British public school accent. 'I'm Lieutenant-Commander Reginald Stockton-Jones, captain of the Royal Navy submarine, *Unbeaten*. We're lying a couple of miles offshore,' he added, gesturing in the general direction of the ocean with a wide sweep of his arm. 'We're part of the Tenth Submarine Flotilla stationed on Malta.' He indicated the man beside him. 'This is Able-Seaman Saunders. He's the best shot we've got on board. Pretty damn good, wouldn't you agree?'

'Yes, he is,' McIndoe replied absently as he glanced down at the dead German. He tugged the balaclava off his head and suddenly the questions began to tumble from his mouth. 'What's going on? Who sent you? How did you know I'd be here? How did you know about the Germans?'

Stockton-Jones held up his hands defensively. 'Steady on, old boy,' he said with a chuckle. 'It seems that the local Partisans only learnt about the Jerries' plan to capture you after you'd already left Naples. And, as there was no way of warning you in time, they called your superior in Malta, Vice-Admiral Starr, and he immediately contacted the Royal Navy for help. We were the only British sub in the area, and I was given instructions to take a team ashore to bail you out. We only landed about five minutes ago. Our dinghy's hidden in one of the grottoes further down the beach.'

'Why didn't the Germans overpower me when I was laying the explosive charge on the railway line? Why wait until we got here?' McIndoe asked.

'From what I understand, these two had agreed to rendezvous with their Jerry pals here on the beach.' Stockton-Jones noticed the look of anxiety cross McIndoe's face. 'Don't worry, old boy, the local Partisans are dealing with the rest of the welcoming party. I believe they've set up a nice little ambush for them on the outskirts of Naples.'

McIndoe managed a weak smile as his eyes flickered between the two men. 'I owe you both for saving my life,' he said uncomfortably – he'd never found it easy to express sentiment in any form. 'Thanks.'

'Glad to have been of assistance,' Stockton-Jones replied.

'Well, you'll have to excuse me,' McIndoe said after an uneasy silence. 'I've got to get back to Naples. There's obviously a lot of questions that need to be answered.'

'Not possible, old boy,' Stockton-Jones told him. 'You're to come back with us to Malta. Vice-Admiral Starr's orders. He wants you to report to his office at 0900 sharp tomorrow morning.'

'I don't believe it!' McIndoe said in frustration. 'I've still got so much to do here. The Partisans are counting on my help.'

Stockton-Jones gave him a helpless shrug. 'Sorry, but those orders came directly from Vice-Admiral Starr. And he was very insistent that they be passed on to you. I've never actually met him, but he sounds like the kind of man you'd defy at your peril.'

'That's precisely the kind of man he is,' McIndoe retorted with a dejected sigh. 'Well, you know where the dinghy's moored. Lead on, *old boy*.'

Unbeaten had reached the sanctuary of the Allied submarine base on Manoel Island in the early hours of the morning. Like the other submarines housed at the base, it remained submerged to reduce the chances of being sunk during one of the now incessant Axis bombing raids which daily battered the besieged island of Malta.

McIndoe had been taken to his quarters soon after boarding the submarine, where he'd spent the next few hours tossing and turning listlessly on his bunk, desperately trying to get some sleep. Exhausted, he'd eventually managed to drop off around six o'clock, only to be woken an hour later on the orders of Stockton-Jones. Bleary-eyed, he'd gratefully accepted a mug of hot, unsweetened tea from a crewman, and sat thoughtfully on the edge of the bunk as he'd slowly drunk it. After a shave and a quick body-wash, he'd pulled on the roll-necked sweater and flannels which had been brought for him to wear. Stockton-Jones had contacted the duty officer at the submarine base, HMS *Talbot*, and satisfied himself that it was safe to surface next to a motorized dinghy which was already waiting to transport McIndoe the short distance to the mainland. *Unbeaten* immediately submerged again after McIndoe had been transferred to the dinghy.

'You needn't worry about Jerry, sir, they've already been and gone this morning,' the young cadet announced when he noticed McIndoe casting a nervous glance towards the dawn sky. 'From what I can gather, their cabbages didn't do much damage to the harbour this time round. But they'll be back again in a few hours, after they've refuelled and rearmed their planes.'

'I'm sure they will,' McIndoe said grimly.

'This your first visit to Malta, sir?'

'Yes,' McIndoe replied brusquely. The man, sensing that McIndoe wasn't in a mood for talking, left him to his own thoughts.

McIndoe looked around slowly as the small outboard motor propelled the dinghy away from Manoel Island and across Marsamxett Harbour towards the entrance of Grand Harbour. Although he'd read in *The Times* back home about the sustained bombing campaign by the *Luftwaffe*, and seen brief footage of one such raid on a Pathé newsreel, he couldn't have begun to imagine the sheer scale of the devastation which had been caused by the German bombs if he hadn't actually seen it with his own eyes. There was hardly a building along the perimeter of either Marsamxett Harbour or Grand Harbour which hadn't been damaged during the raids of the past two years. In many cases entire blocks of buildings had been reduced to piles of rubble; in some cases these had been destroyed in the space of a few seconds by a single five hundred kilogram bomb dispatched with unerring accuracy by a Stuka or Heinkel dive-bomber piloted by the renowned airmen of the élite *Luftwaffe Fliegerkorps X*.

The dinghy turned into Grand Harbour. Ahead of them lay the shattered remains of the breakwater bridge which had been partially destroyed during a daring night raid by the Italian Navy the previous year. McIndoe remembered the press coverage which had accompanied that singular incident. The Italians' mission had been to penetrate Grand Harbour and destroy an Allied convoy which had recently docked there, but their approach had been detected by an Army radio-location set. One of the two E-boats – the human-torpedo vessels – crashed into the bridge, destroying one of the viaducts. The guns overlooking the harbour had opened fire on the enemy vessels when they had come into range and, within the space of six minutes, most of the craft had been sunk, including the second E-boat which had been heading towards the second viaduct at maximum speed. Fifteen corpses were later recovered from the sea and eighteen Italians taken prisoner.

The numerous forts, which had lain dormant since the last war, were now all operational, and bristling with an assortment of big guns – Bofors guns, nine- and six-inch breech-loaders, as well as the twelve- and six-pounder quick-firing guns – all protruding menacingly from their embrasures. To the west of Grand Harbour were the forts of Tigne and Campbell, to the east St Rocco and Delimara, and straddling either side of the harbour entrance were St Elmo and Ricasoli.

McIndoe looked up in awe at the towering sandstone façade of Fort St Elmo as the dinghy passed alongside it. Built in 1488, the fort had been a relatively small garrison which had been overrun with considerable ease by the marauding Turks during the Great Siege of 1565, resulting in heavy losses amongst the Knights of St John. It was later expanded and fortified, and was now one of the first lines of defence against the waves of German bombers which regularly swept across the island. From where he was seated he could see one of the powerful Bofors guns, as well as two six-pounder quick-firing double-barrelled guns which faced out over the vast ocean.

The dinghy shot underneath the undamaged viaduct and the cadet reduced speed as they approached the first of the wrecks which littered the harbour – the British destroyer, *Jersey*, which had struck a mine and sunk in the harbour entrance the previous year. A short distance ahead lay a cargo ship; only its bow protruded grotesquely above the greasy surface, as if in some last, forlorn attempt to try and free itself from the thick oil slick which covered much of the water in and around the harbour. To his right lay the remains of the British minesweeper, *Fermoy*, which had been sunk by German bombers while undergoing repairs after it had limped into Grand Harbour as part of a much-needed convoy. A hundred yards further on a cruiser lay partially submerged on its side, the water gently lapping over its bullet-scarred hull in the wake of the dinghy which passed close to it. Rubble from damaged and destroyed installations was piled up high on both sides of the harbour, but this didn't seem to deter the hundreds of British soldiers and local volunteers who swarmed around the docks. And from within this apparent confusion, he heard a chorus of voices singing in harmony. He traced the choir to one of the dry docks, and smiled to himself at the sight of a grinning British engineer, stripped to the waist, conducting the unlikely ensemble with a spanner from the bow of a damaged cruiser. The dinghy had barely gone another fifty yards when he heard yet more singing, this time emanating from a group of locals who were unloading desperately needed supplies from one of the few cargo ships which had managed to evade the packs of U-boats which lurked in the unseen depths of the Mediterranean. It was almost as if the two choirs were in good-humoured competition to see who could out-sing the other. This stubborn resilience in the face of such adversity only added to McIndoe's ever-increasing admiration for this tiny island and its people. It was no wonder that the German *Luftwaffe*, despite their superiority in the air, had never managed to bomb the island into submission, not with that kind of unbreakable spirit and determination ranged against them.

The dinghy was manoeuvred against the foot of a bomb-damaged jetty and a length of rope was used to tether it to a rusted metal ladder. McIndoe grabbed on to the ladder and climbed up to the jetty, where an NCO, dressed in a khaki uniform, saluted him stiffly. 'Sergeant Pearson, sir. Vice-Admiral Starr sent me to collect you.'

14

'What regiment are you with, Pearson?' McIndoe asked as they walked towards a Bedford MWG which was fitted with a standard twenty-millimetre Polsten gun in the rear.

'I'm with the Intelligence Corps, sir. Sixty-ninth Field Section,' Pearson replied.

'Been stationed in Malta long?' McIndoe asked, climbing into the passenger seat.

'Four months, sir,' Pearson said as he started up the engine. 'And every day's been hell.' He shot a sidelong look at McIndoe. 'Don't get me wrong, sir. I wouldn't swap this assignment for anything. Sooner or later we're going to win the battle for the Mediterranean, and I want to be around when it happens. It'll be the turning point of the war, sir, you mark my words.'

'You could be right there, Pearson,' McIndoe agreed thoughtfully. 'What are conditions like out here? Is it as bad as it looks?'

'We're literally living from day to day at the moment, sir,' Pearson replied, turning the vehicle into one of numerous narrow streets which dissected the bomb-ravaged capital. 'Rationing's been in force for the past four months now. We desperately need the convoys to get through, and not only for the food supplies. We're now so chronically short of ammo that, apart from the guns that are being used to protect the ships in the harbour and those on the three RAF bases, only half the Bofors guns can be in use at any one time. All the other heavy guns have been rationed to three rounds per Jerry raid. And if these raids carry on at this rate, you can be sure it won't be long before the big guns around the harbour and on the airfields will be rationed as well. The situation's become critical, sir. I know a lot of the men are getting really frustrated because of these limitations. But it's not them I feel sorry for. We're at war with Jerry. Our troops will have to learn to take the rough with the smooth. It's the locals I really feel for. This isn't their war, is it? And they're the ones who are taking the brunt of the bombing. Day in, day out. It never stops. Only you never hear them complain. They just get on with their lives as best they can. I've got nothing but admiration for them, sir. They should all get medals. Every last bloody one of them.'

'You smoke, Pearson?' McIndoe asked, pulling a packet of cigarettes from his pocket.

'You're a gentleman, sir,' Pearson said, gratefully plucking a cigarette from the packet. 'We're rationed to forty a week now. And what with all this bombing going on, most of us smoke our quota within the first couple of days. It's the only way to steady our nerves, which means we're all pretty much on edge by the end of the week.' He held up the cigarette. 'You don't mind if I keep it for later, sir?'

'Not at all.'

Pearson slipped the cigarette into his tunic pocket. 'You a married man, sir, if you don't mind me asking?'

'No, I'm not married,' McIndoe replied.

'It's the best way, especially at times like this,' Pearson said philosophically as the towering presence of Fort St Elmo came into view ahead of them. He swerved to avoid a scattering of loose bricks which had become dislodged from a pile of rubble at the side of the road, then turned the MWG sharply into the entrance of the fort and came to a halt in front of the boom gate. A soldier emerged from a small hut and checked Pearson's authorization before raising the boom gate to allow them through. Pearson drove into a cobbled courtyard, careful to detour around a jagged bomb crater before pulling up in front of a wooden door. Switching off the engine, he vaulted nimbly out of the vehicle, where he was again challenged by an armed soldier. Satisfied with Pearson's ID, the soldier stepped aside to allow them past. The door opened on to a flight of steps which fed down to an underground labyrinth of corridors. This was the heart of the intelligence network on the island which monitored wireless and radio transmissions between the various *Luftwaffe* and *Kriegsmarine* units and their respective bases across the

Continent. Invaluable information which could be passed on to the War Office in London and used to decide future military and naval strategies against the Axis. Pearson rapped sharply on one of the closed doors, then opened it and stepped inside. A uniformed Wren smiled at McIndoe when he entered the room behind Pearson. She got to her feet and saluted him without losing the smile. 'It's good to see you again, Lieutenant McIndoe.'

'And you, Janet,' McIndoe replied. He'd known Sergeant Janet Cross for as long as he'd known Starr. She was Starr's personal secretary, and she travelled everywhere with him. There had been a wave of malicious, but totally unfounded, rumours within the SOE of there being more than just a working relationship between the two of them – rumours which McIndoe had never once believed. The rumours had ceased abruptly after she had married a Canadian airman at the end of 1941. Her parents had both been killed during a German bombing raid over Coventry in 1940, and it had been both fitting and appropriate that Starr should have given her away at the wedding.

'I'll leave you to it, sir,' Pearson said, snapping to attention and saluting McIndoe. 'And should you need anything while you're on the island, you know where to find me.'

'Thanks, Pearson, I'll be sure to bear that in mind,' McIndoe said. He waited until Pearson had left the room before turning back to Janet. 'You're looking well. How's Richard?'

'He's still stationed down in Surrey,' she told him. 'He contacted me last night to say that he'd taken his total number of "confirmed kills" to seven yesterday afternoon when he shot down an Me109 over the Channel.'

'Good for him,' McIndoe said stoutly. He'd first met Flight-Lieutenant Richard Cross at the wedding, and the two men had struck up an immediate rapport.

'I'll let His Lordship know you're here,' she said, gesturing to the inner door behind her.

McIndoe smiled to himself. She always referred to Starr as 'His Lordship', but the term was used affectionately. He guessed that Starr knew about her nickname for him, but he'd never let on to any of the men that he did. And none of them would ever say it to his face. Most were wary, some even frightened, of his quick temper. But McIndoe had always got on reasonably well with him. The secret was to speak your mind in front of him. He didn't necessarily agree with you, which could lead to one of his thunderous outbursts, but he still admired you for your candour all the same. McIndoe recalled the words of one unfortunate colleague, describing Starr after feeling the full wrath of his anger: '. . . He has the face and expression of a bucolic, a mind like a rapier, and a deep-rooted intolerance of those who waste either time or speech.' McIndoe knew he couldn't have put it better himself.

'You can go through now, Lieutenant,' Janet said, indicating the open door.

'Ah, McIndoe, come in,' Starr said gruffly, beckoning him into the room. 'Tea?'

'Thank you, sir.'

'Two teas, Janet,' Starr said, and waited until she'd left before gesturing to the chair in front of his desk. 'Sit down, man. Sit down.'

McIndoe sat down, then looked around slowly at the array of maps and charts of the Mediterranean which covered the sandstone walls as Starr gathered together the papers on his desk and slipped them into a folder. Vice-Admiral Edmund Starr was a large, corpulent man in his mid-sixties, with a naturally ruddy complexion and a full head of thick white hair. He was rarely seen without a pipe within arm's reach.

'Near thing in Italy, McIndoe,' Starr said as he took a wad of tobacco from the leather pouch in front of him and tamped it firmly into the mouth of his favourite briar pipe. 'Lucky for you the Royal Navy was in the area.'

'Yes, sir, it was,' McIndoe agreed. 'But I still don't know how the Gestapo were on to me so quickly. I can only assume that they were tipped off by someone in the Partisans.'

'Quite so,' Starr replied. 'It seems that the money currently on offer for the capture of an SOE operative in Italy proved too much of a temptation for one of the Partisan officers in Naples. Fortunately his treachery came to light in time for us to instigate a plan of our own to prevent anything happening to you.'

'I appreciate that, sir. But why was I pulled out? I still had . . .' McIndoe trailed off when Starr began to wave his pipe admonishingly at him.

'You should know better than to question my orders,' Starr chided him. 'And anyway, you'd obviously outstayed your welcome in Naples. I'll be sending in another operative to continue the good work.'

'What about the bomb I planted on the railway line, sir? Did it go off?'

'Unfortunately the Germans were on to that from the start. Not only did they dismantle it, but now they've got a "fog signal" intact to analyse back in Berlin.' Starr sat back in the chair as a rare smile crossed his puffy face. 'Of course, what they didn't know was that the Partisans had already mined the line further down the track. The train was derailed and a large quantity of the munitions it was carrying were destroyed in the ensuing explosion.'

'At least some good's come out of it all,' McIndoe said with evident satisfaction.

There was a knock at the door and Janet Cross entered with their refreshments. She placed the tray on the desk then retreated, closing the door again behind her.

'When did you get in to Malta, sir?' McIndoe asked as he added a dash of milk to his tea.

'Yesterday. They gave me this office to use. I suppose it's adequate.'

McIndoe looked around at the spacious surroundings. It seemed more than adequate to him, but he knew better than to say anything, even in jest. Vice-Admiral Sir Edmund Starr wasn't a man particularly known for his levity.

'What brings you out here at such short notice, sir?' McIndoe asked.

'You,' Starr replied matter-of-factly.

McIndoe paused as he was about to take a sip of tea, then slowly lowered the cup and placed it carefully in the saucer. 'Me, sir?'

'I was going to pull you out of Naples within the next twenty-four hours anyway. What happened last night merely brought my plans forward. I need you for another mission. In Sicily.'

'But Sicily isn't my territory, sir,' McIndoe protested.

'Don't you think I know that!' Starr retorted indignantly. 'I've brought you in because right now I don't have anyone else to use.'

'What about Percy Dankworth? He's our main operative in Sicily.'

'Dankworth was injured on assignment last week. He'll be out of action for the next few months.' Starr paused to draw deeply on the stem of his pipe. 'You're our most experienced operative in Italy. And we're going to need experience on this one. That's why I've recalled you.'

'What exactly is it that I'll be doing, sir?'

'At the moment I can't divulge the exact nature of your mission. Suffice to say that, within the last couple of days, the War Office in London has received some very disturbing information which could ultimately affect the outcome of the war here in the Mediterranean.' Starr sucked thoughtfully on his pipe, as if trying to choose his words carefully before he spoke again. 'US Military Intelligence have also been involved, and it's been decided that we should pool our resources and work together on this mission. Your contact here in Malta will be Major Nick Ravallo. Our American cousins seem to rate him very highly. You've also been assigned a team of SOE operatives. You've worked with them all before, so there should be no problem there. They're on their way to the island as we speak. Once you've established contact with Ravallo and your team, we'll talk further. Pearson is waiting outside to drive you to the airbase at Luqa. It's about six miles from here. You'll find Major Ravallo there. He flew in there early this morning. That's all for now, McIndoe.'

McIndoe got to his feet. 'This must be pretty important for you to have come out here personally to brief me, sir.'

'It is,' Starr replied, the pipe hovering inches away from his mouth. 'Believe me, it is.'

TWO

The RAF's three main airfields on Malta were at Ta'Qali, in the centre of the island; and at Hal Far and Luqa to the south. The runways at Ta'Qali and Hal Far were grass-surfaced, which had often caused problems for the nimble fighters during the wet season. Luqa, which was the closest to the capital, Valletta, was the only airfield with tarmacked runways. The construction of Luqa airfield had been completed in April 1940, and had become operational a month later.

The aftermath of the German bombing raid earlier that morning was still evident as Pearson drove the MWG into the complex at Luqa. The bomb craters which scarred the airstrip were being filled in frantically by ground personnel with an assortment of gravel and rubble, while an old, battered steam-roller trundled reliably behind them, levelling the material to ensure that the incoming fighters could land and refuel, ready for their next sortie against the enemy. It was a never-ending cycle which was invariably repeated after every raid. It had become a way of life for the servicemen stationed there.

McIndoe noticed the manned Bofors guns which were situated strategically around the airfield, as well as several of the protective pens housing the precious collection of Hurricanes and Gloucester Gladiators. Some pens were built with blocks of stone gathered from surrounding buildings which had been destroyed in previous raids, while others were constructed from rows of four-gallon petrol cans filled with earth and sand. Several of the pens were empty, their valiant occupants currently patrolling the skies over the island. All pens, irrespective of whether they housed a fighter or not, were covered with camouflage netting in an attempt to deceive the German dive-bombers into believing that there were more aircraft stationed at the airfield than was the case. The endless art of deception . . .

Pearson brought the MWG to a halt outside the commanding officer's hut. McIndoe got out and waited until Pearson had driven off before knocking on the door.

'Come,' a voice boomed from behind the door.

McIndoe pushed open the door into a small, sparsely furnished room with a single desk and chair. A large blackboard stood against the far wall; on it was listed the status of all the airmen currently stationed on the base. The man behind the desk looked up from his paperwork and frowned at McIndoe. 'Yes, can I help you?'

'I'm Lieutenant McIndoe, sir. I believe Vice-Admiral Starr called to say that I was on my way over here.'

'Stately 'Omes of England, right?' the man said with a smile, referring to the nickname which had been given to the SOE because of their penchant for commandeering lavish country mansions to use as training bases for their operatives. He got to his feet and extended a hand towards McIndoe. 'Wing-Commander Winstanley. Welcome to Luqa.' He gestured to the wooden chair against the wall.

'Thank you, sir,' McIndoe replied, then pulled up the chair and sat down.

Winstanley resumed his seat, leaned back, and swung his feet up on to the desk. He eyed McIndoe for a few moments, then snapped his fingers together. 'Of course. Sam McIndoe. I thought I recognized your face when you came in. You're the rugger player, aren't you? The Scottish international?'

'Yes, sir, I've been fortunate enough to have played rugby for my country,' McIndoe replied with modest pride.

'I saw you play at Twickenham in '38. You scored that last-minute try which won Scotland the Triple Crown, didn't you?'

McIndoe just smiled – it was a glorious moment that he'd never forget for the rest of his life.

'I should have you court-marshalled right now,' Winstanley said good-humouredly. 'Dammit, McIndoe, you broke every English heart in the stadium that day. But I'll tell you something – it was a brilliant try all the same. Absolutely breathtaking the way you out-sprinted our English wing three-quarter to score in the corner. Nobody ever thought you'd beat him for pace. Not a flank forward.'

'I've always had pace. I actually played on the wing until I was fifteen,' McIndoe told him. 'It was only when I attended a rugby clinic that a professional coach suggested I would be more suited as a breakaway flank forward. I often wonder whether I'd ever have achieved the same success had I continued to play on the wing? I guess I'll never know.'

'What a pity you were born on the wrong side of the border,' Winstanley said after a thoughtful silence.

'I'd say that all depends on which side of the border you're on,' McIndoe replied with a wry smile.

Winstanley pondered McIndoe's reply for a moment then smiled too. 'Cigarette?' he asked, pulling a packet from his pocket and extended it towards McIndoe.

'Thank you, sir,' McIndoe said, plucking one from the packet.

'I believe you're here to see Major Ravallo?' Winstanley said.

'Yes, sir, I am. Do you know where I can find him?'

'The mess hall,' Winstanley replied. 'He's been there since he first arrived, regaling the men with colourful stories of his childhood in Brooklyn. He's quite a character is

Major Ravallo. He's also a lifesaver. He brought three bottles of Jack Daniels with him from America. With the severe rationing in force out here at the moment, the stuff's like liquid gold to us. He gave me a bottle and donated the other two to the staff bar. That's one sure way to win over the men.' The telephone rang. Winstanley answered it and put his hand lightly over the mouthpiece. 'You'll have to excuse me. The mess hall's not far from here. It's just past the dispersal huts. You can't miss it. A section of the roof was blown away by a Jerry bomb a couple of days ago.'

McIndoe left Winstanley to his call and walked to the dispersal huts – where the pilots on standby waited in constant readiness to scramble their fighters at the first sign of the next incoming Axis raid – then on to the damaged mess hall. A German bomb had landed short of the building, leaving a sizeable crater in the ground, but the resultant explosion had ripped away a section of the roof. A tarpaulin had been secured temporarily over the gaping hole to prevent the rain from getting in. Broken slates still lay scattered haphazardly across the grass where they'd fallen. He ground his cigarette underfoot and entered the building.

He heard the sound of laughter coming from behind the closed door at the end of the corridor. Pushing open the door, he peered inside and saw a group of men gathered in an informal semi-circle at the far end of the room. An American voice came from behind the cordon of bodies. He crossed to where the men were standing and it was then that he got his first look at Major Nicky Ravallo. McIndoe already knew that Ravallo was twenty-seven years old – a year younger than himself – and with his swarthy good looks and tousled black hair he could easily have been mistaken for a swashbuckling hero from one of those instantly forgettable propaganda films which were being dutifully churned out by Hollywood every month. Even his clothes had a theatrical look about them. A battered brown leather bomber jacket, turned up at the collar; a monogrammed cream scarf wrapped loosely around his throat with the end flung casually over his shoulder; and a pair of baggy cream flannel trousers tucked into a pair of polished brown leather boots.

'You married, Major Ravallo?' a Yorkshire voice called out from the crowd.

'Do I look married?' Ravallo countered with a bemused smile.

'How can you tell whether someone looks married or not?' came the puzzled reply.

'Only a married man would have to ask that question,' Ravallo called back, and the Yorkshireman waved aside the gentle ribbing he received from his colleagues around him. It was then that Ravallo saw McIndoe, recognizing him from the photograph which had been included in the dossier he'd been given by his superiors to read on the flight to Malta. He nodded in acknowledgement to McIndoe, then clapped his hands together. 'Gentlemen, I'm afraid this is where I have to get off. It's been great talking to you all. Hopefully we can do this again sometime. Preferably in Berlin with the victorious Allied flags flying over the Reichstag.' There was a cheer of approval, then the crowd parted to allow Ravallo to make his way across to where McIndoe was standing. 'It's good to meet you,' he announced as the two men shook hands. 'My superiors at Military Intelligence speak very highly of you.'

'I hope I won't disappoint them, sir,' McIndoe replied.

Ravallo took McIndoe's arm and led him out of earshot of the others. 'You can drop the "sir" for a start. Call me Nicky.' He sighed deeply at the sight of McIndoe's uncertain expression. 'You British are all the same. You always have to do everything by the book, don't you? You're all so goddamn formal. Jesus, just loosen up a bit. And that, Lieutenant, is an order.'

'We British are very good at taking orders,' McIndoe said with a self-deprecating smile.

Ravallo sat down at the table furthest from the door. 'So, what do they call you? Samuel? Sam? Mac?'

'Sam or Mac,' McIndoe replied as he sat on the wooden bench on the other side of the table. 'But just not Sammy. That makes me sound like a bloody parrot.'

Ravallo laughed, then leaned back against the wall and raised one foot up on to the bench. 'You're Scotch, right?'

'I'm Scots,' came the soft but firm reply. 'Scotch is a drink.'

Ravallo sensed the underlying tension in McIndoe's voice. 'My apologies if I offended you. I can assure you it was quite unintentional.'

'Theoretically you're right to call me Scotch,' McIndoe told him. 'It's just that most people from Scotland prefer to be called either Scots or Scottish. But then you weren't to know that, were you?'

'I do now,' Ravallo assured him. 'So, where did you learn to speak Italian?'

'Glasgow University. I graduated there with a first in the Classics and a second in Italian.' McIndoe noticed the frown crease Ravallo's face. 'At an American university I'd have majored in the Classics and minored in Italian.'

Ravallo whistled softly in admiration. 'You're obviously one smart son-of-a-bitch.'

'I don't know about that,' McIndoe replied modestly. 'How about you? Were you ever at university?'

'I wasn't exactly what you'd call the academic type,' Ravallo said. 'I couldn't wait to finish school. The only reason I stuck it out was because my parents had made so many sacrifices over the years to make sure I got a proper education. We were a typical poor Italian family living in Brooklyn. My parents were immigrants but I'm a New Yorker born and bred. My father's been a shoemaker all his life. My mother . . .' he trailed off with a shrug. 'Hell, my mother did anything she could to bring that little bit more money into the house. At least she can take it easier now that it's just two of them at home.'

'It can't have been easy being an Italian boy growing up in a predominantly Irish neighbourhood.'

'It wasn't. I used to get regular beatings from the Irish kids on our block,' Ravallo said, instinctively touching his nose as he thought back to his childhood. 'In desperation I joined up with a boxing club over on Coney Island. It was owned by an ex-pro whose only claim to fame in over fifty professional fights was that he'd once gone three rounds with Jack Sharkey at the Yankee Stadium. He taught me how to look after myself. Who knows, I might even have turned pro myself had I not been drafted. The army opened up a whole new life for me. That's how I ended up in Military Intelligence.'

McIndoe had liked Ravallo from the moment they'd met. He could often judge a man's character just by the way he shook hands. Ravallo's grip had been firm but not overpowering, and although he had the suave good looks of a film star, there was nothing pretentious about him. You got what you saw. It had also quickly become evident to McIndoe that Ravallo was the sort of person who was completely up front about himself; he had that kind of friendly, easy-going disposition which automatically made those around him feel at ease.

Yet, on reflection, their personalities were complete opposites. McIndoe had always been quiet and reserved, preferring to keep his thoughts to himself. There were those who regarded him as too intense for his own good, and it had already been speculated by some of the country's leading sportswriters that his continued reluctance to be regarded as 'one of the lads' would ultimately cost him the chance of ever captaining his country at rugby. Those kind of negative comments had always hurt him – especially as he knew deep down that they were probably right. But there were those who admired his style of quiet, disciplined leadership –

especially his superiors at the SOE's headquarters at Baker Street in London.

Suddenly the droning wail of the air-raid siren started up and the two men leapt to their feet and ran outside. Dozens of the base's ground crew – many of the off-duty servicemen dressed only in khaki shorts and boots – were running to their stations, while the duty fighter-pilots spilled from the dispersal hut, some still struggling to secure their leather flight caps over their heads as they sprinted towards the pens where the Hurricanes and the Gloucester Gladiators were housed. To the uninitiated eye it appeared as if complete pandemonium had set in. But only to the uninitiated eye. Both McIndoe and Ravallo realized that each man had a specific duty to perform during these relentless attacks on the base, and would know exactly what he had to do. And, although desperate to assist in any way they could, they knew that they'd only be getting in the way if they tried to help.

'And just what the bleedin' 'ell d'you two gents think you're doing?' a Cockney voice demanded behind them. 'Waitin' in line for tickets for the show? If you want to keep your 'eads then you'd better get 'em down pretty damn sharpish.'

They looked round to find a short, red-faced man standing behind them. He wore the rank of corporal on the shoulder of his khaki tunic. He handed them each a protective steel helmet. 'Wing-Commander Winstanley's compliments. He asked me to look out for you. He said you'd probably be hangin' around like a couple of knotless threads. Looks like he was right. Now, *gentlemen*, if you'd care to follow me I'll get you the best seats in the 'ouse. I promise you, you won't miss any of the action.'

By the time McIndoe and Ravallo had put on the steel helmets and hurried after the man to the sanctuary of a trench close to the mess hall, a deep, ominous rumbling had filled the skies as the German aircraft approached the island;

shimmering silhouettes looming ever larger on the cloud-speckled horizon. Then came a distant booming sound as the first of the coastal Bofors guns opened up on the raiders, and puffs of black smoke began to pepper the rich azure sky around the aircraft, like paint being splashed wantonly across an artist's canvas. McIndoe watched mesmerized as the German aircraft – clustered in a 'beehive' formation – came into focus as they reached Grand Harbour. The 'beehive' was a basic aerial formation whereby the fast, agile fighters would form a close protective cordon around the bombers as they carefully honed in on their targets, allowing them to peel away and engage any enemy aircraft which threatened the bombers. When this happened, the 'beehive' would then reform, with fighters from within the cluster moving out to keep the shape of the formation. In this instance it was a wave of Messerschmitt 109 fighters protecting a mixture of Stuka and Heinkel bombers.

'They got no fear, them Jerry pilots,' the corporal said as the first of the RAF Hurricanes sped down the runway before lifting off the ground. 'They'll keep their shape up there until they've reached their target. Don't matter 'ow many of 'em get shot down in the process, they won't scatter. It weren't like that with the Eyeties though. They don't 'ave the 'eart for a fight. They just turned tail the moment our ack-ack guns opened up on 'em. Most of their cabbages landed 'armlessly in the sea. That's probably why they were replaced by these Jerry bastards. Like I said, they don't know no fear. But then, dyin' for their bloody Fatherland is supposed to be a great sacrifice, ain't it?'

'You almost sound as if you admire them,' Ravallo said, watching as another Hurricane took off from the nearest runway.

'I admire 'em for their courage, sir,' came the sharp response, 'not for nothin' else.'

The two Bofors guns on the edge of the airfield erupted into life as the first of the sleek Messerschmitt fighters came into range. Then, without warning, a Stuka dropped from the centre of the formation and dived towards the airfield. A Hurricane, which had just taken off, immediately banked sharply in a desperate attempt to try and intercept the bomber before it could release its deadly cargo over the base. A Messerschmitt peeled away from the 'beehive' to engage the Hurricane. The Messerschmitt pilot opened up with the twenty-millimetre cannons which were fixed forward on the wings, but the Hurricane arced sharply before levelling out again behind the Messerschmitt. But, in doing so the Hurricane had lost sight of the Stuka. The Hurricane's twenty-millimetre cannons crackled into life, and seconds later a pall of black smoke began pouring from the back of the Messerschmitt. It spiralled uncontrollably towards the ground and exploded in a searing ball of fire on an open field close to the airfield.

The Stuka pilot seized his chance and dived down towards the runway like a fearsome bird of prey closing in on its helpless quarry. The barrel of the entrenched twelve-pounder gun nearest to the runway swung towards the Stuka but, before it could open up, a lone Messerschmitt skimmed low across the runway, raking the dug-out with cannon-fire. All four members of the gun-crew in the dug-out were caught in the scything fusillade, and the gunner slumped forward over the gun as the Messerschmitt arched upwards to confront the approaching Hurricane. The Stuka released its cluster of bombs which landed with unerring accuracy on the runway. The Stuka levelled out and, as it began its climb back towards the protective cloak of the 'beehive', a second Stuka broke away from the formation and dived towards the ground, intent on inflicting further damage on another runway. With the Hurricanes and Gloucester Gladiators already engaged in ferocious dog-fights with the Messerschmitts high above the island, and the Bofors gun pounding relentlessly into the very heart of the 'beehive', the lone Stuka was allowed to dive virtually unchallenged towards the airfield.

McIndoe looked at Ravallo. Each anticipated the other's reaction and, before the corporal could stop them, they'd scrambled out of the trench and were sprinting towards the dug-out. The same Me109 which had earlier attacked the dug-out was now chaperoning the Stuka after seeing off the spirited but inferior Hurricane. The Messerschmitt swooped low over the airfield, and opened up on the two men. The bullets chewed into the ground around them, the Messerschmitt shot past them, and Ravallo looked round in horror when McIndoe stumbled and fell heavily to the ground.

'I'm fine,' McIndoe shouted to him above the crescendo of gunfire which seemed to encompass them from all sides. 'Just get that damn Stuka.'

Ravallo sprinted to the protective circle of sandbags which surrounded the gun emplacement and vaulted nimbly into the dug-out. He could see that the gunner was dead. Pushing the body off the gun, he turned the barrel on the Stuka and braced himself to fire . . .

McIndoe scrambled into the dug-out after Ravallo. He crouched down; he could see the look of intense concentration on Ravallo's face as he carefully followed the Stuka in the sights. He also saw a glimmer of apprehension in Ravallo's eyes, but he knew better than to say anything. He wiped the sweat from his forehead, then squinted up at the Stuka as it continued its screeching dive towards the airfield. He swallowed anxiously as he waited breathlessly for Ravallo to fire. The Stuka was well within range now – why wasn't he firing? Still Ravallo hesitated. McIndoe's eyes flickered between Ravallo and the Stuka, willing him to open fire before the dive-bomber could release its deadly cargo over the airfield.

Suddenly Ravallo drew back from the gun, his eyes wide and staring, his hands clutched on his head. McIndoe shoved Ravallo away from the gun; as he lined up the Stuka in the sights he saw to his horror that the Messerschmitt had wheeled round and was diving towards the dug-out again. He blinked away the sweat that burnt into his eyes, then fired off several rounds which exploded harmlessly in the sky to the right of the Stuka's ungainly black fuselage. And still it kept coming. Closer and closer . . .

As the Stuka levelled out after its near-vertical dive, McIndoe realized that it was ready to discharge its lethal consignment. Yet the pilot seemed to hesitate. McIndoe was momentarily puzzled by this, then he realized that, if the bombs were discharged too quickly, they would destroy the Messerschmitt which was already skimming low across the airfield towards the dug-out. He had to make those few priceless seconds count. He knew he wouldn't get another chance. Suddenly the Messerschmitt's two twenty-millimetre cannons crackled in to life and a row of bullets peppered the ground in a parallel line on either side of the runway. He found that he had to draw on all his inner strength just to keep his concentration on the Stuka when all his instincts were screaming at him to turn the gun on the Messerschmitt as it homed in on the dug-out. He knew that if he were to break his concentration now and make the mistake of looking at the Messerschmitt, he'd never manage to line up the Stuka again in the sights before it had unloaded its bombs over the runway. He fired repeatedly at the Stuka but without success, and all the time the chatter of the Messerschmitt's guns grew ever louder as the Me109 closed in on the dug-out.

Suddenly the Stuka banked sharply to come in behind the Messerschmitt, and for a split second the vast expanse of its black undercarriage and gull-shaped wings were exposed in the eye of the sights. McIndoe loosed off several more rounds in quick succession. One round hit home, shearing off the tip of the Stuka's left wing as if it were made of plywood. The doomed aircraft plunged helplessly towards the ground.

McIndoe flung himself to the floor of the dug-out and wrapped his hands over his head as a fusillade of bullets from the Messerschmitt's cannons ripped into the protective sandbags around him. Then the Messerschmitt shot low overhead and was gone. He was still struggling to his feet when he heard the deafening explosion as the Stuka crashed into one of the pens and burst into flames. He raised his head cautiously and saw the Messerschmitt climbing away from the airfield, returning to the pack which was already heading back towards their base in Sicily. The raid was over.

He stared after the retreating formation until the sound of a fire-engine shattered his thoughts. It sped towards the twisted remains of the Stuka which was now blazing fiercely out of control in the stone pen.

'You OK, sir?'

McIndoe looked up to find the corporal peering down anxiously at him from the rim of the dug-out. 'Yes,' he replied, then gestured around him. 'Get some medics on the double, Corporal. We've got wounded men down here.'

'Yes, sir,' the corporal replied, and hurried away.

It was only then that McIndoe saw Ravallo, slumped against the dug-out wall. He was cradling his left hand against his stomach. On closer inspection, McIndoe saw the blood which was slowly soaking the front of Ravallo's shirt. 'Nicky?' he said anxiously, crouching down in front of Ravallo, 'you've been hit.'

Ravallo looked up slowly at McIndoe. 'It's just a flesh wound,' he said in a barely audible voice. 'It's nothing.'

'Let me see.'

'Forget it,' Ravallo retorted irritably, then gestured to the youth lying beside him. He'd already given the youth his scarf to help stem the flow of blood which had been pumping from the gaping bullet-wound in his chest. The scarf was now soaked in blood. 'Mac, this guy needs a medic. Fast.'

'Not any more,' McIndoe replied softly as he closed the dead soldier's eyelids.

'Oh, Jesus, no,' Ravallo said despairingly as he stared at the dead soldier. 'He was just a kid, that's all. A goddamn kid.'

Two medics arrived and quickly went to work on the two surviving members of the gun-crew. McIndoe climbed from the dugout, then reached down a hand and helped Ravallo out after him. He saw the blood dripping steadily from the tips of Ravallo's fingers.

'You're bleeding badly there, Nicky,' McIndoe said, gesturing to Ravallo's hand.

Ravallo turned his hand over and McIndoe winced at the sight of the gash across the base of Ravallo's thumb. 'A bullet nicked me, that's all. Like I said, it's nothing.'

'You'll still need it seen to, otherwise you could get an infection in the wound,' McIndoe told him firmly.

'There are others who need medical attention a lot more than I do,' Ravallo replied, wiping his bloodied fingers down his shirt. 'We need to talk, Mac. About what happened back there.'

'We'll talk after you've had that wound seen to,' McIndoe said as another fire-engine raced towards the smouldering shell of the burnt-out Messerschmitt on the edge of the airfield.

Ravallo could see the determination in McIndoe's eyes, and realized that it would be pointless to try and argue with him. 'OK, I'll go and have it looked at if that's what it's going to take to get you to listen to what I've got to say.'

'Yes, it is,' McIndoe told him.

Ravallo was about to say something, thought better of it, then turned away and walked slowly towards the field hospital.

'I hear you were a bit of a hero out there today.'

'No more than any other man on the base, sir,' McIndoe replied, scrambling to his feet when Wing-Commander Winstanley entered the room.

'That's not what I heard,' Winstanley said as he crossed to his desk and sat down. He gestured for McIndoe to sit down again. 'We certainly owe you a debt of gratitude, McIndoe. If that Stuka had been allowed to unload its bombs on the airfield, it could have put us out of operation for the rest of the day. That might not sound much to you, but if that meant we couldn't land our fighters, then they'd have had to be diverted to the airfields at Ta'Qali or Hal Far. And that would have left us very vulnerable to the next Jerry raid.'

'You think they'll be back again today, sir?'

'You can count on it,' Winstanley said. 'And next time we could be their main target. From what I can gather they concentrated this attack mainly on Grand Harbour, and in particular the submarine base at Manoel Island. We got off pretty lightly.'

'Have you heard any news about my men, sir?' McIndoe asked.

'Yes, we received confirmation earlier from Gibraltar that their plane took off on time.' Winstanley looked at his watch. 'They've been in the air for just over nine hours now. All being well, they should get here within the next couple of hours. I've got a crew out there right now, filling in the bomb craters on one of the runways. Don't worry, they'll have it completed before your men get here.'

'I don't doubt it for a minute,' McIndoe replied.

Winstanley fished out the bottle of Jack Daniels and two tumblers from his bottom drawer. 'Can I tempt you to a "wee dram" as you'd say north of the border?'

'I'd have preferred the real stuff but, under the circumstances, I suppose that American imitation will have to do,' McIndoe said with a smile.

'Splendid,' Winstanley replied, breaking the seal on the bottle. He poured out two measures and handed one of the tumblers to McIndoe. There was a knock at the door. 'Come,' he called out.

That's human nature, Nicky. It's happened to me before. You can't always tell how you're going to react to a certain situation until it actually happens to you. We both know that it could just as easily have been the other way round had I reached the dug-out first.'

'I hear what you're saying, Mac, but there's more to it than that.' Ravallo sat back against the desk and folded his arms across his chest. 'How much do you actually know about me?'

'Basically, nothing.' McIndoe took his cigarettes from his pocket and held out the packet towards Ravallo.

'I'm trying to quit the damn things,' Ravallo muttered, but he was quick to take one all the same. 'I'm not a field man like you,' he announced after McIndoe had lit the cigarette for him. 'I've been stuck behind a desk ever since I first joined Military Intelligence. For the last couple of months I've been based at our embassy in Gibraltar, intercepting and analysing Axis intelligence here in the Mediterranean. Before Gibraltar I was stationed at Pearl Harbor. I was there when the Japs attacked the naval base on the seventh of December last year. I'd been the duty officer the previous night at the Military Intelligence HQ on Ford Island, and I was in the process of handing over the shift to Garry Mitchell, my best friend at Military Intelligence, when the Japs attacked. The base was on a low state of readiness. Within ten minutes of the attack the *Arizona* had been sunk by a single torpedo. Twelve hundred men perished with her. Then the *West Virginia* went down. Then the *California*. You couldn't see anything in front of your face, that's how thick the smoke was over the island. All you could hear was the relentless pounding of the Jap bombs and the incessant rattling of machine-guns as the Zero fighters fired on anyone or anything that moved in the blazing water.

'We were pinned down in our HQ. There was nothing we could do. We must have been there for about twenty minutes, flat on our stomachs, when the smoke lifted long enough for us to see that the crew of the ack-ack gun outside our HQ were down. We couldn't tell whether they were dead or alive, but we knew we had to do something. We tried to use the smoke as cover but, as fate would have it, a Zero saw us and homed in for the kill. We'd both learnt how to operate anti-aircraft guns during our basic army training, so I volunteered to man the gun while Garry checked on the casualties.'

Ravallo rubbed his hands slowly over his face. 'It wouldn't fire, Mac. To this day I don't know whether it jammed on me or whether it had been damaged in the attack. All I know is, it didn't work. I had the Zero lined up perfectly in my sights, but there wasn't a damn thing I could do about it. It couldn't have been more than fifty yards away from us when the wing-cannons opened up. I ducked down behind the gun, already convinced that I was going to die. Perhaps you were right earlier when you said that the devil looks after his own. Someone certainly looked after me that day, because I didn't even get so much as a scratch. Garry was killed instantly. If he'd volunteered to man the gun instead – who knows – it could have been him here telling you the same story, only from his point of view.'

'And seeing that Stuka through the gun sights today brought it all back again to you?' McIndoe concluded after a lengthy silence.

'Yeah,' Ravallo replied tight-lipped. He straightened up and crossed to the window again. 'I know it's no excuse, Mac, but at least now you know why I froze out there today. Pearl Harbor will haunt me for the rest of my life.'

'Only if you let it,' McIndoe said. 'You have to learn to live with it, Nicky, and the only way to do that is to confront your fears head on. Because if you don't, those fears will just eat away inside you like a cancer. I know – I saw it happen to a colleague of mine in the Firm – what we call the SOE. He was one of our top operatives in France. He'd witnessed the execution of an entire village at the hands of the Germans. It was obvious just how much the massacre had affected him, but he refused to admit that anything was wrong. He should have been retired from the field, but for some inexplicable reason his handler decided to send him back for one last mission. By then he'd become so obsessed with what had happened at the village that he couldn't even concentrate on his work any more. He was tailed by the Gestapo from the moment he landed in France and, without knowing it, he led them to four senior members of the French Resistance. All four were interrogated at length, then shot by the Gestapo. He disappeared shortly after that and his body turned up the next day in a back street in Paris. The Gestapo certainly had no reason to kill him. The Resistance denied any involvement in his death, but it's my guess they killed him to prevent him from betraying any more of their people. And can you blame them? His handler was relieved of his post, and it was only after some very delicate negotiating by our senior officers that the leaders of the French Resistance agreed to continue working with the Firm.'

'Is that a roundabout way of saying that you think I need to see a psychiatrist?' Ravallo asked.

'You're strong enough to be able to whip this by yourself, Nicky,' McIndoe told him as he stubbed out his cigarette in the ashtray on Winstanley's desk. 'After all, you've already taken the first step towards breaking down those psychological barriers just by getting behind that gun today.' He finished his drink then got to his feet. 'I could do with stretching my legs. Fancy a walk? Perhaps we can be of some use out there.'

'Sure, why not?' Ravallo replied, opening the door. 'What time are you expecting your colleagues to get in from Gib?'

'Winstanley reckons they should get here within the next couple of hours.'

'As long as we don't get another visit from our German friends, out to spoil your little reunion,' Ravallo said as he emerged from the hut.

McIndoe cast a despairing look up at the clear blue sky, then closed the door behind him.

There were no air-raids over the island during the next ninety minutes, which allowed the ground personnel to patch up one of the runways in advance of the scheduled arrival time of the RAF's Bristol Blenheim Mk V from Gibraltar.

McIndoe had received word from the radio room of the impending arrival of his colleagues, and now he and Ravallo were standing outside Winstanley's hut, their hands shielding their eyes, watching as the converted bomber touched down at the far end of the runway. The pilot steered the plane – which had been fitted with two extra-long-range fuel tanks – carefully across the bumpy ground, finally bringing it to a halt a hundred yards away from the hut.

'You say that you've worked with all these guys before?' Ravallo asked as the ground crew moved into action around the stationary plane.

'Several times. They're four of the best men we have in the Firm. But then Starr said the operation was important.'

'It is,' Ravallo replied.

McIndoe cast a sidelong glance at Ravallo. 'You know what this operation's about?'

'Sure. Our respective superiors at Military Intelligence and at the SOE have been working together closely on it from the start.' Ravallo noticed the look of expectancy on McIndoe's face as he waited for him to continue. He shook his head. 'Forget it, Mac. You'll get briefed by your side. It's more than my life's worth to venture anything up front. Not only would I get a roasting from my own superiors, I'd also be sure to get carpeted by your Vice-Admiral Starr. And, from what I hear, you don't get on the wrong side of him if you can possibly help it.'

'His bark's a lot worse than his bite,' McIndoe said.

'Well, I sure as hell don't want him barking at me,' Ravallo countered quickly. 'Trust me, you'll be briefed soon enough. You'll have to be for this operation to work. It's all about precision timing. That's all I can say at the moment.'

'Fair enough,' McIndoe conceded.

'So who exactly are these guys?' Ravallo asked as the first of the SOE operatives appeared in the open cabin doorway.

McIndoe smiled to himself as the man tossed his rucksack to a member of the ground crew before jumping to the ground. He was in his mid-thirties with a short, stocky physique and thick black hair greased back over his head. 'That's Sergeant Cliff Evans, but everyone just calls him "Taffy". He keeps the men in line. He's also the best explosives man we've got in the Firm. He runs his own demolition company in Swansea. Very successfully by all accounts, although you wouldn't believe that when it's his turn to get in a round of drinks. And they say we Scots are tight with our money.'

A second man appeared in the doorway, then vaulted nimbly to the ground. He was taller than Evans, with a thin face, a pencil moustache and wiry black hair. 'Bruce Hillyard,' McIndoe said. 'He's a professional acrobat.'

'You mean like in the circus?' Ravallo replied in surprise.

'That's right. He's known as "The Spider". If you need someone to climb up the side of a watch-tower and take out the guard without a sound, Bruce is your man. He's the perfect silent assassin.'

'That's Neville Johnson,' McIndoe said when a third figure emerged from inside the plane: a tall, gangly man with sombre features and thinning brown hair. At the age of thirty-eight, Johnson was the oldest member of the team.

'He's a schoolteacher from Nottingham. Teaches English. He's as dour as he looks.'

'Does he also have a special talent?'

'A *very* special talent: a photographic memory. The great thing about working with Neville is that you never need to carry any incriminating documents on your person when you're behind enemy lines. Neville will have them all memorized in his head. The most detailed grid map imaginable; a numerical list of enemy troops and hardware – it makes no difference. He'll have it all stored up here,' McIndoe said, tapping the side of his head. 'But perhaps even more important than that, you've also got complete peace of mind, knowing that he won't let you down when you need him to recall something he's already memorized.'

'He sounds invaluable,' Ravallo agreed.

'He's one of the Firm's most sought-after operatives. Everybody wants to work with him.' McIndoe's eyes turned back to the open cabin doorway and a grin slowly spread across his face as the last member of the team emerged from the plane: a man in his late twenties with a swarthy, unshaven face and a mop of tangled black hair. 'And that is Monsieur Georges Passiere – the laziest son-of-a-bitch you'll ever have the misfortune of meeting,' he said with a good-humoured chuckle.

'A Frenchman?'

'He was recruited from the Free French eighteen months ago. I've known Georges longer than any of the others. We've been through quite a few scrapes together. But, like I said, lazy beyond belief. If you can't find Georges, the first place to look for him would be in the nearest bed. He spends more time sleeping than anyone I've ever known. It's unbelievable.'

'Sounds like a useful recruit,' Ravallo said contemptuously.

'He's a holder of the *Croix de Guerre* and also the best radio operator we've got in the Firm,' McIndoe retorted. 'What he doesn't know about Allied and Axis radio-transmitters isn't worth knowing. Sure, he may spend his spare time sleeping, but when he's on duty he's as professional as any man in the team. So don't knock him, Nicky. Not in front of me.'

'I stand corrected,' Ravallo said quickly.

'*Comment vas-tu, patron?*' Passiere shouted cheerily to McIndoe as the four men crossed the open ground towards them.

'*Bien, bien,*' McIndoe replied, gripping Passiere's extended hand.

Passiere grinned mischievously as his eyes flickered to Ravallo. 'His Italian may be perfect. But his French . . . Well, that still needs a lot of work.'

McIndoe shook hands with the others, then introduced them to Ravallo.

'So where are you from, Major?' Hillyard asked.

'New York. And you guys call me Nicky.'

'You got it, Nicky,' Hillyard replied with a grin.

McIndoe cursed Ravallo silently when he felt Hillyard looking at him as if waiting for him to follow suit, and tell them to call him 'Sam' or 'Mac'. He was damned if that was going to happen. And if they didn't like it, that was their tough luck . . .

'So what are we doing out here, boss?' Evans asked in his soft Welsh accent.

'I don't know,' McIndoe replied. 'Vice-Admiral Starr hasn't briefed me yet.'

'Starr's out here?' Hillyard asked in surprise. 'It must be something pretty important to get him to leave Baker Street.'

'Do you know why we're here, Major?' Johnson asked Ravallo.

'No, he doesn't,' McIndoe retorted quickly, casting a side-long glance at Ravallo. 'He's as much in the dark as I am.'

'Yeah, that's right,' Ravallo agreed, playing along with McIndoe. 'And call me Nicky.'

'Yes, sir,' Johnson muttered.

McIndoe knew that Johnson was the one man in the team who wouldn't call Ravallo by his first name. Just as he'd always referred to him as either 'Lieutenant' or 'sir', he'd certainly respect Ravallo's rank as well. Johnson was a pious man who had a reputation for being a strict disciplinarian with his students, which was one of the reasons why he'd been able to relate to the regimented structure within the confines of the military. Evans and Hillyard had always called McIndoe 'boss', and Passiere referred to him as *patron* in front of others, though he would occasionally call him 'Sam' if they were alone.

'So how was the flight from Gibraltar?' McIndoe asked.

'Well, apart from Hillyard's incessant yapping, not too bad,' Evans replied.

'Someone had to keep up your spirits,' Hillyard said cheerily.

'The chiefs-of-staff should use you as a secret weapon and let you loose amongst the Germans,' Johnson said with a despairing shake of the head. 'They'd surrender soon enough rather than have to listen to your endless chattering.'

'Perhaps they should send you instead,' Hillyard snorted. 'The Jerries would be begging for mercy if they found themselves having to look at your miserable mug all day.'

'Well, I'd better call in and let Vice-Admiral Starr know you've arrived,' McIndoe said. 'I'm sure you can entertain Major Ravallo while I'm gone.'

'We'll leave the entertainment to Abbott and Costello here,' Evans said, jabbing his thumb towards Hillyard and Johnson. 'Me, I could do with a drink. I'm absolutely parched.'

'You buying?' Ravallo asked with a good-humoured grin.

'It's always been customary at the Firm for the new man to get in the first round,' Evans was quick to point out.

'And if Taffy had his way, every round after that as well,' Hillyard added dryly.

McIndoe smiled to himself as he watched them head off in the direction of the mess hall, then he strode briskly towards Wing-Commander Winstanley's hut to phone in his report to Starr.

THREE

'His Lordship wants to see you,' Janet Cross said to McIndoe after he'd introduced her to Ravallo. 'Alone.'

'That sounds ominous,' McIndoe said.

'I should warn you that he isn't in the best of moods right now,' she added. 'He's been that way ever since I put a call through to him from Wing-Commander Winstanley.'

'You'd better tell him I'm here,' McIndoe said to Janet.

Ravallo put a hand lightly on McIndoe's arm as Janet knocked on the door and entered Starr's office. 'Remember, Mac, his bark's a lot worse than his bite.'

'You obviously haven't heard his bark,' McIndoe replied, then followed Janet into the office.

'Thank you, Janet, that will be all,' Starr said gruffly, then waited until she'd left and closed the door behind her before addressing McIndoe. 'I got a call earlier from Wing-Commander Winstanley at the Luqa air-base. He seems to think you're something of a hero after your antics today. In fact, he even wants to put your name forward for a commendation.'

'I'd hardly go that far, sir – '

'And neither would I!' Starr thundered across McIndoe's words. 'I'd be sorely tempted to suspend you if I didn't need you for this forthcoming operation. What if something had happened to you today while you were playing the hero? It would have jeopardized the future of this whole operation.

You're the most senior man we've got in the Mediterranean. That's why I pulled you out of Italy. I didn't do it so that you could go running about some air-base shooting at enemy aircraft.'

'Sir, with all due respect, the gun-crew were down and, if we hadn't taken over when we did, that Stuka would have put out the runway for the rest of the day,' McIndoe replied defensively.

'I realize that this might come as something of a shock to you, McIndoe, but the ground crew at Luga have managed, with some considerable success I might add, to deal with these *Luftwaffe* raids for the past two years – without your assistance.' Starr paused, then resumed in more measured tones. 'A lot of time and money went into your training. You're a member of an élite team now, not a gunner at an air-base. Just remember that, next time you get the urge to be a hero.'

'Yes, sir,' McIndoe said tight-lipped. That was the closest Starr would be getting to an apology. What did he have to apologize for? Not that he was particularly surprised by Starr's reaction. It was well known within the Firm that Starr liked to cocoon his senior operatives until they were needed for some dirty mission which nobody else wanted to do.

'What do you make of Major Ravallo?' Starr asked as he opened a drawer and removed his leather tobacco pouch.

'Can I speak freely, sir?'

Starr looked up at him and nodded. 'You know that goes without saying. What is it? Don't you two get on?'

'No, sir,' McIndoe was quick to assure him. 'In fact, I get on very well with Nicky.'

'Nicky?' Starr retorted, his face screwed up as if he'd just bitten into a particularly acidic slice of lemon. 'He told you to call him that?'

'He told all the men to call him Nicky, sir.'

'Those Americans have no sense of decorum whatsoever,' Starr bristled disdainfully. 'He's a senior officer in the military, for God's sake. Doesn't that mean anything to him?'

'You'd have to ask him that yourself, sir,' McIndoe replied, amused that Ravallo's indifference to military protocol had so rankled Starr.

'I'll do no such thing!' Starr shot back indignantly. 'Now, you were going to say something about . . . Major Ravallo?'

'He's a desk man, sir. This will be his first field assignment. If this is such an important operation, shouldn't we be insisting that the Americans send us someone with some kind of field experience?'

'You've got the field experience, McIndoe,' Starr replied as he tamped tobacco into his pipe.

'In other words, I'm supposed to carry him, is that it?' came the angry reply.

Starr's eyebrows shot up at the tone of McIndoe's voice, but he didn't speak until he'd lit his pipe. 'Did Major Ravallo tell you that he'd been at Pearl Harbor when the Japanese attacked the base last December?'

'Yes, sir.'

'Did he also tell you that he was awarded the Congressional Medal of Honor for dragging two injured men to safety from a gun emplacement while under fire from a Japanese Zero?'

'No, sir, he didn't,' McIndoe replied in surprise.

'He may not be a field man, but from what I've been told you can rest assured that he'll pull his weight.' Starr picked up the telephone and rang the outer office. 'Janet, ask Major Ravallo to come through, will you?' He listened momentarily to her, then sat back in his chair. 'Ah, he's arrived too, has he? Splendid. Have them both come through.'

McIndoe looked round when the door opened, and broke into a wide grin when he saw the man who followed Ravallo into the room. Sub-Lieutenant Charles Higgins was two years older than McIndoe, with a thatch of fine blond hair and the kind of boyish good looks which invariably drew admiring glances from women wherever he went. But they meant nothing to him; he'd been happily married for over ten years and had a daughter who absolutely doted on him. Higgins was officially attached to the Special Boat Squadron – the SBS – but had been 'loaned' to the SOE for a one-off assignment. That had been ten months ago, and he was still seconded to the SOE. Nobody knew how Starr had managed to hold on to him for so long, but there were certainly no complaints – there were few men around who could pilot a torpedo boat with the skill and expertise of Charlie Higgins. McIndoe could vouch for that, having already worked with him on several covert operations in the past.

'You know Lieutenant McIndoe, don't you?' Starr said to Higgins.

'Yes, sir,' Higgins replied, and pumped McIndoe's hand warmly. 'Good to see you again, Mac.'

'Likewise,' McIndoe replied. 'How's the family?'

'Great, thanks. Little Emma's seven now,' Higgins replied with a smile. 'She's becoming quite a handful these days.'

'I can well believe it,' McIndoe said, then turned back to Starr and gestured to Ravallo. 'This is Major Ravallo, sir.'

'Thank you, Lieutenant, but I had managed to work that out for myself,' Starr said, scowling at McIndoe. He nodded a curt greeting in the American's direction. 'Good to have you aboard, Major.'

'Thank you, sir. And, before I forget, I was told by one of my superior officers – General Harry Liebowitz – to remind you that he's still holding your marker for the twenty dollars you lost in the officers' poker game when you were last over in Washington.'

'Yes, quite,' Starr muttered, shifting uncomfortably in his chair and quickly clearing his throat. 'Pull up a chair and sit down,' he said gruffly, and waved to the chairs against the wall.

'Poker?' Higgins whispered in amazement to McIndoe as they helped themselves to a chair. 'Bridge, I can believe. But poker?'

McIndoe put his hand to his mouth to suppress a smile, then took a deep breath and purposely avoided making eye-contact with Higgins when he placed the chair in front of Starr's desk and sat down.

'Nicky, cigarette?' Higgins said, proffering the packet to Ravallo.

'I'm trying to give the damn things up,' Ravallo retorted, but quickly put a restraining hand on Higgins's arm as he was about to withdraw the packet. He smiled and helped himself to one. McIndoe took one as well.

Starr waited until they'd all lit up before speaking. 'Well, now that you all appear to have finally settled, perhaps we could have your report, Higgins?'

'Yes, sir,' Higgins replied, removing a folder from the battered leather briefcase he'd brought with him. He opened it on his knees and, after leafing through several pages of typed script, he pulled out a blueprint which he handed to McIndoe. 'You recognize that, Mac?' he asked after McIndoe had unfolded it.

'Sure, it's a diagram of an MTB,' McIndoe replied.

'An MTB?' Ravallo enquired, peering at the blueprint in McIndoe's hands.

'A motor torpedo boat,' Higgins told him. 'In the States you call them PTs – patrol torpedo boats.'

'I'm with you now,' Ravallo said. 'So what's so special about this . . . MTB?'

'Nothing special. It's your standard sixty-foot Vosper,' Higgins said, then took a second blueprint from the folder and handed it to McIndoe. 'The same MTB after a few structural alterations.'

'It's basically little more than a shell,' McIndoe said, comparing the two blueprints.

'To the uninitiated eye, perhaps,' Higgins replied. 'But what I see is an MTB stripped of all but its essential components. The galley and the chart room have been stripped bare, and the wheelhouse has been equipped with only the minimum of navigational instruments. Powerful short- and long-range radio-transmitters have been installed in the wireless room, and the engine room's been modified to cut down on the number of crew needed to run it. As you know, the MTB's one real drawback was its range limitation due to the high fuel consumption of the engines. Well, that problem's been eliminated in this design. The three American Packard marine engines have been replaced with two smaller, lightweight Rolls-Royce engines, which were specially commissioned for this particular vessel from the same people who designed the Hawker-Hurricane engine. Smaller, but with a far better fuel consumption rate than either the Packards or even our own British Hall-Scotts, which were the ones used on the first MTBs. The three main fuel tanks have been left intact, but the two reserve tanks have been taken out. Also, as you can see, the port and starboard Vickers machine-guns are still in place, as is one of the two twenty-millimetre Oerlikon anti-aircraft guns. It's situated on the stern. All the other weapons have been removed. Including the torpedoes, of course.'

'In other words, it's been built for speed,' Ravallo concluded.

'You've got the key word there, Nicky. Speed,' Higgins agreed. 'A normal MTB can reach a speed of up to around forty knots on the open sea. This little beauty's already done fifty in the English Channel. It's a significant increase, considering that the German *Schnellboote*, the equivalent of our own MTBs, has a top speed of near enough thirty-six knots. OK, so it may not carry the same awesome array of weapons that the *Schnellbooten* have, but fifteen knots can be just as useful on the open sea. And because it's lighter, manoeuvrability will be that much easier in the event of a torpedo attack.'

'Will these engines now become standard in your MTBs to give them that extra speed on the open sea?' Ravallo asked.

'Unfortunately not,' Higgins replied. 'The Rolls-Royce engines were built specifically with a light, buoyant craft in mind – they're just not powerful enough for a fully equipped MTB. It's not as if we didn't try it, though.'

'*We*?' McIndoe said suspiciously.

'Who else do you think could have pushed her to fifty knots without damaging the engines?' Higgins asked with a grin.

'I should have guessed,' McIndoe replied, then looked at Starr. 'Is this an SOE prototype, sir?'

'No, actually it belongs to the SBS. We've just, shall we say, "borrowed" her for the next few days. The SBS were really quite agreeable to the whole idea.'

'How did you manage to pull that off, sir?' McIndoe asked in amazement. 'The SBS are usually very protective of their equipment, especially their prototypes.'

Starr puffed on his pipe before answering. 'In this case it wasn't so much who I knew, rather than what I knew about them. Let's leave it at that, shall we?'

'You mean you blackmailed them?' Ravallo said with a chuckle.

'I'd prefer to think that we came to an understanding, Major,' Starr replied. 'I've assured them that Sub-Lieutenant Higgins will compile a detailed report of the vessel's handling and performance for their boffins to study back in London. They can only benefit from it. All in all, I'd say they've got themselves a pretty good deal.'

'Where's the MTB now?' McIndoe asked.

'It's moored in one of the submarine pens on Manoel Island,' Higgins told him. 'We couldn't risk leaving it out in the open, not with the hammering the harbour's getting from the Jerry bombers every day.'

'Sir, you still haven't told us anything about the operation itself,' McIndoe said, a hint of frustration creeping into his voice as he handed the blueprints back to Higgins.

Starr opened the folder in front of him. 'The Americans have an operative in Sicily right now, who's been gathering together information on the military hardware which the Germans have been steadily building up over the last few months on the island. Your first task will be to go to Sicily tonight and bring this operative back to Malta for a complete debriefing. Only then will I know how to proceed with the next stage of the operation.'

'I assume you know this guy?' McIndoe said, casting a sidelong glance at Ravallo.

'Gal, actually,' Ravallo corrected him. 'And yeah, I know her well.'

'A woman?' McIndoe replied in surprise.

'Her name's Lieutenant Stella di Mauro. She's our top operative in Sicily.'

'An Eyetie?' McIndoe said scornfully. 'I might have guessed. I hope you're paying her well for this information?'

'And just what the hell's that supposed to mean?' Ravallo demanded as he jumped angrily to his feet.

'Major Ravallo, sit down!' Starr ordered.

'I didn't come all this way just to have your people insult my colleagues,' Ravallo snapped as he swung round to face Starr. 'Stella's risked her life to get the info you wanted. I think she deserves better, don't you?'

'Nicky, I'm sorry. I was out of line,' McIndoe said, putting a hand lightly on Ravallo's arm.

Ravallo jerked his arm away and glared at McIndoe. 'Stella may have been born in Sicily, but now she's as American as I am. She also happens to be a valued member of Military Intelligence, and gets paid a salary just like the rest of us. Satisfied now?'

'Last night, Lieutenant McIndoe was betrayed by a senior Partisan which almost led to his capture by the Gestapo,' Starr told Ravallo. 'Had it not been for the timely intervention of the Royal Navy, he wouldn't be here right now apologizing to you for his rash outburst. It's not the first time that it's happened to him, and sadly it probably won't be the last either. I realize that the vast majority of Partisans would willingly lay down their lives in the struggle to liberate their country from the Germans, but once you've had your fingers burnt, you tend to become that little bit more cynical. It's one of the perils of working in the field, Major.'

Starr's put-down wasn't lost on Ravallo. He raised a hand of acknowledgement to McIndoe. 'I guess you've got every right to be suspicious. It's just that Stella . . .' he trailed off with a quick shrug and retook his seat.

McIndoe was furious with himself for letting his emotions get the better of him. It wasn't like him to be so blunt – Starr was right though, his cynical outburst had stemmed from his brush with the Gestapo the previous night. The scars of betrayal were still fresh in his mind. But even so, it was still no reason for that kind of unprofessional conduct. He knew that Starr would have something to say to him about it afterwards but, as he pushed any thoughts of that from his mind, he was already beginning to wonder to himself whether Ravallo's defence of his colleague went deeper than just professional respect. *It's just that Stella* . . . Had Ravallo been about to reveal something of a personal nature to them before changing his mind? Although intrigued, McIndoe chose not to pursue the matter any further.

'You'll leave Manoel Island at 2200 hours tonight and rendezvous with Lieutenant di Mauro off the Sicilian coast at 0100 hours tomorrow morning,' Starr told them. 'Higgins already has the coordinates for the rendezvous. Major, you and Lieutenant McIndoe will report back here with Lieutenant di Mauro on your return. Now, I suggest that you brief the rest of your team, then get your heads down for a few hours' sleep. It's going to be a long night for you all.' He closed the folder. 'Thank you, gentlemen, that will be all for now. Good luck.'

'Thank you, sir,' McIndoe said, then got to his feet and replaced his chair against the wall.

'McIndoe, a word before you go,' Starr called out as the three men moved to the door.

McIndoe closed the door behind Ravallo and Higgins. As he turned back to Starr he suddenly felt like a naughty schoolboy waiting for his punishment in the headmaster's study. 'I know I was out of line, sir. It won't happen again,' he said, anticipating Starr's reason for wanting him to remain behind.

'Somewhat blunt, perhaps, but understandable under the circumstances,' Starr replied to McIndoe's surprise. 'You spoke your mind, McIndoe, and you know I like that in a man. For what it's worth, I've never actually met Lieutenant di Mauro, but from what I can gather she's regarded as a first-class field operative by the top brass in Military Intelligence. No, that's not what I wanted to speak to you about. I thought you should know that I've already endorsed Wing-Commander Winstanley's request to forward your name to the War Office for a commendation.'

'Thank you, sir,' McIndoe stammered, such was his amazement at Starr's turnabout after the way he'd torn into him earlier about his actions at the air-base.

'Don't get me wrong, McIndoe, this doesn't mean that I condone what you did,' Starr was quick to point out. 'It was damn foolish and irresponsible on your part. But having said that, I've no intention of allowing my personal feelings to jeopardize your chances of being decorated for bravery, especially after Wing-Commander Winstanley spoke so highly of you.'

'I appreciate that, sir. Thank you.'

'That's all, McIndoe,' Starr said, then turned his attention to a folder on his desk.

'Well, here it is,' Higgins announced with a theatrical wave of his arm. 'Officially known as the MTB Prototype 149.'

The sleek, streamlined sixty-foot vessel rocked gently in the oily waters of the illuminated underground cavern as the rippling waves lightly caressed the hull. The superstructure, deck, thin radio mast and weapons were painted a dull, lifeless shade of black which appeared to absorb the reflection of the cavern lights. The compact bulletproof bridge – housed forward of the radio mast – was also painted black, save for the single small window with the angled spray-deflector directly above it. The perfect night camouflage.

'How many crew are there in the engine room?' Passiere asked.

'Two – the chief engineer and his assistant, who'll also double as the stoker,' Higgins replied. 'Fewer bodies, faster boat.'

'That is good, considering that we would have needed at least another two crewmen in the engine room had it been a standard MTB,' Passiere said.

'Except this isn't a *standard* MTB, Frenchy,' Higgins reminded him. Passiere had been called 'Frenchy' ever since he'd first joined the SOE. It had only been a couple of months later that he'd discovered, to his horror, that his nickname was British slang for a condom! But the more he'd fought against the nickname, the more it had stuck. That had been almost eighteen months ago now and, although he didn't like the monicker, he'd learned to live with it.

McIndoe watched as Higgins boarded the MTB, then climbed the metal stairs to the wheelhouse. Like the others, McIndoe was dressed in a black polo-necked jersey and black flannels, with a black balaclava tucked into one of his shoulder epaulettes. McIndoe looked past the wheelhouse to the towering bridge of the Royal Navy submarine, *Unique*, which was moored on the opposite side of the yawning underground cavern. A second Royal Navy submarine, *Ursula*, lay at anchor behind her. The *Ursula* had sustained superficial damage to her conning tower after being caught on the surface and strafed by a German U-boat, and a dozen Royal Navy maintenance engineers, all dressed in lightweight khaki overalls, were working feverishly to try and repair the damage before daybreak so that she could join a planned sortie against a small German convoy which was headed for North Africa with much-needed fuel and ammunition for Rommel's battle-weary troops. He wondered where the submarine *Unbeaten* was at that moment. Was she submerged off Manoel Island for the night, or prowling the depths of the Mediterranean, looking to add to the twenty-five thousand tons of German shipping she'd already sent to the bottom of the ocean?

'You planning to stand there all night, Mac?' Higgins called out good-humouredly from the wheelhouse door.

It was only then that McIndoe realized the others had already boarded the vessel. He grinned ruefully at Higgins and climbed aboard.

'Cast off,' Higgins shouted, then looked across at Evans who'd already taken up a position behind the revolving spotlight which was mounted on the bow. 'You know the drill, Taffy. Keep your eyes peeled for any mines.'

'You can count on it, Charlie boy,' Evans assured him.

Higgins beckoned Johnson and Hillyard to the foot of the stairs, and gestured to the two spotlights which were secured to the deck on either side of the wheelhouse. 'I want you each to man one of them and keep a constant lookout for mines until we're clear of Grand Harbour. I don't care how far away the mines may look to you, if you pick them up in the spotlight then they're already too close.'

Ravallo waited until Johnson and Hillyard had left to take up their posts before climbing the stairs to the wheelhouse. 'Just how serious is the threat of mines around here?'

'Serious enough,' Higgins replied as he started up the engine. 'The Jerries drop magnetic mines in and around Grand Harbour every time they bomb the island. The coastal-defence units go out after every raid and blow up as many of the mines as they can find, but inevitably a few will slip through the net. That's why we need the lookouts. If they spot a mine early enough it can be blown up before it can do any damage.'

'And who's the team's marksman?' Ravallo asked.

'Mac,' Higgins replied, gesturing to McIndoe who was standing silently in the doorway behind Ravallo.

'I might have guessed,' Ravallo said, looking at McIndoe.

McIndoe was armed with a Lee Enfield rifle which he'd taken from the small, but well-stocked, arsenal which was situated in what had been the galley below, deck. He already knew his way around the boat, having arranged for Higgins to give him a tour that afternoon while the others had been resting.

'Well, I'd better get down there in case I'm needed,' McIndoe said, closing the wheelhouse door behind him and descending the stairs to the deck. He crossed to the bow. Evans already had the powerful spotlight trained on the murky waters, even though the vessel still hadn't left the sanctuary of the cavern. He glanced up at the wheelhouse, but couldn't see Ravallo from where he was standing. They'd barely spoken since the incident in Starr's office that afternoon. Yet he hadn't sensed any particular animosity in Ravallo's attitude towards him when the team had been taken by boat from the mainland to the underground cavern on Manoel Island. Admittedly, he and Ravallo hadn't been seated next to each other on the boat – Ravallo had wisely chosen to sit between Evans and Passiere, whereas he'd been forced to listen to Johnson complaining bitterly that he hadn't been able to get back to sleep that afternoon after being rudely woken by yet another German bombing raid over Valletta. McIndoe had been greatly relieved to reach Manoel Island – he'd forgotten just how irritating Johnson's complaining could be, especially as there had been no way for him to make a quick exit. Was Ravallo still angry with him for criticizing Stella di Mauro? It was so hard to tell with him. Ravallo had appeared to be his chirpy, gregarious self as he'd laughed and joked with Evans and Passiere in the boat. But, after seeing Ravallo's ability to switch personalities with such ease at the airfield, he was no longer sure what the man was thinking or feeling. *You're overreacting*, he was quick to tell himself, yet he couldn't seem to shake off the notion that Ravallo was using his affable personality to hide something about himself. Did it involve Stella di Mauro? *Did it matter?* What if there was something between them? It was none of his business . . . unless it happened to encroach on the operation itself.

The MTB emerged slowly from the cavern into the tranquil waters of Grand Harbour. McIndoe looked up in awe at the breathtaking sight of the thousands of strafing searchlight beams which pierced the heart of darkness above and beyond the island, slivers of blinding light constantly dissecting each other, like a mélange of free spirits guarding the night sky against any evil. Stray beams washed reassuringly across the vessel as it made its way carefully across the harbour towards the breakwater; with such a diffusion of light illuminating the waters around them, the spotlights had suddenly become surplus to requirements, at least for as long as they remained within the confines of Grand Harbour.

'Mine ahead,' Evans shouted through his cupped hands to Higgins in the wheelhouse.

McIndoe cursed himself silently for being distracted by the delicate tapestry of interwoven spotlights over the island, and followed Evans's pointing finger. A magnetic mine bobbing menacingly in the water not fifty yards ahead of him. He raised the rifle to his shoulder.

'Mine!' came Hillyard's warning from the starboard side.

McIndoe could hear the anxiety in Hillyard's voice, and immediately ran to where Hillyard was using a wooden prod to delicately push the mine away from the hull of the boat.

'Why the hell didn't you see it earlier?' McIndoe demanded to know. 'Another few seconds and we'd all have bought it.'

'I didn't see it until the last moment. It was floating in the middle of that oil slick,' Hillyard replied guiltily as he continued to keep the mine at bay while Higgins steered the vessel carefully around it.

'Boss, it looks like this little bugger's following us,' Evans shouted to McIndoe. 'You're going to have to put it out of our misery before it gets any closer.'

'I've got it, Mac. You worry about that one.'

McIndoe looked round to see Ravallo, armed with a Lee Enfield, sprint towards the bow. Hillyard winced as the wooden prod slipped and he wiped the back of his hand nervously across his forehead, knowing only too well that these volatile mines could go up at the slightest provocation. He didn't take his eyes off the mine as he followed it towards the stern, the prod still trailing in the water. Then, gritting his teeth, he eased the tip of the prod against the side of the mine and drew his head back, as if that would somehow save him from the blast if the mine were to prematurely explode.

'You're doing fine there, Bruce. Just a few more seconds and then it'll be out of range and I can pick it off,' McIndoe said, brushing away a trickle of sweat which had seeped into the corner of his eye.

A shot echoed out across the harbour, followed a second later by a shuddering explosion as Ravallo's shot scored a direct hit on the mine. Evans let out a whoop of delight and Hillyard cursed furiously under his breath when the resultant swell of water dragged the mine away from the tip of his prod. McIndoe was quick to put a reassuring hand on Hillyard's arm. 'We're clear of the mine. Let it go now.'

'You won't get any arguments from me on that, boss,' Hillyard told him with obvious relief.

McIndoe waited until there was a safe distance between the boat and the mine, then raised the Lee Enfield to his shoulder, lined up the target in the sights, and squeezed the trigger. The mine detonated in an eruption of water, and both men instinctively stepped back from the railing as a fine spray whipped across their faces. It was then McIndoe noticed that Ravallo had been watching him. 'Thanks for the help, Nicky,' he said softly.

'No problem,' Ravallo replied.

'So where does a desk man learn to shoot like that?' McIndoe asked.

'It was all part of basic training,' Ravallo told him.

McIndoe crossed to the metal stairs at the side of the wheelhouse and sat down on one of the treads. 'Nicky, about what I said at the briefing. I'm sorry.'

'Forget it, Mac,' Ravallo replied. 'We all say things on the spur of the moment. You had every right to be suspicious of Stella after what you went through last night.'

'But it still wasn't right for me to go shouting my mouth off like that. It's obvious by the way you came to her defence that you and Stella . . .' McIndoe trailed off uncomfortably, knowing he'd already said too much.

'What exactly are you trying to say, Mac?' Ravallo asked, then a faint smile crept across his face. 'You think I came to Stella's defence because she's my girl? Let me tell you why I stood up for her this afternoon – because I've got the greatest respect for her as a field operative. She's a consummate professional. The best there is, in my opinion. I should know – I'm her controller in Gibraltar.'

'You mean you're her handler in Military Intelligence?'

'Handler, controller: it's the same thing. A word of warning though, Mac. She doesn't expect any special favours just because she's a woman. Don't make the mistake of treating her with kid gloves. She sure as hell won't thank you for it. Remember that.'

'I will,' McIndoe assured him, pulling a packet of cigarettes from his pocket and pushing one between his lips. Ravallo helped himself to a cigarette from the packet as well. 'You know, I've never seen you with any cigarettes of your own,' McIndoe said, lighting it for him.

'Why would I carry any on me when I'm trying to give them up?' Ravallo replied with a questioning frown.

'I guess there's no answer to that,' McIndoe said. He got to his feet and climbed the stairs to the wheelhouse door where he paused to look around him. The vessel was now clear of the harbour and the main risk of floating mines. Even so, the spotlights remained trained on the water. There was no reason to take any unnecessary risks. 'How's it going, Charlie?' he asked on entering the wheelhouse.

'Good,' Higgins replied without looking at him. 'That was some nifty shooting just now. Both of you.'

McIndoe looked round to find Ravallo in the doorway behind him. For a moment he was puzzled as to how Higgins had known that Ravallo was there when he hadn't taken his eyes off the water. It was only when he crossed to where Higgins was standing that he noticed Ravallo's reflection in the window.

'Mac, I think there's something you should know,' Higgins announced, breaking the silence. 'This will be my last run for the Firm. Naturally I'll see the operation through to its conclusion, but I'm being posted to North Africa next month as the team leader of an undercover SBS commando unit.'

'And is there a promotion included with this posting?' McIndoe asked with a knowing smile.

'I'll be promoted to lieutenant,' Higgins replied. In the Royal Navy, a lieutenant was the equivalent of a captain in the army.

'You'll be my superior then, you son-of-a-bitch. I'll have to salute you,' McIndoe said good-humouredly.

'I'll insist on it,' Higgins said with a grin. 'I'll tell you, though, I've had some great times with the Firm. I'm certainly going to miss it.'

'When did the posting come through?' McIndoe asked.

'When I was testing this little baby back in England. My superiors wanted me to take up the post straight away, but naturally Starr had other ideas. So they came to an agreement that I'd finish this assignment before being transferred to North Africa.'

'You deserve it, Charlie,' McIndoe told him. In fact, this promotion's well overdue.'

'The irony of it all is that my superiors only dangled a promotion in front of me to lure me away from the Firm.'

'Don't knock it, buddy,' Ravallo said, entering the conversation for the first time. 'These days far too many of the top brass spend all their time hidden away in protective bomb-proof bunkers while millions of innocent civilians are being left to the mercy of enemy bombers. No, you take what you can from those bastards.'

'Steady on, that's a bit strong,' McIndoe said.

'Is it?' Ravallo replied. 'I have the greatest respect for any officer, irrespective of his rank or nationality, who issues his orders from the battlefield. A man who's prepared to fight and, if necessary, die with his men. But I've got nothing but contempt for those officers who play genocidal war games with soldiers' lives from the safety of some underground bunker thousands of miles away from the front lines. I'm sorry if that rubs you up the wrong way, Mac, but I always call it as I see it.'

'So it would seem,' McIndoe said.

'Mine ahead!' Evans yelled from the bow.

'I'll get it,' Ravallo said, moving to the door. He paused in the doorway as a grin spread across his face. 'Jesus, it's good to finally get out of that goddamn office.'

Higgins slowed the boat and carefully manoeuvred a wide berth around the illuminated mine which was pitching and falling in the rolling waves. They both watched as Ravallo took up a position beside the spotlight and raised the Lee Enfield to his shoulder. He fired too quickly and the bullet went wide of its intended target. Ejecting the spent cartridge, he lined the mine up in the sights again, but it was lost momentarily under a wave as he pulled the trigger, and his second shot missed as well. The spotlight failed to pick up the mine in the wake of the wave and Evans panned the beam frantically across the water in a desperate attempt to locate it again.

'Mac!' Higgins hissed anxiously, following the course of the beam as it strafed across the dark water. 'Do something!'

'Nicky can handle it,' McIndoe assured him in a calm voice.

Ravallo spotted the silhouette of the mine to starboard and swung the rifle away from the beam, firing into the darkness. A moment later there was a shuddering explosion which rocked the boat violently and a cascade of water washed across the deck.

'Christ, how close was that?' Higgins said in horror.

'Close enough to have blown us out of the water if he'd missed,' McIndoe replied sombrely.

They both exchanged bewildered expressions when Evans began to laugh as he pointed to starboard. McIndoe moved to the door and saw that Johnson had taken the full force of the wave which had swept over the side of the boat.

'Look at me, Lieutenant,' Johnson said bitterly as McIndoe descended the stairs. 'I'm absolutely soaked. I'll be lucky if I don't catch pneumonia after this.'

'Go and get changed,' McIndoe told him. 'There's some dry clothes below. I'll man the spotlight until you get back.'

Johnson disappeared through the hatchway, still muttering to himself at his misfortune. Ravallo shook his head slowly to himself. 'How the hell did he ever get into the SOE?'

'Not all our operatives are trained assassins. We've each been brought in to fulfil a specific job. As I told you at the airfield, Neville's speciality's his photographic mind. Though that doesn't mean he can't handle himself in a fight or use a weapon effectively should the need arise. So don't knock him, Nicky. He's a good man to have on your side.'

'You think a lot of these guys, don't you?' Ravallo said.

'They're the best,' McIndoe replied matter-of-factly.

'Who is the best, *patron*?' Passiere asked as he emerged through the open hatchway on to the deck.

'Not you, that's for sure,' McIndoe replied with a smile. 'Well, what do you think of your wireless room?'

'Very impressive,' Passiere replied.

'And so it should be. I had a look earlier. You've got some of the best British radio equipment down there, Georges.' McIndoe had always refrained from calling Passiere 'Frenchy', knowing how much he disliked the nickname. Although Passiere had never mentioned it, McIndoe's gesture hadn't been lost on him. 'So what brings you topside?'

'My orders are to maintain radio silence until we have picked up Lieutenant di Mauro. Naturally I will be monitoring all German radio-transmissions once we get within range of the island, but now that I have familiarized myself with the equipment, there really is not much to keep me down there.'

'You could always have a sleep?' Ravallo said, straight-faced.

'There are no bunks on this boat,' Passiere snorted in disgust. 'And anyway, I had a long sleep this afternoon.'

'Good, then you can man the spotlight and keep a lookout for mines until Johnson returns,' McIndoe told him.

'I certainly walked into that one,' Passiere grumbled.

McIndoe and Ravallo returned to the wheelhouse.

'Another few minutes then we'll have to switch off the spotlights,' Higgins announced. 'The Germans have spotter planes patrolling the skies day and night. We'd stand out like a Christmas tree down here.'

'What about mines?' Ravallo asked anxiously.

'We'll shortly be entering the main shipping channel. I've already plotted the same course that was trawled by the Royal Navy minesweeper, *Abingdon*, for a small supply convoy which got through to Valletta three days ago. It's the most recent chart we've got. Of course some mines could have drifted into the area since then, but the chances of us hitting one must be pretty remote to say the least. Having said that, the risk will further diminish the closer we get to Sicily. The Germans regularly send out *Schnellbooten* to blow up any stray mines which might have drifted out of the shipping channel towards the island.'

'Roll on Sicily,' Ravallo said as he placed his rifle on the wooden bench which was bolted to the wall opposite the window.

The door opened and Passiere peered into the wheelhouse. 'Johnson is back now, *patron*. Is there anything else you want me to do while I am up here?'

'Yes there is,' Higgins said, glancing over his shoulder at Passiere. 'I'm going to open her up shortly, so see to it that all the spotlights are switched off. We don't want to advertise ourselves, do we?'

Passiere closed the door again behind him, and McIndoe watched as he crossed to where Evans was still scanning the illuminated water for any sign of floating mines. Evans listened to Passiere, then looked up questioningly at the wheelhouse. Higgins nodded, drawing his finger sharply across his throat to signify that he wanted the light cut. Evans cast a last look out to sea before reluctantly switching off the spotlight, and the two men left the dark, shadowy bow, disappearing from sight around the side of the wheelhouse.

Shortly afterwards, Passiere returned to the wheelhouse to tell Higgins that his orders had been carried out.

'So are we finally going to see what this boat can really do?' Ravallo asked.

'I'll push her to the limit – but only for a short distance,' Higgins said. 'These engines may be powerful, but they're also very sensitive. They respond brilliantly to short bursts at top speed, but they can't sustain that speed over a long distance. That was the one drawback we encountered during testing. Don't forget, this is still a prototype. The boffins back in Portsmouth wanted another few weeks to work on the engines, but you know how insistent Starr can be when he wants to get his own way.'

'Now you tell us!' Ravallo said.

'I could keep her at a steady speed of forty-five from here to Sicily if I wanted to, Nicky,' Higgins was quick to tell him. 'That speed alone would put us out of sight of any pursuing *Schnellboote*. It's just that these engines still need some minor adjustments which would allow her to maintain her top speed indefinitely. Why don't you two go for'ard and I'll give you a demonstration of what she can do?'

'Yeah, why not?' Ravallo said, moving to the door. 'Coming, Mac?'

McIndoe followed him down the stairs, then called the others together and explained what Higgins intended to do. They all moved to the bow. McIndoe looked up at the wheelhouse and gave Higgins a thumbs-up sign. 'Grab hold of the railing, chaps,' McIndoe said. 'I've got a feeling we're going to be in for quite a ride.'

He wasn't wrong. For the next thirty seconds the hypnotic effect of the rushing waters and the gigantic bow-waves, coupled with the sheer physical shock of the bone-jarring vibrations of the deck as the vessel pulsed effortlessly through the dark waters, parting all before it as if it were some omnipotent deity, was stunning in its breathless magnificence. The effect was like some drug which had infused both mind and body; McIndoe felt as if he'd been taken up and beyond the spectrum of mere mortality. Then, just as suddenly as it had begun, the speed decreased and the rush was over.

McIndoe looked at the faces around him and could see that the hypnotic effect had been the same on all of them. Even Neville Johnson had a distant look in his eyes and a dreamy smile on his face. 'So, what do you think?' McIndoe asked.

'All I know is that the earth sure moved for me,' Ravallo replied with a contented smile. 'Anyone got a cigarette?' The others laughed, and Evans took a packet of cigarettes from his breast pocket, holding it out to Ravallo who helped himself to one. 'What amazed me most was that there hardly seemed to be any noise coming from the engines, even when she was at her peak speed,' Ravallo said to McIndoe. 'Just a low hum. How did they manage to muffle the engines so effectively?'

McIndoe took a cigarette and lit it. 'I had a closer look at the blueprints earlier this evening. From what I can gather, these engines had already been finely tuned for noise reduction even before they were installed. They aren't actually secured to the hull; they're on spring and rubber mountings, and further insulated with cork and layers of long-haired wool. The exhaust is fitted with a suppressor, and the two propellers have been specifically designed for minimum turbulence in the water.'

'But there has to be some kind of ventilation system down there for the engine to breathe,' Johnson said. 'And that would mean a certain amount of noise escaping, irrespective of how well insulated the casing might be.'

'There are two narrow inlet pipes which run from the engines to the bow. They're probably right underneath us,' McIndoe said, tapping his foot on the deck. 'The engine draws and expels air through these pipes. And, as you heard, they're very effective.'

'Now I can see why the SBS wanted to keep the boat under wraps until they were ready to use it themselves,' Hillyard said. 'When it comes down to it, it's almost as silent as a midget sub.'

'Well, the demonstration's over,' McIndoe announced, clapping his hands together. 'Georges has already had a good look below deck, so he's just volunteered to give the rest of you the official guided tour.'

'*Merci, patron,*' Passiere said facetiously.

'Then, after that, Bruce can make one of his famous brew-ups,' McIndoe said. He turned to Ravallo. 'He makes the best cup of tea in the whole unit.'

'Tea?' Ravallo said, pulling a face. 'Isn't there any coffee on this tub?'

'Sorry, Nicky, no coffee,' McIndoe replied with an apologetic shrug. 'Rationing, you understand.'

'Tea it is then,' Ravallo said reluctantly. 'No milk, no sugar. Just hot.'

'Let's get this tour out of the way so that we can settle down to some serious poker. I bought a couple of packs of cards when I was in Valletta this afternoon,' Evans said, patting Passiere on the back as they followed Hillyard and Johnson towards the open hatch.

'Poker?' Ravallo mused, and a slow smile spread across his face.

'I know they'd be glad to have you sit in with them,' McIndoe told him. 'They've really taken to you.'

'What about you, Mac? Are you in for a few hands?'

'I think I'll stay topside and keep Charlie company in the wheelhouse,' McIndoe replied as they moved away from the bow. 'I've never been very lucky at cards. And contrary to the old saying, not very lucky in love either.'

'Stop it, you're breaking my heart,' Ravallo said with a grin as they reached the stairs leading up to the wheelhouse. 'You know where I'll be if you need me.'

'Let's just hope I don't need you until we arrive at the rendezvous.'

'See you later,' Ravallo said, then made his way carefully along the wet, slippery deck towards the hatchway.

'Good luck,' McIndoe called out after him.

Ravallo paused and looked round at him. 'Luck's for amateurs, but I'll be sure to pass on your good wishes to the others. They might just need them,' he said, grinning.

FOUR

'Are you sure this is the right place?'

'I've told you already, Nicky, these are the coordinates I was given by Starr before we left Valletta,' Higgins said. 'It's not my fault if your people can't keep to their part of the deal.'

For a moment McIndoe thought Ravallo was going to turn on Higgins, but he just exhaled deeply and slumped down on to the wooden bench, raking his fingers through his hair before looking up at McIndoe. 'What the hell's keeping her?'

McIndoe didn't reply. For the past twenty-five minutes the MTB had been lying at anchor off the coast of western Sicily. An uninhabited stretch of coastline which, according to intelligence reports, was patrolled only by soldiers on foot. The nearest town was the coastal port of Gela and, from where he stood, McIndoe could just make out a speckle of lights scattered dimly across the distant horizon. But his mind wasn't on Gela or the lights. Although none of them had yet mentioned the possibility that something might have happened to Stella di Mauro, he knew that it would certainly have crossed their minds since they'd first dropped anchor.

There was now a noticeable tension between Higgins and Ravallo. Higgins was rightly concerned that, the longer the boat remained exposed in the open sea, the greater the risk was of them being attacked by one of the numerous U-boats which were known to patrol the coastal waters at night. But Ravallo had insisted from the start that they remain at anchor and, although Higgins was master of the vessel, Ravallo was still in overall command of the operation. Higgins had wisely decided to bite back his anger, knowing better than to question an order from a superior officer. McIndoe had managed to keep the peace so far, but with each passing minute he could sense that the tension between the two men was steadily increasing. And he certainly didn't want to be caught in the middle if it did flare up.

He crossed to the wheelhouse door and looked down at Evans, who was standing motionless on the bow, a Sten gun in his hands, his eyes riveted to the dark waters beyond the boat. Johnson, who was similarly armed, was the starboard lookout. McIndoe couldn't see Hillyard, who had taken up a position on the other side of the wheelhouse. They would all be well aware of the dangers, and it was testament to their professionalism that none of them had once questioned the enforced delay. At that moment McIndoe felt damn proud of his men.

Higgins, though, was still unhappy. 'How long are we going to remain at anchor out here?' he demanded.

'Until Lieutenant di Mauro gets here,' Ravallo retorted.

'You may be in charge of this operation, but my first responsibility is to the men on this boat,' Higgins said, looking across at Ravallo who was still seated on the bench. 'If anything happens to them because – '

'Like you said, I'm in charge of this operation,' Ravallo cut in sharply. 'Remember that.'

'I just hope she's worth it,' Higgins said angrily as he turned back to the wheel.

McIndoe grabbed Ravallo's arm as he sprang to his feet. 'Sit down, Nicky.'

'I don't have to – '

'Sit down!' McIndoe repeated, more forcefully. Ravallo pulled his arm free from McIndoe's grip and sat down again. McIndoe held up a finger as Higgins was about to speak. 'Not another word, Charlie. Not another word.' It was then he noticed Evans peering up anxiously at the wheelhouse, alerted by the sound of the raised voices. Quickly he raised his hand to signal that everything was under control. He turned back to Ravallo and Higgins. 'There are three men out there who've remained at their posts ever since we dropped anchor. You can be sure that they're just as concerned as we are about the possibility of being attacked. Have you heard them complaining? Have you heard them bickering amongst themselves?'

'What's your point, Mac?' Higgins demanded.

'You're both supposed to be officers in élite military units, only right now I don't see much evidence of that. You've been squabbling for the last twenty minutes like a couple of children. You're not exactly inspiring much confidence in the men, are you? And isn't that what being an officer is all about?'

McIndoe knew he'd overstepped the mark the moment he'd opened his mouth by taking a senior officer to task in that way. But he didn't regret it. Not for a moment. It needed to be said if only to clear the air, even though Ravallo would be quite justified in bringing a charge of insubordination against him when they returned to Valletta.

For a few moments neither man said anything, then Ravallo slowly got to his feet. 'I guess I'm just not used to this kind of hands-on pressure you guys come up against out here in the field. In the past I've always been able to handle my problems from the comfort of my office. It may be a lot easier that way, but it's also a hell of a lot more boring.'

'I can understand your concern for Lieutenant di Mauro – I'd be feeling exactly the same way if I were in your shoes – but the fact remains that we just can't wait out here indefinitely for her,' Higgins told him. 'We have to weigh up the risks in this kind of situation. And that means putting the safety of everyone aboard this vessel first.'

'I hear what you're saying,' Ravallo said, looking at his watch. 'We'll give her another ten minutes.'

Higgins glanced at McIndoe who nodded. 'OK, another ten minutes,' Higgins agreed. 'But if she still hasn't showed up by then, we return to Malta.'

McIndoe watched Ravallo leave the wheelhouse and make his way down on to the deck. It was so difficult to read what really lay behind Ravallo's mask. McIndoe had always thought that *he* was good at hiding his emotions, but Ravallo was a master at it. McIndoe tended to withdraw into his shell, thereby dissuading people from approaching him, but then everyone knew that something was troubling him anyway. Ravallo, though, was able to hide everything behind a gregarious, outgoing personality. It made McIndoe think of a circus clown, hiding his emotions behind the painted smile. Was that what Ravallo was doing? Or was he just reading too much into it? Ever since they'd left Valletta he'd been trying to catch a glimpse behind the façade in a vain attempt to try and discover Ravallo's true feelings towards Stella di Mauro. Ravallo appeared angry at her rather than concerned about her, but again the face of a circus clown materialized in McIndoe's mind and smiled mockingly at him. Perhaps when she finally came aboard it would become more apparent. *If* she came aboard . . .

'I shouldn't have gone off at him like that,' Higgins said. 'It's only natural that he'd be worried sick about her. I would, if it were one of my lads. And with her being a woman, that just makes it even worse, doesn't it?'

'I never took you for a chauvinist, Charlie,' McIndoe replied.

'It's only natural that he'd worry more about a woman in this kind of situation,' Higgins said defensively.

'What are you suggesting? That there's something between them?'

'Now who's being the chauvinist?' Higgins said. 'Why can't a man and a woman work together without it spilling over into the bedroom? It happens all over the world, Mac. What makes you think this is any different?'

'I don't. It was just a thought, that's all.'

'Somehow, I don't think so,' Higgins mused. 'He seems too professional to get involved with one of his operatives.'

'That's what he said,' McIndoe said.

'There you are then,' Higgins said with a triumphant smile. 'When you've been married as long as I have, you tend to know these things. It's a kind of a sixth sense, I guess.'

'Sure, Charlie,' McIndoe said in a less-than-convinced tone of voice.

'She's now thirty minutes late,' Higgins said, his face becoming serious as he looked anxiously at his watch. 'What if she's been captured? How long could she hold out under interrogation? She could be giving the Germans our exact location as we speak. I don't like it, Mac, not one little bit. We should have been out of here long ago. Not offering ourselves as target practice for some bloody U-boat.'

'Don't you think I'm just as worried about it as you are?' McIndoe replied. 'But this is Nicky's command and we have to follow his orders.'

'That's another thing that rankles me, having to take orders from a desk man,' Higgins said bitterly. 'Between us, we've got over twenty missions under our belts. Yet this is his first field operation. It doesn't seem right, does it?'

'If you feel that strongly about it, make an official complaint to Starr when we get back to Valletta. Who knows, you might even get transferred to your new command in North Africa that bit quicker.'

'That's a cheap shot, Mac,' Higgins snapped.

'No cheaper than your dig at Ravallo,' McIndoe replied.

'Look!' Higgins said excitedly, and grabbed McIndoe's arm as he pointed towards the shore.

McIndoe had already seen it. A light flashing intermittently in Morse code. 'This . . . is . . . Star-ling,' he read out loud. 'Do . . . you . . . read . . . me?'

Ravallo used a pen torch to signal back: This is Home Base. I read you.

'On . . . my . . . way,' McIndoe interpreted again.

'That's Stella,' Ravallo called up to them in the wheelhouse.

'Or a trap,' Higgins said.

'I'm going down on deck to direct operations from there. You just worry about getting us out of here as soon as I give you the signal.'

'You can count on it,' Higgins told him.

McIndoe descended the stairs and called his team together. 'This could be a trap. I want you to remain at your posts, but only activate the spotlights if I give the order.'

'If it is a trap, do we also have to wait for your order to open fire?' Hillyard asked.

'Not if you're shot at first,' McIndoe replied. 'But for all we know, Lieutenant di Mauro could be wearing a German uniform as part of a disguise. Just use your common sense, that's all.'

'It's not a trap,' Ravallo insisted when McIndoe crossed to where he was standing. 'Shortly after I arrived at Gibraltar HQ we arranged for a list of code names to fall into enemy hands. They were supposedly those used by American field operatives in Italy, Sicily and Greece. But all the code names were false. Only the Germans didn't know that, so if Stella had been captured, she'd have given them one of the code names on the list. And the Germans would have used the false code name to contact us. No, Mac, that's Stella out there.'

'I'll believe that when she's safely aboard and we're on our way back to Malta,' McIndoe replied.

'I was already beginning to fear the worst, I really was. I would have had a lot of explaining to do to my superiors if anything had happened to her.'

'Is that all you're bothered about? That you'd be up in front of your superiors if she'd been captured?'

'Of course I care about what happens to my operatives, but you have to learn to keep your distance,' Ravallo said. 'As I told you before, you can't let your emotions get in the way of the job. To you it may seem cold-hearted, but it's the only way.'

McIndoe didn't reply. He could relate to what Ravallo was saying. He'd never allowed himself to get too close to any of his colleagues at the Firm. They were acquaintances rather than friends. All his friendships lay outside of work . . .

'I can hear an outboard motor, sir,' Johnson called out to McIndoe.

Moments later, a twelve-foot skiff was spotted approaching the boat. There were two shadowy figures in the skiff, but it was impossible to make out their features in the darkness. McIndoe dropped the Jacob's ladder over the side of the hull, but it was only when the skiff drew closer that it became apparent that they were both dressed in loose-fitting woollen sweaters and baggy flannels. The figure seated in the bow was also wearing a woollen cap tugged firmly down, and it was this one who grabbed hold of the ladder when the skiff drew alongside the boat. Johnson already had his Sten gun trained on the figure Ravallo helped aboard.

'You're late!' Ravallo said angrily. 'You of all people should know better than to keep a boat waiting in enemy waters.'

'I'm sorry, Nicky,' came the plea in a soft, husky, feminine voice. 'The truck ran out of gas before we reached the beach. We had to cover the last couple of miles on foot.'

'You ran out of gas?' Ravallo said with stinging sarcasm. 'How original.'

'Well, it's true,' she replied, going on to the offensive. 'The truck had a leak in the gas tank. These things happen, Nicky. Perhaps not in your perfect world, but they sure as hell happen in the real world.'

McIndoe was taken aback by her tone of voice. Not many men would have dared to stand up to a senior officer like that, yet here she was prepared to slug it out verbally with Ravallo, giving as good as she got. Yet there was no trace of insubordination in her voice. She was just telling it as it was.

'Boss, there's something out there,' Evans called to McIndoe from the bow as he peered anxiously into the gloom beyond the boat. 'It sounds like . . . creaking wood.'

'Hit the lights,' McIndoe yelled.

The starboard and bow spotlights illuminated the dark water around the boat, picking out the three cockleshell rowing boats, each containing three armed Germans wearing lifejackets over their tunics. The soldier seated in the bow of the lead boat, who was wearing the rank of sergeant, barked out an order. A volley of bullets peppered the side of the MTB. One of the bullets shattered the starboard spotlight. In that instant McIndoe saw a German MP .38 submachine-gun swing towards Stella and Ravallo. He didn't know whether they'd seen it or not, and there wasn't time to find out either: he only had a split second to react. He hurled himself at Stella, who was standing with her back to him, and tackled her around the legs. She lost her balance, falling heavily against Ravallo, and the three of them crashed to the deck as a row of bullets scythed over their heads. McIndoe didn't need to issue the order to fire as Evans and Johnson opened up with their Sten guns. Hillyard turned the deck-mounted Vickers machine-gun on the lead boat. The German sergeant was killed instantly and his body toppled lifelessly into the water. The other two were hit several times; they slumped against the side of the boat which was already beginning to take in water through the bullet-holes in the hull.

Higgins started up the engine and, having already had the anchor weighed when Stella first boarded the vessel, swung the MTB in a sharp arc, racing towards the two rowing boats which were caught in the glare of the bow spotlight like helpless rabbits in the headlights of an oncoming car. Evans, who was lying flat on the bow deck, fired at the hapless Germans who now found themselves in an unenviable quandary. Should they continue the fight, or bale out before the rowing boats were mowed down by the MTB? Two of the Germans in the front boat decided that discretion was definitely the better part of valour, and leapt into the water moments before the MTB hit it. There was an agonizing scream as the remaining soldier was crushed under the bows. Higgins then swung the vessel in a sharp racing turn close to the remaining rowing boat, and the resultant wave buffeted the small craft with such force that one of the Germans lost his balance and toppled into the water. Whether it was bravado or some last, misguided attempt to carry out his orders, it was hard to judge, but one of the two remaining Germans opened fire on the wheelhouse. The bullets chewed harmlessly into the bullet-proof window and Evans returned fire, killing the two Germans.

For a brief moment an eerie silence descended over the scene, before McIndoe scrambled up on to one knee and peered cautiously over the side of the boat. He counted five dead soldiers floating in the illuminated water, the waves lapping eagerly at their lifeless bodies. Two more were clinging to an upturned rowing boat. Both couldn't have been much older than eighteen. One had blood streaming down the side of his face. Two Germans were still unaccounted for – presumed dead. 'Charlie, can you bring us in closer to those two in the water?' Higgins gave him a wave of acknowledgement. McIndoe beckoned Evans towards him. 'We're going to haul those two out of the water. Keep your gun trained on them. If they try anything, shoot them.'

'With pleasure,' Evans replied.

'Mac?' Ravallo said behind McIndoe. 'Stella says that the Germans have got at least one *Schnellboote* moored at Gela harbour. We don't want to hang around here too long.'

'We're not,' McIndoe told him. 'We're going to pick up these two to take back for questioning, then we're out of here. Believe me, I don't want to be here any longer than you do.'

Higgins brought the MTB alongside the upturned rowing boat, and McIndoe shouted in German for the two men to grab hold of the Jacob's ladder. They exchanged apprehensive glances, but neither of them made an attempt to grab for the ladder.

Ravallo cursed under his breath, then pulled the Sten gun from Johnson's hands and fired a short burst into the water close to the rowing boats. 'Either you come aboard now, or I'll kill you in the water,' he snarled at them in German. 'It's your choice.'

The German nearest the MTB grabbed hold of the ladder and climbed up the side of the hull. Evans hauled him roughly over the railing and Johnson quickly frisked him for any concealed weapons. The second German struggled up the ladder next, and Hillyard pulled him over the railing, dumping him unceremoniously on to the deck. Johnson frisked him as well. Both were unarmed.

'Take them below,' McIndoe said. He gestured to the bloodied German. 'And patch him up.' He watched as Evans and Hillyard bundled the two youths through the open hatchway, then he gave Higgins a thumbs-up sign to start back for Malta. 'That was a good bluff,' he said to Ravallo. 'I'll have to try that one next time.'

'Who said I was bluffing?' Ravallo replied, then turned to Stella. 'We need to talk.'

'You can use the chart room below,' McIndoe told him.

'Give us a few minutes alone, Mac,' Ravallo said. 'I need to clear up a few things for myself. Then come down and join us. You've just as much right to know what the hell went wrong tonight.' He grabbed Stella's arm and they disappeared through the hatchway.

McIndoe climbed the stairs to the wheelhouse. 'Any damage to the engine room?'

'No damage reported,' Higgins replied. 'Did we sustain any personnel injuries out there?'

'No,' McIndoe replied. 'Perhaps the prisoners will be able to shed some light on how they knew about the rendezvous here tonight.'

'What are you suggesting, Mac? That they were working on inside information?'

'At the moment I'm not suggesting anything. All I know is that they knew exactly where and when we'd be meeting Stella. Perhaps they tailed her. Who knows? Nicky's with her now. Hopefully he'll be able to find out something.'

'So what's she like?' Higgins asked.

'To be honest, I haven't even seen her face yet. All I know is that she seems pretty spirited to say the least.'

'Well, the main thing right now is that we've got out in one piece and with only minimal structural damage to the boat,' Higgins said.

'We're not out of trouble yet,' McIndoe said.

'No *Schnellboote* could hope to catch us out here on the open sea. And even a U-boat couldn't track us at this speed. That's the beauty of her. When she's on the move, she's in a class of her own. It's when she's lying at anchor that she's just as vulnerable as any other stationary vessel.'

McIndoe nodded. 'I'd better go and check on our prisoners,' he told Higgins. 'See you later.'

'Sure,' Higgins called out after him.

McIndoe made his way below deck. The door nearest to the stairs was closed. Ravallo and Stella were inside. He went to the cabin at the end of the passage where he found the two Germans slumped against the wall, their hands secured tightly behind their backs with two lengths of rope which Evans had found in the engine room. Their eyes were wide and apprehensive as they stared fearfully at their captors. 'How is he?' McIndoe asked, gesturing to the injured prisoner who now had a bandage wrapped tightly around his head.

'He'll live,' Evans said, closing the lid of the medical kit and getting to his feet. 'It's a nasty cut all the same. He'll need to see a doctor when we get back to Valletta.'

'Have you tried to question them yet?' McIndoe asked.

'Name, rank and number,' Hillyard snorted. 'That's all they'll give us.'

'Can't say I'm surprised,' McIndoe said. 'Look at them. They're petrified. You can bet they'd never even fired a gun in anger before tonight.'

'Some baptism of fire,' Hillyard retorted. 'You want us to carry on questioning them?'

'It can't hurt, although I doubt they'll be able to tell us anything useful,' McIndoe said. 'They'll probably just have been carrying out orders.'

'If they know anything, we'll get it out of them,' Hillyard said, then smiled coldly at the two Germans. 'A few more bruises won't be noticed after their little escapade tonight.'

McIndoe grabbed Hillyard's arm and led him out of earshot of the prisoners. 'You don't so much as lay a finger on them. Is that understood?'

'They may need a little persuading to tell us what they know.'

'You heard what I said,' McIndoe hissed.

'But other officers – '

'I don't care about the other officers,' McIndoe cut in angrily. 'I've heard about some of your interrogation methods, and quite frankly they disgust me. I'm certainly surprised that other officers have allowed it in the past, but that's not the point right now. As far as I'm concerned, I won't tolerate any kind of physical abuse of prisoners by soldiers under my command, and if I hear that you've blatantly disregarded my orders, you'll be on the next plane back to Blighty, where you'll find yourself up in front of a board of enquiry on a charge of insubordination. Is that clear?'

'Perfectly clear,' Hillyard replied humbly.

McIndoe walked back down the passage and paused outside the closed door. He listened for the sound of voices from inside the cabin and, on hearing none, rapped sharply on the door. 'Who is it?' Ravallo called out.

'It's McIndoe. Is everything all right in there?'

There was no reply, then moments later came the sound of a key being turned in the lock. The door opened and Ravallo gestured for him to enter the cabin. Stella was sitting at the table, her hands cupped over her face, a half-smoked cigarette smouldering in the ashtray at her elbow. An Italian Beretta pistol lay beside a packet of cigarettes on the table in front of her. 'Stella, this is Lieutenant Sam McIndoe,' Ravallo said, indicating McIndoe beside him. 'He's the head of the British SOE unit that we've been assigned to work with out here.'

Stella lowered her hands and looked up at McIndoe. It was the first time he'd seen her face, and even the harsh glare of the deck-head light couldn't mar her flawless beauty: the smooth olive complexion, the classical high cheekbones, the small patrician nose, the sultry pale blue eyes and the lustrous silky black hair which hung loosely on her shoulders.

Stella stared back at him for a few seconds, then reached for her cigarette and sat back in the chair. 'I'm sorry about what happened tonight,' she said in her soft, husky voice after drawing deeply on the cigarette.

'Was it your fault?' McIndoe asked, studying her face carefully for any signs of subconscious guilt. None was apparent.

'Nicky seems to think so,' she replied at length. 'And he's the one they'll believe back in Gibraltar. They always believe him. Don't they, Nicky?'

'Somebody let slip the rendezvous tonight,' Ravallo said tersely.

'Well it wasn't me,' Stella replied, a hint of anguish seeping into her voice for the first time. She took several short puffs on the cigarette, then ground it out in the ashtray. 'I don't know how the Germans found out about the rendezvous, but it certainly wasn't through any lapse of security on my part. My conscience is clear on that score.'

Ravallo stared thoughtfully at the floor for several seconds, then looked up at McIndoe. 'We still haven't thanked you for saving our lives tonight, Mac. If you hadn't knocked us to the deck when you did, we'd both be dead.'

'That was you?' Stella said, her eyes lingering on McIndoe.

'It was an instinctive gesture, that's all. I hope I didn't hurt you.' McIndoe gave her a sheepish grin. 'I'm sorry. That must have sounded very patronizing.'

She suddenly grabbed the pistol off the table and swung it on McIndoe. He stood frozen to the spot, his eyes wide and unbelieving, his mouth open in a silent scream. He wanted to dive to the floor, to evade certain death, but it felt as if there were lead weights tied to his feet. Then a single shot rang out and he instinctively flinched, fully expecting to feel the searing pain as the full force of the bullet hammered into him. Nothing happened. The bullet had missed him.

'What the hell . . . ?' McIndoe was vaguely aware of Evans shouting from the corridor. It was as if he was in a daze, his mind still reeling from what had just happened.

'He's dead.'

Ravallo's voice seemed to snap McIndoe out of his trance, and when he looked round he saw a German soldier sprawled in the passage opposite the open doorway, the commando knife still clenched in his lifeless hand. Blood seeped from the single bullet-hole in his chest. His uniform was soaking wet and a pool of water had already collected around the body. Hillyard, Johnson and Passiere, who'd all been alerted by the sound of the shot, hovered above Ravallo and Evans, who were both crouched over the body.

'I'm sorry, Sam,' Stella said with an apologetic smile, the pistol now hanging loosely at her side. 'He just suddenly appeared behind you. I saw the knife in his hand but there wasn't time to warn you. I had to shoot, otherwise he'd have surely killed you.'

'I'm certainly glad you did,' McIndoe said, the obvious relief of his narrow escape evident in his voice. 'You saved my life.'

'*Touché,*' she said with a smile.

'Where did he come from?' Evans asked.

'Isn't he one of the prisoners?' Ravallo asked.

'Not a chance,' Evans replied. 'They're both still tied up in the other cabin.'

'He's obviously one of the two Germans we couldn't account for at the rendezvous,' Hillyard deduced. 'He must have climbed on board before we left.'

'Bruce, I want you and Neville to conduct a thorough search topside in case the other German has also managed to slip aboard,' McIndoe said to Hillyard as his eyes flickered accusingly between the members of his team. But his anger was directed more at himself than at any of them.

'Right away, boss,' Hillyard replied, and the two men disappeared up the stairs.

'Georges, I want you to check down here,' McIndoe said to Passiere, who immediately set off to carry out his orders. 'Taffy, keep an eye on the prisoners. If the other German is aboard, he may try and free them.'

Ravallo eased the knife from the dead man's grasp, then entered the cabin and tossed it on to the table. 'Close call, Mac.'

'Too close,' McIndoe agreed. 'It's my fault. I should have had the boat secured before we left the rendezvous.'

'You couldn't have known this would happen.'

'Stella's right. You're being too hard on yourself,' Ravallo told him. He took a cigarette from the packet on the table, and lit it before pulling up a chair and sitting down. 'I still say the leak originated from your side, Stella. What about the guy who brought you out to the boat tonight?'

'Angelo's one of the most trusted Partisans in the whole organization,' Stella said. 'That's why he was chosen for this assignment.'

'One of the most trusted Partisans in the whole organization?' Ravallo said sarcastically. 'What's that, if not a euphemism for a spy?'

'Sorry to disappoint you, Nicky, but he didn't know about the rendezvous until after we'd left Gela,' Stella shot back. 'I only filled him in once we were already on the road. And before you start accusing any more of the Partisans, none of them knew about the rendezvous either. Not even the leader. Only I knew about it.'

Hillyard appeared in the doorway. 'Nothing topside, boss. And, judging by the pool of water on the stern deck, he must have been hiding there, waiting for us to go below before making his move.'

'But Johnson was up there all the time,' Ravallo said. 'And there's only the one hatch that leads down here. How come he never saw anything?'

'It's pretty dark up there with the spotlights off,' Hillyard told him. 'We had to use torches to see our way around. The German could easily have slipped past Neville without being seen.'

'OK, that's all,' McIndoe said. He dismissed Hillyard with a curt flick of the hand.

'There is another possibility,' Stella said after Hillyard had gone. 'What if your man already knew that the German was topside and let him pass?'

'What are you implying?' McIndoe asked indignantly. 'That Johnson's working in collaboration with the enemy?'

'Apart from myself, the only other people who knew in advance about the exact location of the rendezvous are all aboard this boat,' Stella said, holding McIndoe's stare. 'Even my superiors didn't know these coordinates. I only transmitted them through to Nicky shortly before he left Gibraltar. I used the new code system which he recently devised which is known only to the small group of operatives he runs. So even if the Germans had managed to intercept the transmission, they still couldn't have made any sense of the code.'

McIndoe moved to the door and shouted, 'Taffy?'

'Boss?' Evans said, emerging from the cabin at the end of the passage.

'Where's Neville?'

'Topside, I think,' Evans replied.

'Tell him I want to see him now!' McIndoe ordered.

An anxious Johnson arrived moments later. 'You wanted to see me, Lieutenant?'

McIndoe stood directly in front of him. 'Why did you remain topside after the rest of us came below?'

'Actually, I was . . . well . . .'

'Spit it out, man,' McIndoe demanded.

'I was on the bridge with Sub-Lieutenant Higgins,' Johnson said guiltily. 'I'm sorry I didn't see anything, sir.'

'It's not your fault,' McIndoe replied, then smiled quickly to try and put Johnson at his ease. 'That's all, Neville. You can go now.'

Johnson looked uncertainly at each face in turn before leaving.

'He could have been up there distracting Higgins, couldn't he?' Stella said.

'Perhaps Charlie Higgins is his accomplice?' McIndoe said contemptuously. 'And why not Georges Passiere as well? After all, he had access to the wireless room. He could have radioed ahead to the Germans to tell them when we'd reach the rendezvous. Why not just accuse all of us? Who knows, perhaps Nicky is in league with us as well.' He looked at Ravallo. 'Well, Nicky? Are you also a Nazi spy?'

Ravallo's jaw hardened but he said nothing.

'I know it wasn't me!' Stella shot back defiantly.

'I need some air,' McIndoe said tersely, and strode briskly from the cabin.

Ravallo glared at Stella, then got to his feet and went after McIndoe. He found him on deck, his hands clasped tightly around the starboard railing. 'She has a knack of ruffling feathers, Mac. I guess that's what makes her . . .'

'So good?' McIndoe finished the sentence when Ravallo's voice trailed off.

'Yeah, I was going to say that.'

'What if she is right?' McIndoe said without taking his eyes off the water. 'What if there *is* a Nazi spy on board?'

'Do you suspect anyone?'

'I'd trust each and every one of these men with my life,' McIndoe was quick to reply. 'I've worked with them all before on several important operations, and never once have I ever had any reason to question their loyalty. I can't believe that any of them could be working for the enemy.'

'Yeah, well, the fact still remains that somebody tipped off the Germans tonight,' Ravallo said softly. 'Question is, who?'

McIndoe pulled a packet of cigarettes from his pocket and extended it towards Ravallo without looking round at him. There was no response. He glanced sideways and found that Ravallo had disappeared as silently as he'd arrived. He pushed a cigarette between his lips and lit it. Suddenly he was alone with his thoughts. And he certainly had a lot to think about . . .

'That's a very serious accusation to make, Lieutenant di Mauro,' Vice-Admiral Starr said to Stella after he'd listened to the disturbing events which had occurred earlier that night. 'Especially as you have no evidence to back up these allegations.'

'All I know is that I didn't breach the security regulations, sir,' Stella replied, her eyes flickering between McIndoe and Ravallo who were seated on either side of her in Starr's office. 'And the only others who knew about the rendezvous were Lieutenant McIndoe and his team.'

'And Major Ravallo,' Starr added.

'If you knew Nicky like I do – '

'Oh, spare me the sentimentality, Lieutenant,' Starr cut across Stella's words.

'Sir, I was only – '

'That's enough, Stella!' Ravallo interceded furiously. 'Until we get to the bottom of this, we're all under suspicion.'

Stella bit back her anger and folded her arms tightly across her chest.

'I can understand your reluctance to believe that Major Ravallo could be involved in anything so despicable as treason, Lieutenant di Mauro, but I feel exactly the same way about my own operatives,' Starr said, gesturing in McIndoe's direction. 'I've come to know them all personally, and they're a damn fine bunch of lads. But the fact remains that there was a leak and we need to find it and plug it before it threatens to scuttle this whole operation before it's even begun.'

'Will we be replaced, sir?' McIndoe asked.

'That remains to be seen,' was all Starr would venture on the subject. 'What have you done with the two Germans you fished out of the sea?'

'We handed them over to the Military Police after we got back to Valletta, sir,' McIndoe told him.

'Did you get anything out of them?'

'All they would give us was their name, rank and number, sir,' McIndoe said. 'I don't think they knew anything anyway.'

'I'm sure we'll find out soon enough after they've been interrogated by the Intelligence Corps,' Starr replied. He looked at his watch. 'Well, it's already gone four-thirty. Get some sleep. There's a vehicle waiting outside to take you to the house where you'll be billeted for the duration of your stay in Malta. I'll be studying Lieutenant di Mauro's report later this morning before deciding how best to proceed. Thank you, that will be all for now.' Starr pointed the stem of his pipe at McIndoe as the three of them got to their feet. 'A word before you leave.'

'We'll wait for you outside,' Ravallo said to him, following Stella from the room and closing the door behind him.

'What do you make of all this, McIndoe?' Starr asked. 'Do you think Lieutenant di Mauro's on the level?'

'If she's not, then she's playing the role of the wounded party to perfection.' McIndoe shook his head. 'No, I think she's telling the truth.'

'I tend to agree with you. She's a very direct, straight-talking young woman, isn't she? And if she is on the level, then that means the leak had to have come either from Major Ravallo or from someone in your team.'

'It certainly looks that way, sir,' McIndoe agreed reluctantly.

'I intend to instigate an internal investigation into this matter. But if I don't find the source of the leak, then you and your team will be suspended pending a formal investigation. And that would mean I'd have to call in another team to take over from you. I certainly hope it doesn't come to that, McIndoe. I chose this team personally as I believed it was the best for the operation.' Starr put down his pipe and rubbed his eyes wearily. 'Go on, get some sleep.'

'You look like you could do with some sleep yourself, sir,' McIndoe said.

'I certainly could, but right now that's the furthest thing from my mind after what happened tonight.'

'What time do you want me to report back here, sir?' McIndoe asked.

'I'll send for you,' Starr replied. 'But until this matter has been cleared up satisfactorily, you and the others will be confined to your barracks. They'll have already been told by the MPs who've been posted outside the house. They won't let any of you leave without my express permission.'

'I understand, sir.'

'That's all, McIndoe,' Starr said, reaching for the folder which contained the decoded report which Stella had compiled on the German military build-up on Sicily.

'Good-night, sir,' McIndoe said as he left the room.

Starr removed his glasses, then massaged the bridge of his nose with his thumb and forefinger. 'Not so far, it isn't,' he said softly to himself as he stared at the closed door, then, slipping his glasses on again, he opened the folder in front of him and began to read.

FIVE

By the autumn of 1941, Hitler had become convinced that the war in the Mediterranean was a serious drain on Axis resources which could be better used elsewhere, particularly against the Russians on the Eastern Front. Yet he had been shrewd enough to realize that it would be foolhardy, if not suicidal, to relinquish the stranglehold he still had on Italy and Greece, especially to his fellow dictator Mussolini, whose Army he regarded as lazy, disorganized and lacking any real aggression, and whose Navy he felt had become so in awe of the British that it had become fearful of even putting to sea. He had realized then that his only option was to bring in a proven general, one who was totally loyal to him, to co-ordinate all the Axis operations in the vast Mediterranean theatre. The man he had chosen was fifty-six-year-old Field-Marshal Albert Kesselring.

Kesselring had taken up his new position at the end of November 1941, and his official title was *Oberbefehlshaber Sud* – commander-in-chief, South. Kesselring was a career soldier who had managed to win over the initially hostile Italian armed forces with a combination of tactful diplomacy and a deep understanding of their wounded pride, which he knew resulted from the countless ignominious defeats which they had suffered at the hands of the Allies since first entering the war in June 1940. He was by nature a friendly, approachable man, who took a genuine interest in the welfare of his troops, and it was this genial personality which had given rise to his nickname, 'Smiling Albert'.

It was now February 1942, and Field-Marshal Albert Kesselring wasn't smiling as he sat behind his desk in his spacious office at *Wehrmach's* headquarters in Rome. His face was flushed with rage as he listened with mounting anger to Major Gustav Rembold, who was nervously recounting the bungled attempt by his men to capture the British MTB and its crew the previous night.

'So of the nine men you sent on this operation, one survived; two are missing, presumed dead; two more were taken prisoner, and the remaining four were killed,' Kesselring said bitterly, his voice rising indignantly with each damning statistic.

'Yes, sir,' Rembold replied uncomfortably, his eyes now fixed on his polished boots.

'I can't believe this incompetence!' Kesselring thundered, banging his fist down on to the desk. 'You were given ample time to prepare your strategy after the tip-off we received last night. I've heard a lot of good things about you since I've been here in Rome, which was why I chose you to handle this operation. You've let me down badly, Rembold, and you should know by now that I will not tolerate this kind of failure under my command.'

Rembold swallowed anxiously. 'It won't happen again, sir.'

'You're right, it won't.' Kesselring sat forward, his hands clasped together on the desk as he stared at the officer in front of him. 'Tell me, Rembold, what do you know about conditions on the Eastern Front?'

'I . . . I've heard reports, sir,' came the stammered reply.

'So have I, and they're not particularly pleasant by all accounts,' Kesselring said. 'Word is that Russia's in the grip of a long cold winter. But then you'll be finding that out for yourself soon enough. Your transfer papers for the Eastern Front will be through by the end of the week. I'd suggest that you prepare for it a lot better than you did for the operation last night.'

'Yes, sir,' Rembold replied fearfully.

'Now get out!'

Rembold saluted stiffly and left the room.

The telephone rang. Kesselring snatched up the receiver. 'Yes?' he barked tersely into the mouthpiece.

'*Generalleutnant* Student's here, sir,' his adjutant told him from the outer office.

'Ah, good,' Kesselring said. 'Show him in, will you?' He replaced the receiver, then looked up when he heard the sharp rap on the door. 'Enter.'

The door opened and a tall, angular-faced man was ushered into the room. The door was closed again behind him. Lieutenant-General Kurt Student came to attention and Kesselring returned the salute. Neither gave the Nazi salute. Both were professional soldiers who had avoided any involvement in party politics since Hitler first came to power in 1933. Though neither man was a member of the Nazi Party, they were nevertheless committed fascists with a fierce hatred of communism.

'Good to see you again, Kurt,' Kesselring said, getting to his feet and extending a hand of greeting towards Student.

'And you, sir,' Student replied as he shook Kesselring's hand.

'When did you get in from Crete?' Kesselring asked, resuming his seat.

'About an hour ago. I came straight here from the airport.' Student spoke hesitantly, the result of a serious head wound he'd received in Holland in 1940. A sniper's bullet had almost killed him; he'd spent six months in a German hospital recovering from his injuries. Few who knew him regarded his speech impediment as a disadvantage. Kurt Student was widely respected as one of the finest and most innovative military minds in the German *Wehrmacht*; a brilliant tactician. He was widely credited with introducing airborne troops and troop-carrying gliders into the war, and had masterminded the airborne assault on Crete in May 1941 by *Sturmgruppe* of the élite Parachute Regiments who had captured the only air-base on the island from a vastly superior number of enemy troops, holding their ground against all odds until reinforcements arrived. A week later the Allies had been forced to retreat from the island in some disarray. It turned out, however, to be a Pyrrhic victory for the airborne forces, who sustained heavy casualties with over forty per cent of their number killed during the campaign. Hitler had regarded these losses as unacceptably high, and had told Student that he would never again sanction another airborne operation. Although a limited number of paratroopers were subsequently used in Italy in 1944, Crete proved to be their last major offensive of the war.

'The officer who came out of here looked as if he'd just been condemned to a firing squad,' Student said as he sat down.

'Close enough. He'll be up to his knees in mud on the Eastern Front by the weekend. The *Führer*'s always saying he wants more troops in Russia, and I'm only too happy to oblige him whenever I can.'

Kesselring lit a cigarette, then explained the fiasco of the previous evening. 'It's not so much that he failed, but rather in the way that he failed. He didn't think the operation through properly. He sent a bunch of young, inexperienced soldiers up against a crack team of enemy operatives. Only the sergeant had any real military experience. What good was that? Major Rembold was regarded by many as one of the most promising young officers stationed here in Italy. That's why I chose him. Perhaps it's just as well that I found out now about his limitations, rather than later when he was a field commander.'

'The Eastern Front will either make him or break him, just as it's done to many an officer in the past few months,' Student said.

'If he pulls another stunt like that over there, he won't live to regret it. And it won't be the enemy who'll kill him.' Kesselring tapped the ash off the end of his cigarette. 'The Eastern Front is full of tough, uncompromising soldiers. The type of veterans who've fought in countless campaigns across Europe. If an officer can win their respect, there's nothing they won't do for him. But if he can't, there's nothing they *will* do for him. And those are the officers who end up getting shot in the back by their own men.'

'You almost sound as if your sympathy lies with the soldiers, sir,' Student said.

'There's nothing more dangerous on the battlefield than an officer who abuses the power of rank to cover for his limitations as a military strategist. And experienced soldiers can see through that kind of deception very quickly.' Kesselring took a long drag on his cigarette then shook his head. 'Don't get me wrong, I don't condone that kind of mutiny, but that doesn't mean that I can't understand why it still happens.'

'It would have been quite a coup for you to have captured an entire British SOE unit,' Student mused after a thoughtful pause.

'At least it would have been something Field-Marshal Rommel couldn't have claimed to have achieved in North Africa,' Kesselring retorted. He smiled quickly at Student and stubbed out his cigarette. 'But the operation failed, and that's all there is to it.'

Student knew of the intense rivalry which had existed between Kesselring and Rommel, ever since Kesselring had first arrived in Italy. Rommel, with his flamboyant style of leadership and his numerous successes against the Eighth Army in North Africa, had quickly become a firm favourite with the chiefs-of-staff in Berlin. It had got to the point where the *Führer* would invariably take Rommel's side, especially when it came to the thorny issue of the lack of supplies getting through to the Afrika Korps. The supplies were routed through the Mediterranean, and Student had heard rumours that both Kesselring and the German naval commander-in-chief of the Mediterranean, Vice-Admiral Weichold, were taking much of the flack for the losses being sustained by these convoys at the hands of the Allied submarines. Yet at the same time, Kesselring wasn't being given the credit he deserved for the continuing U-boat successes against the Allied convoys in the area. Fewer and fewer of these convoys were now getting through to Malta; those that did manage to slip past the U-boat wolf-packs inevitably came under heavy and sustained fire from the *Luftwaffe* within hours of reaching Grand Harbour.

'Field-Marshal Rommel and I may not always see eye to eye, Kurt, but there's no disputing his brilliance as one of the greatest strategists of mobile warfare the world has ever known,' Kesselring said, as if reading Student's thoughts. 'He's still the only man capable of defeating the Eighth Army in North Africa.'

'But we'd need total control of the Mediterranean if more supplies are to get through to his troops,' Student replied. 'And that means the occupation of Malta.'

'That's what I told the joint chiefs-of-staff when I met with them in Berlin last week. They agreed in principle with me. Even Field-Marshal Rommel and I agree on that,' Kesselring said with a wry smile. 'But the *Führer* and *Reichsmarschall* Goering disagree. The *Führer* wants Malta neutralized, but we have different ideas on how best to achieve that end. As far as I'm concerned, it can only be achieved by occupying the island – that way we would be assured of both sea and air superiority in the Mediterranean, but the *Führer* is reluctant to pull out troops from other fronts to make up the invasion force. He has reservations about an invasion of Malta after the losses we sustained on Crete last year. He still believes that Malta can be bombed into submission.'

'You know what the *Führer* is like, sir. He won't budge once he's made up his mind about something,' Student said.

'So I thought,' Kesselring replied. 'But shortly before I was due to leave Berlin, I was told to report to the *Führer's* bunker for a further briefing. It seems our esteemed commander-in-chief of the Navy, Admiral Raeder, made a very eloquent speech in favour of a full-scale invasion of the island when the *Führer* had held a meeting with his chiefs-of-staff the previous day. So, with Admiral Raeder, Field-Marshal Rommel and myself all in favour of an invasion, the *Führer* has given his provisional agreement for it to go ahead later in the year. It's already been given a code name: "Operation Herkules".'

'Congratulations, sir,' Student said with a broad smile.

'Not so quick, Kurt,' Kesselring said, holding up a hand. 'The *Führer* has asked me to draw up the contingency plans for the invasion which I'm to present to him and his chiefs-of-staff in Berlin next week. If he approves it, Operation Herkules will proceed as planned. If not, it'll be scrapped. That's why I asked you to fly out here at such short notice. An airborne assault would certainly be a possibility. And that's your particular area of expertise, Kurt. I'll be bringing in several of my advisors to help me put together a viable plan which I can present to the *Führer*.'

'When will you be holding the briefing, sir?' Student asked, unable to keep the excitement out of his voice. He never thought he'd be involved in the planning of another airborne operation, not after the assault on Crete.

'It'll be sometime within the next few days. I've decided to hold it at the Grand Hotel in the Sicilian capital, Palermo. I'll need a team to secure and guard the area around the building for the duration of the meeting.'

'You could use the Gestapo, sir,' Student suggested. 'They've got a battalion stationed in Palermo. They'd be ideal for the job.'

'No, I don't want the Gestapo there,' Kesselring replied firmly. He'd always regarded the Gestapo as a necessary evil in the occupied territories, but he'd never made a secret of the fact that he abhorred the methods they employed to suppress local resistance. 'If I were to use them, then you can be sure their top brass would want to be in on the briefing as well. They like nothing better than to poke their noses in where they're not wanted, especially when it occurs within their jurisdiction. I want a unit brought in from the outside – and you know that I hold the Paratroop Regiments in the highest regard. I've heard numerous reports in the last few months from other senior officers that many of your para-troopers have distinguished themselves as élite tactical infantry units since their regiments were disbanded after the invasion of Crete. I want your best man brought in on this one, Kurt. He can pick his own team. I don't care where they are right now, I want them to assemble on Sicily as soon as possible. Do you have anyone specific in mind?'

'I know just the man for the job, sir,' Student said, nodding his head. 'Major Hans Riedler.'

'I've heard of this Riedler. He was one of your protégés, wasn't he?'

'Yes, sir. He was given the Knight's Cross With Oak Leaves, Swords and Diamonds for his part in the capture of Crete. He's one of the finest soldiers I've ever known. Very much in the mould of his late father. I had the honour of serving with Helmut Riedler in von Richthofen's Flying Circus during the last war.'

'Do you know where Riedler is at present?' Kesselring asked.

'The last I heard his unit had been transferred to the Eastern Front. But I don't know exactly where, though.'

'Leave that to me. I shouldn't have any trouble clearing his transfer with General Paulus, the commander-in-chief of the Sixth Army on the Eastern Front.' Kesselring smiled to himself. 'Friedrich Paulus owes me a few favours any-way.'

'You'll have to clear it for his unit to leave with him as well, sir,' Student said. 'I can tell you now that Riedler won't go without them. He's very loyal to his men.'

'Perfect. The sooner they reach Palermo and secure the hotel, the sooner we can get the meeting under way.'

'General Paulus won't be too pleased to lose someone of Riedler's calibre, sir,' Student said.

'But I'll be sending him a good replacement in Major Rembold.'

'I hardly think General Paulus will see it that way after the way Rembold bungled the operation last night,' Student snorted.

'Who's going to tell him?' Kesselring replied with a faint smile as he reached for the telephone on his desk.

Major Hans Riedler didn't flinch as another shell landed perilously close to the trench. The walls of the makeshift shelter shuddered from the force of the explosion, and a shower of soil rained down from between the rows of wet and warped wooden slats which creaked ominously overhead as they struggled to contain the burdening weight of rain-sodden thatch laid across them as token protection for the men from the hazardous weather conditions outside.

He sat alone in his cramped quarters: a small, dank room illuminated by a single kerosene lamp. In the only dry corner lay a threadbare palliasse and a single blanket. He sat motionless on a wooden chair close to the doorway which was partitioned off from the rest of the shelter by a filthy bed-sheet. His uniform was torn and splattered with dried mud, and his steel helmet was tugged down firmly over his head – it was now mandatory for everyone to wear their helmets inside the shelter after an incident in which one of his men had been killed by a falling wooden slat in the main body of the shelter. Just another fatality. Seventeen days earlier, Riedler had arrived on the Eastern Front with forty-seven paratroopers from the Third Parachute Regiment, regarded as one of the most élite airborne units. Fourteen of them were now dead and another nine had been seriously wounded. Six of the wounded had since been transferred to a German field hospital – but that had been five days ago. The same day that the field telephone had been destroyed by a stray shell. And with the radio-transmitter also out of action, they were now completely isolated. Their token force of cold and dispirited men would be no match for a heavily armed Russian patrol. How much longer could they hope to hold out under these appalling conditions?

Riedler slowly got to his feet and retrieved the dog-eared chart from the floor. He'd thrown it there in a rare moment of temper – or had it been an act of helpless frustration? Their position had been circled several times in black pen. It showed them to be about fifteen miles west of Saratov in the south of the country. They had initially been sent to the Eastern Front to act as a reconnaissance team, scouting ahead for the advancing Sixth Army. Many of the men had quickly become bitter and disillusioned with this thankless task. They regarded themselves as élite paratroopers who had distinguished themselves across Europe; now they were being used as little more than expendable cannon-fodder for the plodding foot soldiers whom they regarded with such contempt. It had taken all of Riedler's considerable leadership qualities to hold his unit together under these exceptionally trying circumstances; despite the rising number of desertions being recorded on the Eastern Front, not one of his men had attempted to desert his comrades.

Riedler pushed aside the bed-sheet draped over the doorway and emerged out into the corridor. Three men were seated on upturned steel buckets, playing out a game of poker. They made to get to their feet to salute him, but Riedler gestured for them to remain seated, walking to a doorway at the other end of the corridor. It was also partitioned off by a grimy bed-sheet. He pushed aside the sheet and, as he stepped inside, was immediately struck by the overpowering smell of antiseptic which seemed to permeate the whole room. An assortment of medical tools lay on a bloodstained sheet on the wooden table in the corner of the room. A row of palliasses lined the floor. Three were occupied. Riedler always made a point of visiting the wounded whenever he could. Morale was vital, even amongst those who couldn't fight.

'Morning, Major,' the medic said as he put down the week old copy of *Neuesten Nachrichten* which a scouting patrol had come across in a deserted house some days earlier.

'Morning,' Riedler replied, 'how are the men today?'

'Buchwald and Heymann are stable, sir, but Weber's condition is becoming critical. He desperately needs proper medical attention,' the medic told him. 'He's in a lot of pain. I'm using morphine to help deaden the pain, but at this rate I'll have run out of morphine within the next forty-eight hours. And that's only if I use it on Weber. If there are any more casualties, I don't know what I'll do. My supplies are already running desperately low.'

'So are the food rations,' Riedler said. 'Two of the men found a dead horse close to the trenches. They wanted to cut it up for meat, but there was no way of knowing whether it was contaminated or not. What if the Bolsheviks had deliberately poisoned the horse? I had to have the carcass burnt in case the men went ahead and cooked the meat. As you know, some of the men have already gone down with dysentery. We certainly couldn't cope with an outbreak of food poisoning as well.'

'It's only a matter of time before the dysentery spreads throughout the whole unit, sir,' the medic told him. 'And there's nothing I can do about it, not with the limited medical supplies at my disposal.'

'You can only do your best,' Riedler said, patting the medic on the arm.

'You'd think that someone in command would have realized by now that we'd been cut off from the rest of the division. Surely they'll have sent out a search party to look for us? It's been five days now. Are we just going to be left out here to die?'

'I'm going to have a word with Weber,' Riedler said, purposely avoiding an answer. He crossed to the row of palliasses against the wall. Buchwald and Heymann appeared to be asleep. He crouched down beside the third man. Although still only in his early twenties, Stefan Weber was already a veteran of the airborne assaults on both Greece and Crete, and had been awarded the Iron Cross, First Class, after the successful airborne assault on the heavily fortified Allied fortress of Eban Emael in Belgium in 1940.

Weber had been seriously wounded five days earlier when he'd stepped on an anti-personnel mine while out leading a scouting patrol. The medic had been forced to amputate his left leg above the knee in order to save Weber's life. Weber had been in and out of a feverish coma for the past twenty-four hours and, although the fever had finally broken earlier that morning, it had left him weak and vulnerable to secondary ailments. He'd already contracted influenza, and Riedler knew it would only be a matter of time before he was struck down with the dysentery which was now so prevalent in the camp. And it was doubtful whether he had the strength left to fight that off as well . . .

'It's good to see you, sir,' Weber said with a weak smile as he wiped his hand across his clammy forehead. 'You don't want to get too close to me . . . not in my condition.'

'And since when do you give me orders, Lieutenant Weber?' Riedler replied with a gentle smile. 'How are you feeling this morning?'

'I'm not sure whether I'd be up to a parachute jump right now, sir,' Weber said with a half chuckle.

'And I went to all that trouble of having your parachute prepared for you,' Riedler replied good-humouredly.

'They were good times, weren't they, sir? Belgium. Greece. Crete. Especially Crete. I still don't understand why the *Führer* saw fit to disband the Paratroop Regiments after Crete. We might have lost a lot of men, but at least we achieved our objective and captured the island. And I thought that the end justified the means.'

'Ours is not to reason why, Stefan,' Riedler said.

'No, ours is only to blindly obey and die,' Weber retorted. He began to cough violently before managing to regain his composure again. He wiped the spittle from his lips. 'Death doesn't scare me, sir. But to die like this. In these conditions. Under these circumstances. It's not right. It's just not right.'

'Somehow I never took you for a defeatist,' Riedler said. 'You're not dead yet, Stefan.'

'I'm under no illusions, sir. I know I lost a lot of blood during the operation on my leg. I don't have the strength to fight off any secondary infections. Then again, perhaps I don't want to any more. The Parachute Regiment was my whole life.'

'You've got a wife waiting for you back in Germany. Doesn't Anna mean anything to you?'

'More to the point, sir, would I mean anything to her like this?' came the bitter reply.

'I remember your wedding reception. It was some party, wasn't it? But you know what I remember most about it? The way Anna kept stealing glances at you whenever the two of you were apart. And it wasn't your uniform or your medals she was looking at. It was you. Do you honestly think she'd stop loving you just because you've been wounded? Because if you do, you don't deserve a woman like that.'

'It's just that . . .' Weber trailed off with a helpless shrug, then his eyes flickered past Riedler towards the figure who had entered the room. 'We've got company, sir.'

Riedler had guessed who it was even before he looked round. Whenever he saw his second-in-command, *Hauptmann* Jürgen Franke, he always thought of the army recruitment posters back home depicting the ideal military conscript as a youthfully handsome, blond-haired, blue-eyed Aryan. Franke was the epitome of Hitler's image of the

Herrenvolk. The only flaw to his boyish good looks was the faint duelling scar on his right cheek which he proudly boasted he'd received at the military academy in Bavaria, where he'd excelled both as a swordsman and as a student.

Franke was fervent Nazi who, a month earlier, had been transferred from the élite Koenen unit – one of the German special forces units known collectively as 'Brandenburg' which had served with such distinction in North Africa – as a belated replacement for Lieutenant Karl Müller, Riedler's brother-in-law and his former second-in-command, who'd been killed during the airborne assault on Crete. Franke was unquestionably the most fearless and dedicated officer Riedler had ever known – but that didn't mean he liked him. But his feelings went deeper than just a dislike of Franke and his blinkered ideological views. He knew Franke had been sent to spy on him after he'd spoken out on more than one occasion against what he regarded as some of the more unjust policies of the ruling Nazi Party. It was obvious that SS paranoia was everywhere. Not that Franke was aware of Riedler's true feelings towards him. Riedler had made sure for the sake of continued harmony within the unit that he kept his personal dislike of Franke to himself. And it seemed to have worked, so far . . .

'You've been injured, sir,' the medic said, noticing the film of blood which seeped from a wound under Franke's helmet. It had already cut an uneven groove through the grime on the right-hand side of his face, and had stained the collar of his mud-spattered battle-tunic.

'It's nothing,' Franke replied dismissively, and waved away the hovering medic.

'You've been out in the trenches dodging those shells again, haven't you?' Riedler said with a smile.

Franke grinned back at him. 'It's hell out there, sir – but I love it.' He crossed to the foot of the palliasse and looked down at Weber. 'You look much better this morning, Stefan.'

'Looks can be deceptive, sir,' Weber replied.

'You know I envy you, Stefan,' Franke said. 'You'll go home to a hero's welcome.'

'I'll also be going home without my left leg,' Weber retorted, struggling to contain the anger which was building up inside him. Like Riedler, he disliked Franke. But unlike Riedler, he'd never made any attempt to hide those feelings.

'You made a great sacrifice for the *Führer* and for the Fatherland,' Franke told him. 'There is no greater honour than that.'

Riedler shot Weber a stern look before he could reply. Weber exhaled deeply but said nothing. Riedler led Franke to the doorway, 'I don't think Weber's in the mood for one of your propaganda speeches right now. Was there any particular reason for your coming here, other than to try to cheer him up?'

'Can we talk outside, sir?' Franke asked.

Riedler emerged out into the corridor and noticed that the three men who'd been playing poker earlier were now gone. Only the upturned buckets remained. 'Well, what is it?'

'I've just received word from the lookout that there's a truck approaching, sir,' Franke replied. 'It appears to be one of ours.'

'It could be a trap,' Riedler said.

'I've already put the men on standby. Not that we could do much against a sustained attack from the Russians, not with the limited amount of ammunition we've got left.'

'I'm well aware of the shortage of ammunition, Captain,' Riedler said. He gestured the length of the corridor. 'Let's go and see what's going on, shall we?'

Franke ducked into a tributary corridor and led the way to an open doorway which emerged out into the grim reality of the exposed trenches. Riedler followed him out into the light drizzle; his boots immediately sunk into the soft, macerated mud. He could feel the drag on his feet with every tired footstep. The soldier on guard outside the doorway automatically saluted the superior officers. Yet there was no recognition on his mud-streaked face; only a look of haunting betrayal. A betrayal of a Parachute Regiment by the chiefs-of-staff in the comfort of their warm bunkers sunk deep beneath the bomb-scarred streets of Berlin. A betrayal few of them would ever forget and even fewer would ever forgive . . .

'It stopped somewhere in there, sir,' the soldier told Riedler, gesturing to a decimated grove of trees which stood bare and forlorn a few hundred yards from the trench. 'That's the only protection for it around here.'

'And nobody's emerged from the trees since it arrived?' Riedler asked.

'No, sir,' the soldier replied.

'What kind of truck was it?' Riedler asked.

'It looked like an Opel Blitz troop-carrier, sir,' the soldier replied. 'Do you think it's been sent to get us out of here?'

'It's possible,' Riedler said thoughtfully, without taking his eyes off the trees. 'Question is, why?'

'I don't understand, sir,' Franke said.

'Why wasn't it sent in with the usual tank support?' Riedler said. 'That suggests to me that, if the High Command want us out of here, they want it done fast. Or at least some of us. In these kind of conditions, those trucks can only carry between twelve and fifteen men at most. Any more than that and the extra weight could result in it becoming bogged down in the mud. That would mean two trips to get us all out of here. So why not send two trucks? No, there's more to this than meets the eye. And I'd certainly be interested to find out what it is.'

'Sir, look,' the soldier said, pointing to a figure who had emerged from the trees and was standing hesitantly at the edge of the clearing. He was dressed in the uniform of a junior German officer and was holding a white flag in his hand.

'Hold your fire!' Riedler shouted to the paratroopers lining the trench, who already had their rifles trained on the lone figure. All the men were armed with FG.42 rifles which had been manufactured in limited numbers for use exclusively by the Paratroop Regiments. He turned to the soldier beside him. 'Go out and bring him back here.'

The soldier scrambled up the wooden ladder which was positioned against the side of the trench, and zig-zagged his way across the clearing to where the man was standing. Both men ducked down as a shell exploded in the distance, then they ran back to the trench. The newcomer, a fresh-faced youth who was wearing the rank of lieutenant on his spotless uniform, was the first down the ladder; he snapped his heels together and gave a Nazi salute on seeing the insignia on Riedler's tunic. Riedler returned the salute by touching the tips of his fingers to the side of his head.

'Major Riedler?' the lieutenant asked.

Riedler nodded. 'How did you know where to find me?'

'A spotter plane was sent up to locate your position, sir.'

'How long ago was that?' Riedler demanded.

'Earlier this morning, sir. It didn't take them long to pinpoint your position, given that they'd already been given your last known coordinates.'

'We've been out here for five days now!' Riedler said angrily. 'And in that time I've lost four men and another three have been wounded. One seriously. We're down to the last of our rations and we're almost out of ammunition and you're saying that we could have been pulled out of here at any time.'

'I . . . I wouldn't know about that, sir,' the lieutenant stammered nervously. 'I . . . I'm just carrying out my orders.'

'Which are?' Franke demanded.

The lieutenant fumbled with the button on the breast-pocket of his tunic, then removed a sealed envelope which

110

he extended towards Riedler. 'I was told to deliver this to you in person, sir.'

'On whose orders?' Riedler asked, plucking the envelope from the lieutenant's fingers.

'General Paulus, sir.'

Riedler tore open the envelope and removed the sheet of official notepaper. His eyes went to the co-signatures at the foot of the page. Field-Marshal Albert Kesselring and General Friedrich Paulus. He read the communiqué silently then handed it to Franke. 'Have you read the letter?' Riedler asked the lieutenant.

'No, sir,' the lieutenant replied. 'It was already sealed in the envelope when I received it. My orders are to see that fifteen of your men, including yourself and *Hauptmann* Franke, are taken to the air-base at Kharkov. A transport plane is waiting for you there – but I don't know your ultimate destination. I was also instructed to tell you that only battle-fit men were to be considered for transportation. The rest of your men, including the wounded, will be pulled out of here within the next forty-eight hours.'

'So it says in the communiqué,' Riedler replied as Franke handed the letter back to him. 'Weber will be going with us as well.'

'Who's Weber?' the lieutenant asked.

'Lieutenant Stefan Weber was seriously injured by an antipersonnel mine five days ago,' Riedler told him. 'He needs urgent medical attention.'

'I'm sorry, sir, but my orders were not to take any of the wounded on the truck,' the lieutenant said. 'General Paulus was very insistent on that.'

'Lieutenant Weber may not survive another forty-eight hours,' Riedler told him. 'He's coming with us.'

'General Paulus – '

'I'm prepared to take full responsibility for Lieutenant Weber,' Riedler cut in sharply. 'And that means explaining my actions personally to General Paulus if necessary.'

'I have my orders, sir,' the lieutenant replied resolutely.

Franke drew his Walther P. 38 pistol and pressed it underneath the young officer's chin. 'Out here Major Riedler is in command. If he gives you an order, you'll obey it without question. If not, you'll be shot for insubordination.'

'Nobody's going to be shot for insubordination,' Riedler was quick to intervene as he pushed the pistol away from the lieutenant's face. 'Captain Franke, I want you to draw up a list of the men we'll be taking with us. Bring it to me when you've finished.'

Franke reholstered his pistol, saluted, then disappeared back into the shelter.

'Sir, I understand your concern for Lieutenant Weber,' the young officer said, 'and I'd be the first to take him with us, along with the rest of the wounded men if it were possible, but there just isn't space in the truck for them. It's going to be cramped enough as it is with fifteen men in there. Time is of the essence here. We have to leave the wounded behind, sir.'

'How many of you are there in the truck?' Riedler asked.

'Just the driver and myself, sir.'

'Then if it's space you're worried about, you can stay behind until the reinforcements arrive,' Riedler told him. 'That way we could get Weber in to the truck.'

'I don't . . .' the lieutenant trailed off when he heard the whistling sound of an incoming shell and he ducked down, his hand clamped tightly over his steel helmet. Seconds later the shell detonated close enough for them both to be caught in the resulting deluge of mud which rained down over the trench.

'It's been like this for the past five days,' Riedler said when the lieutenant looked up apprehensively at him. 'Incessant shelling, twenty-four hours a day. We're out in no man's land here with our forces on one side and the Russians on the other. That much is obvious from the way the shells are coming in from all directions. Only we don't know who's who out there. The battle-lines change daily on the Eastern Front. That's why we've been forced to sit it out here. We couldn't risk breaking out in case we walked straight into a Bolshevik camp. I hear they like to skin their prisoners alive. Personally, I preferred to take my chances with the shelling. But as you'd be the most senior officer here after Captain Franke and I have gone, it would be your decision whether to remain here until reinforcements arrive, or whether to try and make for the sanctuary of a German unit. I'd say you'd have a fifty-fifty chance of success.'

'I . . . I'm sure we . . . can make room for Lieutenant Weber in the truck, sir,' came the fearful reply.

'I'm sure we can, but the more I think about it, the more unfair this all seems to me,' Riedler told him. 'I can't just leave the rest of my men here, not knowing whether they will be pulled out after I've gone.'

'General Paulus gave his word, sir,' the lieutenant assured him.

'From the comfort of his headquarters, and we both know just how bad communications can be on the Eastern Front. No, I need to know that the rest of my men will be transported out of here as well. And the only way to ensure that would be for you to remain behind here with them. That way, after we've been taken to the airfield, the truck can be refuelled and sent back for the rest of you. I'm sure you can persuade the driver to do that, can't you?'

Franke emerged from the shelter before the ashen-faced lieutenant could reply and handed a sheet of paper to Riedler. 'I've coordinated the list with the medic, sir. None of these men have been to see him in the last five days. It doesn't necessarily mean that they're a hundred per cent fit, but it's the best we can do at such short notice.'

Riedler ran his finger down the list, then nodded in agreement and handed it back to Franke. 'I want these men ready to leave in ten minutes' time.'

'I'll see to it right away, sir,' Franke told him. 'What about Lieutenant Weber?'

'The lieutenant's very generously agreed to remain behind with the rest of the men until the truck returns for them. That way there will be space for Weber in the truck.'

'That is very generous, sir,' Franke agreed with a knowing smile.

The young lieutenant ducked down nervously as another shell exploded a short distance from the trenches. Franke grabbed his arm roughly, pulled him to his feet, and bundled him unceremoniously into the shelter. He paused in the doorway and slowly scanned the dark, overcast sky. It was then that Riedler saw the look of sadness in Franke's eyes, almost as if he were reluctant to be leaving the hellhole which had served as their temporary home for the past five days. But then, knowing of Franke's fanatical devotion to his *Führer* and to his Fatherland, it really didn't surprise him at all . . .

SIX

'Morning.'

'Morning, boss,' Evans and Hillyard chorused together as McIndoe entered the dining room. Johnson just nodded in greeting, as was his way.

'Sleep well, Mac?' Ravallo asked.

'Not particularly,' McIndoe replied tersely. He moved to the window and tweaked back the net curtain. A Bedford MW with two MPs seated up front was parked outside the gate. 'I see we're still under house arrest.'

'How long is this going to go on for?' Evans asked.

'How the hell should I know?' McIndoe retorted sharply, then put a hand lightly on Evans's shoulder before sitting down beside him at the table. 'I'm sorry, Taffy, I didn't mean to snap at you like that. I'm just as frustrated about this as you are.'

'I realize that, boss,' Evans said in a placating tone.

'So what delights do we have for breakfast?' McIndoe asked, reaching for the teapot in the centre of the table.

Hillyard picked up the bell and rang it in the direction of the open door. 'We've even got our own cook here. Starr thinks of everything.'

A middle-aged woman entered the room and crossed to the table, where she placed a plate in front of McIndoe. On it was a large spoonful of scrambled eggs, two rashers of bacon, a sausage and half a grilled tomato. He waited until the woman had left before pushing the plate away from him. 'We should be on army rations like the other military personnel stationed here on the island. None of this is available to them. It's not right that we should be given special privileges, especially when the locals are having to scrape together food to survive.'

'Take it while you can, Mac, that's what I say,' Ravallo said.

'You would say that, Nicky,' Stella said from the doorway. She was dressed in a pair of unflattering khaki fatigues, no make-up, and with her tousled raven hair loose on her shoulders. Yet she still managed to look absolutely stunning. She crossed to the table and sat down. 'Sam's right. Why should we be given special privileges when there are thousands of locals, and in particular children, who are suffering dreadful ailments like bacillary and amoebic dysentery as a direct result of the deficiencies in their diets? And you think it's right that we should eat like royalty while they have to go without?'

'That's hardly going to change anything, is it?' Ravallo retorted, gesturing to the food on McIndoe's plate.

'It's the principle that's the issue here, Nicky,' Stella replied. 'You of all people should know that after the penury of your childhood in Brooklyn.'

'The one thing I learnt from my childhood was never to let food go to waste,' Ravallo told her. 'But don't worry, the next time I'll make sure that I throw it in the garbage bin. Out of principle, of course. Will that make you happy?'

Evans caught Hillyard's eye and surreptitiously indicated towards the door with his head. Hillyard touched Johnson on the arm and got to his feet. 'Would you excuse us?' he said with a quick smile. 'We've got a few things to do.'

'I'll come with you,' Ravallo said, pushing back his chair and standing up. He looked down at McIndoe. 'If Starr wants me, I'll be around. It's not even as if I can leave the house.'

Stella waited until the four men had left the room, then rubbed her hands over her face. 'I should have known better than to bring up Nicky's childhood. I realized that the moment I mentioned it. He's always been very defensive about it. And it doesn't help that most of his colleagues in Military Intelligence come from affluent families who could afford to put their sons through university. That gave them a distinct advantage when they joined Military Intelligence. Nicky's had to start out from the bottom. It can't have been easy for him, but it shows the kind of guy he is to have got where he is today. And the resentment towards him from a certain section of his peers certainly hasn't helped either. You know the type. The All-American youth who captained the college football team, dated the prettiest cheerleader, graduated with a law degree and ended up marrying the daughter of some senator on Capitol Hill.' She poured herself a cup of tea, then looked across the table at McIndoe and gave him a triumphant smile. 'But Nicky will have the last laugh. He's already being groomed to become the youngest ever head of Military Intelligence. Then watch his detractors squirm in their All-American shoes.'

'You think a lot of him, don't you?' McIndoe said, holding her stare.

'I have the greatest respect for what he's managed to achieve, if that's what you mean,' she replied, chuckling softly and shaking her head to herself when she saw the uncertain look on McIndoe's face. 'Don't start jumping to conclusions, Sam. Nicky and I have a purely professional relationship. And that's how it'll stay.'

'The nature of your relationship with Nicky has nothing to do with me,' McIndoe said. Once again he moved to the window and looked out into the street. The MPs were still there.

'You're still smarting with me about what I said last night, aren't you? I'm sorry if it hurts, Sam, but I still believe that you've got a traitor in your team. And I'm damned if I'm going to take the fall for him.'

'It's strange that we've never had any problems before you arrived on the scene,' McIndoe said as he turned away from the window. 'Who knows, perhaps it was Nicky who tipped off the Germans.'

'I know it wasn't Nicky,' Stella said.

'And I know it wasn't anyone in my team,' McIndoe countered.

Stella was about to say something, thought better of it, then strode from the room.

McIndoe sat down slowly at the table and buried his head in his hands. How could he be so sure that the traitor wasn't someone in his team? He knew he couldn't, and that was what really bothered him. He hadn't had any sleep the previous night – he'd spent the hours tossing and turning restlessly in his bed, unable to think of anything else. But each time he'd gone through the names – and God knows how many times he'd done that in the small hours of the morning – he just couldn't believe that any of them could be a German spy. It just didn't seem possible. These were all proven men who had had unblemished careers in the Firm. Evans and Passiere had even been decorated for bravery in the field. Yet he knew only too well that, if Starr couldn't find the traitor, they would all be regarded with understandable suspicion which would put an end to any future they may have had with the Firm. They wouldn't be trusted any more. That included himself . . .

'Mac?'

McIndoe looked up to find Ravallo standing on the other side of the table. 'Sorry, Nicky, I didn't hear you come in.'

'You OK?' Ravallo asked.

'No,' McIndoe replied bluntly. 'I didn't get a moment's sleep last night. I couldn't stop thinking about the possibility that one of my team could be a traitor.'

'You and me both, buddy,' Ravallo replied.

'If you were looking for Stella, I'm afraid I sent her away with a flea in her ear,' McIndoe told him. 'We haven't exactly got off on the right footing.'

'Don't worry about Stella,' Ravallo said with a dismissive flick of his hand. 'As you've already seen, she's not one to mince her words. But then that's what I like about her. A girl after my own heart. Actually, I came to find you. I've just bumped into Sergeant Pearson in the kitchen. He's here to take the two of us over to HQ for a briefing with Starr.'

'You think that Starr's discovered the identity of the traitor?' McIndoe asked, getting to his feet.

'I guess there's only one way of finding that out, isn't there?'

'Yes, I've found your traitor,' Starr said in reply to McIndoe's question. He jabbed the stem of his pipe at the two chairs in front of his desk. 'Sit down, both of you.'

McIndoe sat down anxiously on the edge of the chair, his eyes riveted on Starr's face. 'Well, sir, who is it?'

'It was the Partisan who brought Lieutenant di Mauro to the rendezvous,' Starr replied, glancing down at the report on his desk. 'Angelo Sciarro.'

'But Stella only told him about the location of the rendezvous once they were on the road,' Ravallo reminded him. 'How could he have communicated their position to the Germans if he was never out of her sight until she reached the boat?'

'My guess is that he left the coordinates for the rendezvous in the truck,' Starr replied. 'The Germans could have followed the truck at a discreet distance without Lieutenant di Mauro knowing it. The truck conveniently runs out of fuel and di Mauro and Sciarro have to complete the last couple of miles on foot, which would not only have given the Germans time to retrieve the coordinates, but also to get themselves into position to launch an attack on the MTB the moment she was safely aboard.'

'This is all speculation, sir,' Ravallo said.

'How the Germans came by the coordinates is still speculation,' Starr agreed, 'but half an hour ago I received word from Giancarlo Massimo, the leader of the Partisans in Sicily, that Angelo Sciarro's body was found in a hotel room in Gela. He'd been shot once through the head. A piece of paper was found in one of his pockets. On it was a name and a telephone number. The name was Colonel Ernst Brausch, head of the Gestapo in Sicily. The number has since been verified by one of our operatives in Berlin as being that of Brausch's private line at Gestapo headquarters in Palermo. That seems pretty conclusive proof as far as I'm concerned.'

'Thank God for that,' McIndoe exclaimed, then held up a hand towards Starr. 'I didn't quite mean it like that, sir . . .'

'I know what you meant, McIndoe, and believe me, I feel the same way.' Starr handed a folder to McIndoe. 'It's all in there. I also learnt that he was a heavy drinker who used to associate with a known German collaborator in his hometown of Gela. God knows why the Resistance ever used him, but Massimo seemed to hold him in high regard.'

Ravallo got to his feet and thrust his hands into his pockets. He walked slowly to the door where he paused momentarily before turning back to Starr. 'So I was right after all. Stella was responsible for the leak. I can only apologize for having doubted the integrity of your men, sir, and I'd quite understand if you now wanted to have her taken off this assignment.'

'I think you're being a bit hard on her, Major,' Starr said. 'I certainly don't blame her for what happened. She couldn't possibly have known about Sciarro's treachery, otherwise I'm sure she'd have taken the necessary steps to deal with the situation. She struck me as a very intelligent and headstrong young woman when I met her earlier this morning. I have no reason to want her taken off the assignment. McIndoe, how do you feel about it?'

'I agree with you, sir. Not only is she intelligent and headstrong, but her specialist knowledge of Sicily and the local Partisans will be invaluable to us when we reach the island.' McIndoe sat back and folded his arms across his chest. 'That is, after you've briefed us on just what exactly it is you want of us once we do get there.'

Starr raised his bushy eyebrows questioningly at McIndoe's tone of voice, then puffed thoughtfully on his pipe for some time before finally speaking. 'Very well, now that I've satisfied myself that none of you were involved in the incident last night, I can brief you in more detail on your assignment.' He looked at Ravallo, who was still standing at the door. 'If you'd care to sit down, Major.'

Ravallo resumed his seat. When McIndoe held out a packet of cigarettes towards him, he hesitated – then plucked a cigarette from the packet. Starr waited until both men had lit up before opening the folder in front of him. 'The War Office in London has received some very disturbing information in the last few days that the Axis are putting together the final plans for a full-scale invasion of Malta. I don't have to tell either of you of the strategic importance of this island in the continuing battle for the Mediterranean. If the Axis were to gain control of Malta, it would give them outright air and sea superiority over the Mediterranean. And with the Axis controlling the Mediterranean, the Allied convoys couldn't use the route any more, and that would leave our troops completely isolated in North Africa. In effect, their supply lines would be cut. No incoming fuel for their tanks, no ammunition for their guns but, even more importantly than that, no fresh rations for the men. How long could they hold out against a rejuvenated Sixth Army under those conditions? And if North Africa were to fall to the Germans it would be a damaging body blow to the Allied cause. Who knows just where that could ultimately lead?'

'In other words, we could lose the war if Malta were to fall,' Ravallo concluded.

'Not necessarily, but with the way things are going against the Allies right now, especially in North Africa and on the Eastern Front . . . Well, let's just say I wouldn't like to predict the outcome.'

'How did the War Office find out about the invasion plans?' McIndoe asked.

'That's classified top secret, McIndoe,' Starr told him brusquely. 'But I can assure you that this information is very reliable indeed.'

It wouldn't be until after the war that McIndoe would discover that this sensitive information, together with countless other vital Axis cipher communiqués, had been intercepted at the top-secret base at Bletchley Park in London, then deciphered by the boffins who operated 'Colossus', a highly effective computer which had been encrypting the numerical cipher codes of the German Enigma electromechanical computer since 1941. This operation was given the very highest security classification, 'Ultra'.

'Field-Marshal Kesselring, the commander-in-chief of the Axis forces here in the Mediterranean, has scheduled a top-level meeting of his chiefs-of-staff tomorrow in the Sicilian capital, Palermo, to finalize the plans for the invasion. It's to be known as "Operation Herkules". He'll then be travelling to Berlin in the next few days to present the details of Operation Herkules to Hitler. And if Hitler gives it his approval, the wheels will then be set in motion. In fact, there's already disturbing signs of a steady military build-up on the island of Sicily. Lieutenant di Mauro's report showed that only too clearly. That would suggest Kesselring's confident of his plan being given the go-ahead once he takes it to Berlin. Why else draft in all that extra military hardware, unless he intends to use it as an invasion force?' Starr paused to puff on his pipe. 'I don't know how much you know about the situation here on Malta, but the fact is that right now the defences are so depleted that we'd be in no position to repel an Axis invasion. If Kesselring were to send his troops in tomorrow, Malta would fall into enemy hands within a matter of days.'

'Obviously the Germans don't know that, otherwise they'd already have invaded the island,' Ravallo said.

'Obviously, and that's all we've got going for us right now.' Starr picked up a coded communiqué he'd received earlier that morning from SOE headquarters in London. He stared at it for some time before slowly replacing it on his desk. 'What I'm about to tell you is in the strictest confidence. It doesn't leave the confines of this room.' Both men nodded. Starr chewed on the stem of his pipe, as though still reluctant to tell them. He finally laid the pipe in the ashtray on his desk. 'Next month, fifteen Spitfires are due to arrive here aboard the aircraft carrier, *Eagle*, to bolster the island's fragile defences. Any Axis invasion would almost certainly be preceded by a sustained bombing campaign but, with the Spitfires in place, it would make it that much harder for the *Luftwaffe* to carry out their nefarious task. Not only that, Kesselring's far too shrewd a tactician to risk sending in his ground troops unless the *Luftwaffe* already had control of the skies over the island. And those extra Spitfires could just tilt the balance in our favour.'

'So what exactly is it you want us to do, sir?' McIndoe asked.

'Stall Kesselring's invasion plans, at least until the Spitfires have arrived,' Starr replied. 'It's our only chance.'

'And how do we do that, sir?' McIndoe continued.

Starr removed a photograph from the folder and handed it to McIndoe. 'The man standing on Himmler's immediate right is Major Otto Schenk – or, to give him his correct Gestapo rank, *Sturmbannführer* Otto Schenk. I know it's not a particularly good photograph of him, but it's the only one the Americans have of him on file. And that's one more than we've got. Then again, Schenk doesn't exactly court publicity. You'll understand why when I tell you that he's one of only five senior officers based at Gestapo head-quarters in Berlin whose sole job it is to carry out spot-checks on Gestapo bases in the occupied territories. He's answerable only to Himmler, and has *carte blanche* to go anywhere and to see anything he wants. Their reports can result in even the most senior Gestapo officer being stripped of his rank. So it's hardly surprising that these men should be both feared and reviled by their fellow Gestapo officers.'

'So where exactly does Schenk fit into all this?' McIndoe asked, tapping the photograph with his finger.

'He's due to arrive in Sicily later this afternoon. We already have a rough idea of his movements once he gets there. We know this because we have a highly placed source at Gestapo headquarters in Berlin. That's all I can say. But he is very reliable.' Starr puffed on his pipe before speaking again. 'Tomorrow morning Schenk will be abducted by the Resistance, then smuggled out of the country and flown to London for interrogation. But none of that need concern you.'

'It won't be long before the alarm's raised, sir,' McIndoe pointed out. 'Then the whole island will be crawling with soldiers looking for him.'

'I don't see why,' Starr answered. 'For all intents and purposes, Schenk will still be on the island. Major Ravallo will be taking his place. Ravallo speaks fluent German and he's already made an in-depth study of Gestapo operations to get himself into character.'

McIndoe stared at the photograph, then cast a sidelong look at Ravallo. He shook his head. 'It'll never work. They look nothing like each other.'

'Major Ravallo is confident it'll work,' Starr said. He ges-tured to the American seated beside McIndoe. 'Perhaps we should let him explain. After all, this part of the operation was his idea. And his superiors were impressed enough to give it the go-ahead. Major?'

Ravallo stubbed out his cigarette before addressing McIndoe. 'Schenk's due to leave Palermo early tomorrow morning to visit several of the Gestapo bases along the coast. He's expected to be away for the next few days. Nobody on the island knows exactly where he'll be going. Even we don't know that. And that can only work in our favour. He could turn up anywhere at anytime. That's his brief – to keep these bases on their toes. Added to that, apart from the senior Gestapo officers who'll meet his plane, nobody else on the island knows what he looks like. And, as I won't be going anywhere near Gestapo headquarters in Palermo, why should anyone think I'm not Schenk? I'll also have in my possession a letter of authorization from Himmler that these special officers carry with them at all times. That letter alone can get me access into any building I please. And I mean any building.'

'Including the one where Kesselring will be holding his briefing?' McIndoe deduced.

'The briefing's due to be held at the Grand Hotel,' Starr said. 'It's where Kesselring always stays when he's in Palermo.'

'What are you suggesting, sir? That we steal the plans for the invasion?' McIndoe asked in amazement.

'Nothing so blatant. We photograph them. But I'm not going to go into the details of that right now. It's explained at length in these dossiers for you to read,' Starr said, tapping the two manila envelopes on his desk. 'What we need to do, however, is make Kesselring think that the plans could have been compromised for this to work. With that in mind, it's been decided that the stenographer's handwritten notes will be found discarded in a bin outside the hotel after Kesselring has already taken possession of the typed plans. That will leave Kesselring with a serious dilemma. Should he risk presenting the original plans to Hitler, not knowing whether they've been seen by unauthorized eyes, or should he scrap them and draft a completely new strategy? Imagine what would happen if they were to go ahead with the invasion, only to discover that we'd already seen the plans and were able to counter every move they made. The Germans would sustain substantial losses, and Kesselring would almost certainly be relieved of his command. For that reason alone I believe he'll choose to scrap the plans in favour of a new strategy.'

'And a new strategy would mean going back to the drawing-board,' McIndoe said. 'A time-consuming exercise all round.'

'Exactly,' Starr agreed. 'Giving London the time they need to dispatch those fifteen Spitfires to Malta.'

'Assuming that Kesselring plays it safe, sir,' McIndoe said.

'He will,' Starr said resolutely.

'Why not just steal the plans and make it known to the Germans that we've got them?' McIndoe asked. 'Then they would have no option but to scrap the invasion.'

'It's not as simple as that, McIndoe,' Starr said. He knew that only a handful of senior German officers had been briefed in advance of the meeting, and by stealing the blueprint it would suggest that the Allies had been acting on inside information. A top-level investigation would be instigated and, once the officers concerned were exonerated of any blame, then the inquiry would concentrate on other possible sources of the leak. And if they were ever to suspect that their Enigma codes had been intercepted and decoded by the Allies, they would immediately change their entire communications network. A new system, with new codes, which would render the entire Ultra program useless . . .

'What do you mean by that, sir?' McIndoe asked when Starr fell silent.

'I can't go into details, McIndoe. Suffice to say that it's not viable. This way there's a degree of uncertainty which should work just as effectively.'

'So where exactly do we come into it?' McIndoe asked.

'Your team will act as Major Ravallo's back-up unit. Higgins will drop you off at a prearranged rendezvous, then conceal the MTB until your return.'

'Will we be working with the Partisans?' McIndoe asked.

'Yes,' Starr replied, raising a hand before McIndoe could object. 'I know that could prove risky after the incident last night, but the wheels have already been set in motion. They have to be involved for this to have any chance of working. As you'll realize when you read the dossier.'

'Did Sciarro know about the operation?' Ravallo asked.

'No. I spoke to Massimo a short time ago and he assured me that he's broken down those involved into individual cells and briefed them only on their particular role in the operation. So each cell will be working independently of the others to ensure maximum security. They're all on a need-to-know basis only.'

'Except Massimo,' McIndoe said.

'Giancarlo Massimo is an Oxbridge graduate,' Starr replied, as if that alone put him above suspicion. 'I can personally vouch for his loyalty.'

'Just as Stella vouched for Sciarro's loyalty,' McIndoe said, stubbing out his cigarette. He took another from the packet and lit it. 'It's our necks on the line out there, sir. If Sciarro was working for the Germans, who's to say that they haven't recruited other Partisans to spy for them? We could be walking straight into a trap.'

'You're not going on some boy-scout jamboree, McIndoe,' Starr said angrily. 'Of course there will be risks involved. There always will be in this line of work. But if you don't feel that you can handle the pressure, then I'll have you relieved of your command and bring in someone who can. Nobody's indispensable in this organization. Just remember that.'

'That won't be necessary, sir,' McIndoe said, tight-lipped.

'I'm glad to hear it,' Starr replied. He pushed the two sealed manila envelopes across the desk towards them. 'As I said just now, it's all detailed in there. Standard regulations apply, of course.' He looked at Ravallo. 'That means the contents are to be burnt once they've been consigned to memory. You'll be given the relevant charts and maps appertaining to the operation shortly before you leave for Sicily.'

'When do we leave, sir?' McIndoe asked, picking up the envelopes and handing one to Ravallo.

'Midnight,' Starr said. 'That's all, gentlemen. Thank you.'

McIndoe turned to Ravallo as the two men headed for the door. 'It should be interesting to see how Stella reacts to the news of Sciarro's treachery,' he said.

'I'm sure it will,' Ravallo agreed, before following him from the room.

'I don't believe it,' Stella announced defiantly after McIndoe explained what Starr had told them earlier.

'It sounds pretty conclusive to me, Stella,' Ravallo said.

'For a frame-up, yes,' she retorted.

McIndoe and Ravallo exchanged uncertain glances across the table. The three of them were alone in the room. The others were out, having earlier hitched a ride into Valletta after being informed by the MPs that they were free to leave the house.

'I worked closely with Angelo Sciarro these last few months,' Stella said. 'He was no German stooge. He was a loyal member of the Partisans.'

'So how do you explain him turning up dead in a hotel room with that kind of incriminating evidence on him?' Ravallo asked.

'As I said, it's got to be a frame-up,' Stella replied. 'The Germans were obviously expecting to be successful in capturing us last night. So when things went wrong, they had to act quickly to protect the identity of the real traitor. It's the only logical explanation.'

'I don't buy any of this,' McIndoe said, getting to his feet and moving to the window.

'I know how it must sound, Sam,' Stella said, turning in her chair to look at him. 'But you've got to believe me. Angelo was no informer.'

'You haven't produced a shred of evidence to back up your theory,' McIndoe told her.

'You know I don't have any evidence. It's just a gut feeling, that's all.' Her eyes turned to Ravallo. 'Nicky knows that my gut reactions are rarely wrong. Please, Sam, you've got to believe me. Angelo wasn't the one who betrayed us.'

McIndoe looked at Ravallo, who gave a quick shrug. 'Yeah, she's usually pretty accurate when it comes to her gut feelings. But, for what it's worth, I still think she's way out on this one.'

'What do I have to do to convince you two?' she pleaded.

'Evidence, for a start,' McIndoe told her.

'Do you have to brief your men in full before we leave tonight?' she asked.

'It's standard procedure,' McIndoe replied. 'Why do you ask?'

'Couldn't they be briefed on a need-to-know basis only? That way, if one of them is the spy, he wouldn't be able to tip off the Germans in advance about the operation. I know it's asking a lot, Sam, but what if I am right? We'd be captured the moment we set foot on Sicily. And you can bet that the Germans will be a damn sight better prepared for us than they were the last time.'

'I'm getting tired of these constant accusations against my men!' McIndoe told her. 'You just don't want to admit that you were wrong, do you? There's overwhelming evidence pointing to Sciarro being the spy, and that's an end to it as far as I'm concerned.'

'And what if I am right?' she demanded, breaking the uneasy silence which filled the room. 'You'd be leading us all straight into a German ambush. And you know as well as I do what would happen to us if we were handed over to the Gestapo. Can you really be so sure of Angelo's guilt? Can you?'

McIndoe heard the front door open before he could reply, and shortly afterwards Evans, Hillyard and Johnson entered the room. 'Where's Georges?' McIndoe asked when he realized that Passiere wasn't with them.

'In bed, where else?' Hillyard replied. 'We asked him if he wanted to go into Valletta with us, but he just turned over and went back to sleep.'

'Go and wake him up,' McIndoe said, gesturing to the door.

'You got a thousand-pound bomb handy, boss?' Hillyard quipped.

'Just do it!' McIndoe snapped.

Hillyard raised his hands defensively, then hurried from the room.

'Sit down,' McIndoe said to Evans and Johnson, pointing to the chairs behind him.

'I assume from the way the siege was lifted earlier that Starr's managed to weed out the spy?' Evans said, pulling up the chair beside Ravallo and sitting down.

'Yes, he has,' was all McIndoe would say. He looked round at the doorway when Hillyard entered with a bleary-eyed Passiere. 'I hope I didn't disturb your beauty sleep, Georges?'

'I think I can – '

'Just sit down,' McIndoe cut in irritably, then waited until Hillyard and Passiere had taken their seats before out-lining what Starr had told him about Sciarro.

'It seems an open-and-shut case if ever I heard one,' Hillyard said, the relief evident in his voice.

'It certainly looks that way,' McIndoe replied.

'What exactly is the operation, boss?' Evans asked. 'Did Starr brief you on that as well?'

'Yes,' McIndoe said.

'Finally,' Hillyard muttered. 'So what's it all about?'

There was a pause as McIndoe stared at his feet. Then he looked up at Stella. 'You'll be briefed on a need-to-know basis only.'

'But we've always been – '

'Those are Vice-Admiral Starr's orders,' McIndoe cut across Hillyard's protestations, knowing that none of them would dare to question Starr's authority.

'Still treating us like little children, I see,' Hillyard muttered contemptuously.

'I'm sure he has his reasons,' Stella said, without taking her eyes off McIndoe's face.

'I'm sure he has,' McIndoe agreed, but there was little conviction in his voice. He purposely avoided eye-contact with her as he leaned over the table and stubbed out his cigarette. 'Right, let's get on with the briefing, shall we?'

Built in 1855, the *Grand Albergo* – Grand Hotel – had for many years been regarded as the only place for the rich and famous to stay when visiting Palermo. Situated in the heart of the Sicilian capital, it had been where the German composer, Richard Wagner, had found the inspiration to complete his last opera, Parsifal, a year before his death in 1883. The exterior of the building was painted a delicate shade of cream; the wooden shutters secured over the windows, and the protective steel railings enclosing the small bedroom balconies, were all painted a verdant forest green. The Italian and German flags hung limply from angled poles directly above the entrance – a set of revolving glass doors which led into a spacious marble-floored foyer. This was decorated by four Doric pillars and several life-size marble statues, which stood like milky ghosts from a bygone era beside the red-carpeted staircase that swept up majestically from the foyer to the unseen pleasures on the upper floors. It wasn't surprising that the occupying German Army had requisitioned the hotel for the exclusive use of their senior officers based in Sicily.

Captain Jürgen Franke entered the hotel through the revolving doors and made his way to where Major Hans

Riedler was standing in the centre of the deserted foyer, directly beneath the breathtaking four-tiered crystal chandelier which hung from the ornately carved wooden ceiling high above him. 'We shouldn't have any trouble sealing off the area around the hotel, sir,' Franke told him. 'The local troops who were guarding the area before we arrived seemed to have the situation in hand. There were a few areas where security needed to be tightened, but I've already seen to that.'

'I assume then that the handover has been completed?' Riedler asked.

'Yes, sir. Our men are now installed in and around the hotel. Nobody will get in or out without authorization. I assume that all the staff have already been given clearance?'

'Yes. The hotel was cleared of all non-essential personnel last night. There's only a skeleton staff on duty now. I sent a list of their names over to the local Gestapo headquarters on the Piazza Bologni when we first arrived. I got a call a short time ago to say that all those on the list had been investigated thoroughly by the Gestapo before they were given clearance to work here. And if the Gestapo have given them clearance, that's good enough for me.' Riedler looked at the sheet of paper in his hand. 'There are four possible means of access into the building. The revolving doors over there, the back door which leads into the kitchen, and the two fire exits on either side of the hotel. I want them all manned around the clock.'

'We don't have a lot of men to spare, sir. It can probably be done if they were to work twelve hours on, twelve hours off.'

'I don't care if they have to work twenty-four-hour shifts, I want those doors under constant guard,' Riedler told him.

'I'll see to it right away, sir,' Franke replied, then strode briskly across the foyer and exited the hotel through the revolving doors.

Riedler sat down on the nearest chair and caught sight of his reflection in one of several wall mirrors which lined the foyer. There he was, clean-shaven and resplendent in full paratroop uniform. A far cry from the muddy trenches of the Eastern Front. He smiled to himself, more out of relief than anything else that he was away from there, and he let his mind drift back to the previous afternoon when they'd finally left the hell of Russia behind them . . .

Although he didn't know exactly how far they had travelled in the truck, he'd estimated it to be about thirty miles. Twice the truck had come under attack and he'd felt helpless and exposed as the shells had exploded relentlessly around them. It was a feeling he'd only ever experienced once before when he'd been aboard a U-boat which had been trapped by two British frigates in a Norwegian fjord. The captain had ordered the U-boat to lie motionless at the bottom of the fjord, and it had been nothing short of a miracle that none of the depth-charges had found their target.

A *Tante Ju*, the affectionate nickname given to the ungainly Junkers 52 which had been used extensively by the paratroopers during the airborne assault on Crete – and which had since become one of the more proficient German transport aircraft on the Eastern Front – had been waiting at an air-base near Kharkov in the Ukraine to fly them on to Sicily. On landing at a German airstrip outside Palermo, they had been met by two troop carriers which had taken them to the barracks of the Fifteenth Panzer Grenadier Division, where he and his men had each been afforded the luxury of a hot bath and a nourishing four-course meal – the combination of which had done wonders to boost their flagging morale. But above all it had been the sight of the fifteen sets of clean paratroopers' uniforms laid out neatly in their temporary quarters which had helped to restore much of the pride they'd lost both in themselves and in their unit while serving as infantrymen on the Eastern Front. . .

Riedler's thoughts were interrupted by the sound of an approaching engine. When he looked through the glass doors he saw an official, open-topped staff car pull up outside the hotel. The driver cut the engine, then jumped out from behind the wheel to open the back door; Riedler was amazed to see the familiar but unexpected figure of General Kurt Student step out into the cobbled street. Riedler leapt to his feet, brushed an imaginary fleck of dirt off the front of his tunic, then straightened his cap in front of the mirror before crossing the foyer to meet Student as he entered the hotel. He snapped to attention. Student returned the salute, then extended a hand in friendship.

'I wasn't expecting you to arrive until tomorrow morning, sir,' Riedler said, gripping Student's hand firmly.

'Field-Marshal Kesselring asked me to come down today to check on the security arrangements. Judging by the road-blocks already in place around the hotel, I'd say you have the situation well in hand.'

It was then that Franke entered the hotel through the revolving doors. He came to attention and snapped his heels together as his right arm shot out in a Nazi salute. Student returned the salute. 'This is my second-in-command, sir. *Hauptmann* Jürgen Franke,' Riedler told Student. 'He was serving with one of the Brandenburg units before he joined us.'

'Which unit were you with, Franke?' Student asked.

'Koenen, sir. North Africa,' Franke replied, still standing rigidly to attention.

'One of the best, from what I've heard,' Student said, nodding to himself. 'Major Riedler was very lucky to have got a replacement like you.'

'The honour is mine, sir,' Franke replied without taking his eyes off Student.

'It's good to have met you, Franke,' Student said. 'I'm sure we'll get to talk more over the next couple of days.

Right now, however, I need to speak to Major Riedler alone. Would you excuse us?'

'Sir,' Franke replied, saluting before turning sharply on his heels and striding from the foyer.

'Seems like a good man to have on your side,' Student said, staring after the retreating Franke.

'We'll see,' Riedler replied coldly.

'What's that supposed to mean?' Student asked.

'I think you know what I mean, sir,' Riedler said.

Student held Riedler's stare for a moment, then gestured to the closed doors which led into a spacious conference room off the foyer. It was here that Kesselring was due to hold the meeting the following day. 'Let's go in there. As I said, we need to talk.' Riedler followed Student into the room and closed the doors again behind them. A heavy, elongated oak table stood in the centre of the marble floor, with half a dozen chairs positioned around it. Student tossed his cap on to the table then swung round to face Riedler. 'Perhaps you'd care to explain to me why you blatantly disregarded an order which had been signed by two of the most senior officers in the *Wehrmacht?*'

'It was the only way I could be sure of getting Lieutenant Weber proper medical attention,' Riedler replied. 'And from what I've since been told, he wouldn't have lasted out the day had I not insisted that he be taken to the nearest hospital.'

'And you think that justifies disobeying a direct order?' Student retorted angrily.

'All I know, sir, is that if I hadn't acted in the way I did, Weber would be dead right now,' Riedler said defensively.

'If you're given an order by a superior officer, you obey it!' Student yelled. 'You don't interpret it to suit your own purposes. Is that understood, Major Riedler?'

'Understood, sir,' Riedler replied softly.

'It took a great deal of persuading by Field-Marshal Kesselring to get General Paulus to agree, albeit reluctantly, to release you and your men from the Eastern Front to come here for this assignment. So it's hardly surprising that General Paulus rang Field-Marshal Kesselring personally this morning to express his extreme disquiet at the way you countermanded his orders. Field-Marshal Kesselring is normally a very affable man, except when he feels that his authority is being undermined. You embarrassed him in front of General Paulus and he, in turn, vented his anger on me, since I was the one who put your name forward for this assignment in the first place. But I can live with that. What I can't accept is that your actions brought shame on the good name of the Parachute Regiment. That's something I will not tolerate under any circumstances!'

'We were abandoned in no man's land by the Sixth Army, sir,' Riedler said, struggling to control his anger. Not at Student, but at the feeling of being persecuted for daring to stand up for his men. 'We endured five days of constant shelling from both sides, only to find out later that we could have been pulled out at any time had the *Luftwaffe* bothered to send up a spotter plane to look for us.'

'I don't care if you were constantly shelled for five months, your behaviour was totally inexcusable. And should it ever happen again, you'll be up in front of a court-martial for wilful insubordination. As it is, General Paulus wanted to pursue the matter further, and it was only as a direct result of Field-Marshal Kesselring's tactful diplomacy that no further action will be taken against you. I assured Field-Marshal Kesselring before I left Rome this morning that I'd speak to you about your wholly unacceptable conduct. So, as far as he's concerned, the matter is now closed. Which means, fortunately for you, he won't mention it when he gets here tomorrow morning. You actually owe him a great debt of gratitude because, without his intervention, you wouldn't be here right now. You'd be on your way back to Berlin to explain yourself to a court-martial. Just remember that.'

Student pulled out a chair and sat down. The matter was now closed. 'Tell me, how's your brother these days? Andreas, isn't it? The last time I saw him he was the best man at your wedding. He was very drunk, if I recall, but then weren't most of the guests?'

Riedler wasn't surprised that Student had changed the subject so abruptly. He knew Kurt Student well enough to know that he never held a grudge. He'd said what had needed to be said, and that was an end to it. That was his way, and Riedler had nothing but respect and admiration for the man. 'Andreas was killed at Tobruk last year, sir,' he said.

'I had no idea. I'm very sorry,' Student said softly.

'Two tragedies within the space of a few months. First Andreas in North Africa, then Karl Müller on Crete.'

'Your wife took Karl's death particularly badly, didn't she? But then she always was close to her brother. How is she now?'

'Charlotte's coping a lot better now, sir. We're expecting our first child in the next couple of months. The baby's certainly helped to make it easier for her to come to terms with Karl's death.'

Suddenly the sound of raised voices could be heard coming from the foyer. Riedler pulled open the double doors and crossed to where Sergeant Manfred Kuhn – a tough, uncompromising soldier and one of the most decorated paratroopers in the history of the regiment – was arguing with a man Riedler had never seen before. But the distinctive black Gestapo uniform was no stranger to him. Riedler estimated the man to be in his early forties. The gaunt features and ice-blue eyes gave him a strangely cold, mesmeric appearance. He wore the rank of colonel. Riedler saluted him.

The officer clicked his heels together and his hand shot out in a Nazi salute. 'Good afternoon, Major,' he said as he approached Riedler. 'I am *Standartenführer* Ernst Brausch, head of the Gestapo here in Sicily. Your sergeant was very insistent that I wait by the door while he sought permission to let me into the hotel. I tried to explain to him that the Gestapo don't need permission to enter a building in any of the occupied territories, but he was determined to argue the point with me. I must say, Major, I don't care to be treated in this way.'

'Thank you, Sergeant, that will be all,' Riedler said to Kuhn who saluted him stiffly then returned to his post beside the revolving doors. 'He was only carrying out his orders, sir,' Riedler informed Brausch. 'Orders that came directly from Field-Marshal Kesselring in Rome.'

'I hope you don't have a problem with that, Colonel,' Student said as he emerged into the foyer. 'I doubt very much whether Field-Marshal Kesselring would take kindly to having his orders questioned by the Gestapo.'

Brausch was quick to snap to attention and salute Student. 'I wouldn't have questioned the orders, sir, had I known that they'd been issued by Field-Marshal Kesselring.'

'A misunderstanding, obviously,' Student said with a faint smile. 'So Colonel, what brings the Gestapo here? This is hardly your jurisdiction – '

'I'm surprised that Field-Marshal Kesselring didn't choose to contact me about the security arrangements for the meeting here tomorrow. I could have provided him with one of our *Einsatz-commando* units we have stationed on the island.'

'Field-Marshal Kesselring asked me to handle the security arrangements,' Student told him. 'I'm sure one of your commando units would have been more than capable of providing an excellent guard had they been asked, but I naturally chose from those who've served under my command. And the paratroopers are one of the best battlefield regiments. As I'm sure you'd agree . . .'

Brausch's mouth twitched in a forced smile. 'I'm sure they are, sir.'

'Is that the only reason why you came here today, Colonel? To query the security arrangements?'

Brausch shifted uncomfortably from one foot to the other. 'Sir, it was never my intention – '

'Is there another reason for your being here?' Student cut across Brausch's obsequious protestations.

'Sir, as the senior Gestapo officer on Sicily, I feel that I should have been asked to the meeting here tomorrow morning,' Brausch said.

'The meeting has nothing to do with the Gestapo,' Student was quick to inform him.

'With all due respect, sir, anything that concerns the security of this island is of importance to the Gestapo.'

'This is a military briefing, Colonel, which has nothing whatsoever to do with the internal security of the island. Only a handful of Field-Marshal Kesselring's closest aides will be attending. It doesn't concern the Gestapo. And that's an end to it.'

'I understand, sir,' Brausch said tight-lipped, indignant at being given the brush-off, but knowing better than to question a senior officer.

'I'm surprised that you aren't more concerned about the situation in your own backyard,' Student said. 'I hear that you're shortly due a visit from one of *Reichsführer* Himmler's personal investigators. An internal unit, out to find fault with the very system it created. Certainly an interesting idea.'

'I have nothing to hide,' Brausch replied brusquely, then smiled quickly, as if to cover his sudden outburst. 'I fully support these internal investigations, sir. They help to maintain the consistently high standards which *Reichsführer* Himmler expects from those who are chosen to serve in this organization.'

'I'm sure they do,' Student replied. 'Well, Colonel, if you'll excuse me, I still have a lot of work to do before the day's out.'

'Sir, there is one other thing I feel I should bring to your attention,' Brausch said as Student turned to leave.

'Well?' Student demanded.

'I'm sure you've heard about the failed attempt to capture a British SOE team when it picked up an American intelligence officer off the coast of Sicily two nights ago?' Brausch asked.

'What of it?'

'It was our operative who tipped us off about the rendezvous in the first place. Had the Gestapo been allowed to handle the operation – '

'What's your point, Brausch?' Student cut in irritably.

'That same source told us to expect another Allied sortie on the island within the next forty-eight hours. A joint operation by the British SOE and American Military Intelligence. In fact, the same team who were here two days ago. Only we don't know exactly where, or when, the operation's due to take place.'

'Riedler, come here,' Student barked, gesturing towards him. 'I think you should hear this.'

Brausch repeated to Riedler what he'd told Student. 'We don't know yet why they're coming back, but it would seem too much of a coincidence for it not to be linked in some way with the briefing which is being held here tomorrow.'

'This is very disturbing news indeed,' Student said gravely as he met Riedler's anxious look. 'Do you want more men drafted in to help with the security arrangements?'

'We have men here – '

'No,' Riedler interceded sharply across Brausch's words. 'No, thank you, sir,' he added quickly in a more conciliatory tone. 'My men are more than capable of handling any situation, should it arise.'

'As you wish,' Brausch said.

Student turned to Brausch. 'You said that you didn't know *yet* why they were coming back to Sicily. That would imply that you expect to find out in due course.'

'I will, sir,' Brausch replied with a knowing smile. 'You can be sure of that.'

SEVEN

Had he been erring on the side of common sense by keeping the briefing on a need-to-know basis only, or did he really believe that one of their number was a traitor? It was a question which had been haunting Sam McIndoe ever since the MTB had left Grand Harbour, destined for the pre-arranged rendezvous with the Partisans off the west coast of Sicily. And one he was still no closer to answering. Then again, was there an answer? Or was he blowing it all out of proportion? He knew that all the evidence pointed to the spy being Stella's former contact on Sicily, Angelo Sciarro. So why was there still a nagging doubt lingering in the back of his mind? He found he didn't have an answer for that either . . .

'Knock, knock.'

McIndoe was startled by the voice. Stella stood in the open doorway. Like himself, she was dressed in a pair of black trousers and a baggy black polo-necked jersey. 'How long have you been standing there?' he asked.

'Not long,' she replied. 'Can I come in?'

'Of course,' he replied, gesturing her inside.

She entered the cabin and crossed to the wooden table, where she pulled out the chair opposite him and sat down. She took a packet of cigarettes from her pocket and offered him one. He shook his head. She lit one for herself then tossed the packet on to the table. 'I haven't had a chance to speak to you alone since the briefing at the house. Thanks for believing me, Sam.'

'I don't know what to believe any more,' McIndoe replied, shaking his head in frustration.

'I realize that the evidence is stacked overwhelmingly against Angelo, but I know in my heart that he wouldn't have betrayed the Partisans. I can't explain it, Sam, but I know I'm not wrong about this.'

'I hope you are,' McIndoe replied, but there was no malice in his voice.

'What did Vice-Admiral Starr say when you spoke to him earlier this evening?'

'He gave me his full backing to run the operation in my own way, as I knew he would, but I still got the feeling he believes, like I do, that Sciarro was the traitor,' McIndoe replied. 'But when it boils down to it, you have one major advantage over us when it comes to Sciarro. You'd worked closely with him over the last few months. We never even knew him. I guess that's what swayed me.'

'Is this a good time for me to suggest a truce?' she asked with a smile.

McIndoe nodded. 'Truce. Agreed.'

'I know I'm to blame for much of the friction that's occurred between the two of us in the last couple of days. It's just that in a predominantly male-oriented profession like Military Intelligence, there will always be those Neanderthals who resent the fact that a woman can be more successful than them in what they regard as their own domain. Those types would like nothing better than to see me fall flat on my face so that they can point a finger at me and say "I told you so". I've learnt the hard way that I have to give as good as I get. I can't afford to show any weakness in this business. Not when it can be used against me. I know that sounds very cynical, but it's the only way to survive.'

'I know what you're saying. Some of the Firm's best operatives are women. And for a time there was an undercurrent of resentment from a certain section of the men about having to work with them. But Vice-Admiral Starr was quick to stamp it out. He won't tolerate anything like that.'

'You've got a lot of time for him, haven't you?' she said.

'He's a crusty old devil with a mind like a rapier and a tongue to match. But you pull your weight, and there's nothing he won't do for you. And that's the kind of man I'd want in my corner when the going gets tough. I guess in a way he's the closest thing I have to family now.' McIndoe whistled softly to himself. 'That's a pretty scary thought when you stop to think about it.'

'Are your parents dead?' Stella asked.

'My father's dead. He was gassed during the last war and invalided out of the army in 1916. He died ten years later, having never recovered his health. I was very close to him. As for my mother, well, she certainly didn't waste any time finding herself another husband. A Canadian who has a string of nightclubs in Glasgow. They'd been seeing each other secretly even before my father died. He gave her what my father never could – the kind of superficial social acceptability that so often comes with wealth. That's the only reason she married him. I haven't seen or heard from her since the day of my father's funeral.'

'I'm sorry,' she said softly.

'Why? I'm not. None of the family has anything to do with her now.' McIndoe helped himself to a cigarette from the packet on the table. 'OK, so now you know about my parents. What about yours?'

'They're both dead. My mother was American. My father was Sicilian. He was a marine archaeologist.' She paused to take a long drag on her cigarette. 'Well, that's what he liked to call himself. What he actually did was plunder wrecks off the coasts of Italy and Greece and sell the bounty to private collectors on the black market. I know that makes him sound like a complete scoundrel, and I guess he was, but I absolutely adored him. As a child I used to go out on the boat with him whenever I could. Usually weekends and school vacations. His crew were a motley bunch of renegades, but they always treated me like a little princess. He was killed diving off Sardinia. The authorities put it down to an accident. I was never convinced, though. Not only was he an excellent diver, but at the time of his death he owed a lot of money to several shady characters on the Italian mainland.

'After his death my mother took me to live in America. She had a brother who was in the military in Washington. That's where we settled. She died three years ago. She was only forty years old. The coroner said it was a heart attack. In a way he was right. She died of a broken heart. She never got over my father's death. I went to Sicily to bury her beside my father – it's what she'd always wanted – but when I got back home it was too late for me to enrol at the university, and my uncle offered me a job as a temporary secretary at the military base so that I could make some extra money to keep me going until I went to university the following year. It was through him that I was first introduced to a senior officer at Military Intelligence. Well, to cut a long story short, that's how I managed to get into this business in the first place.'

'That's not like you to cut a long story short,' Ravallo said from the doorway, and winked at McIndoe as he entered the cabin. 'How come I never got the abridged version when you reeled out your life-story to me? Hell, I could have spent those extra hours on the golf course.' He ducked out of the way of her playful punch, then pulled up the third chair, turned it round, and sat astride it. 'It's nice to see that you two are finally able to have a civilized conversation without constantly baring your fangs at each other.'

'We've called a truce,' Stella said, looking at McIndoe.

'For the moment . . .' McIndoe said. His eyes turned to Ravallo. 'I didn't know you were a golfer.'

'If my intentions were as good as my game, I'd be a champion by now,' Ravallo replied with a grin. 'But I'm getting better with each game. Do you play?'

'Whenever I can,' McIndoe said. 'We'll have to get together for a game sometime.'

'You're on,' Ravallo readily agreed.

'Where are the others?' Stella asked, changing the subject. Sport had never much interested her.

'The last time I looked in, Hillyard was in the radio room reminiscing about life in the circus,' Ravallo replied. 'Johnson was there as well, complaining because he'd heard it before. I think Passiere's given up trying to boot them out. Evans is topside. It's his turn for lookout duty. I've just been talking to Charlie Higgins. He said we'll be arriving off the Sicilian coast within the next ten minutes.'

'In that case we'd better go topside. I'll get the others and meet you both on deck.' McIndoe stubbed out his cigarette, then got to his feet and went to the radio room where he passed on Higgins's message.

'Then what happens?' Passiere asked.

'You know that this operation's being conducted on a need-to-know basis only, Georges,' McIndoe replied. 'And I've already told you that you'll be staying behind with Sub-Lieutenant Higgins when the rest of us go ashore. What happens once we reach the mainland doesn't concern you.'

'I still do not understand why I have to stay here,' Passiere retorted sharply, a spark of anger flashing in his Gallic eyes. 'The boat is going to be moored in some cave until you get back. I will not be able to use any of this radio equipment when it is there. There will be too much interference. You know that I am the best radio operator in the Firm, so why bring me on this operation if I am not going to be needed?'

McIndoe looked at Hillyard and Johnson, then jabbed his thumb over his shoulder. 'Get your stuff and report to Major Ravallo topside.' He waited until they'd left the cabin, then sat down on one of the vacated chairs. 'Don't ever question my orders like that again in front of the men.'

'I want to know – '

'Never again!'

'I am sorry, *patron*, it will not happen again,' Passiere assured him.

'Contrary to what you may think, Georges, you're actually a very important part of this operation,' McIndoe said. 'You're our link with Starr. It's imperative that he's kept abreast of the situation. I'll be contacting you every six hours to update you on the progress of the operation. You'll then send my report back to Starr in Malta.'

'I have already told you, *patron*, the radio equipment will not work inside the cave,' Passiere replied with a hint of irritability in his voice.

'Sub-Lieutenant Higgins will take the boat out of the cave every six hours. He's understandably concerned, though, that the boat could be seen by a spotter plane, especially during the daylight hours, so you'll only have ten minutes before he returns the boat to the cave.'

'Ten minutes?' Passiere snorted.

'I'll keep my reports as short as possible. Three minutes maximum. That will give you ample time to send them to Malta.' McIndoe saw the uncertainty on Passiere's face. 'You've just finished telling me that you're the best radio man in the Firm. Now's your chance to prove it. Ten minutes, Georges. That's all the time you're going to get.'

Passiere nodded before McIndoe continued. 'We'll establish contact in the usual way by using our own coded passwords to identify ourselves. If I don't use my password, or if I fail to make contact with you at the given time, then Sub-Lieutenant Higgins has orders to abort the operation and return to Malta.'

'And if I fail to give you my password, then you will know that something is wrong at this end,' Passiere concluded.

'That's right.' McIndoe took a sheet of paper from his pocket which he handed to Passiere. 'That's a copy of a numerical code recently introduced by the German *Wehrmacht* here on Sicily. All our transmissions will be made in German using that code. That way there's less chance of the Germans becoming suspicious should any of our transmissions be intercepted by one of their listening posts. It's not foolproof by any means, but hopefully it will deceive them into believing that it's just regular Army radio-traffic. It's a chance we have to take.'

'Where did you get this from?' Passiere asked in amazement.

'The Partisans gave it to Stella when she was last here,' McIndoe replied. 'I don't know how they managed to get it or break the code, but it's been authenticated by our own boffins back home.'

'So not only will we be able to fool the Germans into believing that it's just part of their own radio-traffic, but I'll also be able to listen in and decode their transmissions,' Passiere said.

'Exactly. I want you to memorize the code and then destroy the list.' McIndoe indicated the array of radio equipment which lined the walls of the cabin. 'We've all been taught the basics of radio operations as part of our training, but this is a pretty sophisticated set-up in here, and you're the one man who knows how it all works. That's why I need you to stay behind on the boat.'

'I understand, *patron*,' Passiere replied. 'I just wish you had told me this earlier.'

'Need-to-know basis,' McIndoe reminded him. 'And if it's any consolation, the others will only be briefed on the next stage of the operation once we've reached the mainland.' He moved to the door. 'It's essential that you and Sub-Lieutenant Higgins work closely together, Georges. I don't have to tell you what would happen if the Gestapo were to get their hands on us. You saw the results of their brutality when the Germans invaded France two years ago.'

'And never to be forgotten for as long as I live,' Passiere said softly. He got to his feet and crossed to where McIndoe was standing, embracing him quickly. 'God be with you, *mon ami*.'

'I'd happily settle for God and a bit of luck,' McIndoe replied with a fleeting smile, then he left the cabin and made his way up on to the deck. It wasn't ideal conditions for a night operation, but it could have been a lot worse. The moon, which periodically disappeared behind the low clouds which drifted idly across the star-speckled sky, cast a weak shaft of light across the calm sea. All the lights on the boat had been switched off in advance of their arrival off the Sicilian coast, and even the wheelhouse was now shrouded in darkness. With one hand gripped firmly on the railing, McIndoe negotiated his way carefully along the gently rolling deck to where the three shadowy figures were crouched down on the bow. Evans, Hillyard and Johnson. All were dressed in black and each had a black rucksack at his feet. 'Where's Nicky and Stella?' he whispered, dropping down on to his haunches beside them.

'Up there talking to Charlie,' Evans replied, gesturing towards the wheelhouse.

'We'll be arriving at the rendezvous shortly,' McIndoe said, pointing to the three rucksacks. 'I take it you're all ready and packed?'

'For what?' Hillyard hissed. 'You still haven't told us what we're supposed to be doing out here.'

'You'll be briefed in due course,' McIndoe assured him.

'Have the Yanks been briefed yet on the operation?' Hillyard asked.

'Yes,' McIndoe replied.

'It's all right for some,' Hillyard muttered.

'We went through all this before we left Malta,' McIndoe said in exasperation, then took a deep breath to steady his rising anger before continuing in a subdued tone of voice. 'I don't like the situation any more than you do, but those are the rules and I expect you to abide by them. This will be one of the most dangerous operations we're ever likely to undertake for the Firm, and that means we're going to have to work together as a team if we're to have any chance of pulling it off. There's no place for dissenters where we're going. So if any of you aren't happy about that, then now's the time to speak up, and you can damn well stay behind on the boat.'

Nobody said anything. McIndoe gazed out over the dark waters as he struggled to find the words he needed to try and reassure them, but he knew that whatever he said would only have sounded hollow and patronizing. They had every right to be bitter and resentful about the way he was handling the operation. He'd worked with them all before, often deep behind enemy lines, and each time they'd proved themselves to be total professionals. He'd even been tempted to suggest at his last meeting with Vice-Admiral Starr that, under the circumstances, a new team should be flown over from England to work with Ravallo, but he'd known that it really wasn't feasible, not with the meeting between Kesselring and his chiefs-of-staff due to take place in Palermo later that day. There wasn't time to turn back now.

'Boss, look!' Evans said, grabbing McIndoe's arm and pointing towards the shore.

McIndoe saw the beam of the small spotlight flashing intermittently in the distance. It came from one of the caves which lined that dark and forlorn stretch of rugged Sicilian coastline. Although the light couldn't be seen from the land, there was always the possibility that it would be spotted by an enemy vessel at sea. It wasn't a message in Morse code. Just five flashes, at three second intervals, to be repeated twice – the signal that it was safe to bring the MTB into the cave where two Partisan commandos were waiting to take them to the shore. Three flashes, similarly delivered, was the signal that it wasn't safe for them to approach the cave. For a moment McIndoe felt an uneasy churning in his stomach when he only counted three flashes of light, but he quickly reminded himself that he hadn't seen the whole transmission. He waited breathlessly for the signal to be repeated: one . . . two . . . three . . . four . . . five.

Higgins turned the MTB sharply to starboard and made towards the light, already knowing the exact location of the cave from the detailed charts he had in the wheelhouse. Ravallo descended the metal stairs silently and crossed to where they were crouched down on the bow. 'You see that?' he asked.

Evans nodded. 'Five flashes. Coast clear.'

'I want both the port and starboard Vickers guns manned until we're safely inside the cave,' McIndoe said, pointing to Johnson and Hillyard.

'You think it could be a trap?' Johnson asked suspiciously.

'We're in enemy waters now. We can't take any chances,' McIndoe replied. 'Taffy, you've got the twenty-mil Oerlikon on the stern. And remember, no lights unless authorized either by Major Ravallo or myself. Now go on, man your posts.'

'Well, this is it, Mac,' Ravallo said after the others had left them on the gently rocking bow. 'Into the valley of death and all that, eh?'

'Preferably not,' McIndoe replied with a half-smile. 'I'd settle for a successful operation and quick exit out of here.'

'That's not asking much, considering what we've come here to do,' Ravallo replied with gentle sarcasm, then he cast a sidelong glance at McIndoe. 'You scared, Mac?'

'The day I don't get scared going behind enemy lines is the day I apply for a desk job before I get myself killed through overconfidence,' McIndoe replied. 'How about you? Are you scared?'

'Damn right,' Ravallo replied, then gave McIndoe a broad grin. 'But isn't that what it's all about? I can already feel the adrenaline pumping through my veins. What a great feeling, though. It's like a drug, isn't it? It's only now I realize just what I've been missing while I've been stuck behind a desk all this time. I don't want to go back to that life again. No, this is living, Mac. Really living.'

'A danger addict in the making if ever I saw one,' McIndoe said.

'You think I'm crazy, don't you?'

'You have to be a bit crazy to be in this game, Nicky,' McIndoe replied. 'Let's face it, what person in their right mind would willingly go behind enemy lines knowing what would happen to them if they were caught? Yet it never ceases to amaze me that there's still this misguided illusion back home of there being something inherently romantic about being a covert operative working behind enemy lines. I only wish those people could see pictures of what the Gestapo have done to colleagues of mine who've been captured in occupied countries like France and Holland. Bodies broken and twisted from days of brutal, inhuman torture. Maybe then they'd finally come to realize that there's nothing romantic about any of this. We're just ordinary people like them, not a bunch of comicbook heroes out for personal glory.'

'Shatter the illusion and you take away the dream,' Ravallo said. 'And sadly in many cases the dream is all they have left to keep their spirits alive. It's all about propaganda, Mac. And isn't that the most powerful illusion of all?'

McIndoe sensed someone behind him, and when he turned round he noticed Stella standing at the foot of the stairs. She was staring at Ravallo, a wistful smile on her lips, as if mesmerized by the emotion behind his words. Her eyes flitted to McIndoe and the smile broadened fleetingly, then she grabbed the railing and moved towards them. They stood silently on the bow as the MTB entered the cave. It was virtually impossible to see anything in the enveloping darkness the deeper the MTB ventured into the cave and, although McIndoe had all but dismissed any thoughts of their being drawn into a trap, there was still a hint of uncertainty lingering in the back of his mind. With only a single route out of the cave, it would be the perfect place to lay an ambush.

McIndoe quickly pushed the negative thoughts from his mind. Higgins finally cut the whispering engines, then opened the wheelhouse door and called out to Evans in German to drop the anchor. It had been agreed before they left Malta that nobody would speak any English once they reached Sicily. It was essential that they remained in character, as even the slightest mistake could jeopardize the whole operation. Depending on the situation, they would be permitted to speak either German or Italian – but no English.

McIndoe's eyes were beginning to adjust to the darkness when he heard the sound of creaking wood to starboard, and when he looked round he saw that Hillyard already had the Vickers gun trained on the water. He crossed to where Hillyard was poised behind the gun, his finger resting lightly on the trigger, and peered down into the gloom beyond the boat. For a moment he couldn't see anything in the darkness, although now he could also hear the sound of a pair of oars being dipped rhythmically in and out of the water. Then the silhouette of a rowing boat emerged from a narrow tributary in the cave and moved towards the boat. Moments later, a second rowing boat followed it out into the main body of the cave. McIndoe waited until both boats had drawn up alongside the starboard hull, then beckoned Stella towards him.

The Partisan leader, Giancarlo Massimo, had earlier furnished Starr with the names of the two men who would be meeting the boat. Men that Stella would know. Starr had then sealed the names in an envelope which McIndoe now had in his pocket. McIndoe slit open the envelope, removed the sheet of paper and handed it to Stella. He signalled to Evans who shone a flashlight on the lone figure seated in the nearest of the two rowing boats. Stella nodded to McIndoe. She recognized him. Evans then trained the beam on to the second man, who instinctively put his hand to his face to protect his eyes from the dazzling glare. For a moment Stella couldn't see his features properly, but when Ravallo ordered him to lower his hand, she nodded again to McIndoe. They were the two names on the paper. Ravallo struck a match beside her and she held the paper over the flame. Within seconds it had been consumed in the flames and she let light wind whisk the charred remains from her fingertips.

'Nicky, you and Stella go with Evans in the first boat,' McIndoe said to Ravallo. 'I'll bring up the rear with Johnson and Hillyard.'

'Sure,' Ravallo agreed, then he grabbed the two rucksacks which were lying at the foot of the wheelhouse stairs and handed one of them to Stella. She took a woollen cap from her rucksack, coiled her hair up on top of her head, then pulled the cap down firmly over her head. Evans shouldered his own rucksack and released the Jacob's ladder down the side of the hull. Ravallo gestured for him to go first.

Higgins emerged from the wheelhouse, descended the stairs and extended a hand towards McIndoe. 'Take care, Mac.'

'You too, Charlie,' McIndoe said, gripping his hand warmly.

'And make sure you keep an eye on our American friends while you're at it,' Higgins said as Ravallo followed Stella over the side of the boat. 'They're OK, those two. Especially Stella. She's something else, isn't she? I have to admit, it's not very often that I – '

'Then let's keep it that way, shall we?' McIndoe interceded quickly as he wagged a finger at him. 'And anyway, you're a married man. You shouldn't be looking.'

'Surely I'm allowed to window shop, as long as I'm not tempted to buy?' Higgins replied as he led McIndoe out of earshot of the others. 'Not like you, eh, Mac?'

'What's that supposed to mean?' McIndoe asked with a suspicious frown.

'We're ready to go,' Hillyard called out to McIndoe from the railing.

'Go on, I'll follow you,' McIndoe replied, then turned back to Higgins. 'Just what are you trying to say, Charlie?'

'Between you and me, she likes you. In fact, she likes you a lot. She told me in so many words when we were on the bridge together.'

'Just like that Wren back in Portsmouth who also liked me a lot and who turned out to be a happily married woman.'

'Come on, Mac, that was a genuine mistake, but – '

'But nothing,' McIndoe cut in quickly, and tapped him lightly on the chest. 'I'll see you when we get back.'

'I know I'm not wrong this time,' Higgins called out after him.

McIndoe cast a despairing look over his shoulder, then slipped on his rucksack and climbed down the Jacob's ladder into the waiting rowing boat. He nodded in greeting to the Partisan, who retrieved a Beretta submachine-gun from the bottom of the boat and handed it to him. Hillyard and Johnson were similarly armed. The man used one of the wooden oars to push the rowing boat away from the MTB, then he began to dip the oars into the water as he went in pursuit of the leading rowing boat which had already reached the mouth of the cave. Within a couple of minutes they emerged from the bowels of the cave and McIndoe suddenly felt very exposed on the open sea. Any passing German patrol on the clifftops would spot them right away. And what chance would they have to defend themselves in such a cramped, slow-moving vessel? He took some comfort in the knowledge that there were Partisan snipers secreted within the thick foliage which enveloped much of the area around the cliffs, but it still left him with a distinctly uneasy feeling – a feeling that he knew would disappear only once they were safely ashore . . .

'Lieutenant, do you hear that!' Johnson hissed as he grabbed McIndoe's arm.

'No, what . . . ?' McIndoe trailed off when he heard what sounded like a distant rumble of thunder. Only he knew it wasn't thunder. It was the low growl of aircraft engines. More than likely German night bombers. And the rumble was steadily growing louder with each passing second. He looked across at the other rowing boat, but as he was gesturing frantically towards the sky, the half-moon sneaked out from behind a low cloud and illuminated the two boats like some giant celestial spotlight. Ravallo stabbed a finger towards the nearest cave, and McIndoe watched anxiously as the two Partisans communicated with each other using a form of sign language he'd never encountered before. It seemed to work, as both rowing boats were turned towards the cave.

McIndoe could feel the mounting apprehension writhing in the pit of his stomach as the sinister sound of the engines grew ever closer. He knew that if they didn't reach the sanctuary of the cave in time they'd easily be spotted from the air, and their position would be radioed through to the nearest German command centre. They wouldn't get very far if the whole area was saturated with enemy soldiers looking for them. He glanced at Hillyard and Johnson. Anxiety was etched on their moonlit faces. Each powerful stroke of the oars brought the rowing boat that bit closer to the mouth of the cave, but there was still no guarantee that they'd make it in time. He cast a despairing look towards the horizon, but it was too dark to see the approaching aircraft. Just as well really, he thought to himself, because the moment he saw the aircraft in the sky it would already be too late for them to escape detection. He could see the look of grim determination on the oarsman's sweating face as he dipped the oars repeatedly into the waves and gritted his teeth as his arms shuddered with the effort of dragging them through the water. McIndoe could see that the man was doing everything he possibly could to propel them towards the cave, but he still felt the urge to rip the oars from his hands and take over the rowing himself. He knew it wouldn't help them reach the cave any faster, though. If anything, it would only hinder their progress. He guessed that he was probably stronger and certainly a lot fitter than the oarsman, but that would have counted for nothing if he couldn't synchronize the movement of the oars through the water. And that's where the oarsman had the advantage over him. Experience always triumphed over enthusiasm.

The oarsman slumped forward in exhaustion once he'd manoeuvred the rowing boat safely into the cave. The other rowing boat had already entered the cave ahead of them. McIndoe leaned forward and patted him on the arm. Relief? Gratitude? Both, probably.

The man looked up at McIndoe, still sucking in deep mouthfuls of air, and managed a weak smile as he drew his forearm across his sweating forehead. McIndoe instinctively ducked down in the boat when the first of the aircraft passed low over the cave. The rest followed in a close 'beehive' formation. He recognized the sleek, tapered fuselages straight away. A pack of Junkers 88A-1 night bombers which were being escorted by a score of menacing Messerschmitt fighter planes.

'Where did they come from?' Hillyard asked, staring after the retreating aircraft as they headed out over the open sea towards their final destination: Malta.

'More than likely the Gerbini airfield in Catánia,' the Partisan replied. 'It's the *Luftwaffe's* main air-base here on Sicily. We've tried several times to disrupt their operations through sabotage, but it's well fortified and we've yet to be successful. But we will succeed.'

McIndoe found himself nodding in agreement. There was no trace of arrogance in the man's voice, just a quiet confidence in himself and the Resistance. 'You look shattered,' McIndoe said, reaching out a hand towards the nearest oar. 'I'll row us to the shore.'

'No,' the man replied firmly as he eased the oar from McIndoe's hand. 'We all have our role to play, however small it may seem to you. This is mine.'

McIndoe realized he'd inadvertently offended the man with his offer of help, but wisely chose not to say anything in his defence, knowing that any apology could add further insult to injury. The oarsman lined up his two oars in the water, then began to row with carefully timed strokes after the lead boat, which had already left the cave. The rest of the journey was conducted in silence, and when they reached the shallows, four silhouettes ghosted out from behind a cluster of rocks and ran the short distance to where the rowing boats were now bobbing in the shallow water. They paired off to steady the two rowing boats, and McIndoe gestured surreptitiously to Hillyard to remain seated rather than jump out to help them. He didn't want to cause any more offence. Once the boats had been manoeuvred closer to the beach, they were invited to get out. McIndoe was the first out into the knee-deep water, and he waded the short distance to the shore. The others were quick to join him. The rowing boats were pushed back out into deeper water, and the two oarsmen began to row away from the shore.

'Close thing with those bombers,' Ravallo said to McIndoe.

'Too close,' McIndoe replied as he instinctively cast his eyes upwards.

'So what happens now?' Ravallo asked, looking around him.

'I guess we're in their hands now,' McIndoe said, gesturing to the four Partisans as they emerged from the water.

One of the men gestured for them to follow him, and they traipsed up the wet sand after him. His three colleagues retrieved their rifles from behind the rocks and brought up the rear. The man led them to a narrow path which dissected the thick undergrowth on the edge of the beach. It had to be negotiated single-file, and they all realized that the path would provide an ideal place for an ambush. It was this uncertainty in mind that had their eyes constantly flitting between the shadowy walls of tangled undergrowth on either side. Every crunching footstep on the shingled pathway sounded like a deafening crash in the silence around them. Even resorting to moving on tiptoe didn't seem to make any difference.

McIndoe, who was following closely behind the point man, was greatly relieved when the path finally emerged out on to an unlit road. An Alfa Romeo eight-ton truck was parked nearby. The passenger door swung open and a man leapt out, landing nimbly on his toes. He clapped his hands together, then held out his arms in a gesture of fraternal greeting. For a worrying moment McIndoe thought the man was going to embrace him, but to his relief Stella brushed past him and the man enveloped her in an affectionate hug. He kissed her on both cheeks, then beamed in delight as he held her at arm's length. He said something to her that McIndoe couldn't quite hear as she wagged a finger of admonishment at him. Putting his arm around her shoulders, he led her towards the others. It was only then that McIndoe saw his face. He estimated the man to be in his early fifties, with a large, aquiline nose and a face craggy and weatherbeaten from years of constant toil under the hot Sicilian sun.

Stella gestured to Ravallo. 'This is Major Nick Ravallo. He's the senior officer on this operation. Nicky, this is Giancarlo Massimo, leader of the Partisans here on Sicily.'

'Nicky Ravallo,' Massimo said, pumping Ravallo's hand warmly. 'Stella has told me so much about you, ever since you first arrived in Gibraltar.'

'All good I hope?' Ravallo said with a smile.

'Well, that would be telling, wouldn't it?' Massimo replied with a broad grin.

'This is Lieutenant Sam McIndoe, British SOE,' Ravallo announced, indicating McIndoe beside him.

'I have heard a lot about you too, my friend,' Massimo said, shaking McIndoe's hand. 'Vice-Admiral Starr speaks very highly of you. But don't tell him I told you that. He'd never forgive me.'

McIndoe had quickly warmed to Massimo, with his gravelly voice and bluff character. He could easily understand how a man like Massimo could inspire the confidence and respect needed to lead a resistance movement. McIndoe then introduced the rest of the team to Massimo, who nodded in greeting as he logged each name in his head. He wouldn't forget their names after that. 'There's a farmhouse about ten miles from here where you can rest until daybreak,' Massimo told them. 'We have a hot meal waiting for you there.'

'Then what are we standing around here for?' Hillyard asked, patting his stomach. 'I'm famished.'

'Are there any German patrols in the area?' Ravallo asked.

'Not in the immediate vicinity,' Massimo replied. 'We've been keeping them busy over the past few hours. Don't worry, we won't be troubled by them tonight.'

'Are you driving the lorry to the farmhouse?' McIndoe asked as he walked with Massimo towards the stationary vehicle.

'No, I've brought a driver with me,' Massimo replied. 'Why do you ask?'

'I was hoping I could have a word with you in private before we reached the farmhouse,' McIndoe said.

'Then, my friend, I will drive and we can talk,' Massimo replied. He pulled open the passenger door and spoke briefly with the driver, who clambered out and made his way to where the others were getting into the back of the truck.

Ravallo walked over to the two men. 'I take it you guys are sitting up front?'

'I've got a couple of things I want to discuss with Signor Massimo before we get to the farmhouse,' McIndoe replied.

'Why are the British always so formal?' Massimo said, throwing up his arms in despair. 'I think it's because you are afraid to offend. Am I right?'

'You've probably hit the nail on the head there,' McIndoe replied with a rueful smile.

'Please, all my friends just call me Giani,' Massimo said. He turned to Ravallo. 'Are you going to ride in the front with us? There is plenty of room.'

'No, I think Mac wants to talk to you alone,' Ravallo said, looking at McIndoe. 'I'll hitch a ride with the others in the back.'

'He's very much as Stella described him,' Massimo said after Ravallo had walked off. 'He seems like a good man. I like him.'

'That makes two of us,' McIndoe agreed.

Massimo checked that everyone was in the back of the truck and that the flap was securely locked, then he climbed into the cab where McIndoe had already taken his seat. He started the engine, engaged the gears, switched on the lights, then pulled away from the side of the road. 'They call you "Mac"?'

The question caught McIndoe by surprise. 'Yes, it's my nickname.'

'Then I'll call you Mac,' Massimo decided as he slipped the engine up another gear and pressed his foot down on the accelerator. 'You want to talk about Angelo Sciarro, don't you?'

'Yes,' McIndoe replied. 'Vice-Admiral Starr believes that Sciarro tipped off the Germans about our operation here a couple of nights ago. And, let's face it, the evidence against Sciarro does seem pretty conclusive, doesn't it?'

'And what do you believe?' Massimo said without taking his eyes off the road.

'I wish I knew,' McIndoe replied. 'Right now I'm stuck on the fence. That's why I wanted to talk to you. From what Stella's told me, you probably knew Sciarro better than anyone else.'

'That's true. We go back a long way.'

'He had a drink problem, didn't he?' McIndoe said, casting a sidelong glance at Massimo to gauge his reaction. He wasn't particularly surprised when there wasn't one.

'Yes, he drank,' Massimo said at length. 'He drank to try and forget that the Gestapo murdered his parents before dumping their naked bodies in the street as a warning to others against trying to resist their occupation of the island. I hardly think a man who'd lost his parents like that would then willingly cooperate with the very people who killed them, do you?'

'Yet his drinking partner was a known German collaborator,' McIndoe continued.

'You already seem to be convinced of his guilt, so why are you even bothering to ask my opinion?' Massimo queried.

'I'm just putting forward the evidence that I've been given.'

'Then don't forget about the piece of paper that was found in his pocket with the private number of the head of the Sicilian Gestapo written on it. I agree, the evidence appears very convincing to anyone who wasn't close to Angelo. I know that there are many in the movement, including several of my senior colleagues, who've already condemned him as a traitor.'

'And what makes you so sure he wasn't?' McIndoe asked.

'Because I knew him better than any of them,' Massimo replied. 'It may not sound like much of a defence to you, but to me it's more convincing than all this so-called evidence the Gestapo have used to frame him. I don't care if you were to produce even more incriminating evidence against him: nothing you say will ever make me change my mind. Angelo had his problems, granted, but that doesn't make him a traitor. You wanted my opinion, that's it.'

'So you think he was framed to protect the real collaborator?'

'All I know is that Angelo wasn't a German spy. You make of that what you will.'

Once again, McIndoe knew that he'd managed to offend a potential ally. It was fast becoming a habit with him. Only this time the ally was a powerful one. But what was he supposed to have done? He'd wanted Massimo's input on the Sciarro incident. Now he had it – and it still left him lonely and isolated on the fence. Who to believe? What to do? How to handle the next part of the operation? How long before he'd have to tell the men why they'd been sent to Sicily? He knew the longer he held out, the less they would trust him. And a lack of trust could lead to an understandable dissatisfaction which could filter through into the operation. He couldn't afford that. Not with so much at stake.

Suddenly he wished he were elsewhere. He knew just the place as well – the rugby field on a typically cold, wet and windy Saturday afternoon in Glasgow, his rain-soaked shirt clinging to his sweating torso, his studs desperately raking the macerated turf as he sought to get a firm grip to help balance the heaving pack, yelling encouragement from the side of the scrum as his forwards pushed relentlessly towards the opponents' try line. Then a sudden breakaway on the blind side of the scrum; the wet, slippery ball tucked firmly under his arm; a dummy pass to fool the opposition's wing three-quarter; a body swerve to evade the fullback's lunging tackle; and finally that feeling of sheer euphoria which always came from diving over the goal line and touching the ball down for a try. So many good memories . . .

'That's the farmhouse up ahead.'

Massimo's voice shattered McIndoe's wistful reverie. It was only then that McIndoe realized they were now travelling along a narrow dirt road which was bordered by a wall of thick foliage. It was a bumpy ride, and the truck continually swayed from side to side as the wheels slipped in and out of the uneven ruts which had been carved into the hard ground from years of constant use. Although the road itself was bathed in the creamy reflection of the pale moonlight, McIndoe still couldn't quite make out the building which was partially obscured by a column of tall pine trees, and only when the truck negotiated the final bend was he able to see the structure clearly ahead of them. With its solid timber walls, thick thatched roof and covered porch, it reminded him of one of those frontier farmsteads that always seemed to come under attack from gangs of marauding Indians in every other Hollywood western.

Massimo followed the road to the back of the farmhouse and parked the truck inside an empty garage. He switched off the engine, pushed open the driver's door, jumped to the ground and lowered the flap at the back of the truck. Once everyone had been assembled in the yard, the garage doors were closed and padlocked. The truck had served its use.

'Who lives here?' Evans asked, gesturing to the single illuminated window which looked out over the yard.

'A couple who've helped us in the past,' Massimo told him. 'Their son was a Partisan. He was killed in a shootout with a group of local fascists last year. The man who actually pulled the trigger had once been his best friend. That's what the Germans have done to us since the occupation. They've turned family against family, friend against friend. Nothing's sacred here any more.'

'Come on, let's go inside,' Stella said, breaking the silence.

'Where are the uniforms?' Ravallo asked Massimo.

'They're in the barn over there,' Massimo said, pointing to a building situated some distance from the farmhouse. 'It's locked though. Do you want to go inside?'

'Yes, I'd like to check them to make sure they're the right ones,' Ravallo replied, taking a flashlight from his rucksack. Massimo handed him the key.

'What uniforms?' Hillyard asked McIndoe after Ravallo had headed off towards the barn.

'They're for the next phase of the operation,' McIndoe told him. 'I'll explain it all once we've had something to eat.'

'This is getting like one of those infernal children's puzzles where you have to join up the dots to get the whole picture,' Hillyard said bitterly. 'Only at least the children have all the dots in front of them before they start. We have a right to know what you're getting us into here, boss.'

'That's the last time you speak to me like that,' McIndoe said in a soft, menacing voice as he levelled a finger of warning at Hillyard. 'So unless you want to find yourself back in the trenches, I suggest you keep your comments to yourself.'

Evans grabbed Hillyard roughly by the arm and pulled him away from McIndoe before he could say anything else. 'He understands perfectly,' Evans assured McIndoe, without releasing his powerful grip on Hillyard's arm.

'And I thought I told you before we left the boat not to call me "boss" once we got ashore,' McIndoe continued. 'The others seem to have remembered. I'd be grateful if you'd try and do likewise.'

'It won't happen again,' Evans said, jerking Hillyard's arm sharply. 'Will it?'

'No,' Hillyard muttered with a dark scowl. He looked at Massimo. 'Is there a toilet around here? I think I'd better go and cool off before I say something that's going to land me back in the trenches again.'

'It's over there,' Massimo said, pointing to a wooden hut at the bottom of the yard.

Hillyard jerked his arm free of Evans's grip and strode towards the shed. Evans watched him leave, then shook his head. 'I'm sorry about that, sir,' he said to McIndoe. 'I know I should have kept him in line. I guess we're all a bit on edge at the moment.'

'Don't I know,' McIndoe replied. 'I'm just as frustrated as the rest of you about these conditions that have been forced on us, but those are my orders and that's all there is to it. If I were to disobey Starr, I'd be the one sent to the trenches.'

'He only said what we're all feeling inside, sir,' Johnson said, falling in line beside McIndoe as he walked towards the back door. 'The difference being that he's never been shy to voice his opinion. But then that's always been his way, hasn't it? That's what makes him who he is. Change him, and he'd almost certainly lose that edge which has made him such a good soldier.'

'He's lucky to have friends like you and Taffy,' McIndoe said to Johnson as they entered the kitchen.

'I think that's a bit strong, sir,' Johnson replied, raising a finger as if he'd reverted back to being a schoolteacher and was gently admonishing one of his pupils. 'I have a great respect for him. But I wouldn't say we were actually friends. Certainly not in the conventional sense of the word.'

'There's nothing conventional about this line of work, is there?' McIndoe replied. He cast a quizzical look in Johnson's direction before crossing to where Massimo was waiting to introduce him to the elderly couple who owned the farm. Their name was Andoni, but Massimo didn't mention McIndoe or any of the team by name. The couple appeared to accept this without explanation, as if it weren't the first time this had happened to them.

'Giani says you're English?' Signor Andoni asked, shaking McIndoe's hand.

'British, actually,' McIndoe replied affably.

'It's not the same?' Signor Andoni queried further.

'Not quite, no,' McIndoe replied. The last thing he wanted to do was explain the geography of the British Isles to a couple who'd probably never even heard of the other three countries. 'Have you lived in Sicily all your lives?' he said, changing the subject before they decided to pursue the geography lesson.

'Yes, indeed,' Signora Andoni told him. 'My husband was actually born in this very room. He's lived here all his life.'

'That's quite remarkable,' McIndoe replied.

'We have been married now for forty-seven years,' she told him proudly. 'And never a cross word in that time.'

McIndoe smiled politely, then noticed that Stella was watching him from the other side of the room, a faint smile on her lips. He gave her a 'save me' look as Signora Andoni began to recount how she'd come to meet her husband all those years ago.

Stella appeared beside McIndoe. 'Whatever you've got in the oven certainly smells delicious, Signora Andoni. What is it?'

'Nothing very fancy, I'm afraid. Just a tray of lasagna,' she replied, gesturing to the assortment of chairs which had been placed around the battered wooden table in the middle of the room. 'Why don't you all sit down and I'll serve it up?'

'That would be wonderful, thank you,' McIndoe said as the others took their seats around the table.

'We don't have the same strict rationing here that you have in Malta,' Signora Andoni said as she opened the oven. 'It's probably the only good thing to have come out of the occupation.'

'Yet every morning my wife and I still look out to sea with a deep sense of envy, because we know that, despite all the terrible hardships those wretched people are having to endure in Malta, at least they haven't been subjugated and forced to live as virtual prisoners in their own country. I would gladly swap places with them if that meant we still had some control over our own destiny.' Signor Andoni's voice suddenly broke and he wiped his hand quickly across his moist eyes. 'I'm sorry. You must think me a foolish old man.'

'On the contrary,' Stella said as she steered him gently to the nearest chair. She sat down beside him. 'You're a remarkably brave and courageous man, Signor Andoni, and if only more Sicilians had been prepared to help the cause even half as much as you and your family have done since the occupation, then maybe our country wouldn't be in this intolerable situation right now. It's all very well for them to say that there's nothing they can do, but unless they're actively participating in the struggle against the German occupation, then they're really no better than the enemy collaborators they're always so quick to denounce in public.'

'You would have liked our son: he had the same driving passion inside him as you do,' Signor Andoni said to her. 'We were both very proud of him.'

'And I'm sure he was just as proud of you,' Stella replied.

Signora Andoni distributed the food around the table.

'This is delicious,' Evans announced between ravenous mouthfuls.

'There's plenty more if you want it,' Signora Andoni said as she placed a freshly baked loaf of bread in the middle of the table.

'I'll be the first in line,' Evans assured her, and was about to reach for the bread when he noticed Hillyard hovering uncertainly in the doorway. He could tell by the nervous expression on Hillyard's face that something was wrong. 'What is it?' he asked as he reached for the Beretta submachine-gun that was propped against the wall behind his chair.

'Don't touch that!' a voice barked venomously in German from behind Hillyard. Before any of the others had time to react, four armed German soldiers had brushed past Hillyard and trained their Karabiner rifles on them. Hillyard was shoved forward into the kitchen, and it was only then they saw the German officer with the Luger pistol pressed firmly into the back of Hillyard's neck. 'Get their guns,' the officer snapped at the nearest soldier.

'How dare you come into my house!' Signor Andoni spluttered angrily as he struggled to his feet.

'Sit down!' the German officer barked at him.

Stella reached out a hand and touched Signor Andoni lightly on the arm. When he looked down at her she gestured for him to sit down. He glared at the Germans as he slowly retook his seat. Once all the rifles had been gathered up, the officer despatched two of the soldiers to search the rest of the farmhouse.

'Put your hands on the table,' the officer commanded, shoving Hillyard away from him and ordering him to sit down and do the same.

'The bastards were waiting for me when I came out of the toilet,' Hillyard said to McIndoe. 'I couldn't do anything about it.'

'Be quiet!' the officer shouted.

McIndoe's mind was racing as he desperately sought a way out of their current predicament. Yet, however he looked at the situation, it didn't look good. He thought of Ravallo. But what could he possibly do against five armed Germans? Maybe more. There was no way of knowing whether there were more outside in the yard. All considering, of course, that the Germans hadn't already come across him in the shed. And if they had, what had they done to him? He suddenly sensed that Stella was staring across the table at him. Their eyes met and he guessed by her anxious expression that she was thinking along the same lines. Nicky Ravallo appeared to be their only chance now. It didn't look good at all . . .

The soldiers returned to the kitchen. 'The rest of the house is empty, sir,' one of them announced.

'Then one of them is still missing,' the officer replied.

'No, there's not,' an authoritative voice announced from the doorway. 'My men found him out in the shed. He's been dealt with already.'

The officer swung round and came to attention on seeing the senior Gestapo officer in front of him. McIndoe glanced across at Stella, but there was no recognition in her eyes at the sight of Nicky Ravallo dressed as a major in the Gestapo. Like the others around the table, she knew it was imperative not to blow his cover by appearing to recognize him. Ravallo ignored the officer's salute and stepped into the kitchen, his hands clasped tightly behind his back. He'd been tipped off about the Germans by half a dozen armed Partisans who'd materialized silently from the surrounding trees as he'd been about to leave the shed. Any thoughts of storming the farmhouse had quickly been discounted in favour of Ravallo's more conservative plan of impersonating a Gestapo officer. Not only would it gain him access to the farmhouse, it would also allow him to find out just how much the Germans already knew about the operation. The Partisans had secreted themselves in the yard, close to the kitchen door, awaiting his signal. But for the moment he had to assume his new role, and the only way he could pull it off with any degree of success was to go on to the offensive. He slowly looked at the faces around the table, then turned to the officer. 'Your name?'

'*Hauptmann* Rohmer, *Sturmbannführer*,' came the instant reply.

'You've done well, Rohmer,' Ravallo said, then he let his eyes drift up to the German soldiers guarding his colleagues. One of the soldiers made the mistake of glancing nervously at him. 'Keep your eyes on the prisoners!' Ravallo yelled at him, then swung round on Rohmer, the glint of anger still apparent in his eyes. 'Do you know who your prisoners are?'

'I recognized Massimo straight away,' Rohmer said with evident pride. 'I believe the others are the enemy agents we were told might try and infiltrate the island. But I would have found out the truth soon enough. I would have made them talk.'

'How did you come to capture them?' he asked Rohmer.

'It was very fortuitous, *Sturmbannführer*,' Rohmer told him. 'We'd become separated from our unit after an ambush by the local Resistance. We were trying to find a shortcut back to the barracks when we saw two rowing boats landing on the shore. There are only the five of us, and I didn't think we could apprehend them all on the beach, so I made the decision to follow them discreetly and to strike when they were least expecting it.'

'Very commendable,' Ravallo replied. 'Did you see where the rowing boats came from?'

'No, *Sturmbannführer*,' Rohmer replied. 'We only saw them when they reached the shore.'

'Have you radioed through for reinforcements?'

'We have no radio with us,' Rohmer replied.

'No matter. I have more than enough men outside to deal with this. I'll see to it that the prisoners are taken into custody. And, of course, I'll ensure that your part in their capture is made known to my superiors. It may even result in a promotion for you.'

'Thank you, *Sturmbannführer*,' came the obsequious reply.

Ravallo noticed a look of uncertainty in Rohmer's eyes, as if he wanted to say something but wasn't sure how best to word it in case he incurred the wrath of the Gestapo officer. 'If you've got something on your mind, Rohmer, then let's hear it. I can't read your thoughts.'

'I . . . I mean . . . we . . . my unit . . . we had no idea that there was a Gestapo unit active in this area,' Rohmer stammered uncertainly. 'We . . . we weren't told about it.'

'And why should you have been told?' Ravallo retorted indignantly. 'The Gestapo isn't answerable to your unit, or to any other military unit of the *Wehrmacht*. We are answerable only to *Reichsführer* Himmler in Berlin.'

'I'm sorry, *Sturmbannführer*, I didn't mean to insinuate anything by that.'

Ravallo eyed him coldly, then unclasped his hands from behind his back. As he reached up to adjust his cap, he noticed Rohmer's eyes go to his bandaged left hand. Rohmer quickly looked away when he realized that Ravallo had seen him. Satisfied, and greatly relieved that this small pocket of German soldiers appeared to pose no real threat to the operation, Ravallo decided it was time to make his move. He turned towards the door, flicked open the catch on his belt holster and removed his Luger pistol. It was the signal for the Partisans to close in on the kitchen.

He swung round and pressed the barrel of his pistol into Rohmer's back. Before Rohmer could react he'd been disarmed. Ravallo then locked his arm tightly around Rohmer's throat and pushed the barrel up into the soft flesh under his chin. The four German soldiers found themselves in a dilemma as they looked uncertainly from Rohmer to the prisoners. Then, realizing they'd been duped, one of them turned his rifle on Ravallo and ordered his colleagues to keep their weapons trained on the prisoners.

'Tell them to put down their guns,' Ravallo said to Rohmer, digging the barrel harder into his skin.

'You kill me and they'll kill you,' came the disdainful reply.

'Possibly, but there's a group of Partisans outside with their weapons already trained on your men,' Ravallo informed him. 'I may be killed, but so too will you and your men the moment I'm hit. It's your choice, Rohmer.'

The soldier who had his weapon trained on Ravallo saw the barrels of three rifles outside the door, which were aimed directly at his head. He knew the moment he pulled the trigger he'd be dead. It wasn't much of an incentive to continue holding out. He slowly lowered his rifle and let it fall to the floor.

'Stand your ground!' Rohmer ordered. 'You surrender now and they'll kill you.'

A second soldier dropped his weapon. The other two exchanged anxious glances, then slowly extended their weapons in surrender. They were quickly disarmed and frisked. Ravallo released his hold on Rohmer's throat, pushing him away from him. Hillyard grabbed him roughly, slammed him face first into the wall, and frisked him as well. They were all unarmed.

'Get them out of here,' Ravallo ordered.

'I should have known,' Rohmer said as Hillyard led him towards the door.

'What should you have known?' Ravallo asked as Rohmer drew abreast of him.

'You're the American, aren't you?'

'Am I?' Ravallo said, struggling with the uncertainty which surged through his stomach. How did Rohmer know who he was? Was it a guess? Or was there more to it than that? He suddenly felt distinctly uneasy.

'Your hand,' Rohmer said quietly, nodding in the general direction of Ravallo's bandaged left hand. 'This morning all *Wehrmacht* officers received a communiqué from Gestapo headquarters in Palermo to say that one of the enemy agents had a bandaged left hand. The American, Major Nick Ravallo. I should have known the moment I saw it. I should have known.'

'Take him away,' Ravallo said to Hillyard in a barely audible voice, then he moved to the table and sat down opposite McIndoe. Before he could say anything, a single shot rang out from the yard.

They were both on their feet in an instant and darted out into the yard. Rohmer lay dead on the ground, blood seeping from a gunshot wound in the stomach. Hillyard stood over him, the offending rifle still clutched in his hand. 'What the hell happened?' McIndoe demanded.

'He made a grab for the gun,' Hillyard said. 'We struggled and it went off. I didn't mean to kill him. It just went off.'

'That's what happened,' one of the Partisans behind Hillyard said, and there was a general murmur of agreement from his colleagues. 'It wasn't his fault. It was either him or the German.'

'Get the truck out of the garage,' Massimo said, tossing the keys to the nearest man. 'Load the body in the back. I want it weighed down and dumped at sea.'

'What about them?' McIndoe asked, gesturing to where Evans and Johnson, together with a handful of Partisans, were guarding the remaining four Germans. The prisoners gathered in a nervous huddle in the centre of the yard, their eyes fixed fearfully on the dead officer at Hillyard's feet.

'Don't worry, my men will deal with them,' Massimo replied.

'In other words, they'll be executed,' Ravallo said.

'Do you have a better idea, Nicky?' Massimo asked with a hint of sarcasm in his voice. 'Because if you do, I'd like to hear it.'

'He's right, Nicky, there's no other choice,' McIndoe said, grim-faced. 'I don't like it any more than you do, but they've seen you wearing the Gestapo uniform. That means they already know too much.'

'We can't take prisoners,' Massimo said. 'Not only don't we have the manpower to guard them, but what if one were to escape and raise the alarm? It could jeopardize the whole operation.'

'Welcome to the reality of the front line, Nicky,' Ravallo said contemptuously to himself, then turned to McIndoe and Stella. 'I want to see you both in the kitchen. Now.'

When McIndoe and Stella entered the kitchen, they found that Ravallo had already asked the Andonis to leave the room. He sat alone at the table.

'What is it?' Stella asked, pulling up the chair beside him and sitting down.

'Did you hear what Rohmer said to me about my hand?' Ravallo asked. They shook their heads. When he told them a look of horror crossed their faces as the realization of the truth hit them with all the force of a descending sledgehammer.

'That's right,' Ravallo said, 'Angelo Sciarro couldn't possibly have known about the injury to my hand, could he? So it would appear that Stella's been right about him all along. The Gestapo have gone to great lengths to protect the identity of the real spy. How many people who knew about my injured hand also knew about this operation?'

'There's no doubt in my mind now that we've got a German spy in our midst,' McIndoe said. He buried his head despairingly in his hands.

'We've got to abort the operation now,' Stella said to Ravallo.

'We can't,' McIndoe said, raising his head to look at her. 'If we abort the operation now, Kesselring and his chiefs-of-staff will have a free hand not only to plan but also to execute the Axis invasion of Malta. And you know as well as I do that the island's defences are chronically depleted right now. They couldn't possibly repel a major Axis offensive. The island would fall within a week, leaving the Axis with total control of the Mediterranean. And where would that leave our troops in North Africa? We don't have a choice, Stella. We have to see this through to the end.'

'Mac's right, there's far too much at stake for us to turn back now.' Ravallo looked at his watch, then pushed back his chair and got to his feet. 'We're going to have to change our plans. We can't stay on here, not after what happened tonight. There's every chance that the Germans will send out a scouting party to search for their missing colleagues.'

'What do you suggest?' McIndoe asked.

'You and your men change into your German uniforms,' Ravallo replied. 'Then we've got to get out of here.'

'I have to brief them about the operation, Nicky,' McIndoe said. 'I can't put it off any longer.'

'Then what's to stop the spy from relaying it all back to his German masters?' Stella countered.

'Who's to say that the spy's necessarily one of them?' McIndoe said. 'It could be Charlie Higgins. Or Georges Passiere. It could be one of us. There's no way of knowing, at least not until they slip up and reveal their true colours.'

Ravallo raised a hand in Stella's direction before she could reply. 'This has obviously put us all on edge. I agree with Mac. The others have to be briefed. They can't be expected to go in blind.'

'Then brief them shortly before we reach Palermo,' Stella suggested.

'There you go again, insinuating that – '

'Mac, please,' Ravallo interceded quickly. He looked at Stella. 'I can understand your concern. Believe me, I share it as well. But it'll be safe for Mac to brief his men after we leave here. That way the spy won't be able to pass a message on to the Germans without having to first make some excuse to get away from the others. And if that were to happen, one of us could follow them and monitor their actions.'

'Assuming that *one of us* isn't the spy,' McIndoe added caustically.

'I realize there's going to be a certain amount of suspicion between the three of us from now on – it's only natural – but it's imperative that we hold together as a team,' Ravallo said. 'We can't afford to let on to the others that there's a spy on board. Not only would it alert the real spy, but it would also create an atmosphere of mistrust and suspicion which could have them turning against each other. That's the last thing we need right now.'

'It makes sense,' McIndoe agreed. 'After all, the three of us have already been fully briefed on the operation. And if one of us is the German spy, then the chances are that we'll already be walking into a carefully laid German trap.'

'I think it would also be prudent if you were to limit the information you passed back to Passiere,' Ravallo said. 'There's no need for him to know the precise details of the operation. After all, it's not as if he's even involved directly with it.'

'Agreed,' McIndoe replied. He took a packet of cigarettes from his pocket and offered one to Stella. She took a cigarette and he lit it for her. He then stuck one between his lips and lit it before pushing the packet back into his pocket.

'And what about me?' Ravallo asked.

'I thought you were trying to give them up,' McIndoe said, tossing the packet to him.

'I will, one day,' Ravallo replied as he pulled a cigarette out of the packet and pushed it between his lips. 'But it sure as hell won't be today.'

EIGHT

He'd been standing guard at the main gates since midnight. It was now six o'clock. Two hours left of his shift, then he could climb into bed and get some welcome sleep. There had been several occasions during the night when he'd found himself struggling to stay awake, and it had only been by splashing cold water over his face from a natural spring close to the driveway that he'd managed to stave off the encroaching drowsiness. He stifled another yawn and was about to reach into his tunic pocket for a cigarette when he heard a rustling sound in the undergrowth behind him. He instinctively tightened his grip on the submachine-gun and was still turning to investigate when a hand was clamped tightly around his mouth. His head was jerked back roughly and he was still struggling fiercely against the grip when he saw the steel blade flash across the front of his face. The finely sharpened blade sunk deep into the flesh below his left ear and sliced downwards across his exposed throat . . .

Lino Venucci kept his hand over the guard's mouth, waiting until the soldier stopped shuddering in the final spasms of death before dragging the body into the foliage at the side of the driveway. He slipped the bone-handled knife back into the sheath on his belt, then rummaged through the dead man's pockets until he found the key to open the gates. Straightening up, he stared down dispassionately at the body at his feet, but felt no remorse whatsoever about what he'd done. He never did. This was the seventeenth German soldier he'd killed since the occupation – he'd memorized the details of each kill and kept them buried away in some dark recess of his mind – and he would continue to dispatch them until Sicily was once more returned to its people.

He heard the sound of footsteps coming from the dense undergrowth, and in one fluid movement he'd grabbed his submachine-gun, bringing it up from his side into a firing position. His body tensed in anticipation as the noise grew closer, then he exhaled deeply in relief when the familiar figure of Mauro Conte appeared. He let the gun fall back to his side. Like him, Conte was wearing the uniform of a German soldier. Conte was his partner in the Sicilian Resistance. They'd always worked well as a team, despite having little in common with each other.

'It's done,' Conte told him.

Venucci knew Conte meant that he'd neutralized the guard at the rear of the property. Conte never used words like 'kill' or 'assassinate' to explain his actions, nor did he ever refer to what he did for the Resistance in the first person. It was just his way. Venucci knew Conte had been having trouble psychologically in dealing with some of the covert operations the two of them had carried out against German targets. Not that he ever talked about it though. He was a loner who kept very much to himself. But Venucci was the one person who could see past the façade. Which was why they worked so well together . . .

Venucci emerged from the undergrowth and paused to look up at the silhouette of the lavish double-storey mansion which stood prominently on the gentle slopes of the verdant hillside overlooking the driveway. The mansion, which belonged to a wealthy countess who was a generous benefactress of the Italian Socialist Party, had been requisitioned by the Gestapo shortly after the Germans occupied the island, and was now used exclusively by them to accommodate visiting senior Gestapo officers. One such officer was *Sturmbannführer* Otto Schenk, who'd spent the night in the mansion after flying in from Berlin the previous evening.

Venucci unlocked the gates then, cupping his hands over his mouth, made the call of the night owl. Moments later, five shadowy figures emerged from the darkness of the trees on the opposite side of the road and slipped through the gates. They were dressed in black and their faces were smeared with camouflage cream. Like Venucci and Conte, they were Partisans based in Palermo. The five men disappeared silently into the undergrowth, their target the staff quarters – an L-shaped building situated behind the mansion – where the four off-duty German guards, as well as the household staff, were billeted. Although all the staff had been carefully vetted and approved in advance by the Gestapo, the Resistance had still managed to place one of their own operatives inside the mansion. Many of the senior Partisans thought that, at the age of eighteen, Gina Roetta was too young to have been given such a heavy responsibility, but there was no denying that her detailed reports on the flow of Gestapo traffic to and from the mansion had proved invaluable to the movement in the last few months.

Now Venucci and Conte had to wait for her signal to let them know that the five-man team had penetrated the staff quarters and overpowered the sleeping occupants. It had been agreed at the initial briefing some days earlier that the prisoners would be taken away for interrogation once Venucci and Conte had successfully completed their part of the operation. But that was assuming it all went according to plan. They knew it was imperative to isolate Schenk if they were to have any chance of capturing him alive, yet all it would take was one of the guards raising the alarm to throw the whole operation into jeopardy. Venucci looked at Conte, who seemed lost in his own thoughts as he stared at the house. Conte's face was expressionless. It didn't surprise Venucci. But he knew that, behind the bland exterior,

Conte would be feeling just as apprehensive as he was. It was only natural under the circumstances.

'Look!' Conte hissed, grabbing Venucci's arm tightly. Venucci followed Conte's pointing finger and saw the slight figure who'd emerged from the side of the mansion. It was Gina Roetta. They waited anxiously for her to give them the prearranged signal. Nothing. For a horrifying moment they thought that something had gone wrong in the staff quarters, even though neither of them had heard the sound of gunfire. Then casually she removed the white hand-towel which was tucked into the top of her apron, using it to dust down the front of her tunic before draping the towel over her shoulder and disappearing back around the side of the building. An innocuous gesture to anyone who might have been watching. But for Venucci and Conte it was the signal they'd been waiting for. It was now safe for them to approach the house.

Venucci followed Conte to a pathway which was bordered by a blaze of colourful flowerbeds at the end of the driveway. The path ended at a flight of stone steps which took them on to the spacious gravel courtyard at the front of the mansion. Parked in the courtyard was a black Gestapo staff car, a three-litre Adler Diplomat. The two *Hakenkreuz* – swastika – pennants hung limply on either side of the bonnet. The two men exchanged distasteful glances as they passed the car. As they reached the corner of the building, Venucci held up his hand. He pressed himself against the wall and peered cautiously around the corner. He could see the staff quarters. The curtains were drawn across the windows. Nothing stirred. He nodded to Conte, then slipped round the side of the building, pushed open a wooden gate, and made his way across the yard to an open door at the side of the house.

Gina Roetta was sitting alone in the kitchen smoking a cigarette. She looked up sharply when Venucci appeared in the doorway and smiled at her. She smiled back fleetingly at him, then got to her feet and followed him out into the yard.

'Where's Schenk?' Venucci asked.

'Upstairs in his bedroom.' She noticed Conte hovering behind Venucci, and nodded in greeting to him. 'I've just taken his breakfast up to him. He was already dressed in his uniform, so it's safe to assume that he'll be ready to leave shortly. His driver's up there as well. The bastard's been hanging around in here with me for the last half an hour, waiting for his master to call him.'

'Any trouble?' Venucci asked, gesturing to the staff quarters in the distance.

'None at all. I laced the guards' supper last night with finely ground sleeping tablets. They were in no condition to put up a fight this morning. The building was secured without incident.'

'Then it's all going according to plan,' Conte said.

She looked round on hearing the sound of uneven whistling emanating from the hallway. She peered through the open kitchen door and cursed softly when she saw the figure standing in the foyer. 'It's Kraewel. Schenk's driver.'

'Good. We can deal with him now,' Venucci said. 'Can you get him to come out into the yard?'

'Leave it to me,' she replied.

'Hey, come here,' she called out from the kitchen to Kraewel, purposely injecting some urgency into her voice.

The man hurried into the room. 'What is it?' he demanded.

'There's someone out there,' she said, sounding nervous. 'I was standing at the sink when I saw a movement through the window. I saw him clearly . . . it was a man dressed in black. He ran into the bushes behind the staff quarters when he saw me.' She grabbed Kraewel's arm. 'I'm scared. He had a gun.'

'Wait here,' Kraewel told her as he removed his pistol from the holster on his belt. He jerked his arm free, then crossed to the door and stepped out into the yard. He sensed someone behind him but, before he could react, Venucci caught him viciously across the back of the head with the

180

butt of his submachine-gun. Kraewel was unconscious before he crumpled to the ground.

Gina emerged from the kitchen and stared contemptuously at the unconscious figure, then she suddenly lashed out with her foot, catching him viciously in the ribs. Venucci pulled her away before she could deliver another kick. She eyed Venucci coldly. 'The bastard couldn't keep his hands off me this morning.'

Venucci tightened his grip on her arm when she tried to break free to kick Kraewel again. He caught Conte's eye and nodded to Kraewel. 'Take him to the staff quarters. I'll meet you out front.'

Conte hoisted the unconscious man on to his shoulders and headed off towards the staff quarters. Only then did Venucci release his grip on Gina's arm. She disappeared back into the kitchen.

Venucci walked back to the forecourt, where he took a packet of cigarettes from his pocket and lit one. He knew from the plans of the house that all the bedroom windows on the second floor faced out over an undulating valley at the rear of the house. And, even if he were to be seen from one of the upper floor windows, the German uniform would guarantee his cover. He looked up slowly at the façade of the building and smiled contentedly to himself. The net was finally closing around *Sturmbannführer* Otto Schenk . . .

Otto Schenk stared at his reflection in the cheval mirror. He knew he was handsome. He certainly didn't need the succession of beautiful women he regularly entertained in the élite nightclubs of Berlin to tell him that. Not that he really cared what they thought of him, or anything else for that matter – they were there merely to satisfy his sexual penchants. He knew there were those who would call his penchants sadistic and perverse, but none of the women had ever complained about being whipped in the privacy of his sumptuous Berlin flat. They knew better than to speak out publicly against a senior Gestapo officer. The repercussions against them would have been swift and severe. Like his colleagues, he revelled in the power that came with the honour of serving under the inspired leadership of his mentor, *Reichsführer* Himmler, at the *Geheime Staatspolitzei's* headquarters on the Prinz Albrechtstrasse in Berlin. But, as one of the selected few who'd been chosen personally by the *Reichsführer* to ensure that the Gestapo's high standards were maintained in the occupied countries, his power was now vast. How many times had he seen the look of abject fear in the eyes of even the most powerful *Gauleiter* when he'd arrived unexpectedly in one of the occupied countries to carry out an internal audit? They may have held the superior rank, but he had the ear of the *Reichsführer*, and in the eight months since his appointment to the job, he could say truthfully that the *Reichsführer* had yet to question any of his findings . . .

He crossed to the bedside table and poured himself a coffee from the solid silver pot on the stainless steel tray which Gina had brought up a few minutes earlier. She was undeniably pretty. Perhaps when he returned from his tour of the island, he'd amuse himself by beating her just like he did those pseudo-socialite whores back in Berlin. He had the necessary accoutrements with him. He never travelled without them. Ignoring the cooked breakfast that she'd prepared for him, he consumed a single slice of buttered toast with the black coffee, then went through to the adjoining bathroom to wash his hands. He slipped on a pair of black leather gloves, then picked up his valise from beside the bed and left the room. He descended the spiral staircase and looked around irritably for his driver on reaching the foyer.

'Kraewel!' he yelled. No response. He swore furiously, then strode briskly into the kitchen, where Gina jumped to her feet and hid the cigarette she'd been smoking behind her back. 'Have you seen Kraewel?'

'Kraewel, sir?' she replied with a feigned frown. It was essential that she continue the pretence of the naïve, inno-

182

cent country girl that she'd been playing ever since she'd first arrived at the mansion.

'My driver, Sergeant Kraewel!' Schenk thundered. 'Have you seen him?'

'Yes, sir,' she stammered, nodding her head. 'He was in here a couple of minutes ago. I . . . I think he's waiting for you in the car.'

'I ordered him to wait for me in the foyer. Why am I bothering to tell you this anyway? Damn peasant girl.' Schenk departed the house through the back door and walked the short distance across the yard to the wooden gate leading out on to the forecourt. His hand froze on the handle as he looked down across the sprawling lawn to the towering wrought-iron gates at the end of the driveway. He'd been told there would be a twenty-four-hour guard at the gates. So where was the guard? It was with an apprehensive sense of unease that he drew his Luger from the holster on his belt and pushed open the wooden gate. He placed his leather case against the side of the building then, pressing himself against the wall, swung round to face the forecourt, the pistol gripped tightly in his extended hand. His sense of unease immediately turned to one of rage when he saw the guard seated on the stone steps beside the staff car, smoking a cigarette. 'What are you doing here?' he screamed in fury as he stormed towards Venucci. 'I'll see to it that you're court-martialled for dereliction of duty. Get back to your post!'

Venucci carefully stubbed out the cigarette on the plinth of the nearest of two magnificently hand-carved stone lions which stood at the foot of the steps. Getting to his feet, he waited until Schenk was within range before slamming the butt of his submachine-gun viciously into his stomach. Schenk cried out in pain and the pistol fell from his grasp as he stumbled backwards. He had to grab on to the bonnet of the staff car to prevent himself from losing his balance and falling to the ground. Venucci scooped up the pistol and slipped it into his belt. Conte emerged from his concealed position behind the steps, and crossed to where Schenk was now down on one knee with his hand clasped tightly over his stomach. He was struggling desperately to catch his breath.

'Get up, you bastard!' Venucci snarled in German. He grabbed Schenk by his collar and hauled him to his feet. He shoved him roughly against the side of the car, pressing the barrel of the submachine-gun against the side of his neck as he quickly frisked him for any more weapons that he may have been carrying. He was unarmed.

'Who are you?' Schenk hissed between clenched teeth, having already deduced from Venucci's thick accent that he wasn't German.

'Partisans,' Venucci replied, and smiled triumphantly when he saw the look of naked fear flash across Schenk's face. He slammed the butt of the submachine-gun into Schenk's midriff again, and he would have struck him a third time as he fell to his knees had Conte not grabbed him and pulled him away.

'That's enough,' Conte snapped. 'You want to beat him up, that's fine by me. But later. Right now we've got to get out of here. Now come on, let's get him into the car.'

Venucci reached down to yank Schenk to his feet. But lashing out suddenly with his fist Schenk caught Venucci painfully on the side of the face. Venucci stumbled backwards and lost his balance. As he fell heavily to the ground the Luger spilled from his belt and landed within Schenk's reach. Grabbing the pistol, Schenk dived quickly for cover behind the nearest stone plinth in the second before Conte opened fire on him. A volley of bullets peppered the side of the plinth, and Schenk jerked his head back as a sliver of masonry nicked his cheek. He absently wiped away the tear of blood, then swung the pistol on Conte who had loomed up from behind the staff car, the submachine-gun raised to fire. Schenk got off two shots in quick succession; both bullets struck Conte in the chest and he collapsed to the ground

184

without a sound. Slowly straightening up Schenk trained the pistol on Venucci who was still lying on the gravel courtyard, struggling to clear his head. Schenk sneered derisively to himself at the look of desperation on Venucci's face. The Italian was looking round frantically for his submachine-gun, which was nowhere in sight. Schenk was going to enjoy personally interrogating Venucci at Gestapo headquarters in Palermo. Then, when he had the answers he wanted, he'd kill him. Very slowly. Very painfully.

He only saw the movement at the last moment but, before he had time to react, a row of bullets ripped unevenly across his chest, each one searing through his flesh like the thrust of a red-hot blade. He was slammed back against the side of the plinth and, although he couldn't sense any feeling in his hands, he heard the pistol clattering on to the steps. He turned his head slowly towards his assassin. Gina Roetta glared back defiantly at him, Conte's submachine-gun cradled in her hands. For a moment Schenk stared in disbelief at her through his glazed eyes, then an ironic half-smile touched his bloodied lips. All his adult life he'd held women in complete contempt, using them purely as a means of satisfying his own selfish pleasures. Fate had dealt him his final hand. And all he could see now was the Joker laughing at him. It was his last, self-deprecating thought before his lifeless body slid down the side of the blood-splattered plinth.

Venucci struggled to his feet, hurrying to pick up the fallen Luger which he pressed against Schenk's neck as he felt the carotid artery for a pulse. He looked up at Gina and shook his head. Letting the weapon fall from her hands, Gina began to sob uncontrollably as she stared in horror at Schenk's body, unable to comprehend what she'd just done.

Venucci next hurried over to where Conte lay close to the staff car. It was obvious that Conte was dead even before he went through the empty motions of checking for a pulse. Finding none, he gently closed Conte's sightless eyes, then looked round as two of his colleagues appeared breathlessly in the courtyard behind him, alerted in the staff quarters by the gunfire, their submachine-guns at the ready. Realizing there was no further danger, they lowered the weapons and ran over to where Venucci was now standing over his partner's body.

Venucci explained what had happened, and one of the men crossed to where Gina was standing and put a consoling arm around her shoulders, leading her away from Schenk's body.

'What do we do with him?' the other man, Luigi, asked Venucci. He prodded Schenk's body with the tip of his boot.

'We can't leave him here,' Venucci told him.

'The van's due to arrive in the next twenty minutes to take the prisoners to the safe house,' Luigi said. 'We could put the body in there and get rid of it later.'

'No, I don't want any of the German soldiers to know that Schenk's dead,' Venucci replied. 'If one of them were to escape – '

'They're not going anywhere,' Luigi interceded indignantly.

' – it could blow the whole operation,' Venucci completed his sentence. 'We can't take that chance. No, I'll take the body with me in the staff car and dispose of it later. Come on, help me put him in the boot.'

Venucci searched Conte's body and found the car keys that Conte had taken earlier from Kraewel's tunic pocket. He opened the boot. Luigi helped him to carry Schenk's body to the back of the staff car, and together they bundled it unceremoniously into the boot. 'I'll take Gina with me,' Venucci said.

'She's in no state to go with you,' Luigi said. 'I'll go with you. We've got the situation under control in the staff quarters. They won't miss me now, not with the van due here shortly.'

'You wrap her in cotton wool now and she'll never get over this,' Venucci told him. 'I'm taking her with me. She has to face this herself, Luigi. Trust me, it's the only way.'

'This is her first kill, Lino. There's a hell of a difference between shooting straw dummies on a target range, and shooting down a man in cold blood. She needs to talk it out. We've got counsellors who can help her do that.'

'She needs to confront her own fears, Luigi,' Venucci replied. 'And she has to do it alone.'

'She's far too young to have been involved in any of this,' Luigi hissed his disapproval. 'She's still only a child.'

'It's got nothing to do with age. I've seen girls younger than her kill German soldiers without a second thought. It's all about what's in here,' Venucci said, hitting his chest with his clenched fist. 'And she's got the heart for our struggle. She's proved that already.'

'No, Lino, leave her be,' Luigi replied.

'I want to go with you,' Gina said softly behind them.

Luigi turned to her. 'You're in no condition – '

'I want to go,' she cut defiantly across his words. The tears were gone. Now there was only a cold and dispassionate look in her eyes.

Venucci unlocked the passenger door for her, then moved round to the driver's side and tossed the submachine-gun on to the back seat. He was about to get behind the wheel when he paused to look across the roof at Luigi. 'You can count yourself lucky that you're staying behind here. I've still got to explain the dead body to the British when they arrive in Palermo.'

'They wanted him alive, didn't they?'

'They were going to send him to London for interrogation,' Venucci replied.

'It was either him or you,' Luigi said. 'You know that.'

'Try telling that to them,' Venucci said as he climbed into the staff car, started the engine, and pulled away from the steps.

McIndoe sat silently at the table in the kitchen of the safe house in the Kasr, the Arab quarter of the city, as Venucci recounted the events of the morning which had culminated in the death of Otto Schenk. Only once did McIndoe look at Gina Roetta who was standing by the door; that was when Venucci explained how Schenk had met his end. She'd lowered her eyes, unable to hold McIndoe's penetrating stare. When he'd finished speaking, Venucci braced himself for the backlash as his eyes flitted nervously between the four figures seated around the table with him.

For a moment nobody spoke, then Giancarlo Massimo got to his feet and put a reassuring hand on Venucci's shoulder before crossing to Gina. He spoke softly to her and she left the room, closing the door behind her. McIndoe's eyes went first to Ravallo then to Stella. Neither acknowledged him as they stared at the empty coffee cups on the table in front of them. Then he looked at Venucci. But there was no anger or resentment in his eyes, just a resigned acceptance of what had happened.

'I am sorry, signore,' Venucci muttered apologetically.

'Me too,' McIndoe replied.

'We did try to capture him alive but circumstances . . .' Venucci trailed off, knowing just how hollow his excuses would sound. Best to keep his mouth shut.

'What did you do with Schenk's body?' Ravallo asked.

'We buried it in a forest on the outskirts of the city, signore.'

'I assume you stripped the body of all identification?' Ravallo continued.

'*Si, signore,*' Venucci was quick to assure him. 'We removed his uniform as an added precaution.'

'Good thinking,' Ravallo told him. 'Do you still have the uniform with you?'

'It was burnt, signore,' Venucci replied. 'I gave Signore Massimo all the personal belongings we found on the body.'

'Including his briefcase?' Ravallo asked.

'*Si, signore.*'

'I've got that,' Massimo said from the door.

'I'd like to see it,' Ravallo said, getting to his feet. 'It should contain the letter of authorization from Himmler which would have given Schenk access to all areas of the island.'

'I'll get it for you,' Massimo said. He paused as he was about to open the door. 'Do you have any more questions for Venucci?' he asked.

'Not at present,' Ravallo replied, and Stella and McIndoe both shook their heads, so Massimo gestured to Venucci who gratefully departed the room after him.

'That girl couldn't have been any more than seventeen or eighteen at the most,' Ravallo said with a sad shake of the head. 'She shouldn't be put in that kind of situation. Not at her age.'

'The unfortunate truth is that war transcends all age-barriers, Nicky,' Stella replied. 'She's got just as much right to fight for her country as anyone else on this island.'

'I agree, but what I'm trying to say is that she shouldn't have had so much responsibility piled on to her shoulders at such a young age,' Ravallo said. 'She should have been weaned into the movement gradually, not thrown in at the deep end. But it's not just the Partisans who are guilty, it's all the Resistance movements in all the occupied countries. I've seen what the Gestapo do to girls of her age who are caught working for the underground. And most of them are caught because of their inexperience in the field.'

'I bet she's got more field experience than you have, Nicky,' McIndoe said, and raised a hand before Ravallo could say anything. 'I agree, it's far from ideal. But often there just isn't time to train them properly. If they can point a gun and pull the trigger, then they're ready to be sent out against the Germans. And just remember, Nicky, nobody was ever press-ganged into joining the Partisans. They all volunteered. It was their choice.'

Ravallo was about to speak when he saw Massimo standing in the doorway, a battered leather valise in his hand. He had no idea how long he'd been there. Massimo crossed the

189

room and placed the valise on the table. He took an envelope from his pocket and handed it to Ravallo. 'That's what they found in his pockets. I don't know if it will be of any use to you.'

'We'll find out soon enough,' Ravallo said, spilling the contents of the envelope on to the table.

Massimo walked to the door, then stopped to look back at Ravallo. 'I agree with you, Nicky. Gina shouldn't have to be forced to bear so much responsibility on her shoulders. But unfortunately not everyone was prepared to stand up and be counted when the Germans occupied our island. Our resources are scarce. They always have been, which means that we have to deploy our people wherever we can. Gina may not have the field experience, but she more than makes up for that in courage. I couldn't be more proud of her if she were my own daughter. Perhaps you'll understand those sentiments one day.'

Ravallo stared at the doorway after Massimo had left. 'Perhaps I will,' he mused. He reached for the valise but found it locked. Poking through the contents of the envelope, he picked out three keys to try on the valise. One of them opened it.

'I'll leave you to it, Nicky,' McIndoe said as he got to his feet. 'I'd better go and look in on the others.'

'The last I saw, they were playing cards in the lounge,' Stella said.

'Figures,' McIndoe said with a wry smile. 'I'll see you later.'

'See you, Mac,' Ravallo replied absently as he rummaged through the valise in search of the letter.

McIndoe left the room and made his way down the hall to the lounge door. Evans, Hillyard and Johnson were seated around a small coffee table playing poker. He was about to go in, then decided against disturbing them. He knew he still wasn't too popular with them after the way he'd handled the pre-dawn briefing. He'd had to evade their more pertinent questions with woolly answers and, when pressed to explain himself further, he'd been forced to pull rank and fall back on the now familiar 'need-to-know basis' reply. In retrospect, he knew he could have handled the briefing a lot better. That much had been evident by mixed emotions mirrored on their faces when it was over. Anger. Frustration. Hurt. The hurt had certainly cut the deepest. But what choice did he have without revealing the truth to them?

He made his way to the front door and emerged out on to the porch. The Partisan on guard duty was sitting on the porch steps, a Fucile rifle laid across his knees. He nodded in greeting to McIndoe, taking a last drag on his cigarette before stubbing it out carefully and slipping it back into the packet he'd taken from his shirt pocket. Getting to his feet, he slung the rifle over his shoulder, then walked across the small clearing in front of the patio, disappearing into the row of trees which obscured the safe house from the road.

McIndoe sat down in one of the two wicker chairs on the patio, then swung his legs up on to the low wooden railing which encompassed it. He was about to reach into his pocket for his cigarettes when he remembered that he'd left them in his rucksack. He thought momentarily about going to fetch them, but dismissed the idea. He was smoking too much anyway. Clasping his hands behind his head, he closed his eyes and let his mind drift back over the past few hours . . .

Once the briefing was over, they'd departed from the farmhouse wearing the German uniforms that had been left for them in advance of their arrival on the island. Apart from Ravallo, McIndoe was dressed as the only other officer in the party: a captain in the *Wehrmacht*. Stella had been given an oversized tunic and, having previously removed all traces of make-up, and with her hair piled up on her head and carefully concealed underneath a peaked cap, she'd been able to pass herself off as a youthful German soldier. And, sandwiched between Evans and Hillyard in the back of an Opel Blitz troop carrier, she'd blended easily into her role. It had proved the perfect disguise. Johnson, who was regarded as one of the best German speakers in the Firm, was appointed as the official driver of the officers' staff car. Both vehicles had been captured some weeks earlier, during an ambush by members of the underground in the south of the country. The number plates had been changed to those corresponding to a similar staff car and troop carrier which were currently in service on the island. Nothing had been left to chance.

With the way their luck had been running since they'd left Malta, he'd fully expected to have encountered problems on the road. That they hadn't was down solely to Nicky Ravallo. For the first time since meeting him, McIndoe had understood why Ravallo had been chosen for this particular assignment. His chilling portrayal of Otto Schenk was both mesmerizing and more than a little frightening. It was almost as if the Gestapo officer McIndoe had read about in the US Military Intelligence file was actually in the back of the car with him. The file had been compiled by a former high-ranking Gestapo officer who'd defected to the Americans the previous year. And, just like Schenk, who, it was claimed in the file, rarely indulged in small-talk with fellow officers, Ravallo didn't court conversation on the journey, preferring to stay in character at all times. On the few occasions when he had been called upon to break his self-imposed silence, invariably at one of the *Wehrmacht* roadblocks along their route, he'd merely had to identify himself to be waved through by the nervous soldiers. McIndoe doubted whether Schenk himself could have improved on Ravallo's menacing performance.

They had reached the safe house in the early afternoon. The staff car and troop carrier were then driven away to be doused in petrol and torched. Another two burnt-out vehicles wouldn't arouse any suspicions in a city whose streets were already littered with such wrecks. It was imperative, in order to add further authenticity to his cover, for Ravallo to use Schenk's official Adler Diplomat staff car when he was driven to the hotel that evening. The staff car was currently hidden in a lock-up garage somewhere in the city. He didn't know where, though. Even Massimo hadn't been told its location. It would be delivered to the safe house once Massimo had received word that the meeting at the hotel was over.

They'd already learnt from Venucci that the hotel was being guarded around the clock by a crack team of élite German paratroopers who'd been flown in especially from the Eastern Front just for that task. He was well aware that they would be a very different proposition to the nervous young soldiers they'd encountered earlier at the roadblocks. These kind of paratroopers were in a league of their own. Hardened, battle-weary veterans, with more decorations between them than almost any other unit in the *Wehrmacht*. Many had been decorated personally by Hitler in Berlin. Their pride came from their fierce loyalty to their country. They didn't fear anyone, not even the Gestapo, and they would certainly challenge Ravallo's authority once he arrived at the hotel. It was going to take an exceptional performance from him to outsmart them.

McIndoe opened his eyes as the final thought flashed through his mind. It should have been a worrying thought. But somehow it wasn't. Not after what he'd witnessed that afternoon. If there was one person who could pull this off successfully, it was Nicky Ravallo.

It was the first good feeling he'd had in a long time. Even with the undercurrent of suspicion and uncertainty that constantly plagued his subconscious, was it really too much to hope for that the operation was finally beginning to turn in their favour?

'Well, unless anyone has anything else to add to what's already been said, I believe that concludes our business here today,' Field-Marshal Kesselring said as he looked at the faces around the table. Those senior officers present, each of whom had their own personal aides in close attendance, were his chief-of-staff, Marshal Deichmann; his liaison officer on Sicily, General von Senger und Etterlin; the naval commander-in-chief of the Mediterranean, Vice-Admiral Weichold; and, seated on his immediate right, General Kurt Student. When nobody ventured any further comment, Kesselring clapped his hands together in a gesture of obvious satisfaction. 'Good. This has been a most constructive meeting, and I've every confidence that the *Führer* will see it that way too when I present Operation Herkules to him in Berlin next week. And if, as I believe, we are given the go-ahead to implement the plan, then I predict that Malta will fall within a matter of weeks. And I don't have to tell any of you the strategic importance of having control over the entire Mediterranean theatre. I certainly hope I don't, seeing as that's what we've been discussing here for the past eight hours.' There was a ripple of laughter. He closed over the folder in front of him, then sat back in his chair.

'I believe that some of you are intending to fly back to Rome tonight, but I hope that you'll be able to find the time to dine with me in the restaurant before you leave.' There wasn't a man in the room who would dare to turn down Kesselring's invitation, even if it meant delaying or rescheduling prearranged flight plans in the process. And Kesselring knew that only too well. 'Splendid,' he announced with a broad smile, 'I look forward to it. We'll meet in the bar first for an aperitif at, shall we say, seven o'clock?' There was a general murmur of agreement. 'Thank you, gentlemen. Until seven, then.' He put a hand lightly on Student's arm as the meeting began to disband around them. 'Ask Riedler to come through.'

Kesselring looked up as Student returned with Riedler. He nodded in response to Riedler's salute. 'This is the first chance we've had to talk since I arrived on Sicily. I wanted to say how impressed I've been with the security arrangements here at the hotel. You've done an excellent job at such short notice. I can assure you it won't go unnoticed once I get back to Rome. You're far too good a soldier to be serving as a reconnaissance scout for some infantry battalion on the Eastern Front. I know that Field-Marshal Rommel is constantly on the lookout for experienced soldiers for his special forces in North Africa. Would that interest you, Riedler?'

'Only if my men were transferred to North Africa as well, sir,' Riedler replied.

'You can only take that kind of loyalty so far in the military, Riedler,' Kesselring told him. 'A good officer knows when it's time to move on to a new challenge.'

'Yes, sir,' Riedler replied respectfully.

Kesselring sensed the lack of conviction in Riedler's voice, but chose not to pursue the matter further. Instead he gestured to a middle-aged woman who was seated in the corner of the room. 'That's Sergeant Schmidt. She's my stenographer. I brought her with me from *Wehrmacht* headquarters in Rome to take notes of the meeting here today. She'll start to type up her notes once we've left. I want you to post two of your best men outside the door while she's in here. They're not to admit anyone unless it's first been cleared with me. I mean *nobody* – not even my senior officers or any of their aides. And if there are any problems, you're to contact me without delay. Is that understood, Riedler?'

'Yes, sir.' Riedler glanced across at the woman. 'How long do you anticipate her being here?'

'A couple of hours at the most,' Kesselring replied. 'She'll be typing up the report that I'll be presenting to the *Führer* in Berlin next week. That's why it's essential it's not seen by any unauthorized personnel before then.'

'Of course, sir. Will she take the report to you once she's typed it up?'

'No,' Kesselring replied. 'We have a senior orderly stationed here at the hotel. His name's Pizzoni. He'll collect the report from her once she's finished and bring it directly to me. He'll also remove her notes, as well as those notes made by myself and my fellow officers during the meeting, and destroy them. But that needn't concern you. Your only concern is the security of this room. See to it, Riedler.'

Riedler came to attention, then left the room.

'He's a good soldier, sir,' Student said, staring at the open doorway after Riedler had gone.

'A little sentimental, perhaps, when it comes to his loyalty to his men, but on the whole I think you made a good choice in choosing him for this assignment,' Kesselring said as he got to his feet. 'I want you to stay here until the guards arrive to secure the room.' He picked up the folder and crossed to the door where he paused to look back at Student. 'I'll see you in the bar at seven.'

'Yes, sir.'

Kesselring ran his hand over his thinning hair as he nodded thoughtfully to himself. 'All in all, I'd say it's been a very fruitful day indeed.'

'We're already halfway there, sir,' Student replied. 'Now it's up to you to convince the *Führer* that Operation Herkules will succeed.'

'I think you can confidently rely on me to do that, Kurt,' Kesselring said with a knowing smile before disappearing out into the corridor.

Lieutenant Bruno Pizzoni was being blackmailed. And he knew there was nothing he could do about it if he wanted to see his wife and four-year-old daughter alive again . . .

In what had appeared at the time to be totally unrelated incidents, the families of two Italian officers serving on Sicily had been abducted by the Partisans in the last three days. The Partisans had demanded that the officers help them sabotage two rail installations on the island in return for the safe release of their families. Both officers had dutifully informed their superiors of the situation, and had been told to play along and go to the prearranged meeting. The Partisans had had the rendezvous areas under surveillance, and had been able to spot the plain-clothes Gestapo officers who infiltrated the area in advance of the meeting. The meetings had been aborted, and on both occasions the Resistance had executed their hostages. The Gestapo, in retaliation, had rounded up a dozen Partisan sympathizers and executed them in public.

Although Pizzoni had heard about the incidents, he'd taken little notice of them, until he'd returned home the previous evening to find two Partisans waiting for him. His wife and daughter weren't in the house. It was only when the situation had been explained to him that the two previous abductions suddenly made sense. The Resistance had chosen the two officers carefully, knowing full well they were committed fascists who would never accede to their demands. But the demands had just been a ruse. It went deeper than that. The two previous abductions had been carried out to prove to Pizzoni that the Resistance would have no qualms about killing his family if he were to breathe a word of what had happened to the Germans. It had also proved just how uninterested the Germans had been in locating the officers' families. And that's what had hit home the hardest. Pizzoni had had to choose where his true loyalties lay – with the Germans or with his family? It hadn't been a difficult choice under the circumstances . . .

He dialled the number which he'd already committed to memory and let it ring four times. He replaced the handset. There was no going back. Not any more . . .

NINE

Nobody answered the telephone when it rang. It stopped after the fourth ring. It was the signal they'd been waiting for – the conference at the hotel was over. Ravallo was the first to his feet. 'I'll go and get dressed,' he announced, having changed out of the Gestapo uniform soon after they'd arrived at the safe house that afternoon.

'And I'll go and tell the others,' McIndoe said to Stella, following Ravallo from the lounge.

He went out on to the porch. Schenk's staff car was parked in the clearing in front of the house. Venucci, who'd brought the vehicle to the house an hour earlier, was now helping Evans, Hillyard and Johnson to clean it. They were all wearing shorts, and both Evans and Hillyard were stripped to the waist. 'How's it going?' McIndoe called out as he descended the steps.

'We're nearly done,' Evans informed him. He was polishing the roof. 'The carpeting inside the boot was the main problem. It was covered in Schenk's blood. Bruce and Venucci have been scrubbing it. They've got rid of most of the blood now.'

McIndoe moved to the back of the car and peered into the open boot. The carpeting was concealed beneath a frothy layer of soapsuds. 'You're going to have to leave it. We've just received the signal from the hotel. The meeting's over.'

'Then I'd better get changed,' Johnson said, tossing his duster across the roof to Evans.

'It's all right for some,' Evans muttered as he caught it deftly with his free hand.

'You're welcome to take my place,' Johnson told him.

'I wouldn't dream of denying you your moment of glory,' Evans said with a lopsided grin.

Johnson muttered something inaudible under his breath, then crossed to the porch and disappeared into the house. 'What are we going to do about this?' Venucci asked as he raked the soap off the carpet with his scrubbing brush. 'There are still some bloodstains we can't seem to get out.'

'What can we do?' McIndoe replied with a shrug. 'I don't see it being a problem, though. There's no reason why anyone should need to look in the boot.'

'What if the guards at the hotel want to check it?' Venucci said. 'They'd be in their rights.'

'Then Nicky will just have to come up with some excuse to explain why it's wet,' McIndoe said. 'He can say that his driver spilt some oil in the boot earlier today.'

'Perhaps we should sprinkle a little oil over the carpet, just enough to give off a faint smell,' Venucci suggested. 'That would give the story credence.'

'Good idea,' McIndoe said. 'Have you got any oil here?'

'I'll go and see,' Venucci said, dropping his scrubbing brush into the bucket at Hillyard's feet.

Hillyard cursed under his breath as the soapy water splashed across his bare legs. Then, wiping the back of his hand across his forehead, he looked after the retreating Venucci. 'He's a good man, that one.'

'He seems it,' McIndoe agreed.

Hillyard squinted up at McIndoe, who was standing above him. 'I've been thinking a lot about what I said to you at the farmhouse last night, sir. I was out of line. I know you were only carrying out Starr's orders by briefing us on a need-to-know basis. I guess I just let my frustration get the better of me.'

'It's been a pretty frustrating time for us all since we left Malta,' McIndoe said. 'What you said at the time was ill-advised, granted, but understandable under the circumstances. Just as long as you don't make a habit of it.'

'No, sir,' Hillyard replied with a relieved smile.

'Finish up here now. I want you all in uniform and ready to leave in twenty minutes,' McIndoe said.

As he headed back to the house, he saw Stella standing in the open doorway, her arms folded across her chest, her shoulder resting against the jamb. She smiled gently at him when he climbed the steps leading up to the porch. 'So Hillyard's finally decided to swallow his pride and apologize for his outburst at the farmhouse this morning.'

'I've got a feeling Taffy had something to do with it,' McIndoe replied as he looked across at Hillyard. 'But then Bruce has never been one to keep quiet about anything. He always says exactly what's on his mind.'

'A bit like you then,' Stella said good-humouredly.

'Except that I've learnt when to curb my tongue,' McIndoe pointed out as he followed her into the house. 'Bruce hasn't. I've always said that he has the potential to become an officer, but he'll never be considered for promotion because of his negative attitude towards authority. But that's the way he is. He'll never change.'

'Perhaps he'll surprise you yet,' she said, entering the lounge.

'I certainly hope not,' McIndoe replied, and noticed the look of surprise cross her face. 'He's driven by that negativity. If he were to suppress it, he'd lose an essential part of his character which would affect his performance in the field. No, it's not worth it.'

Stella slumped down in the armchair by the open window. 'At least the waiting's over,' she said. The change in subject caught McIndoe by surprise. 'We've been our own prisoners for the last twenty-four hours. Stuck in one another's pockets. Nobody's been allowed to go anywhere without a chaperon. It's been hell.'

'It's what we agreed with Nicky before we left the farmhouse this morning,' McIndoe reminded her.

'Sure, but it doesn't mean I've had to like it,' she retorted. 'I've never known so much suspicion and mistrust between three people. God, it's been awful.'

'It's only natural,' McIndoe replied.

'I'm just amazed none of it's rubbed off on to the others.'

'I'm sure it has, only it's not their place to question it,' McIndoe told her.

'Not even Hillyard?'

'He's treading on eggshells right now,' McIndoe said. 'He won't open his mouth again in a hurry. Not with the threat of being hauled up in front of Starr looming over him. He may not respect authority, but he's also no fool. He knows that Starr abhors insubordination more than anything else. And it's not as if it would be the first time he's crossed swords with Starr. He's already on a written reprimand. I doubt he'd survive another brush with Starr. That's why I'd be so loath to put him on report.'

'My God, a chink in the armour of the infallible Sam McIndoe,' she said sarcastically. 'Now there's something you don't see every day.'

'You can cut the snide remarks,' McIndoe snapped, stung by her biting sarcasm. 'I don't like these arrangements any more than you do, but you know as well as I do that it's the only way to safeguard the operation. We let someone stray from the fold, and the next thing we know the Germans have us surrounded.'

Stella stared pensively out of the window after he'd finished speaking, then she drew her knees up to her chest and wrapped her arms tightly around her legs. It was then that McIndoe saw the expression of vulnerability on her face. It was almost as if she had become a child looking at the world through adult's eyes. She was scared. And for the first time she'd allowed him to see beyond the barriers of self-confidence she built around herself in order to survive in a predominantly androcentric world. He felt the urge to hold her tightly against him and reassure her that it would all turn out all right. But would it? And then the opportunity was gone when she got to her feet and moved to the window.

'So much for the bravado,' she said softly in a faltering voice. 'I've never felt like this before. In the past, the enemy was always out there. Staying one step ahead of them was never that difficult. But now the enemy's one of us. And there's nothing I can do. I've never felt so helpless in my life.' She turned to McIndoe, tears welling up in her eyes. 'All this uncertainty's pushing me to the edge, Sam. Right to the very edge.'

Three brisk strides and McIndoe was standing directly in front of her. He hesitated, still uncertain whether to put his arms around her. How would she react? Then, as she looked up at him, a tear ran down her cheek. He pulled her to him, holding her tightly against him. She made no attempt to pull away. Instead she rested her face lightly against his chest. He could smell the delicate fragrance of her perfume as he gently stroked his hand over her newly washed hair. It was then he heard the footsteps in the hallway and the tall, commanding figure of Nicky Ravallo appeared in the doorway.

He was dressed as a Gestapo officer, the peaked cap clutched tightly in a black-gloved hand. His step faltered when he saw McIndoe with his arms around Stella. But only for a moment, then he entered the room and crossed to a wall mirror where he tugged the peaked cap firmly over his head. McIndoe knew that Stella had seen Ravallo, but she didn't try to pull away from him. It was McIndoe who finally, and reluctantly, moved away from her.

'What's wrong with you?' Ravallo asked tersely, looking at Stella's reflection in the mirror as he made a minor adjustment to the position of the cap on his head.

'It's nothing,' she replied, quickly wiping her moist eyes.

Ravallo turned away from the mirror. 'Look at you, for Christ's sake. Go and wash your face before any of the others sees you like that.'

A look of anger flashed across her face as she glared at Ravallo then, wiping her hands quickly across her eyes, she hurried from the room.

'There was no need to speak to her like that,' McIndoe said after she'd gone.

'I told you before, treat her with kid gloves and she won't thank you for it,' Ravallo said.

'I didn't notice her struggling to get free while I was consoling her. Perhaps you don't know her like you think you do.'

Ravallo slowly shook his head to himself. 'Jesus, I should have seen it coming.'

'What are you talking about?' McIndoe demanded.

'You've gone and fallen for her, haven't you?'

'Of course not,' McIndoe retorted quickly. Too quickly, he realized to his own chagrin. But at that moment he honestly didn't know what his exact feelings were for Stella. There was no denying that he'd been attracted to her from the first time he'd laid eyes on her. But love? Having never been seriously in love before, it wasn't as if he had any kind of yardstick to use to measure his tangled emotions. He'd had girlfriends in the past, but the more he thought about it, the more he realized that his feelings for Stella were undeniably stronger than they had been for any of them. Was he falling in love with her? A woman he hardly knew. Suddenly he felt very confused.

Ravallo sat down on the arm of the chair by the window. 'You are in love with her, aren't you?'

'I like her, that's all,' McIndoe replied defensively.

'You're not the first guy to fall for Stella since I've known her. But you're the first I regard as a friend. And that's why I don't want to see you get hurt. I know for a fact that she likes you a lot. But just as a friend. Don't confuse that friendship for something deeper, Mac. It's not. You make a play for her now and she'd turn you down. And that could jeopardize your friendship with her. Is that really worth it?'

'What are you saying, Nicky? That she's got a bloke back in the States? A husband? A fiancé?'

'You should know better than to ask me about Stella's personal life,' Ravallo replied. 'What's written in her file is strictly confidential.'

'In other words, you're saying that she already has someone in her life?'

McIndoe saw the uncertainty in Ravallo's eyes. 'At least answer me that, Nicky.'

'Let's just say that I have my reasons for warning you off her. That's all I can say. You'll have to read into that what you will.'

'Either she's already got a bloke back home, or else you've got your eye on her and you're worried that I'm trying to muscle in on your territory.'

Ravallo laughed heartily, then got to his feet and slapped McIndoe on the back. 'I think you've been watching too many gangster films, Mac. I've already told you, Stella and I have a purely professional working relationship. Imagine if we were to get involved now that I'm her controller in Gibraltar? I'd be worried sick every time she went off on another assignment. And moreover, do you honestly think that our superiors in Military Intelligence back home would have let the two of us work together out here if they knew that we were involved with each other?' Ravallo smiled. 'No, Mac, you're not muscling in on my territory. But take a word of advice from a friend – let it go. It's the only way.'

'Don't you think Stella should be the judge of that?' McIndoe asked.

'The judge of what?' Stella asked from the doorway. She'd freshened up and her face bore no traces of the anguished vulnerability which had been evident in her eyes only minutes earlier. Her mouth tugged in a faint smile as her eyes flitted between the two men. 'The judge of what?' she repeated, this time in a more forceful tone of voice.

Ravallo looked at McIndoe, who was shifting uncomfortably on the balls of his feet. 'Well, Mac, you were saying?'

'Forget it,' McIndoe replied, flush-faced, and he strode from the room.

Stella watched him leave, then turned back to Ravallo. 'What was all that about?'

'Forget it,' Ravallo said, and followed McIndoe from the room.

'Tell you what, guys, why don't I just forget it?' she muttered. She crossed to the table and picked up the packet of cigarettes. It was empty. 'Figures,' she snorted in disgust as she crumpled the packet in her hand. She tossed it back on to the table and went off in search of a cigarette.

McIndoe had barely said a word since they'd left the safe house in the Opel Blitz troop carrier for the five-mile journey into the centre of Palermo. He sat up front with the driver who'd tried on several occasions to strike up a conversation with him but each time McIndoe had only ventured a monosyllabic reply. The driver had taken the hint and fallen silent as well until they reached their destination.

'We're here,' the driver announced as he brought the truck to a halt. The engine was kept running.

McIndoe pushed open the passenger door and climbed down on to the road. In his freshly pressed uniform, he looked every inch the part of a proud captain of the German *Wehrmacht*. He made his way round to the back of the truck. The tarpaulin flaps were pulled down and tied together, shielding from sight the occupants inside. He untied the flaps and pulled them open. Hillyard and Evans, who were both wearing German uniforms and armed with standard infantry rifles, scrambled out of the truck. Stella grabbed McIndoe's hand to steady herself before jumping down nimbly on to the road. Even in an unflattering loose-fitting dress, a pair of scuffed sandals, and without a trace of make-up on her face, she still managed to look beautiful. The clothes had been specially chosen to give her the appearance of a local. It was all part of the plan.

'We'll give you a twenty-second head-start,' McIndoe told her. 'Make sure you're in place when we get there.'

She hurried across the road and ducked into a narrow alleyway where she quickly became aware of an overpowering stench of rotting flesh around her. Putting her hand over her nose to block out the awful smell, she quickened her step and had covered half the distance through the alley when she came upon the decomposing body of a dog which lay beside a collection of rusted metal bins which were overflowing with putrefying refuse. Then, as she turned away, she thought she saw the dog move. She must have been mistaken, she was quick to tell herself. Then the horrifying realization of what she'd witnessed became apparent when a tight ball of writhing maggots tumbled from its half-open mouth and broke apart on contact with the ground. She recoiled in horror when several maggots landed close to her foot and, fighting back the rising bile in her throat, she ran to the end of the alley where she paused to regain her composure.

She looked across at the church on the opposite side of the road. Her eyes went to the belfry which, according to the Partisans, had a perfect view of the hotel and the surrounding area. A lone German soldier stood guard in the belfry. The priest – who'd been evicted from the church the previous afternoon as part of the security arrangements put into effect for the meeting of Kesselring and his chiefs-of-staff at the hotel – had told the Partisans that the church was now a virtual fortress, with every door and window locked from the inside. Entry would be difficult. But essential if they were to monitor Ravallo's progress. That way, if anything were to go wrong, they could abort the operation and withdraw discreetly, without incurring any further losses to the team. And with that thought in mind, she and McIndoe had come up with a plan to gain them access to the church . . .

She heard the sound of footsteps pounding behind her, and looked round to see Evans and Hillyard running down the alley towards her. She darted out from the mouth of the alleyway and ran to the front of the church, where she banged loudly on the solid oak door as if desperate to be given sanctuary from her pursuers. Although she didn't dare look up, she knew that the pounding would have alerted the soldier in the bell-tower above her. She looked round as Evans and Hillyard emerged from the alley. She turned to flee again.

'Halt, or I'll shoot!' Evans called out, his rifle trained on her.

'Don't shoot her,' Hillyard ordered. 'You heard what the captain said. She's to be taken alive.'

Stella darted round the side of the church. As she ran towards the vestry window, she heard the soldier in the belfry call down to Hillyard and Evans, 'What's going on?'

There was a pause before Hillyard shouted back, 'She's a member of the local Resistance. We've got orders to take her in for questioning.'

Stella paused in front of the vestry window and glanced up at the belfry, but all she could see was the tip of the steeple from where she stood. She picked up a brick, crossed herself quickly, then hurled it through the window. She turned away as the glass shattered, then quickly reached through the jagged aperture and opened the window. She pulled herself up on to the ledge and jumped into the vestry.

For a few moments she looked around, and was about to make for the door leading into the nave when suddenly it was thrown open with such force that it slammed back against the wall. A German soldier entered the room, panting, his rifle trained on her. It was the same soldier she'd seen in the belfry. Alerted by the sound of the breaking glass, he'd obviously come down to investigate the noise. The plan seemed to be working . . .

It was then that Hillyard and Evans appeared at the open window and peered into the vestry. 'Keep her there,' Hillyard told him. 'I'm coming in.'

'Nobody comes in here,' the soldier replied without taking his eyes off Stella.

'What are you talking about?' Hillyard demanded. 'I'll climb in through the window, open the back door, then we can take her off your hands.'

'My orders are not to allow anyone in here without the proper authorization,' came the reply. 'And that authorization can only come from my superior officer.'

'What's the hold-up?' a voice called out brusquely. Stella saw McIndoe's face appear at the window. Hillyard explained briefly what he'd been told and McIndoe looked at the soldier. 'I'm Captain Strauss. Seventy-sixth Infantry Division. Who are you?'

'Corporal Neumann, Third Parachute Regiment, sir,' came the respectful reply.

'Neumann, this woman is wanted in connection with a series of bomb attacks on *Wehrmacht* installations here in Palermo. We also believe that she may know something about a possible attempt on the life of Field-Marshal Kesselring while he's visiting the island. Now, either you let us in so that we can take her away for questioning, or else I'll see to it that you're held personally responsible should anything happen to Field-Marshal Kesselring because of your insubordination.'

Neumann swallowed nervously. 'Has Major Riedler been told that Field-Marshal Kesselring's life may be in danger, sir?'

'I believe he was briefed personally this morning by *Standartenführer* Brausch, the head of the Gestapo here in Sicily,' McIndoe told him.

'I'll let you in, sir,' Neumann said reluctantly. He backed slowly towards the door, careful never to take his eyes off Stella, then pulled back the bolt and opened the door.

McIndoe was the first to enter the vestry. He snapped his fingers at Hillyard and Evans. 'Take her away.'

Neumann didn't look at the two men, which allowed Hillyard to steal up silently behind him, clamp a hand over his mouth, and sink a thin, six-inch stiletto blade into his stomach. Stella looked away as Hillyard twisted the blade up sharply between the ribcage and into the heart. Neumann was dead before Hillyard laid him out carefully on the floor. He wiped the blade on Neumann's tunic, then hurried towards the belfry to assume his sentry duty. The original plan had taken into account that the soldiers who were manning the roadblock further down the road would have witnessed the incident outside the church: it was essential to allay any suspicions on their part by making it appear as if Neumann had returned to his post in the belfry. Although not as tall as the dead man, Hillyard would pass as him from that distance, especially as the soldiers at the roadblock wouldn't be expecting the deception.

'Go and get the others. Taffy and I will hide the body,' McIndoe said to Stella.

She picked up the dead German's rifle, then went out into an alley at the back of the church. She gave a thumbs-up sign to the driver of the truck which was now parked at the mouth of the alley. When she returned to the vestry, McIndoe and Evans had already removed the body into the nave.

The truck backed up to the vestry door; the tarpaulin cover at the rear was pushed aside and Venucci jumped to the ground. He was wearing a uniform identical to the one McIndoe had on, and was carrying the rucksack containing the SOE radio-transmitter. The two men who got out behind him were dressed similarly to Hillyard and Evans. Gina Roetta was the last out of the truck. She had on the same baggy dress and scuffed sandals that Stella was wearing. Even their hair was similarly tied in a ponytail. Venucci ushered his colleagues into the vestry, then bolted the door behind them.

'The driver will take the truck round to the front of the church,' Venucci said to McIndoe when he and Evans returned to the vestry.

'You know what to do,' McIndoe said to Venucci.

Gina grinned at Stella like a mischievous schoolgirl, then followed Venucci out into the nave. The other Partisans went after them. Venucci unlocked the front door and she was marched down the steps at gunpoint to the waiting truck. She was bundled unceremoniously into the back of the truck, and Venucci secured the flaps once the other two men had climbed in after her. He slammed the church door shut, looked around at the small crowd who'd gathered to watch the drama unfold, then walked to the front of the truck and climbed in beside the driver. The truck drove off, heading away from the hotel.

McIndoe carefully, and quietly, slid the bolt back into place, then crossed to the rear pew and sat down. 'It looks as if it's worked,' he said to Stella.

'I told you it would,' she replied with a relieved smile as she sat down in the pew opposite him. 'What was all that about an attempt on Kesselring's life?'

'Improvisation,' McIndoe said. 'When I realized we weren't going to get in without the proper authorization, I had to do some fast thinking to bluff our way into the church.'

'Better you than me, sir,' Evans said with a wry smile. 'I couldn't have come up with something like that on the spur of the moment. But then that's why you're an officer and I'm just a peterman.'

'A peterman?' Stella said with a frown.

'A safe-breaker,' Evans said, chuckling at her startled expression. 'Don't worry, I've served my time for my misdemeanours. Now I'm strictly legitimate. I have my own explosives firm in Swansea.' He noticed her frown reappear. 'That's in Wales, Miss.'

'I had no idea you were . . .' she trailed off uncomfortably.

'A con?' Evans finished the sentence for her. 'As I said, I've paid my dues for my dubious past. Now I just blow Jerry safes, amongst other things.'

'He's the best explosives man we've got in the Firm,' McIndoe said to her.

'I'll remember that the next time I forget the combination to my wall-safe back home,' she said with a smile.

McIndoe got to his feet, removed his peaked cap, and raked his hands through his hair. 'Something on your mind, sir?' Evans asked.

'Yes. Neumann said that his commanding officer was a Major Riedler.' They both nodded but didn't say anything. 'It's got to be Hans Riedler. The last I heard he was a captain in the Third Parachute Regiment during the Axis invasion of Crete. I don't know how much you know about the invasion, but the Third Parachute Regiment landed slap-bang amongst the Aussies at Galatas. They took some dreadful casualties, but still managed to reform and hold off the Aussies until reinforcements arrived. Word is that Riedler personally took charge of the remnants of the unit after their commander was killed. He was subsequently awarded the Iron Cross With Oak Leaves, Swords and Diamonds, which is the highest commendation that can be bestowed on a German officer.'

'You almost say that as if you admire him, sir?' Evans said.

'Why shouldn't I? The man's obviously a damn fine soldier who leads from the front.'

'He's also probably a Nazi,' Evans said.

'Not from what I've been led to believe,' McIndoe said. 'He's always been a career soldier with no interest in politics. I'm just surprised that neither of you have ever heard of him before.'

'Nicky would probably know about him,' Stella said. 'Assuming, of course, this is the same Riedler who was at Crete.'

'It's too much of a coincidence for it not to be. I'd stake my life on it.'

'From what you've just told us about him, sir, you might have to do just that,' Evans said.

'We might all have to before this is over,' McIndoe replied with a knowing look in Stella's direction. 'But for the moment all we can do is wait. It's up to Nicky now.'

Ravallo was on the last of the cigarettes he'd found in the packet on the kitchen table. He didn't know who'd left them there, but they'd been an invaluable ally in helping to alleviate the mounting tension of the last hour as he waited restlessly for the call from their contact, Pizzoni, at the hotel to signal that the conference was over. It wasn't so much the uncertainty of what lay ahead which bothered him, it was the damn waiting. But there was little he could do about it.

He was standing at the lounge window of a safe house in the old Arabic quarter of La Kalsa. Not that he could see anything with the drapes closed. He'd left the last safe house in the Kasr in the staff car with Johnson at the wheel shortly after the others had departed in the Opel Blitz truck to initiate their part of the plan. The staff car was now parked inside a lock-up garage at the back of the house to prevent it from being spotted by a passing German patrol. La Kalsa had quickly become a hotbed of insurrection against the reviled German Army who regularly raided the area in force in their endless search for members of the Resistance or those sympathetic to the cause. It was hardly the location he'd have chosen, knowing that the area was teeming with German soldiers and their collaborators, but its close proximity and easy access to the hotel made it an ideal short-term hideout. He hadn't seen Johnson since they'd arrived at the house. Although normally a gregarious person who was happiest around others, he was grateful for the solitude to collect his thoughts. He guessed that Johnson had sensed this. He appreciated the gesture. But now he was ready to take on the daunting challenge which lay ahead of him. And he was confident he could pull it off . . .

The telephone rang, shattering the fragile silence. One. Two. He drew anxiously on the cigarette as it continued to ring. Three. Four. Silence. It was the signal. He grabbed his peaked cap off the table, then moved to the door and threw it open. Johnson was already in the hallway, the keys to the staff car in his hand. Neither man spoke. There was nothing to say. They knew what had to be done.

Lieutenant Bruno Pizzoni's hand was shaking as he slowly replaced the handset after the fourth ring. He clenched his fists tightly together at his sides, desperately trying to calm his frayed nerves. He couldn't afford to let anyone see him like this. He had to get a grip on himself. Sucking in several mouthfuls of air in an attempt to relax himself, he moved to the wall mirror and dusted his hand down the front of his tunic. Then, placing his cap on his head, he left the bedroom on the second floor which he used whenever he was required to stay overnight at the hotel, ignored the lift, and hurried down the red-carpeted stairs to the ground floor. There he paused to look around him slowly. His eyes made contact with the lone receptionist behind the front office desk. He didn't return the man's fleeting smile. His eyes moved on to the soldier who was standing guard beside the revolving doors, then across the vast foyer to the conference-room doors. Two guards there. Both armed. He knew he had no reason to fear them. They couldn't possibly know what was going on. But he did. It would be men like them who'd arrive unexpectedly in the middle of the night and drag him away for questioning if the true nature of his treachery was ever uncovered. He would certainly be taken to Gestapo headquarters on the Piazza Bologni for interrogation. He felt a distinct shiver down his back, as if a pair of jackboots had trampled over his grave. A drop of sweat escaped from under his hat but he brushed it away before it could trickle down the side of his face. He couldn't put it off any longer. It had already been several minutes since the stenographer had rung his room to tell him that she'd completed the typescript for him to take to Field-Marshal Kesselring.

He crossed the foyer to the conference room, his boots echoing across the marble floor. 'Lieutenant Pizzoni,' he announced to the two guards, then removed his identification from his pocket and held it up for them to see. At least his voice had sounded authoritative. That was something in his favour. The two soldiers saluted him, stepping away from the doors to allow him access to the room. As he pushed down the door-handle the relief flooded through him. His hand wasn't shaking. He entered the room, closing the door behind him and smiling politely at the stenographer as he crossed to where she was sitting.

'That's the typescript for Field-Marshal Kesselring,' she said, tapping the sealed folder beside the typewriter. Pizzoni was fluent in several languages, which was one of the reasons why he'd been appointed to the post at the hotel. 'Field-Marshal Kesselring wants it delivered to him personally. If he's not in his suite, he'll either be in the restaurant or the bar.' She got to her feet. 'Well, I'll leave you to it, Lieutenant. It's been a long day and I'm ready to relax in a hot bath. Good-night.'

'Good-night,' Pizzoni said. He picked up the folder and turned it around slowly in his hands. The fact that it was sealed was of little consequence to him. He'd been given an identical seal by the Partisans to replace the one which would have to be broken to get at the typescript. He'd no idea how they'd come by the seal. But then that wasn't important. His instructions were to take the folder to a room on the second floor, hide it underneath the mattress, then burn all the notes made by the officers at the meeting. It was a ritual he performed whenever there was a conference at the hotel. Normally he would deliver the typed notes to the commanding officer first, then destroy the officers' hand-written notes. But not this time. And, if everything went according to plan, when he returned to the bedroom he'd find that the folder had been replaced under the mattress. The seal would be broken, but otherwise the notes would be intact. Which led him to believe that the Resistance intended to photograph the contents of the folder so as not to alert the Germans that they had ever been there. He had no idea how they intended to penetrate the security which had been set up around the hotel. But then that wasn't his concern.

He quickly collected up all the loose sheets of paper which were still strewn across the tables where they'd been left by the German officers. All were to be burnt, except for the stenographer's notes, which would turn up later in a refuse bin at the back of the hotel. It would certainly throw the whole outcome of the meeting into doubt. And, knowing what a shrewd militarist Kesselring was, he would certainly have to re-evaluate the situation. He couldn't take the chance that those notes hadn't been seen by unauthorized eyes. It would mean abandoning the plans which were contained inside the folder and reconvening another meeting at a later date. Pizzoni knew it would cost him his position at the hotel. It would also cost him his rank. He would have lost his dignity and standing amongst his fellow officers, but at least he'd have his family back safely. That was all that really mattered to him . . .

Ravallo was under no illusion about the task which lay ahead of him as the staff car approached the roadblock. It was the first contact he'd have with the élite German para-troopers who had been flown in to guard the hotel. But if these paratroopers had one weakness – which under any other circumstances would have been viewed in a very favourable light – it was that they were regarded as one of the most disciplined units in the *Wehrmacht*. And within the framework of that discipline lay a consummate respect for authority. Ravallo intended to take full advantage of that should the need arise. And he had a feeling it would.

Johnson eased his foot on to the brake when a soldier stepped out into the road and flagged down the staff car. Ravallo saw that the soldier was armed with a Russian PPSh submachine-gun which had obviously been captured on the Eastern Front. The soldier moved to the driver's window and peered in at Johnson. Then his eyes went to Ravallo, and he immediately snapped his boots together and came rigidly to attention. Ravallo returned the salute before winding down the window and holding up his fake Gestapo identity for inspection.

'May I ask the nature of your business here, *Sturmbannführer*?' the soldier asked after checking the ID card.

'No, you may not,' Ravallo replied indignantly. 'Now let me through.'

'I'm afraid I can't do that, sir, not without the proper authorization,' the soldier replied in a firm but polite voice.

Ravallo knew the soldier would have had his orders to challenge anyone wanting access to the hotel. Even a senior Gestapo officer. Now it was time for him to repay his superiors' belief in him when they'd chosen him for the operation. Ravallo snapped his fingers at Johnson – a prearranged signal for just such an eventuality – who jumped out from behind the wheel and opened the back door for him. Ravallo got out of the staff car.

The soldier instinctively stepped back as he took in the tall, menacing figure before him. For a moment Ravallo thought he saw a look of uncertainty in the soldier's eyes. Then it was gone as the man quickly regained his composure. A second soldier approached the staff car and snapped to attention when Ravallo looked at him. Ravallo gave him a curt nod. 'I assume you know who I am?'

'Yes, *Sturmbannführer*,' came the reply.

'Yet still you choose to challenge my authority?' Ravallo said coldly. 'I do not have to justify my actions to you or anyone else. I am answerable only to *Reichsführer* Himmler. Would you dare to question his authority as well?'

'No, *Sturmbannführer*,' the soldier replied as a hesitancy crept into his voice for the first time. 'But we have our orders from our commanding officer. We cannot allow anyone through without the proper authorization.'

'Those are our orders, sir,' the second soldier told him.

'Stand to attention when you address an officer!' Ravallo berated the soldier. 'Who gave you those orders?'

'Our commanding officer, sir. Major Riedler,' the second soldier said.

Ravallo could sense that their nerve was beginning to waver. It was essential he continued on the offensive to keep the upper hand. He crossed to where the second man was standing rigidly to attention, and positioned himself directly in front of him. 'Who is this Riedler anyway? You would dare to put his orders above those of the *Reichsführer*?'

'With all due respect – '

'Silence!' Ravallo thundered, turning away from the two men as if trying to control his fury. Let them sweat a bit. It could only work in his favour. He remained motionless for several seconds, then he swung round again to face them, ready to play his trump card. Reaching into his tunic pocket, he removed the letter which had been found in Schenk's valise. It was written in Himmler's own hand and gave Schenk the authority to go anywhere and see anything he wanted while he was on the island. Anyone daring to question that authority would have to explain themselves to Himmler in person. It certainly wasn't a threat to be taken lightly in view of Himmler's ubiquitous power within the Third Reich. He thrust the letter towards the soldier. 'Read it,' he ordered.

The soldier took the letter hesitantly from him and unfolded it. He shifted uncomfortably on the balls of his feet as he read the contents, then handed it back to Ravallo. He saluted stiffly. 'You may proceed, *Sturmbannführer.*'

'It worked,' Johnson said with a rare smile as he glanced at Ravallo in the reflection of the rearview mirror when they were clear of the roadblock.

'For the moment,' Ravallo replied. 'But you can bet they'll contact Riedler to tell him what's happened. Deceiving them is one thing, but if Kesselring learns about this it's going to be a damn sight harder trying to pull the wool over his eyes.'

'You've got the letter, sir,' Johnson said. 'And even Kesselring can't question its authenticity.'

'But he could question mine. You can be sure he knows a fair amount about the workings of the Gestapo, even though by all accounts he's not too enamoured with the methods they employ. I only have a limited knowledge of the Gestapo. If he were to get into a conversation with me about the Gestapo, I'd be walking barefoot over a bed of broken glass. It would only take one slip-up on my part to blow the whole operation. No, the sooner we're out of here, the better for both of us.'

'Agreed, sir,' Johnson said, then indicated to the hotel ahead. 'Where do you want me to park?'

'At the front,' Ravallo replied. 'Schenk's hardly likely to go sneaking in through the back door, is he? It's essential that I remain in character now that we're so close to the prize.'

Johnson brought the staff car to a halt, switched off the engine, then climbed out and opened the back door. Ravallo got out, smoothed down his tunic, then picked up Schenk's valise and walked purposefully to the revolving doors. In the hotel foyer he was challenged by another soldier. With time now of the essence, he cut to the quick by showing the soldier the letter straight away. The soldier saluted him and resumed his post.

Ravallo paused in the centre of the foyer to get his directions. He'd earlier studied a detailed blueprint of the hotel which the Partisans had procured from a sympathizer at the city hall, and it was now just a matter of spreading the plan out again in his mind. He walked to the lift and was relieved to find that it was already on the ground floor. That meant several valuable seconds had already been saved. Stepping inside, he pressed the button for the second floor. When the cage came to a halt again, he pulled back the grille and stepped out into the corridor. It was deserted. He walked swiftly to a door directly opposite the stairs and removed a key from his pocket. He took his Luger from its holster as he inserted the key into the keyhole, but he knew that if the Germans had laid a trap for him, it would be of little use to him. He had no reason to believe there was a trap: everything seemed to be going according to plan. But there was only one way to find out if his optimism was justified.

Unlocking the door, he pushed it open and peered cautiously into the room. Nobody there. He closed the door again behind him, locked it, then crossed to the bed and slid his hand under the mattress. His fingers touched the folder. He pulled it out, barely able to conceal his excitement, and slit open the seal with the side of his hand. Then, removing a Minox miniature stainless-steel camera from his inside pocket, he sat down on the bed and opened the folder. He scanned the first couple of pages of typed print to establish their credibility. Satisfied that they were genuine, he set about his task without delay.

Captain Jürgen Franke had taken over as the commanding officer of the security detail shortly after seven o'clock that evening, when Riedler had been unexpectedly invited to join Kesselring and his chiefs-of-staff for an aperitif in the bar. Franke was sitting behind the desk in the general manager's office, engrossed in the previous day's edition of the *Volksischer Beobachter*, the official Nazi Party newspaper which he'd found discarded in the corner of the room. A sharp knock on the door startled him and he cursed irritably under his breath before calling, 'Come in.'

The door opened and one of the soldiers who'd been on guard at the roadblock stepped tentatively into the room and saluted Franke.

'What are you doing here, Scherl?' Franke demanded.

'I have something to report, sir,' came the reply.

'Then why didn't you use the field telephone?'

'I thought it best if I were to report either to you or to Major Riedler in person, sir,' Scherl told him. 'Goetz is still on duty at the roadblock.'

'I'm glad to hear it,' Franke retorted sarcastically. 'Now what's so important that you couldn't tell me over the telephone.'

'*Sturmbannführer* Schenk is here, sir.'

Franke immediately sat forward. 'Here, at the hotel?' he asked incredulously.

'Yes, sir.'

'Did he say what he wanted?' Franke asked.

'I asked him, sir, but he refused to divulge the nature of his business. He had a letter from *Reichsführer* Himmler which gave him – '

'Yes, yes, I know about the letters these officers carry with them,' Franke cut in quickly. 'He must be here to see Field-Marshal Kesselring.'

'I assumed that as well, sir,' Scherl said hesitantly.

'What is it?' Franke asked when he saw the uncertainty on Scherl's face.

'Sir, should there be any comeback from *Sturmbannführer* Schenk about the way we conducted ourselves at the roadblock, you will say that we were just carrying out our orders?'

Franke chuckled to himself. 'He gave you a hard time then?'

'You could say that, sir,' Scherl replied, shifting nervously on his heels. 'He was shouting like a madman . . . I . . . I didn't mean to imply that he was mad, sir.'

'I've heard he has something of a reputation for that,' Franke said with a smile. 'But then what do you expect from someone who wields that kind of power?'

'You almost say that as if you envy him, sir.'

'I envy the perks that come with the job. Not the job itself. He'll get the best table and the best service in the top restaurants in Berlin. He'll get the pick of the most beautiful women wherever he goes. A different one every night if he wants. A flat in the best part of the city, probably with a view overlooking the Spree. Exotic food and drink that are rationed to the rest of us. I don't know about you, Scherl, but I certainly wouldn't mind that kind of lifestyle.'

'No, sir,' Scherl replied.

'He's also one of the top swordsmen in the country, did you know that?'

'No, sir, I didn't,' Scherl said.

'Oh yes. He was regarded by many as the finest swordsman ever to have attended the Officers' Academy in Bavaria.'

'Did you know him, sir?' Scherl asked.

'No, he was there some years before me but there was a picture of him, along with the other top swordsmen of their years, in the corridor outside the fencing hall. Our instructor used to boast that he was the only man ever to mark him. Just a slight nick under the left eye but enough to leave a faint scar.'

'There wasn't a scar under his left eye, sir,' Scherl said, shaking his head.

'As I said, it's a very faint scar. You probably didn't notice it.'

'He didn't have a scar, sir,' Scherl replied firmly. 'I should know. We were almost standing toe-to-toe when he was shouting at me. I would have noticed it.'

Franke slowly got to his feet and moved round to the front of the desk. 'Describe *Sturmbannführer* Schenk.'

'About six foot two – '

'The face,' Franke cut in quickly. 'Just the face. That's all I ever saw of him.'

'Angular face; brown eyes; good-looking, I guess,' Scherl said with a quick shrug.

'That sounds like him, but . . .' Franke trailed off and bit his lip pensively as he stared at the carpet. He was suddenly caught in a dilemma. The scar was faint, granted, but Scherl was adamant that there wasn't one. It didn't make any sense. At least to him it didn't. It made him feel distinctly uneasy, especially in light of the warning they'd received from the Gestapo about the possibility of a British SOE team infiltrating the island. What better way of gaining access to the hotel than by impersonating Schenk? But what if he was overreacting? He'd be severely carpeted by Schenk and Riedler if he were wrong, but he knew that as the chief security officer it was his duty to follow up on what Scherl had told him. Also, he was probably the only person in the hotel who could identify Schenk from the photograph which had hung in the academy. He doubted whether Kesselring would know what Schenk looked like. He had to follow his instincts and put his mind at rest, irrespective of the consequences. He grabbed his peaked cap off the desk and moved to the door. He paused to look back at Scherl. 'I want all the exits sealed off until further notice. *Sturmbannführer* Schenk is not to leave the hotel until either Major Riedler or I have had a chance to speak to him. Is that understood?'

'Yes, sir,' Scherl replied.

'See that the guard is doubled on all the exits until further notice. I'm going to speak to Major Riedler.'

Scherl saluted, then hurried from the room. Franke made his way quickly to the bar, where he looked for Riedler amongst the officers who were clustered in small cliques around the room. He finally spotted Riedler seated at a table against the far wall, deep in conversation with General Student and Vice-Admiral Weichold. Riedler noticed Franke hovering anxiously in the doorway, trying to get his attention, and immediately excused himself before crossing to where he was standing.

'Has *Sturmbannführer* Schenk been in here, sir?' Franke asked.

'Schenk?' Riedler replied in amazement. 'You mean he's here at the hotel?'

'Yes, sir.'

'He hasn't been in here as far as I know. Why do you ask?'

Franke explained the situation to him. 'I realize that it may sound very thin to you, sir, but I know that *Sturmbannführer* Schenk definitely has a scar under his left eye. Perhaps Scherl didn't see it – although he was adamant it wasn't there – but I thought it best not to take any chances after the warning we received earlier about the SOE. It would be the perfect way for one of them to get past the roadblock.'

'Wait here,' Riedler said. He went back to the table where he whispered in Student's ear. Student put his glass down and followed Riedler back to Franke.

Franke repeated to Student what he'd already told Riedler.

'He certainly hasn't been in here,' Student told him. 'And that alone makes me suspicious. Whatever his reasons for coming to the hotel, assuming that it is Schenk, you'd have expected him at least to have had the courtesy to introduce himself to Field-Marshal Kesselring before going about his business, whatever that may be.' He put a hand on Franke's shoulder. 'You did right to have all the exits sealed off until we've had a chance to investigate the matter further.'

'If it does turn out to be *Sturmbannführer* Schenk, sir, I doubt he'll see it that way,' Franke said.

'We'll say that I gave the order for him to be detained for further security clearance,' Student said, much to Franke's obvious relief. 'He wouldn't question my authority.'

Scherl hurried into view at the end of the corridor, where he paused to draw breath before striding purposefully to where the three officers were standing. He came to attention in front of them. 'Stand easy,' Riedler told him. 'What is it?'

'*Sturmbannführer* Schenk's in the foyer, sir,' Scherl told him. 'He's kicking up a storm about not being allowed to leave the hotel. I don't know how much longer the men can keep him there without having to physically restrain him. And they're not willing to do that. Not to a senior officer of the Gestapo.'

'Let me handle it,' Student said to Riedler. 'I'll take him through to the manager's office. That is the room you're using as your base, isn't it?'

Riedler nodded.

'I want you and Franke to remain here until he's safely inside the office. Once he's there, Franke can come through to make the identification. If it is him, all well and good. No harm will have been done, apart from a slight dent in his dignity. I regard that as a small price to pay to give us all peace of mind. If he is an impostor, however, we'll have got him cornered in the room. There will be no way for him to escape and alert any of his colleagues who may already be in the vicinity.' He turned to Scherl. 'OK, soldier, let's go and meet this *Sturmbannführer* Schenk.'

Ravallo had realized that something was wrong as soon as he emerged from the lift and crossed to the revolving doors. The guard had been doubled at the main entrance, and his path had been blocked by both soldiers when he'd tried to leave the hotel. He'd berated them furiously for daring to challenge him, all to no avail; even the personal letter from Himmler had made no impression on them. His every tirade was met with the same polite reply: they had their orders to detain him until his security clearance could be verified by their commanding officer. Had something happened while he'd been in the bedroom photographing the contents of the folder? He knew he hadn't made any mistakes. Had Pizzoni let on about the breach of security?

Then why hadn't they come to the room and arrested him there? No, that didn't make any sense. So why the sudden clampdown? Or was he just overreacting? Whatever it was, he knew that he'd have some careful explaining to do before he was allowed to leave the building. He knew that Johnson could see what was happening, but they'd already agreed not to do anything hasty should any problem arise while he was inside the hotel. Sure, he could shoot the two soldiers and make his escape, but just how far would they get in the staff car? And that kind of impulsiveness could put the rest of the team in danger. He'd been made aware of the risks when he'd first accepted the mission back in Gibraltar. Now it was up to him to talk his way out of trouble. Easier said than done, but it was all he had left going for him . . .

'*Sturmbannführer* Schenk?' a voice queried behind him.

Ravallo's arm shot out in a Nazi salute at the sight of a senior officer. He recognized Student from the photographs of Kesselring's chiefs-of-staff which had been included in the dossier forwarded to him by Military Intelligence in Washington. Student touched his fingers to the rim of his peaked cap, then extended a hand of greeting to him.

Ravallo shook it firmly. 'It's an honour for me to meet such a legend, *Herr General*,' Ravallo said, laying on the obsequious charm which Schenk was renowned for when it came to dealing with superior officers.

'We had no idea that you were coming here today, Schenk,' Student said.

'I try, whenever possible, not to give advance warning of where I'm going, *Herr General*,' Ravallo replied. 'It comes with the job.'

'I'm sure it does,' Student said with a genial smile. 'Please, why don't you come through to my office. We can talk more privately in there.'

Ravallo glanced at his watch. 'With all due respect, *Herr General*, I am rather pressed for time. This was just meant to be a brief stop to check on the security arrangements here at the hotel.'

'Excellent. I'd certainly be interested in the Gestapo's assessment of our security set-up here. I'm always open to constructive criticism should the situation merit it.'

'Of course, *Herr General*,' Ravallo said, knowing he had no choice but to obey. He followed Student to the manager's office where he was directed to the armchair against the wall.

Student sat down behind the desk and gestured Scherl into the office before turning to Schenk. 'A drink, perhaps?'

'No, thank you, *Herr General*,' Ravallo said.

'Bring me the drink I left in the bar,' Student said, the code they'd agreed for Scherl to fetch Riedler and Franke and to have two soldiers posted in the corridor, out of sight of the door. Not that Ravallo could have seen them anyway from where he was sitting, but Student had never been a man to take any unnecessary risks. He waited until Scherl had left, then looked across the desk at Ravallo. 'So, tell me, Schenk, what do you make of our security arrangements?'

'From what I've already seen, I certainly can't fault them, *Herr General*,' Ravallo replied. 'But then I didn't really expect to find anything amiss here. Not with you handling the security operation.'

'Oh, but I'm not,' Student was quick to correct him. 'I'm just here for the meeting. All security has been handled by the members of the Third Parachute Regiment under the leadership of Major Hans Riedler. You may have heard of him. He's something of a legend amongst the paratroopers.'

'I've heard of him, but I've never met him,' Ravallo replied.

'Talk of the devil,' Student said as Riedler appeared in the doorway. He gestured him into the office and introduced him to Ravallo. His eyes went to Franke as he stepped into the room. 'And this is Major Riedler's deputy, Captain Jürgen Franke.'

Franke saluted Ravallo. 'I've heard a lot about you, sir. I was at the Officers' Academy in '37. You were regarded as one of the finest swordsmen ever to have passed through there.'

'That was a long time ago,' Ravallo replied. 'Unfortunately I don't practise as much as I'd like to these days.'

'I remember the fencing instructor, Steffenberg, held you in very high esteem,' Franke said.

'Steffenberg?' Ravallo replied with a frown, quickly recalling the section in the dossier on Schenk's time at the academy. 'He was a lecturer in military tactics. Don't you mean Sigfried Preuss? He's been the senior fencing coach at the academy for years.'

'You've certainly done your homework, I'll give you that,' Franke said, then pulled the Luger from his hip-holster and trained it on Ravallo. This isn't Otto Schenk, sir.'

'How dare you – '

'Save it!' Student cut in sharply across Ravallo's outburst as Riedler relieved Ravallo of his pistol. 'Search him.'

Franke shoved Ravallo against the wall and pressed the Luger into his back as he carefully frisked him. He found a sleeve dagger secured to Ravallo's forearm, as well as the miniature camera which was concealed in the inside pocket of his tunic. He handed them both to Riedler. He then spun Ravallo around and ripped the buttons off the front of his tunic. On closer inspection one of the buttons contained a small waterproofed pivot-compass and a second a cyanide capsule. The other buttons were discarded and the two incriminating ones placed on the desk in front of Student.

Ravallo had barely had time to catch his breath, let alone put up any kind of fight when he'd been so expertly frisked by Franke. Suddenly, within the space of a few seconds, his whole cover had been stripped bare. How had Franke known that he wasn't Schenk? Had the two men met before? Franke's name hadn't been mentioned in the dossier. Had it something to do with the Officers' Academy in Bavaria? Not that it really mattered now that Franke had uncovered the deception. There was no point in keeping up the pretence any longer. He knew when he was beaten.

Student tipped the cyanide capsule out into the palm of his hand, then looked up at Ravallo. 'I believe you call this an L-pill. Who are you working for? British Intelligence? American Military Intelligence?'

Ravallo said nothing. Franke clamped his fist around the butt of his pistol and punched Ravallo savagely in the stomach. Franke grabbed Ravallo's hair viciously as he doubled over in pain, forcing him to look up at him. 'Answer the General.'

'Franke, that's enough!' Student barked. 'His driver's sitting in the staff car at the front of the hotel. Get him, but I don't want any force used on him. If their colleagues are watching the hotel, they mustn't suspect for a moment that anything's wrong. Tell him that Schenk's been invited to have a drink with Field-Marshal Kesselring. Invite him in for a drink as well. But no force. Is that understood?'

'Yes, sir,' Franke replied, leaving the room.

Riedler shoved Ravallo down into the armchair, then stepped back in case Ravallo were to try and make a desperate grab for his pistol. Student replaced the cyanide capsule in the button, then picked up the miniature camera and turned it around slowly in his hands. 'I see that you've already used up most of the exposures on the film. Tell me, what exactly is on here?'

Silence.

He shrugged. 'We can get the film developed soon enough. My guess would be that you've photographed the contents of the folder which was supposed to have been delivered to Field-Marshal Kesselring.'

'If that's true, sir, it means that the Italian orderly must be in on this as well,' Riedler concluded.

'Have him brought here,' Student said.

Riedler summoned one of the paratroopers into the room and relayed Student's orders to him. He waited until the soldier had left, then gestured to Ravallo's black leather gloves. 'Take them off.'

Ravallo knew what Riedler was thinking. He thought momentarily about defying him but realized the futility of such an action. The gloves would be removed, with or without his consent. He pulled them off his hands and tossed them on to the desk. He noticed a smug smile tug at the corners of Riedler's mouth when the German saw the bandage wound tightly around his left hand.

'What is it, Riedler?' Student demanded.

'I know who he is, sir. Major Nicholas Ravallo. American Military Intelligence.'

'How do you know that?' Student asked.

'The Gestapo were given a tip-off that Ravallo had injured his left hand during a *Luftwaffe* raid on an air-base in Malta a few days ago,' Riedler told him. 'They passed that information on to us when we got here. It has to be him, sir.'

'Are you Major Ravallo?' Student asked. No answer. 'Where is Otto Schenk? Is he dead?' Student continued, leaning forward and clasping his hands on the desk in front of him. Ravallo remained silent. 'How did you know about the meeting here today?' Still silence. 'Major, it would be in your best interests to cooperate with me. The alternative would be for me to hand you over to the Gestapo for further interrogation. Is that what you'd prefer?' No reply. Student exhaled deeply, then sat back in the chair. 'You will talk. One way or the other, you will talk. I can promise you that.'

Neville Johnson appeared in the doorway, his hands clasped on top of his head. Franke was directly behind him, the Luger pressed into the small of his back. The buttons on Johnson's tunic had been ripped off, and Franke spilled them out on to the desk, along with his sidearm and sleeve dagger, before shoving Johnson roughly towards the chair where Ravallo was sitting.

'Don't say anything,' Ravallo told Johnson in Italian.

'What was that, Major?' Student asked. Not surprisingly, he didn't receive an answer. His eyes went to Franke. 'Any trouble with the driver?'

'No, sir. I frisked him once we were inside the foyer, then I brought him straight here.'

'I assume you're going to be as stubborn as Major Ravallo?' Student asked Johnson. There was no response, not even a flicker of surprise in Johnson's eyes at the mention of Ravallo's name. Student could see that they were good. But there was a way to break them. He picked up the receiver and asked to be put through to Colonel Ernst Brausch at the Gestapo headquarters on the Piazza Bologni.

TEN

'I don't like it,' McIndoe said warily.

'We don't know that anything's wrong down there,' Stella replied. Both were sitting with their backs against the low belfry wall. Neither could be seen from the street below.

'Nicky should have been out of there ten minutes ago,' McIndoe said. 'And why did Johnson go into the hotel? That wasn't part of the plan.'

'He did go into the hotel voluntarily, sir,' Hillyard said, looking at the empty staff car which was still parked at the front of the hotel. 'If he had been in any trouble, he'd have resisted, if only to alert us.'

'That's exactly what the Germans would want us to think if they've captured them,' McIndoe chided him. 'They'll have guessed that the hotel's under surveillance. What better way of lulling us into a false sense of security than by making out Neville's gone into the hotel voluntarily? We don't know what's happening in there now, do we?'

'So why haven't they flooded the area with troops to try and flush us out if they think we're out here?' Stella asked.

'Give them time,' McIndoe replied.

'I think you're overreacting, Sam,' Stella said. 'Why should anything have gone wrong in there anyway? Nobody's going to question the letter Nicky's got with him. No, my guess is that he's probably having a drink with Kesselring right now. It's just the crazy kind of thing he'd do.'

'I'm not so sure,' Hillyard said, craning his neck to look down at the approach road.

'What is it?' McIndoe demanded.

'Troop carriers, sir. Two of them. Both headed this way.'

'I knew it!' McIndoe crossed, doubled over, to the steps that led down to the nave, hurrying down the steps until the floor was visible below him. Although unable to see Evans from where he was standing, he knew the Welshman was on guard at the main door. 'Taffy?' he hissed, unwilling to raise his voice in case it were to carry beyond the belfry walls. It was doubtful whether anyone could hear him above the sound of the approaching trucks, but there was no reason to take the chance. There was no reply from Evans. 'Taffy?' he repeated, this time more forcefully. He heard the sound of approaching footsteps, and Evans appeared directly beneath him. McIndoe gestured for him to come up, then returned to the belfry and crouched down beside Stella. His eyes went to Hillyard. 'What's going on down there, Bruce?'

'One of the trucks has stopped, sir. It's parked diagonally across the road about three hundred yards away from the church. The second truck has been cleared through the roadblock and is now approaching the hotel.'

'Is there any sign of troop movement from the first truck?' McIndoe asked.

'Not as yet, sir, no. All I can see are the two soldiers in the cab section. But no movement from the back.'

Evans arrived breathlessly at the top of the stairs. He crouched down to listen with mounting unease as McIndoe quickly briefed him on the events unfolding in the street below. 'You all know the drill,' McIndoe said when he'd finished. 'We have to abort the operation and pull out before the whole area's swarming with troops.'

'I'm not going anywhere,' Stella told him bluntly.

'What are you talking about?' McIndoe demanded. 'You were there when Starr gave us specific orders to abort – '

'To hell with Starr and his orders,' Stella cut in sharply. 'You know exactly what would happen if Nicky and Johnson were handed over to the Gestapo for interrogation. They'd be tortured for days and then executed. You of all people should know the contempt the Gestapo hold towards Allied spies. You three go if you want, but I'm damned if I'm going to abandon them.'

'I'm the senior officer here, Stella,' McIndoe said, barely able to contain his mounting anger. 'You disobey my orders and you'll find yourself up in front of a court-martial when we get back to Malta.'

'I'll take my chances,' Stella replied, holding McIndoe's withering glare.

'Me too,' Evans said softly from the stairs. 'I'm with you, Miss. I say we bail them out before the Gestapo can get their claws into them.'

'Count me in as well,' Hillyard added.

McIndoe slumped back against the wall. 'This is tantamount to mutiny, do you realize that? Doesn't that mean anything to any of you?'

'You'd better leave now if you want to reach the safe house, sir, before the Germans bring more troops into the area,' Evans said, ignoring McIndoe's outburst.

McIndoe stared in disbelief at Evans. He could have understood Hillyard disobeying an order. But Taffy Evans? It seemed inconceivable. Now his mind was in turmoil. There wasn't time to try and make them change their minds. They'd made their decision. Now it was his turn. Either he played it by the book and returned alone to the MTB, or else he went along with them and risked the full wrath of Starr when he returned to Malta. He knew if he walked away now he'd never be able to live with himself if they didn't make it back safely to Malta. But at the same time, disobeying a direct order from Starr would cost him his pips. It could even cost him his career. A career that was already being tipped by some in Baker Street as having a great future. *It's time to make a decision,* he said to himself. *Are you with them or not?*

'Trouble,' Hillyard called out over his shoulder, shattering McIndoe's delicate train of thought.

'What is it?' Stella replied, as if having now assumed command of the new rebel unit.

'Two Gestapo staff cars have just come into view at the end of the road. They're heading this way. They're being chaperoned by an armoured vehicle. It's a *Panzerspähwagen Sonderkraftfahrzeug* 222, armed with the usual twenty-millimetre cannon and coaxial machine-gun.'

'They're obviously on their way to the hotel to take Nicky and Johnson back to Gestapo headquarters for interrogation,' she said grimly.

'Excellent,' McIndoe announced. All eyes turned to him, waiting for him to expand on his surprise outburst. He raised his eyebrows questioningly at their quizzical looks. 'Would you prefer to try and spring them from the hotel?'

'Does this mean you're with us, sir?' Evans asked with a grin.

'You'd never pull it off without me,' McIndoe replied dryly.

'Thanks, Sam,' Stella said softly.

'Don't thank me yet. We've still got to put together a viable plan to get them away from the Gestapo. And we have to do it before they reach Gestapo headquarters because, once they're inside the Piazza Bologni, it'll be too late to save them.'

'A plan's already been put together,' Stella announced. 'I drew it up earlier with Giani – Giancarlo Massimo – in case something like this happened. Sam, all you have to do is contact him on the radio and say – *send the doctor.* That's all. He'll know what to do.'

McIndoe was about to press her for further details of the plan, but quickly dismissed the idea. There would be time for explanations later. 'Taffy, where's the radio?'

'I left it in the vestry, sir. Do you want me to get it for you?'

'No, I'll contact him from there. I won't be long.'

'I'm coming with you,' Stella said.

'There's no need . . .' McIndoe trailed off when he remembered the agreement he'd made with her and Ravallo at the farmhouse. He wasn't to use the radio without at least one of them in attendance. Although now faced with a desperate crisis which could ultimately cost them their lives, it brought home sharply to him just how divided they still were, underneath the glossy façade of a 'team'. 'Taffy, you wait here with Bruce.'

'I think it would be better if I came with you, sir,' Evans suggested.

'No.'

'But if the Germans were to see Stella dressed like that – '

'Just do as you're told!'

Evans was about to say something, thought better of it, then slumped back against the wall and watched McIndoe hurry after Stella, who'd already disappeared down the stairs.

Standartenführer Ernst Brausch waited for his driver to open the back door, then stepped out of the staff car. His eyes lingered on the group of soldiers who'd alighted from the back of the stationary truck and were now standing around idly awaiting further instructions. He looked beyond the truck and saw that a succession of roadblocks, manned by paratroopers, had been set up to seal off all exits within a two hundred yard radius of the hotel. At least that was something, he thought to himself, then snapped his fingers at the junior officer who was hovering close to him. They both entered the hotel, the junior officer close behind him. Student was waiting in the foyer.

'Have the prisoners said anything since you rang me, *Herr General*?' Brausch asked.

Student shook his head. 'We can't get anything out of them. That's why I called you. It's imperative that we get to the bottom of this as quickly as possible.'

'We will make them talk,' Brausch predicted confidently. 'I contacted *Reichsführer* Himmler in Berlin before I came here. The *Reichsführer* has ordered me to employ any means necessary to find *Sturmbannführer* Schenk. It is possible that he may already be dead, but I would have thought he'd be more use to the enemy alive.'

'We've also arrested the senior orderly at the hotel. He's an Italian officer – Pizzoni. He's been more cooperative than the others. According to him, the Resistance kidnapped his family last night to force him to leave the folder containing the plans in one of the bedrooms for Ravallo to photograph. I think his involvement goes deeper than that though. How else could they have known about the meeting unless they had inside information?'

'That's something we'll find out when you hand him over to us for interrogation, *Herr General*,' Brausch said.

'Take him, he's no use to us. You'll have to excuse me though. I'm due to give a briefing to Field-Marshal Kesselring and his chiefs-of-staff about the events here this evening. The prisoners are under guard in the manager's office. Major Riedler is waiting for you there. You'll deal with him from now on.'

'Of course, *Herr General*,' Brausch said stiffly.

'I want to be kept fully informed on any new developments,' Student told him. 'I'll be staying at the hotel tonight. It doesn't matter what time it is, I want to be told. Is that understood?'

'Perfectly, *Herr General*,' Brausch replied. A chilling smile touched his thin lips. 'With the resources I have at my disposal, I have every confidence of extracting the truth from them before you've even retired for the night. That way your sleep will be undisturbed.'

'I very much doubt that, Brausch,' Student said, walking off in the direction of the restaurant where Kesselring and his senior officers were waiting for him.

Brausch entered the manager's office and nodded absently in response to the salutes given him by Riedler and Franke. His only interest was in the three handcuffed prisoners in the corner of the room. He studied each of them in turn, then sat down and poked a gloved finger through the contents of their pockets which had been placed in three separate piles on the desk in front of him. He picked up the identity papers that American Military Intelligence had produced for Ravallo. Their authenticity impressed even him. Then he opened the letter from Himmler and recognized it as the same one Schenk had shown him when they'd met at Gestapo headquarters the previous evening. He sat back in the chair and pressed his palms together under his chin as he looked at the prisoners. His eyes finally settled on Ravallo. 'Major Ravallo, I am *Standartenführer* Ernst Brausch, head of the Gestapo here in Sicily. But then I'm sure you know that already. I have no desire to see you broken under interrogation, but if you persist in refusing to answer the questions put to you, you will leave me with no alternative. And, let me assure you, everything you've ever heard about our methods of interrogation are true. We will get the truth out of you, one way or the other. Personally, I hope we can resolve this temporary impasse in a civilized manner. But then it's not up to me, is it?'

There was no response. His eyes flickered to Riedler. 'Take the other two prisoners outside. I want to speak to Ravallo alone.'

Franke hauled Johnson roughly to his feet and marched him from the room. Riedler shoved Pizzoni into the corridor after them and closed the door behind him. The two paratroopers on duty outside the office grabbed Pizzoni, and he was ordered to face the wall. Johnson was told to do likewise and he watched out of the corner of his eye as Franke approached Riedler. When they spoke it was out of earshot of their men.

'Why do you think he wanted to speak to Ravallo alone?' Franke asked.

'I don't know, and frankly I don't care either,' Riedler replied. 'The sooner that bastard's off the premises, the better for all concerned.'

'I won't be sorry to see the back of Ravallo either,' Franke agreed.

'I wasn't talking about Ravallo,' Riedler replied. A look of horror replaced the smile on Franke's face. 'I know your true loyalties lie with the Party,' Riedler continued, 'and that's your right. You respect people like Brausch. I don't. And, as a career soldier, I never will. I have nothing but contempt for him and his kind. But then I expect you were told all about my outspoken views by your SS superiors before you were posted to my unit.'

'Sir, I don't know what you're talking about,' Franke replied in amazement.

'Are you going to tell me you were never with the SS?'

'I was with an SS unit in North Africa, sir. You already know that. But if you're implying that I'm some kind of spy sent here . . .' Franke trailed off and shook his head in disbelief. 'No, sir. I'm your second-in-command and my loyalties are with you and this company.'

'I'm glad to hear it,' Riedler said in a less than convincing tone of voice.

The office door opened, and Brausch led Ravallo out into the corridor. He handed Ravallo over to the two paratroopers, then made his way to where Riedler and Franke were standing. 'Before leaving Malta, Ravallo's colleagues were given specific orders to abort the operation should any of them be caught. It's my guess that they've already left the area and are heading back to Malta with their tails between their legs.'

'Did Ravallo tell you that, *Herr Standartenführer*?' Franke asked.

'That is no concern of yours,' Brausch told him firmly. 'In light of this information, however, I've already issued orders for security to be tightened at all railway stations, roadblocks and ports across the country. They won't get far.' He snapped his fingers at the two paratroopers who were guarding the prisoners. 'Take them away. But I want Major Ravallo to ride in my car. We can talk more privately in there.' He waited until the prisoners had been led away, then turned to Riedler. 'You can be sure there will be a full investigation into this serious breach of security.'

'I'd welcome it,' Riedler replied. 'I know I've got nothing to hide.'

'I'm glad to hear it, because I intend to lobby Field-Marshal Kesselring to allow an external Gestapo unit to handle the investigation. Preferably one from Berlin. You can explain yourself to them.'

'As I said, I've got nothing to hide. I don't honestly see how any of my men could have known that Ravallo was an impostor. Had it not been for Franke's vigilance, Ravallo would have got away. I think you'll find the investigation will be centred more around how the Resistance managed to get hold of a letter in the *Reichsführer*'s own handwriting which gave the bearer unlimited access to all military installations here in Sicily. You'd have thought, considering the very nature of the meeting here today, that the local Gestapo would have had the foresight to have forwarded a photograph of Schenk to us, especially in light of your earlier warning about the possibility of an SOE operation somewhere on the island. But as I said, I welcome any investigation, irrespective of who carries it out.'

'I've heard a lot about you, Riedler,' Brausch said disdainfully. 'Your disrespectful insubordination towards your superior officers. The way you flout or just blatantly disregard your orders. You may be regarded in some quarters as a war hero after the assault on Crete last year, but that doesn't wash with me. You're just another soldier as far as I'm concerned and, quite frankly, I don't like you or your attitude.'

'Believe me, the feeling's mutual,' Riedler replied as his eyes went to the Iron Cross on Brausch's chest. 'You know, I can still remember a time when you had to earn your medals by risking your life in battle for your country. Things have certainly changed. Berlin's obviously not too fussy about who they decorate these days.'

'I won this helping to clear the ghettos of Warsaw,' came the indignant reply.

'Yes, I've heard all about the Gestapo's brave heroism during the Polish campaign. Rounding up defenceless civilians and executing them in front of their families. You must be really proud of yourself.'

'How dare you speak to me like that!' Brausch snapped, his whole body shaking with rage. He sucked in several mouthfuls of air, struggling to contain his surging fury, before levelling a finger at Riedler. 'You've gone too far this time. I'll see to it that you're put on report for gross insubordination to a superior officer. I'll have your head for this, Riedler. I swear I will.'

'I'd be more worried about my own head if I were you. Correct me if I'm wrong, but I was under the impression that your men were supposed to have been protecting Schenk while he was over here. If it's true, then they've failed miserably, haven't they? And, from what I've heard, the *Reichsführer* doesn't take too kindly to that sort of incompetence. The next time we see each other we could be on the Eastern Front. Who knows, you might even get a chance to earn that medal after all.'

Brausch glared furiously at Riedler, then strode briskly down the corridor and disappeared from view. The soles of his boots echoed across the foyer; then there was silence. There was a look of disbelief on Franke's face when he addressed Riedler. 'Sir, you could lose your command if *Standartenführer* Brausch files a report against you. No military tribunal would tolerate that kind of insubordination towards a superior officer.'

'Brausch's finished and he knows it. He'll be far too pre-occupied with trying to save his own neck in anticipation of the outcome of the investigation to be bothered about filing some report against me. But even if he should decide to do so, it would still only be his word against ours. The tribunal would see it as little more than the word of a bitter man in the final death throes of his waning power.' Riedler looked Franke directly in the face. 'Unless, of course, you chose to testify against me and to abandon all your previous loyalties to your commanding officer.'

Franke smiled faintly to himself, then looked up as if addressing someone above him. 'I was certainly surprised when I heard that *Standartenführer* Brausch had chosen to file an insubordination report against Major Riedler, sir. After all, I was with them at the time and never once did Major Riedler ever say anything that could have possibly warranted this action. I do, however, remember *Standartenführer* Schenk saying that he didn't like Major Riedler. For some reason he seemed to resent Major Riedler's successes on the battlefield. Far be it from me to speculate, sir, but could this have been the spiteful reaction of an embittered man, especially in view of the Gestapo's own investigation which proved beyond any doubt the negligence of his men in providing adequate protection for *Sturmbannführer* Schenk on his recent visit to Sicily?'

'You've just become the key defence witness should the need arise,' Riedler said. 'Come on, we've still got work to do.'

The smile faltered on Franke's face as he watched Riedler walk away. So Riedler knew he'd been sent by the SS to spy on him. What Riedler couldn't know was that he'd been ordered to send monthly reports back to Berlin detailing his commanding officer's movements. Riedler's contempt towards the Party hierarchy and the defenders of the state like the Gestapo and the SS was now regarded by many in Berlin as being dangerous; incitative to the men under his command. And now Franke had all the ammunition he needed to have Riedler shot down in flames. He'd personally witnessed Riedler's disgraceful show of insubordination and, with the added support of Brausch's report, he knew that the proper authorities in Berlin would pursue the matter vigorously until they had Riedler up in front of a court-martial. And, unlike his previous brushes with authority, this time the tribunal would dismiss all the glowing character references from those senior officers who'd rallied to his defence in the past. That's when Franke would play his hand – for the prosecution. But there was more to it than just that. A much bigger prize at stake. He'd been promised command of the Third Parachute Regiment if he could give his superiors the documented proof they needed to clip Riedler's wings. And now he had that proof . . .

'You've certainly got it all worked out,' McIndoe said grudgingly to Stella after she'd outlined the plan to spring Ravallo and Johnson from the Gestapo.

'It's not foolproof by any means, but it's the best we could come up with in the time available,' she replied.

'Don't you think you could at least have told me about it?' McIndoe continued. 'I am, after all, the commanding officer in Nicky's absence.'

'I know you always like to play it by the book . . . well, you did before now. That's why I couldn't risk telling you, not when Vice-Admiral Starr had given specific orders for us to abort the operation if Nicky was captured.'

'She's got a point there, sir,' Evans piped up. 'Let's face it, you weren't too receptive to the idea at first, were you?'

'I've still got my reservations, believe me,' McIndoe told him. 'But it's not as if I've got much choice in the matter. I'm damned if I'm going to go traipsing across Sicily by myself trying to find my way back to the boat. I'd never make it alone.'

'Come on, sir, admit it. You just don't want to miss out on all the fun,' Evans said with a grin.

'Is that what you call it?' McIndoe replied facetiously, then looked across at Hillyard. 'What's going on down there, Bruce?'

'Nothing so far, sir,' came the reply. 'The troops have alighted from both trucks now, but they're still just standing around.'

'It's my guess they're waiting for the Gestapo to leave the hotel before they start to search the area,' Stella speculated. 'It suits us better if they're all together. It'll make an ambush that much easier.'

'So the Partisans are already in place?' McIndoe asked, as if to reconfirm what Stella had already told them.

'They've been in place for the past couple of hours for just such an eventuality,' she replied. 'And, as I've already said, they all know exactly what to do when the time comes. Our only concern will be how to deal with the Germans in the two staff cars. The rest we can safely leave to them. By the time the Germans have managed to bring in reinforcements, we'll be long gone.'

'We've got movement,' Hillyard called out to them. 'Brausch's just emerged from the hotel. He's getting into the back of the second staff car. They're on the move.'

'Let's go,' Stella said to McIndoe and Evans. She followed them to the steps and paused there to look back at Hillyard. 'You know what you have to do?'

'Take out the two guards at the roadblock once the Resistance have launched their attack, then keep an eye on your backs from up here.' Hillyard furrowed his brow uncertainly. 'You're absolutely certain the Resistance know that I'm not a Müller . . . er, a Jerry? I don't want a bullet in my back from one of their damn snipers.'

'How many times do I have to tell you, Bruce? They know you're one of us.'

'God, I hope you're right,' Hillyard replied.

She hurried down the steps and found McIndoe and Evans in position by the front door. McIndoe's hand was resting lightly on the heavy bolt. He looked across at her as she approached them.

'Any minute now all hell's going to break loose out there,' she said, moistening her dry lips with her tongue as the tension mounted with each passing second.

'At least this way we won't miss our cue,' McIndoe said.

'You can count on that,' she replied. 'Good luck. Both of you.'

'Luck's for amateurs, or so Nicky tells me,' McIndoe said with a quick smile, in an attempt to mask the anxiety which was pulsing through his tense body.

'Right now I'll take all the luck you've got,' Evans said with an apprehensive glance in her direction. 'I've got a feeling we're going to need it.'

Ravallo noticed the look of apprehension which flashed across Brausch's face when the *Panzerspähwagen Sonderkraftfahrzeug* 222 – the Gestapo's special-purpose armoured vehicle – was forced to brake sharply at the head of the small convoy. A blinkered horse had emerged from the alley at the side of the church. It was pulling a battered, unpainted wooden cart in its wake; an old man in a flat cap and a threadbare jacket was at the reins. The old man seemed totally oblivious to the presence of the armoured vehicle, until the hatch door was thrown open and a junior officer appeared, berating him furiously and ordering him sharply to get out of the way.

Ravallo had already dismissed the idea of an ambush – the team had orders to abort the operation should he be taken prisoner. Brausch's initial anxiety seemed to have gone and he appeared more at ease now, having scanned the surrounding area and satisfied himself that there was no apparent threat to the convoy, but he still held the Luger tightly in his gloved hand, his eyes constantly darting around him as the junior officer in the armoured vehicle continued to yell angrily at the old man who was now desperately trying to manoeuvre the horse back into the alley. It was then Ravallo noticed the four German soldiers who had emerged from the alley and were running to where the old man was still struggling with the horse. One of the men was an officer – wearing the rank of captain – but Ravallo couldn't see his face which was obscured by the rim of his peaked cap.

Brausch wound down his window and shouted to the officer to clear the road. The officer turned to Brausch and saluted him, and Ravallo was able to see his face for the first time. For a moment he thought he must be mistaken. He could have sworn it was Venucci! Then the streetlight illuminated his face for a split second. It *was* Venucci.

Ravallo's mind was racing as the excitement surged through him, but he was careful not to allow any emotion to reach his expressionless face. He watched as Venucci gestured for the old man to dismount from the cart. One of the soldiers helped the old man down off the cart and, as he shuffled towards the alley, Venucci swung round on the armoured vehicle, pistol drawn, and shot the junior officer. One of the Partisans jumped up on to the side of the armoured vehicle, dropped a primed grenade through the open hatch, then slammed the lid shut and leapt back down on to the road.

Brausch was already yelling at his driver to reverse away from the ambush when the ground shuddered as the grenade detonated inside the armoured vehicle. The force of the explosion blew open the lid and a thick pall of black smoke spiralled up into the night sky from the doomed vehicle. It was then the Partisans opened fire from their concealed positions behind shuttered windows and on rooftops overlooking the street.

The fusillade of bullets rained down on to the helpless German soldiers who were still amassed around the two stationary trucks. Within seconds the whole road had become a killing ground. The sound was deafening as the gunfire echoed all around them. Ravallo looked behind him as the driver struggled desperately to engage the reverse gear, and saw the two paratroopers who'd been manning the road-block now sprinting towards the church. One of them stumbled and fell to his knees, his hand clutched tightly to his chest. There was a look of total bewilderment on his face still as his lifeless body toppled face forward on to the ground. His colleague swung his submachine-gun towards the church belfry, but before he could fire he too was hit. As he stumbled backwards, another bullet ripped through his chest, killing him. Ravallo had no idea who'd shot them, but it was damn good shooting all the same.

The driver had managed to engage the reverse gear, and the wheels shrieked in protest as he revved the engine before reversing away from the first staff car. That was also gunning its engine, waiting to follow them. Ravallo saw the church door swing open and McIndoe, Evans and Stella hurried out on to the steps. Evans immobilized the first staff car by shooting out the two back tyres.

'Get us out of here!' Brausch screamed at his driver, but it was already too late; Ravallo felt the car jolt underneath them as McIndoe shot out the front tyres. Stella darted behind the staff car and took out the rear tyres as well.

Ravallo watched as the driver and the officer in the other staff car threw open their doors and spilled out on to the road, using the armour-plated doors as cover. Evans and Stella were forced to retreat back into the church doorway as a row of bullets peppered the steps where they'd been standing. McIndoe had ducked into the alley where he was being effectively pinned down by the driver's fire. Suddenly the driver cried out in agony and stumbled away from the door as a bullet took him in the shoulder. McIndoe dived low to the ground and cut him down with a short burst of gunfire.

Ravallo noticed the officer look up in horror towards the belfry. He was still swinging his weapon upwards when he was shot in the forehead and killed instantly. Pizzoni scrambled from the back of the staff car. Ravallo watched the Italian look around frantically, his eyes alight with fear, then run towards the alley, his movements impeded by his manacled wrists. A figure appeared from the shadows in the alley to challenge Pizzoni. Stella? His eye went to the church doorway where she'd been standing moments earlier. She was still there. Whoever this woman was, she had on exactly the same clothes as Stella. Then he heard her shout a warning to Pizzoni as he ran towards her. It was then Ravallo recognized her. Gina Roetta. Pizzoni ignored her warning and caught her squarely on the chest with his shoulder, knocking her to the ground. He almost lost his balance but managed to keep his footing. He continued to run towards the alley. She grabbed her fallen submachine-gun and turned it on the retreating figure. This time there was no warning as she shot him in the back.

'Lock your door,' Brausch ordered his driver, digging the pistol into Ravallo's ribs. 'They can't get to us in here. We can hold out until reinforcements arrive.'

'You'd better hope your reinforcements get here quickly,' Ravallo said with a satisfied sneer.

'The car's chassis is armour-plated and the windows are made of reinforced glass,' Brausch replied. 'But if your friends do try anything, you'll be the first to die.'

'Sir, look!' the driver called out anxiously over his shoulder as Evans and McIndoe approached the driver's door, their submachine-guns trained on the windscreen.

Ravallo recognized the small compact black plastic case Evans removed from the rucksack which was slung over his left shoulder. It was known as a 'clam' – an explosive device used by the special forces to destroy cars, light tanks and small boats. He couldn't be sure just what impact it would have on the staff car's armour-plated chassis, but then he doubted whether the two Germans had any idea either. Evans placed the magnetic clam on the driver's door, carefully inserting two yellow time-delay pencils through the narrow openings at the top of the device. He then squeezed the copper tubes at the tip of the pencils to break the inner glass vials to activate the charge. The clam was live. Evans stepped away from the door and held up his index finger towards McIndoe. Both men then retreated to a safe distance, their bodies doubled over as the gunfire continued unabated around them. Ravallo knew there were six colours to signify the different time delays for the pencils. The yellow pencils had a six-hour delay fuse. Evans was calling the Germans' bluff as his signal to McIndoe had obviously meant to signify that the device would detonate in one minute. But would the deception work?

'Sir, if that goes off – '

'They won't dare detonate it,' Brausch cut in angrily as he wiped the sweat from his face with his black gloved hand. 'If they did, they'd know I'd kill Ravallo before they could get to him. They didn't go to these lengths to let him die.'

'They'd certainly kill me before they let you and your butchers interrogate me,' Ravallo countered.

'Quiet!' Brausch snarled. He pushed the barrel of the pistol harder into Ravallo's ribs.

'Sir, we can't just sit here like this. We've got to get out before the bomb goes off,' the driver pleaded.

'Stay where you are. That's an order!'

The driver's eyes flitted nervously to the reflection of Brausch's grim face in the rearview mirror. 'Sir, we have to – '

'Not another word!' Brausch interceded furiously, his breathing now ragged and uneven as he looked across at McIndoe and Evans. 'Don't they realize the door's armour-plated? They can't get in.'

'Then why are you so worried?' Ravallo asked.

'If they detonate that charge, I'll kill you – I swear I'll kill you,' Brausch threatened.

'And here I thought I was your passport out of here. Seems I was wrong.'

'I can't just sit here! I can't!' the driver screamed, fumbling desperately with the handle.

Brausch turned the gun on the driver and shot him in the back. The driver slumped against the door which he'd already managed to unlock; as it swung open his body tumbled out into the road. Ravallo seized his chance and head-butted Brausch as hard as he could. There was a sickening crunch of bone, and Brausch screamed in agony as Ravallo's forehead smashed into his nose. The Luger fell from Brausch's grip as the blood spurted from his broken nose. He tried desperately to retrieve his pistol from the floor, but Ravallo stamped his heel down viciously on to the back of Brausch's hand. Brausch cried out in pain and lashed out with his free hand, catching Ravallo on the side of the head but, as he was about to reach for the fallen pistol again, he saw that both Stella and McIndoe were standing in the open doorway, their weapons trained on him. He slowly sat upright, his hands half raised in surrender. Ravallo cast a sidelong glance at Brausch and allowed himself a smile of satisfaction, more out of relief than anything else. Brausch glared back at him, defiant to the last. But there was no fight left in him any more.

Stella unlocked the back door. She helped Ravallo out of the car, then gestured for Brausch to get out after him. Brausch slid across the seat and carefully stepped out into the road. Once outside, his hand dipped towards his pocket.

'Don't even think it!' McIndoe jabbed the barrel of his submachine-gun into Brausch's stomach. 'Put both hands on your head and keep them there.'

'I was going to get a handkerchief for my nose,' Brausch replied as the blood streamed down his face.

'I said put your hands on your head!' McIndoe repeated. Brausch did as he was told. 'Where are the keys for the handcuffs?'

'In my tunic pocket,' Brausch replied coldly.

Stella opened the breast pocket of Brausch's tunic and retrieved the keys. She unlocked Ravallo's handcuffs, then tossed the keys to Evans to do the same for Johnson, who'd been taken into the sanctuary of the church. Ravallo retrieved Brausch's Luger from where it lay on the floor in the back of the car.

'I am *Standartenführer* Ernst Brausch, and as your prisoner I demand to be treated under the terms of the Geneva Convention.'

'Like hell, you bastard,' Ravallo snarled, and pressed the pistol against the side of Brausch's head.

'No, Nicky, don't . . .' McIndoe screamed in desperation, and he was still reaching for the pistol when Ravallo pulled the trigger. He instinctively threw up a hand as a fine spray of blood splashed across his face, and he stared in numbed horror as Brausch was punched sideways by the sheer force of the shot. His body fell heavily against the side of the car before crumpling to the road. Brausch's legs and arms jerked spasmodically as the blood formed an ever-widening pool around the back of his head. Then Brausch's body stopped convulsing and his head lolled sideways into the pool of blood.

'Jesus Christ, you shot him in cold blood,' McIndoe said in disbelief as he stared at the body. He wasn't even conscious that he'd reverted back to his native tongue. When he spoke again his voice was louder. Angrier. In German. 'We could have used him as a hostage to help us get out of here. Look at him now. He's no use to us like that. What the hell got into you, Nicky? You're no better than them, are you?'

'Sam, that's enough,' Stella said, grabbing McIndoe's arm. 'There will be time for explanations later. Right now we've got to get out of here before the German reinforcements arrive. Come on, both of you.'

Ravallo frisked Brausch's body, more out of hope than anything else, for the miniature camera which had been taken from him at the hotel. It didn't surprise him when he failed to locate it. Student would hardly have let Brausch take it, knowing the sensitivity of the material contained on the film. He pushed the Luger into the empty holster on his belt and hurried after Stella as she disappeared into the alley. Evans gestured to Hillyard in the belfry that they were leaving. He took a grenade from his rucksack and, removing the pin, dropped it into the petrol tank of Brausch's staff car, then sprinted to the safety of the alley. He pressed himself up against the side of the wall; seconds later he heard the explosion as the grenade detonated inside the petrol tank. He waited until the blast had subsided, then peered cautiously around the side of the wall. The twisted shell of the staff car was now straddling the road, burning out of control, effectively blocking the way for any advancing traffic. And with the immobilized armoured car blocking the route from the other direction, it would give the Partisans, who would continue to hold off the Germans until they were clear of the area, precious time to effect an escape. Evans sprinted the length of the alley and almost ran into Hillyard as he emerged through the vestry door; a rifle in one hand, the rucksack containing the radio-transmitter in the other. They grinned triumphantly at each other, then emerged into the adjoining street where the Opel Blitz truck was waiting for them, its engine running. McIndoe, who was crouched closest to the open flap, reached out a hand and hauled Evans up into the back of the truck. Hillyard handed Evans the radio-transmitter, then jumped up into the truck after him. Stella slapped her hand against the glass partition which separated them from the cab. The driver, a taxi-driver with an intimate knowledge of the city and its environs, gave her a wave through the glass panel and the truck rumbled away from the rear of the church. He knew the quickest, and safest, route to the safe house in the Capo quarter; a squalid, shack-infested district which suffered from appalling subsidence due to the lattice of covered rivers and underground canals which ran beneath it.

McIndoe looked across at Ravallo who was sitting with his head bowed on the wooden bench opposite him. He was about to approach Ravallo when Stella stepped in front of him, leading him to an area of the truck which she assumed was out of earshot of Ravallo. They both sat down. She kept her hand on his arm when she spoke. 'Leave him, Sam. I don't know what got into him either. It was totally out of character for him, especially after the way he'd spoken out against the execution of those German soldiers at the farmhouse this morning. But now isn't the time for recriminations. He needs to be alone right now with his thoughts so that he can reflect on what he's done.' She noticed McIndoe glance past her at Ravallo. 'Please, Sam. Leave him, at least until we reach the safe house.'

McIndoe sat back against one of the metal stanchions. 'When it comes down to it, I don't have the authority to question his motives. He's my superior officer. But if I think that he's beginning to crack under pressure, I have the authority to relieve him of his command.'

'Surely it won't come to that?' Stella said, anxiously brushing a loose strand of hair back over her ear.

'I don't know yet, but should the need arise I would hope I could count on your support to back me up. I know my men would stand by me.'

She stared at the floor then reluctantly nodded her head. 'Yes,' she said in a barely audible whisper, 'I'd support you.'

'Come in!' Kesselring shouted in response to the sharp knock on the door.

Riedler entered the office and found Kesselring seated behind the manager's desk. Student was perched on the edge of the armchair against the wall, his arms resting lightly on his legs. Riedler snapped to attention in front of them.

'At ease, Riedler,' Kesselring told him.

'What have you got for us?' Student demanded, sitting back in the chair and folding his arms across his chest.

'An initial casualty report, sir,' Riedler replied, holding up the sheet of paper in his hand. 'Of course, we can't be sure yet of the exact number – '

'Just tell us what you know!' Kesselring interceded tersely.

'Yes, sir. Initial figures are: twenty-nine dead, including *Standartenführer* Brausch and his seven-man Gestapo escort. Another eighteen soldiers wounded. Three Partisans have been found dead and another two have been captured. Naturally we would expect to find more bodies once the surrounding buildings have been searched by the reinforcements who've been drafted in from the local barracks.'

'It's a bit late for them, isn't it?' Kesselring said bitterly. 'Twenty-one soldiers gunned down. Had the order to start the search for Ravallo's accomplices been given earlier, the Partisan snipers would have been discovered and this whole massacre could have been averted. Heads will roll after this fiasco, Riedler. You mark my words.'

'Yes, sir,' Riedler said, shifting uncomfortably on his heels.

Kesselring noticed Riedler's nervousness and shook his head. 'You're not to blame for any of this, Riedler. Your men showed great bravery in the face of such overwhelming fire-power. The fact that none of my chiefs-of-staff or any of their aides were injured is testament to the way you and your men defended the hotel.'

'Thank you, sir,' Riedler replied.

'How many men did *you* lose in the ambush?' Student asked Riedler.

'Three, sir. Goetz and Scherl at the roadblock, and Neumann in the church belfry. Another two were injured in the hotel, but their wounds aren't serious.'

'Something on your mind, Riedler?' Kesselring asked, sensing that Riedler wanted to speak but seemed uneasy about addressing him. 'You know you're free to speak your mind in front of us.'

'It's just that I've never felt so helpless in my whole life, sir,' Riedler told him. 'My unit had the protection of the hotel when the snipers opened fire. Those soldiers out there were just cut down where they stood. Some of them barely out of school. What chance did they have? If only we could have done something to have helped them.'

'Your unit was drafted in for the specific purpose of protecting the senior officers here in the hotel,' Student said. 'That's why you were given strict orders not to leave the confines of the hotel when the ambush started. And, even if your men had ventured outside to try to help those soldiers in the street, they'd almost certainly have been killed as well. It was imperative that the defence of the hotel remained intact. I grieve for the loss of those young lives just as much as you do, but the fact remains that we couldn't risk anything happening to the senior officers here at the hotel.'

'In other words, those soldiers out there were expendable?' Riedler said angrily.

'If it meant protecting the lives of Field-Marshal Kesselring and his joint chiefs-of-staff, then yes, they were,' Student replied bluntly.

'I understand, sir,' Riedler said between clenched teeth.

'The best way to avenge their deaths, Riedler, is to find those responsible. And believe me, we will,' Kesselring told him. 'But first I want Major Ravallo and his colleagues found. I've already initiated armed checkpoints on every road leading in and out of the city. I've also had the security increased at all railway stations and sea-ports. They're not to be allowed off this island. That's where you come in. I want you to lead the hunt for them.'

'Me, sir?' Riedler said with genuine surprise.

'Do you have a problem with that?' Kesselring demanded.

'No, sir,' Riedler was quick to assure him. 'I just thought you'd have wanted to bring in a more senior officer to coordinate the search.'

'I've read your dossier, Riedler,' Kesselring said. 'You've got the field experience that's lacking in many of these officers here in Sicily. They may be able to plan a tactical campaign better than you, but you have the advantage of having actually carried out those campaigns on the battlefield. That insight could prove invaluable in this kind of situation. You can bring in as many men as you want. I'll see to it that you get them.'

'I'd prefer just to use my own unit, sir,' Riedler replied. 'I know them.'

'As you wish,' Kesselring replied. 'I've already arranged for General Student to set up an HQ at the barracks of the Nineteenth Panzer Division here in Palermo. You'll liaise directly with him. All divisions across the island have already been put on full alert. Should any of them come across the enemy unit, General Student will be informed at once. You and your men will then be dispatched to the area to take charge of the situation. Any questions?'

'Just one, sir,' Riedler asked. 'This enemy unit. Are they to be captured, or eliminated?'

'Alive, if at all possible. I'm sure they would prove to be a mine of information about both British and American covert operations in the Mediterranean. But should they try and resist capture, kill them. The main thing is not to let them leave the island. We may have Ravallo's camera, but it's what he may have memorized up here that worries me most,' Kesselring said, tapping his head. 'That dossier contained facts and figures of our military strength here on the island which would prove invaluable to the enemy. It's my guess that he wouldn't have had time to assimilate much, but we just can't afford to take that chance. Does that answer your question satisfactorily?'

'Yes, sir.'

'Dismissed,' Kesselring said.

Riedler saluted him then left the room, closing the door again behind him. Kesselring got to his feet and began to pace the room thoughtfully, his hands cupped over his mouth and nose.

'Something bothering you, sir?' Student asked at length.

Kesselring paused at the door and looked across at Student. 'It's an uneasy feeling I've had in the pit of my stomach ever since I learnt that Ravallo had been captured on the premises. I know you think the orderly, Pizzoni, was more deeply involved in this than he was willing to admit. I'm not so convinced. What if he was telling the truth? What if he didn't tell the Resistance about the meeting? What if the British or the Americans have another source?'

'You mean one of your chiefs-of-staff?' Student retorted in amazement. 'I can't believe that, sir. Their loyalty's beyond question.'

'They were the only ones who knew about the meeting here today. Even their aides weren't briefed until late yesterday afternoon. Personally, I trust them all implicitly.'

'But then how could the enemy have known about the meeting, if not from Pizzoni or one of the chiefs-of-staff ?'

'The exact date, time and details of the meeting were initially transmitted to the chiefs-of-staff by cipher machine,' Kesselring pointed out.

'My God, sir, are you suggesting that British or American Military Intelligence are reading our Enigma ciphers?' Student retorted in horror.

'I know it sounds ludicrous, Kurt,' Kesselring said as he crossed to the desk and sat down again. 'And it probably is. But for my own peace of mind I feel I must investigate the matter further. I'll send a ciphered message on the Enigma machine to my adjutant in Rome. It'll be classified top secret.'

'What will it contain, sir?' Student asked.

'I need to make a couple of phone calls to clarify the information I'll need. I'll fill you in in more detail later.'

'If you are right about this, sir, how can you be so sure that they will take the bait?' Student asked.

'Because I'll make sure the bait's so tempting that they couldn't possibly resist taking it,' Kesselring replied. 'But for the moment our conversation isn't to go beyond the confines of this office. At least that way if I am wrong, no harm will have been done.'

'And if you're right?' Student asked.

'Let's bait the trap first, shall we?'

* * *

Vice-Admiral Starr reached for his pipe and tobacco pouch after he'd finished reading through the decoded transcript of the latest communiqué detailing the events in Palermo which he'd received minutes earlier from Georges Passiere on board the MTB. It hadn't made good reading. The one consolation was that, as yet, there were no casualties amongst the SOE contingent, but Starr knew the Germans would already have launched a manhunt across the island to track them down. It was going to take all of McIndoe's guile and ingenuity as a field officer to get his team back to Malta now. But at the same time, Starr knew McIndoe was probably the one person in the SOE capable of outsmarting the Germans in this kind of cat-and-mouse situation.

It was still uncertain how the Germans had discovered the ruse when Ravallo was inside the hotel, but that wasn't important. What did trouble Starr was the fact that they'd left the hotel empty-handed. The plan had been for the film to have been developed at a safe house in the city, so that Johnson could then have memorized the photographs as an added precaution should anything happen to them or to the negatives before they could be brought back to Malta. Now they had nothing. It had been suggested at an earlier meeting that, because of his photographic memory, Johnson should have gone into the hotel with Ravallo, but the suggestion had been quickly discounted by Johnson himself. With time being of the essence, once they were inside the hotel it would have put tremendous pressure on Johnson to have tried to remember as much as possible in such a short time. He had a photographic memory; he wasn't a speed reader. At the time Starr had acceded the point to him. Now he regretted having not gone along with the idea in the first place. Johnson may not have remembered much, but what he had would have been something. He knew he was being too hard on them. Had the plan worked, Johnson would have had the time to consign the salient points of the dossier to memory. It was the chance he'd had to take at the time. That it had backfired was something he'd have to explain to the War Office. Yet, despite all these setbacks, he still believed they'd done enough to stall an invasion of Malta by several months. Perhaps even permanently . . .

The teleprinter on the table behind him chattered into life. He tamped a wad of tobacco into the bowl of his pipe, lit it, then exhaled the smoke up towards the ceiling as he waited until the message had finished before reaching over and tearing off the paper. He realized its importance straight away. It had been sent personally by the head of the SOE from the sanctity of his Baker Street office in the heart of London, and was encrypted in a special code known only to the two of them. Starr unlocked the bottom drawer of the desk and removed the relevant decoding pad. He spent the next twenty minutes carefully inserting the relevant letters above those on the page then, when he'd finished, he wrote out the complete decoded message on a clean sheet of paper:

Classified: For the eyes only of Vice-Admiral Starr – Valletta, Malta. Have received information from Bletchley Park that 'Ultra' intelligence have intercepted an Enigma communiqué from Field-Marshal Kesselring in Sicily to his HQ in Rome. He has authorized an attack by a U-boat wolf-pack on the Allied convoy – known as Operation 'Fortitude' – due to leave Gibraltar for Malta later tonight. The wolf-pack has orders to lie in wait for the convoy close to the small island of Cani off the northern coast of Tunisia. The precise coordinates have already been passed on to the Admiralty. Estimated time of attack: 0600 hours tomorrow morning. They will arrange for the wolf-pack to be engaged by Allied submarines before the convoy reaches Cani.
End transmission.

Starr burnt both sheets of paper and dropped them into the metal bin beside his desk. He knew only too well how important Operation Fortitude was to the future of the island. It consisted of eight cargo ships carrying fresh food as well as fuel and artillery ammunition, with an escort force of one carrier, two battleships, four cruisers and twelve destroyers. With cholera and dysentery now widespread on the island, the food supplies were essential to the lives of hundreds of locals – especially the children and the elderly who were most at risk; and with some inland artillery batteries now being restricted to three shells per air-raid, the ammunition was desperately needed for the continued protection of the island.

Yet in light of the developments at the Grand Hotel in Palermo, Starr suspected that Kesselring's communiqué could be a trap. It was only natural that Kesselring would be suspicious about the source of the leak. There was already a contingency plan in place to discredit the hotel orderly, Pizzoni, by planting evidence at his home which would prove beyond any doubt that he'd tipped off the Resistance about the details of the meeting at the hotel. But it was imperative that the Germans discover this evidence by themselves. Any other way and it could conceivably be seen as a set-up. And until then all communiqués on the Enigma machines had to be treated with extreme caution, especially those being transmitted within the Mediterranean theatre.

He knew it could be a genuine communiqué between Kesselring and his adjutant, but all his instincts told him that Kesselring was trying to find out whether the Allies were intercepting their messages. Starr had the greatest respect for Kesselring, regarding him as a shrewd military tactician, and this was a very clever move on his part. It meant that if the wolf-pack was intercepted by Allied subs, the convoy delayed or even rerouted to avoid the island Cani, it would confirm Kesselring's suspicions that the Allies had broken the Enigma code. And 'Ultra' was far too important to the Allies to allow that to happen. Which only left one alternative. He could hardly bring himself to think it.

But he knew there was no way around it. If necessary, the convoy would have to be sacrificed to protect the existence of the 'Ultra' programme at Bletchley Park.

It was at that moment that the reality of what he was proposing suddenly hit him like a metal fist slamming mercilessly into his stomach. How many Allied seamen would die if he were to pass his suspicions on to SOE headquarters in Baker Street? Hundreds? More than likely thousands. And how many Maltese would die if the convoy's precious cargo was lost at sea? It would mean even less fresh food getting through to an already desperate population. Less stocks of essential ammunition to help combat the repeated waves of *Luftwaffe* bombers which attacked the island without respite, day and night. An endless cycle of inhuman suffering. How much more innocent blood would he have on his conscience over the next twenty-four hours? And beyond? What price 'Ultra'? What price victory?

A rage of helplessness at his appalling predicament swept through him, and he lashed out in anguish, sending the cup at his elbow crashing against the wall. Sergeant Janet Cross hurried anxiously into the room, alerted by the sound of the breaking crockery.

'Get out!' Starr bellowed at her.

She retreated quickly, closing the door again behind her. Starr stared at the dark rivulets of tea which were trickling down the sandstone wall, then he slowly opened his code book. His hand was trembling as he began to carefully set to paper the communiqué he would send back to his superior at SOE headquarters in Baker Street.

An hour later came the reply from Baker Street. He already knew what it would say even before he set about decoding it.

Classified: For the eyes only of Vice-Admiral Starr – Valletta, Malta. Your report concerning the convoy was submitted to the Cabinet, the War Office and to the Admiralty. I have now received a communiqué from the head of the Admiralty in Whitehall. It reads as follows: In view of Vice-Admiral Starr's disturbing comments regarding the potential threat to the future of the 'Ultra' programme, a decision has been taken at the highest level of government that this programme is to be protected at all costs. It has therefore been decided, in the light of this report, not to dispatch a contingent of Allied submarines from Manoel Island on Malta to engage the U-boats, or to alert the convoy that a wolf-pack will be lying in wait for them off the island of Cani.

May God help them.

End transmission.

ELEVEN

'Do you ever think about dying?'

The question caught McIndoe by surprise, and he pondered it as he reached for the packet of cigarettes on the table. 'I think about it sometimes, sure, but I don't dwell on it unduly. You know what they say about there being a bullet with your name on it? It's fate. Nothing can ever change that. So why let it prey on your mind? Why do you ask?'

Stella drew deeply on her cigarette, then leaned forward and tapped the ash into the glass ashtray on the table. 'I've only ever thought about dying twice before today. I mean really thought about it. The first time was when my father drowned. The second time was after my mother's death. They both died so young. Today was the third time that it really hit home to me. That ambush scared the hell out of me, Sam. I've never been so frightened in my life. When I heard the gunfire outside the church, I didn't want to move it was so loud. I just wanted to stay where I was. I knew I'd be safe in there. It took all my nerve to follow you out into the street when you opened the door. Yet, when we were in the church belfry, I was so psyched up to get out there and get involved. I guess, in retrospect, that was down more to naïvety than anything else. At least the next time I'll know what to expect.'

'Surely you've been in an ambush before?' McIndoe said with a puzzled frown. 'Your dossier says that you've been involved in dozens of military operations here on Sicily. Surely you must have engaged the enemy during that time?'

'Sure. But they were always isolated incidents. Killing a guard at a depot or a rail crossing. But certainly nothing on that scale. I guess that's why it affected me in the way it did,' she said as she stared at the glowing tip of her cigarette smouldering between her fingers.

'I had no idea,' McIndoe said when she fell silent. 'I just assumed that . . . you'd mixed it up close with the Germans before.'

'She's always been too smart to ever let them get that close to her,' Ravallo said from the doorway.

'Nicky?' Stella gasped in horror when she looked at him. 'My God, what happened to you?'

Ravallo, who was now dressed as a major in the Italian army, had a bandage wound tightly around his forehead which slanted down to obscure his left eye. He grinned at her and patted the bandage as he entered the room. 'Good, isn't it?'

'Good?' she retorted in amazement.

'It's not a real injury, for Christ's sake,' he said in exasperation. 'It was Massimo's idea. The Germans are sure to have a description of me which will be circulated to all ports and stations before the night's out. Hopefully this will help to throw them.'

'What about Johnson?' McIndoe asked. 'They'll have a description of him as well.'

'I think you'll find that he's turned for his inspiration to a higher authority,' Ravallo said with a smile, then he stuck his head out into the corridor and called to Johnson. Moments later Johnson appeared, muttering discontentedly under his breath as he gestured disdainfully to the clothes he was wearing. McIndoe smiled at Johnson's obvious discomfort. It wasn't so much that Johnson was dressed as a Roman Catholic priest, which in itself was amusing, as McIndoe knew he was strict Church of England, but the black shirt and trousers were both too large for his scraggy frame. The trousers were rolled up at the ankles and held up by a combination of a thick leather belt and one of Johnson's bony hands, which was hooked tightly under the waistband as if his very life depended on it. The shirt was tucked securely into the trousers, but the sleeves were puffed out around the cuffs and the whole sorry ensemble gave him the unfortunate appearance of a second-rate vaudeville performer who'd seen better days.

'Jesus, just look at me,' Johnson hissed, twisting his fingers tighter around the waistband. 'I look like a bloody clown.'

'Language, Father,' Ravallo reminded him with a mischievous wag of his finger.

'He's right, though,' McIndoe said, getting to his feet. 'He can't go out looking like that. He'd only draw attention to himself.'

'It's all in hand,' Ravallo assured him. 'The trousers will be taken in and there's a jacket he can wear to hide the shirt.'

'I assume this was Giani's brilliant idea as well?' Stella asked.

Ravallo nodded. 'I'm glad you like it, because he's come up with something for you as well. You'll be travelling with Johnson. As a nun.'

'You must be joking!' she replied in disbelief.

'We'll have to split up the team, and not just because of what happened at the hotel,' Ravallo said. 'If the Germans have been tipped off about us, then they'll already be on the lookout for a group of five men and a woman. We have to do everything possible to throw them off the scent. At least this way it'll give us a better chance of evading detection if we are intercepted by a German patrol.'

'Nicky's got a point,' McIndoe said. He crossed to where Johnson was standing. 'Do you know how long these alterations are going to take?'

'It shouldn't take that long,' Ravallo answered for him. 'The girl, Gina Roetta, was training to be a seamstress before the occupation. She'll take up the trousers for him.'

'What about new documentation for Stella and Johnson?' McIndoe asked. 'The original plan was for us all to disguise ourselves as Italian soldiers. Those IDs won't be any use now.'

'New documents are being prepared for them in the basement as we speak,' Ravallo said. 'I've also arranged to have new identity papers as an added precaution. The Germans know what I look like now.'

'But you're still posing as an Italian officer?' McIndoe said.

'It's not the uniform that will give me away, Mac, it's the face. I've already had a new photograph taken for my identity papers. It should be enough to fool them, especially with this bandage over my eye.' Ravallo turned to Johnson and patted him on the arm. 'You've still got to have those alterations done. And take Stella with you. She'll need to get changed as well.'

'Yes, sir.' Johnson looked at Stella. 'Come on, Lieutenant, I'll show you where you can get changed.'

'A nun!' she snorted, following Johnson from the room.

McIndoe sat down in the armchair vacated by Stella. Again Ravallo's mood-swing was startling. It was the first time he'd seen him since they had arrived at the safe house half an hour earlier. Then Ravallo had waited until the others had alighted before climbing from the back of the truck, as silent as he'd been for the duration of the journey from the church. He'd disappeared into the house alone, his head bowed, a look of abject dejection on his face, as if he'd known deep down that the cold-blooded murder of Brausch had been both barbaric and quite unforgivable. McIndoe had even contemplated relieving him of his command. Looking at him now, McIndoe found it hard to believe that this was the same Nicky Ravallo. The spring was back in his step. The twinkle was back in his eye. The confidence was back in abundance. This was the Nicky Ravallo he'd first encountered at the Luqa air-base on Malta. The real one? Or another of his disguises? There was no way of telling.

'You want to talk about Brausch?' McIndoe asked.

'No, but you obviously do,' Ravallo replied. He positioned the coffee table in front of him, and swung his legs up on to it.

'Brausch could have been a valuable hostage for us,' McIndoe said.

'You're not thinking here, Mac. You're letting your emotions get the better of you. We're winging it now. In fact, we've been winging it ever since I was grabbed at the hotel. That means we've entered the realms of improvisation. Like splitting up the team and having Johnson masquerade as a priest and Stella as a nun. You can bet the Jerries will have set up roadblocks right across the island by now. How far do you think we'd have got with Brausch in tow? Do you think he'd have played along with us? He'd have raised the alarm the first chance he got. And you know that.'

'All I know is that you shot him in cold blood,' McIndoe retorted.

'You're dealing in double standards here, Mac,' Ravallo countered, then he swung his legs off the coffee table and turned to face McIndoe. 'What about those German soldiers at the farmhouse this morning? You were the one who was so quick to defend Massimo's decision to have them executed. I was the one who was questioning the morality of that decision, if you remember.'

'They were killed because they saw you dressed as a Gestapo officer,' McIndoe replied. 'What if one of them had escaped and passed that information on to his superior officer? Security would have been tightened around the hotel, and you wouldn't have got near the place.'

'So what you're saying is that, if they hadn't seen me, they wouldn't have had to be killed? In other words, it's my fault that they were executed. Thanks, Mac, that makes me feel a hell of a lot better knowing that.'

'You know damn well what I mean. They were executed to ensure their silence. You can't use that same excuse for killing Brausch.'

'I don't feel any remorse for what I did. None whatsoever. And given another chance, I'd do it again. As far as I'm concerned, there's a hell of a difference between a handful of conscripted German soldiers and a Gestapo butcher like Ernst Brausch. Maybe you don't agree, Mac, but you just think about it for a while. And if you want to make more of it if we ever do get back to Malta, that's up to you.'

Ravallo got to his feet. 'I'm not particularly proud of what I did, but neither do I regret it. It was something that happened on the spur of the moment. Why did I do it? Anger. Bitterness. Disgust. Perhaps it was even fear. I don't know. But it's done. It's in the past. It's time for us to look ahead and try and find a way to get back to the boat. I know that's what I'm going to be doing. I hope I can count on your support as well. Unless, of course, you think I'm cracking under the pressure and feel it necessary to relieve me of my command?'

'Does Stella tell you everything I say to her?' McIndoe asked caustically.

'Stella didn't say anything. I overheard you guys talking in the truck. You'd be surprised how voices carry in that kind of confined space. Well, do I still have your support, Mac?'

'We wouldn't be having this conversation, if you didn't,' McIndoe replied.

Massimo appeared in the doorway. His genial smile faltered as his eyes flitted hesitantly between the two men. He could see by their expressions that he'd come at an inopportune moment. 'I'm sorry, I didn't mean to interrupt anything,' he said, his hand raised in apology.

'You're not interrupting,' Ravallo replied, 'I was just leaving anyway. I've got to look in on Stella and see how she's getting on with her new calling. See you later, Mac.'

Massimo watched Ravallo leave, then turned to McIndoe. 'Is there a problem?'

'No,' McIndoe retorted brusquely.

'That's good,' Massimo replied unconvincingly. He turned to leave.

'Tell me, what will happen to Pizzoni's wife and daughter now that he's dead?'

'If all's gone according to plan, they will already have escaped from the house where they were being held. They're probably being questioned by the Germans as we speak.'

'What plan?' McIndoe asked in bewilderment. 'The whole point of the exercise was for it to appear as though Pizzoni had been working for the Partisans for the past few months. Our boffins at the SOE went to great lengths to manufacture the necessary evidence your people planted at his house last night. As soon as his wife tells the Germans that it was really the Partisans who abducted them, that evidence will be useless.'

'She'll tell them that she and her daughter were abducted by three German soldiers,' Massimo said.

'And why would she say that? It's not true.'

'No, but she doesn't know that. The three men who abducted them were wearing German uniforms. They spoke to each other in German, except for the smattering of broken Italian they used to communicate with their hostages. I'm surprised that Vice-Admiral Starr didn't tell you that. After all, it was his brainchild.'

'No, he didn't tell me that,' McIndoe said in exasperation.

'We purposely allowed them to escape after Pizzoni's death. Naturally it was staged to make it appear as if his wife had outsmarted her captors. So, when she takes the Germans back to the house where she and her daughter were held, all the evidence will point to their own troops being implicated in the abduction.'

'But that doesn't make any sense,' McIndoe said.

'Exactly,' Massimo said with a faint smile. 'You can be sure the Germans will be just as perplexed by it all. They may well suspect it's a ruse by the Partisans – until they uncover the evidence in Pizzoni's house. That's sure to throw them completely. In effect, they'll be left chasing their own tails.'

'Clever,' McIndoe said, recalling how Starr had refused to tell him how the Firm had found out about the proposed top-secret meeting between Kesselring and his chiefs-of-staff at the hotel. This way Starr was deflecting the Germans away from the real source of that information. It intrigued McIndoe. Who had really supplied the information to him? It could only have been one of a handful of people. One of the chiefs-of-staff? One of their aides? He knew it would remain idle speculation unless Starr chose to reveal his source to him. And that was unlikely in the extreme . . .

'If you'll excuse me. I have to make some calls. The sooner you're all safely out of the city and on your way back to your boat, the better it will be for all concerned,' Massimo said as he left the room.

McIndoe reached for the cigarettes on the table and lit one. He heard the sound of approaching footsteps outside in the corridor, and looked round at Stella when she entered the room. She was wearing a nun's black habit and her raven hair was concealed underneath a wimple which was secured over her head. 'Well, what do you think?' she asked.

'You're certainly the prettiest nun I've ever seen,' McIndoe replied with an approving nod of his head.

'That's not quite what I meant, but thanks for the compliment anyway,' she replied, rolling her eyes. 'What I really want to know is, do I look the part?'

'Yes, I think you do,' McIndoe replied truthfully. 'It's Neville that worries me though. I don't see how he's going to manage to pass himself off as a priest. Not in those clothes.'

'I resent that, sir,' Johnson said as he entered the room with Gina Roetta.

McIndoe was amazed by Johnson's transformation. The shirt with the comically bouffant sleeves had been discarded in favour of a flowing black soutane which he wore over the black trousers. The trousers, which were only visible from the calf down, had been taken in and turned up at the ankles. They now looked a perfect fit. A pectoral cross hung loosely on his chest and his thinning brown hair had been greased back over his head. The new look served vividly to highlight his skeletal features and the intensity of his deepset brown eyes; giving him a striking, if somewhat sinister, appearance.

'What do you think?' Gina asked McIndoe.

'He looks more like one of the four horsemen of the Apocalypse than a man of the cloth,' McIndoe replied, then addressed himself to Johnson. 'But what's more important, you look completely different to when you were dressed as a German soldier. And that's what really matters. Where did you get the cassock from? It's certainly an improvement on the shirt.'

'It was amongst the vestments a priest dropped off at the house, sir,' Johnson replied. 'It seemed right as soon as I put it on. Loose fitting. Very comfortable.'

'You know something, I think that hairstyle really suits you,' Stella told Johnson. 'It gives your face a lot more character than it had before. It also gives you an edge. Slightly menacing, if anything.'

'Really?' Johnson said, allowing himself a smile as he stroked his hand lightly over his greased hair. 'Slightly menacing. I like that.'

'Our very own Lon Chaney, the man of a thousand faces,' Hillyard announced as he and Evans entered the room, having overheard Stella's comments from the hall. Both men were dressed as Italian soldiers.

'No, he looks more like Bela Lugosi to me,' Evans said, stroking his stubbled chin with his thumb and forefinger as he pretended to study Johnson with a critical eye. 'Definitely Bela Lugosi. What do you think, sir?'

'I think you should be getting ready to move out,' McIndoe replied sombrely. 'Massimo's making some enquiries about the safest route for us out of the city. We may have to move fast if he can find an opening for us.'

'We're ready, sir,' Hillyard assured him.

'Where's your pack? And your rifle?' McIndoe demanded.

'We left them at the front door, sir,' Evans said.

'Papers?' McIndoe pressed.

Both men patted their tunic pockets. 'ID papers, as well as our three-day leave passes should we be stopped by an enemy patrol,' Evans told him.

'Neville, are your papers in order?' McIndoe asked.

Johnson removed an authentic-looking dog-eared ID which had been prepared for him in the basement by one of the country's leading forgers. He handed it to McIndoe. It was an excellent forgery. McIndoe paged through it, then returned it to Johnson. 'Good. So we're all ready to move out.'

'Where's Nicky?' Evans asked.

'The last I saw he was out on the porch,' Stella told him.

Massimo rapped sharply on the open door to get everyone's attention. 'There's a train leaving for Catánia in thirty-five minutes.'

'Catánia?' Stella replied in surprise. 'But that's on the east coast. Our boat's moored off the south-west coast of the island.'

'Right now you should be more worried about getting out of Palermo before the Germans throw a ring of steel around the city,' Massimo told her. 'There are other trains leaving the station at regular intervals up until midnight, but they're all just local services. You need to put as much distance between yourselves and Palermo in the shortest possible time. The train to Catánia seems your best chance of escape. What's more, the senior ticket conductor is a sympathizer who's helped us in the past. He'll be a useful ally to have on your side in the event of any trouble. So if you want to take the train, I'll arrange for a vehicle to be on hand when you reach Catánia to drive you to your boat.'

'What would our chances be by road?' Stella asked.

'From what I can gather, the German roadblocks are already beginning to cause serious tailbacks on almost every road in and out of Palermo. And those tailbacks can only get worse in the next few hours. As I said just now, you need to get out of here as soon as possible. So the longer you delay your departure from Palermo, the more chance they'll have of finding you.'

'I agree,' McIndoe said, stubbing out his cigarette and getting to his feet. 'Taffy, go and tell Major Ravallo that we've got a train to catch.'

They said their farewells to Massimo at the safe house. It would have been impossible for him to have accompanied them any further, given that his face was displayed so prominently on the wanted posters which the Germans had plastered across the city, together with the tantalizing offer of a very lucrative reward for any information leading to his capture. Not only was the city rife with enemy collaborators, but every roadblock across the country would also have been issued with copies of the incriminating poster. His every move had to be carefully orchestrated in advance to avoid these hazards. As it turned out, he left the house shortly before them. Destination unknown.

Their destination had been the main railway station at end of the Via Roma. It was ironic that the Grand Hotel was less than a mile away, and understandable that the military roadblocks seemed to increase significantly the closer they got to the station. They'd left the safe house in two cars: Johnson, Stella and Gina in a battered, antiquated Fiat befitting the humble wage of a clergyman; while the others had followed at a discreet distance with Venucci behind the wheel of an Italian army TL 37 command car which the Partisans had commandeered the previous day from two dispirited Italian soldiers on the outskirts of the city. The number plates and serial number stencilled on the side of the chassis had since been changed to those of an identical command car currently operating somewhere in the south of the island. This was standard procedure for any military vehicles captured from the enemy, and the Partisans would only use each vehicle for one operation, then it would be gutted before the Germans could uncover the deception.

It turned out to be the same routine at every roadblock: their forged identity papers were carefully scrutinized by some grim-faced soldier, but were of such a high quality that they didn't raise any suspicions, and their vehicles were waved through without further delay. Their enemy turned out to be the clock; a problem not helped by the tailbacks at each roadblock, and it seemed that they wouldn't reach the station in time to catch their train. They eventually made it – with five minutes to spare.

Johnson was the first to arrive. He double-parked the Fiat opposite the brightly illuminated station, put it in neutral with the engine still running, then grabbed the battered suitcase from the back seat and scrambled out from behind the wheel. Stella and Gina got out together and, after embracing each other warmly, Gina kissed her affectionately on both cheeks and climbed into the driver's seat. She slipped the gear out of neutral, then gave them a wave before pulling away and disappearing into the late-night traffic. Johnson grabbed Stella's arm as she was about to step out into the road, and admonished her for not having checked first for any oncoming traffic, as if she were one of his young charges on a school outing. She dutifully looked the length of the road, then turned to Johnson who nodded his approval. She put a hand to her mouth to hide her smile when he took her arm and led her safely to the other side.

Venucci pulled up next to a 'no-parking' sign in front of the station, just as Johnson and Stella disappeared through the main doors. Evans and Hillyard, who'd been sitting in the back with McIndoe, vaulted over the side of the vehicle then reached inside for the Italian army-issue kit-bags they'd been given to replace their own rucksacks. McIndoe patted Venucci on the shoulder, then climbed out of the command car and slung his kit-bag over his shoulder.

'Good luck,' Venucci said, extending a hand towards Ravallo.

Ravallo gripped it tightly. 'You too, friend. And thanks for all your help.'

'It is we who should be thanking you,' Venucci said, then he grabbed the remaining kit-bag from the back of the command car and pushed it into Ravallo's arms. Ravallo was about to go after his colleagues when he noticed Venucci's eyes stare past him and he was suddenly aware of someone standing directly behind him.

'It says quite clearly: "no-parking",' a voice snapped in Italian. 'Are you blind?'

Ravallo turned to find himself face to face with a young policeman. 'Is that some kind of joke?' he demanded.

The policeman gasped in horror at the sight of Ravallo's bandaged eye. 'I'm . . . I'm sorry, sir. I had no idea . . . I didn't mean anything by that. It was just . . . a figure of speech.'

'I lost my eye when we recaptured Benghazi from the Eighth Army last month,' Ravallo informed the nervous policeman. 'I was only released from hospital three days ago. This is my first night back in Sicily in over six months. I was the one who told my adjutant to drop me off here. So if you have a problem with that, I'd be glad to take it up with your superior.'

'No, sir, that . . . won't be necessary,' the policeman assured him.

'Then if there's nothing else, I've got a train to catch. My wife's allowed our two children to stay up past their bedtime just so that they can see me when I get home. I would hate to disappoint them by missing my connection. And so would you. Believe me, so would you.'

The policeman saluted stiffly and hurried away. Ravallo smiled at Venucci, then headed for the stairs. 'Major?' Venucci called out after him. 'Don't forget to send my love to your wife and children.'

Ravallo chuckled softly to himself as he watched the command car drive off, then he climbed the stairs and entered the concourse. It was packed with Italian and German soldiers, many of them already curled up on the wooden benches or stretched out on the cold concrete floor for the night, with their kit-bags as makeshift pillows. He found himself touching his hand to his head several times in quick succession as he passed a row of young Italian soldiers. A new consignment of raw recruits ready to be bloodied in the arid African desert. Many were little more than children dressed up in a military uniform. He could understand the uncertainty evident on many of their young faces. How many of them would never return home? It was such a waste of innocent life.

He was startled when a hand grabbed his arm, and he let out a deep sigh of relief when he turned to find McIndoe beside him. 'What happened to you?' McIndoe demanded. 'I was about to send out a search party to look for you.'

'Just a small brush with the law,' Ravallo replied as he disengaged his arm from the light grip. 'Don't worry. It was nothing. A misunderstanding, that's all. I sent him off with his tail between his legs. So, have you got the tickets yet?'

McIndoe took two tickets from his tunic pocket and handed one of them to Ravallo. 'I sent Bruce and Taffy on ahead to get a compartment.'

'What about Stella and Johnson?'

'As far as I know, they've already boarded the train,' McIndoe told him. 'Come on, let's go. I'll feel a lot safer when we're on the train as well.'

Ravallo looked around him as they crossed to the ticket barrier, where four German soldiers were checking passengers' identity papers and travel permits. He counted at least a further dozen German soldiers patrolling the concourse – mostly in pairs; four standing guard at the main doors;

another two outside the toilets; there was even one standing guard in the only ticket booth still open at that time of night. It was an obvious show of force. Very effective. He took the relevant papers from his tunic pocket when he reached the ticket barrier and handed them to the nearest soldier.

'Your destination, sir?' the soldier asked in Italian as he leafed through the identity papers.

'Catánia.' Ravallo watched with a growing sense of unease as the soldier returned to the photograph and scrutinized it closely before looking up at him. He knew the only way to deal with the situation was to go on to the offensive. 'Is there a problem?' he demanded.

'It's just routine, sir,' the soldier muttered.

'Look, soldier, I've been confined to a hospital bed in Benghazi for the last month. It was hot, smelly and very uncomfortable. For the last three days I've been waiting for a flight back to Sicily, and when I did finally get one we were attacked by a squadron of British Hurricanes when we were halfway across the Mediterranean. Three of our escort fighters and the other transport plane were shot down. It's a miracle that I got back here at all. Now all I want to do is go home and see my family again. Is that really too much to ask?'

The soldier shifted uncomfortably under the onslaught, then handed the documents back to Ravallo. He saluted him stiffly. 'Your papers are in order, Major.'

Ravallo stuffed the papers back into his tunic pocket and crossed to where McIndoe was waiting for him.

'Was that wise, drawing that kind of attention to yourself?' McIndoe asked once they were out of earshot of the soldiers.

'It wasn't exactly as if I had much choice in the matter. I thought he was on to me back there by the way he was staring at the photograph. I had to put him in a corner. It was the only way I could play it.'

McIndoe scanned the four carriages until he saw a familiar face amongst the dozens of soldiers who were leaning out
of the open windows saying their final goodbyes to their
loved ones congregated on the platform. 'There's Taffy. Third
carriage. Let's get out of here.'

'I'm with you there,' Ravallo replied.

He used his kit-bag as a buffer to push his way through
the crowd, and was grateful when McIndoe reached down a
hand towards him from the open carriage door. He thrust
the kit-bag into the extended hand and, after discarding it in
the corridor behind him, McIndoe locked his fingers around
Ravallo's forearm and helped him up into the carriage. A
young Italian soldier tried to push past them to catch a last
glimpse of his girlfriend on the platform but when he saw
the pips on their shoulders he came to attention and saluted
them.

Ravallo returned the salute, then smiled at the young
soldier and gestured for him to step past him. 'Go on, you
probably won't see her again for a long time.'

The soldier beamed gratefully as he squeezed past the two
men. McIndoe picked up Ravallo's kit-bag and pushed it into
his arms. 'It's more likely that he'll *never* see her again.'

'You're all heart, you know that?' Ravallo muttered. He
followed McIndoe along the corridor to the compartment
where Evans and Hillyard were waiting for them.

'How did you manage to get a compartment to yourselves?' McIndoe asked, placing his kit-bag on the overhead
rack. 'The train's packed tonight.'

'It turns out Massimo arranged it with the conductor
once he knew we were taking the train to Catánia,' Evans
replied as McIndoe sat down on the opposite banquette. 'At
least that's what the conductor told us when we boarded
the train. He's tied in somehow with the Partisans.'

'Yes, so Massimo said back at the house,' McIndoe said.

'Here's the conductor now,' Hillyard said as the door slid
open and the official entered the compartment.

'I believe we have you to thank for this,' McIndoe said, gesturing around him.

'Giani Massimo asked me to reserve it for you,' the conductor replied. He handed McIndoe the two newspapers he was carrying. 'I thought you might like something to read to help pass the time. It's a four-hour journey. Unfortunately we stop at almost every station along the way. It can get very tedious.'

'Thank you,' McIndoe said, placing the newspapers beside him on the banquette.

'There is something I should tell you,' the conductor said. He paused when two soldiers passed the open doorway and quickly closed the door. 'The Gestapo have a man on board the train.'

'You think they could be on to us, sir?' Evans asked, looking anxiously at McIndoe.

'If they were, we wouldn't be sitting here right now,' McIndoe replied. 'We'd be having a most unagreeable manicure with a pair of pliers at Gestapo headquarters.'

The conductor smiled weakly and nodded in agreement. 'The Gestapo have a team of agents here in Sicily whose job it is to work the trains. Unfortunately they tend to swap them around regularly on different routes, so it's not always easy to spot them. But this one I know. I've seen him before. They mix with the other passengers, usually in the dining cars, trying to pick up information about the Partisans. Sometimes they travel in pairs, but more often than not it's just one man. They normally reserve a single berth in the first-class section of the train. That way they can be sure they won't be disturbed if they need to send a message back to their headquarters on the portable radio-transmitter they always carry with them.'

'And you can bet he'll already have a damn good description of me,' Ravallo said.

'If we know where he is, why not neutralize him and throw the body off the train?' Hillyard suggested.

'Why don't you just go and tell him that we're here: it would save a lot of trouble,' McIndoe replied sarcastically. 'You're not thinking logically, are you? The moment he misses a transmission, the Gestapo will be swarming all over the train. No, we don't touch him.'

'We have a radio-transmitter hidden in the guard's van,' the conductor told them. 'It's one of a batch the British supplied to the Partisans for the sole purpose of monitoring the Gestapo's transmissions here on Sicily. Of course, the Gestapo have no idea we're listening in to them. So now I can monitor all his calls, assuming the Gestapo haven't altered the frequency again. Normally they change it every two or three days, and sometimes it can take us another day just to locate the new frequency. But they changed it yesterday, so it should be all right. There is one problem though. I can only monitor the calls when I'm in the guard's room.'

'You want one of us there to cover for you?' McIndoe asked.

'It would help,' the conductor said.

'Consider it done,' McIndoe said. He turned to the others. 'It's a four-hour journey. I suggest we each take an hour-long shift in the guard's room.'

'Agreed,' Ravallo said.

'I'll take the first shift,' Hillyard offered. There was no disagreement.

The conductor moved to the door. 'I'll look in on you from time to time and let you know what's going on.'

'Thanks, we'd appreciate that,' Ravallo told him.

'I must go now.' The conductor looked at Hillyard. 'I'll come back in a few minutes, when the train's left the station, and take you to the guard's van.'

McIndoe closed the door behind the conductor, then pulled the blind down over the window. He picked up one of the newspapers and barely had time to read the first column of the lead article when the train shuddered into life and left the station in a choking cloud of thick, impenetrable smoke. He knew they were still far from being safe, but at least they'd taken the first positive step in that direction.

It had already gone midnight when a weary Hans Riedler took the call from a senior officer at Gestapo headquarters on the Piazza Bologni. The officer recounted the gist of what he'd been told by one of their more reliable informers and, realizing it could be a significant breakthrough in their search for the elusive enemy agents, Riedler had woken Franke and despatched him and five of his most experienced paratroopers to meet with the Gestapo's informer at a prearranged rendezvous in the Capo quarter of the city.

Their escort was a *Panzerspähwagen SdKfz* but after what had happened to the Gestapo's armoured vehicle at the church the previous day, its presence was of little comfort to Franke. The only consolation was that the crew of the armoured vehicle knew their way around the narrow, ill-lit streets of the Capo. Franke wasn't a man easily scared, but the deeper their *Kübelwagen* penetrated into the quarter, the more uneasy he became. Not that he allowed his emotion to show in front of the men. An officer had to lead by example.

When the armoured vehicle came to a stop ahead of them, the driver of the *Kübelwagen* pressed his foot gently to the pedal and pulled up behind it. The hatch of the *Panzerspähwagen* was thrown open and a young officer pulled himself up through the aperture and pointed to an unlit alley about twenty yards further down the road. Franke got out of the passenger seat, his favoured twin-magazine MP.40 submachine-gun in his hand. The nauseating smell of rotting garbage was overpowering, but this was of little concern to him as he scanned the shadowy doorways on either side of the street. He was far more worried about the possibility of an ambush. One sniper. One bullet. That was all it would take to kill him. It was a particularly sobering thought, especially as the Capo was a known stronghold of the Sicilian Resistance.

Satisfied that the area appeared safe, Franke gestured for two of the paratroopers to take up positions at the back of the *Kübelwagen*, and for the other two to accompany him. The two paratroopers flanked him as he made his way cautiously towards the alley, their submachine-guns clutched tightly across their chests. He raised a hand as they reached the mouth of the passage way, and one of the men produced a torch, switched it on, and stroked the powerful beam across the darkness. His hand froze when the beam illuminated a shabbily dressed figure standing by the wall at the far end.

'Kuhn, check the alley,' Franke ordered. Sergeant Manfred Kuhn produced another torch and made his way to a collection of rusted drums outside the single doorway in the passage. He checked behind the drums. Nobody there. He shoved his palm firmly against the padlocked wooden door, but it held firm and he instinctively drew his foot back as a rat darted out from a hole at the foot of the door and disappeared behind the nearest drum. He then made his way to the man, who was now cowering nervously against the wall, a trembling hand shielding his eyes from the glare of the torch beam which was still trained on him from the mouth of the alley.

'Are you Verga?' Kuhn asked in Italian.

The man nodded, then jabbed a finger anxiously towards the source of light. 'Tell him to switch off the torch. If I am seen talking to you, I will be killed.'

'The light stays, so you'd better get used to it,' Kuhn told him. The hollow sound of Franke's boots echoed on the cobbled pavement as he approached the two men. 'This is him, sir,' he said to Franke, reverting back to his native tongue. Riedler had sent Kuhn to interpret for Franke, as he was one of the few paratroopers in the unit capable of communicating effectively in Italian.

'You have the money?' Verga asked, rubbing his thumb and forefinger together in front of Franke.

'Tell him he'll only be paid if his information proves useful to us,' Franke said.

Kuhn translated Franke's words into Italian, then grabbed Verga by the front of his threadbare overcoat and hauled him away from Franke. 'You talk to me. Is that clear?'

'I don't care who I talk to, as long as I get my money,' Verga replied.

Franke eyed Verga disdainfully. The filthy clothes, the unwashed hair, the black fingernails, the suppurating sores around his mouth. The man was totally repugnant to him. Franke slipped on his black leather gloves as if they might somehow protect him from this malodorous night creature. He took Kuhn to one side. 'According to Major Riedler, Verga phoned his contact at Gestapo headquarters and told him he'd seen Massimo leave a house in this quarter shortly before a group of Italian soldiers were driven away from the same house by a member of the Resistance. There's a good possibility these soldiers could have been Ravallo and his team. Tell him I'm not interested in Massimo, only in the soldiers. Show him the artist's drawings of Ravallo and his colleague and see if he recognizes either of them. And find out the exact location of the house.'

Kuhn took the two drawings from his pocket, handed them to Verga, then raised his torch to illuminate them clearly. 'Was either of these men amongst the soldiers you saw leaving the house earlier tonight?'

Verga chewed a black fingernail thoughtfully as he studied the faces carefully, then tapped the drawing of Ravallo. 'Two of them were wearing officers' uniforms. One had a bandage over his left eye. It could have been this man, but I am not sure. The man was handsome, like him.'

'So he thinks it might have been Ravallo,' Franke said once Kuhn translated what Verga had told him. 'Where did they go?' Franke queried.

'I don't know,' Verga replied when Kuhn asked him. 'I was on foot. They left in an army command car. I wasn't able to follow them.'

'How did you happen to be there at that particular moment?' Kuhn demanded.

'I had heard a rumour earlier tonight that Giancarlo Massimo was at the house,' Verga replied.

'So why didn't you inform the Gestapo straight away?'

'You have to understand that I hear so many rumours. Most of them are just that – rumours. The Gestapo will only pay me for factual information. That's why I went to the house to see for myself. Once I'd established he was there, I contacted the Gestapo.'

'But by then he'd already gone,' Kuhn said.

'That was regrettable,' Verga said with a dispassionate shrug.

'Wasn't it?' Kuhn replied contemptuously. 'Where's the house?'

'It's not far from here.'

'Show us,' Kuhn said.

A look of fear flashed through Verga's eyes, then he quickly shook his head. 'No. I cannot be seen with you. I will explain – '

'You'll show us,' Kuhn repeated, this time more forcefully.

'It would be too dangerous – '

'Shut up!' Kuhn snarled, and slammed Verga painfully against the wall. He kept one hand gripped tightly around the front of Verga's soiled shirt and indicated to Franke behind him. 'That's my superior officer. He served with the Special Forces in North Africa. Rumour has it that a patrol he was leading captured two British divers trying to mine a destroyer off the coast of Alexandria. He got the information he wanted from them. Then he killed them. Only he didn't use a gun or a knife – just his bare hands. Word is it took them three days to die in the most excruciating and agonizing pain imaginable. And these were hardened soldiers. I'd hate to think what he could do to a little weasel like you if you were to get on his wrong side.' He smiled coldly at the petrified expression on Verga's face. 'But, as I said, it was just a rumour. And from what you've told me, you don't seem to have much faith in them, do you? Do you really want me to tell my captain that you're refusing to cooperate with us?'

'No, please, I'll show you the house,' Verga responded with a renewed eagerness in his voice. 'I'll take you there now.'

'What's going on?' Franke demanded.

'Just a misunderstanding, sir. He'll take us to the house. He says it's not far from here.' Kuhn grabbed Verga's arm and followed Franke back to the *Kübelwagen*.

Franke spoke briefly to the officer in the armoured car, then got into the vehicle. 'Get the exact directions from him, then we can move in,' he told Kuhn.

'What about the *Panzerspähwagen*?' Kuhn asked.

'It stays here, at least for the time being,' Franke replied. 'If there is anyone in the house, I want them taken alive for interrogation. We need to approach the house as quietly as possible. Stealth and surprise are the key factors here. That's why I don't want the armoured car involved at this stage. It's too noisy.'

Kuhn passed on Verga's directions to the driver, who started up the *Kübelwagen* then pulled out from behind the armoured car and drove to the end of the street. There he turned right and continued on for a couple of hundred yards before reaching the junction of a second intersection. According to Verga's directions, the safe house was a hundred yards further down the road. Franke drew his finger across his throat to signal the driver to switch off the engine and to kill the lights. Then he got out, his twin-magazine MP.40 submachine-gun in his hand, and crouched down as he listened carefully to the alien sounds around him. A raised voice from an adjoining house. A distant engine. Then another engine, this time closer. Two dogs barking incessantly in a neighbouring street. He slowly scanned the semi-lit street to his right. It appeared to be deserted. There was no real way of knowing whether they were being drawn into a carefully planned ambush, although all his instincts told him that they were in no immediate danger. Whatever else he may have thought of Verga, his unswerving loyalty to the Gestapo appeared to be beyond question. He finally stood up and gestured to the four paratroopers to disembark from the back of the vehicle.

Kuhn hurried over to him. 'What about Verga?' he whispered.

'He stays here with Hoffman,' Franke replied, jabbing a thumb towards the driver. 'And tell Hoffman to kill him at the first sign of any trouble.'

'You think it could be a trap?' Kuhn asked.

'No, but that doesn't mean we're going to be any less vigilant when we approach the house,' Franke replied. 'I'm certainly not prepared to take any unnecessary risks. Are you?'

'No, sir,' Kuhn said. He returned to the *Kübelwagen* to pass Franke's instructions to the driver.

Franke detailed two of his men, Brandt and Meisner, to circle around to the back of the house and then to await further orders. The other two – Kuhn and Hausser, a young paratrooper whom Riedler held in high esteem – followed Franke as he ran, doubled over, to the sanctuary of a garden wall further down the deserted street. There were no lights on in the house behind them. He indicated the safe house which was now only twenty yards away. The house was also in darkness. He wiped the sweat from his forehead with the back of his sleeve, then indicated to Hausser to advance to the wooden fence at the front of the house. Hausser darted through the open gate and sprinted across the road, then dropped down on to one knee in front of the wooden fence, from where he carefully surveyed the overgrown garden and the windows which looked out over the street. Satisfied that the area appeared secure, he indicated this to Franke, who gave Kuhn the signal for them to close in on the house.

They quickly exited through the gate and ran silently to where Hausser was crouched down beside the fence. Franke scanned the length of the deserted street, then got to his feet again and ran up the narrow pathway to the house. Taking up a position on one side of the front door, he gestured to Kuhn and Hausser to advance. Kuhn was first up the pathway. He pressed himself up against the brick wall on the other side of the door – his torch in one hand, his submachine-gun in the other – ready to enter the house. Hausser brought the sole of his boot up savagely against the door; although they heard the wood splinter under the impact of the blow, the door held firm. Hausser kicked the door again and this time it gave way. Kuhn, a vastly experienced entry-man of numerous house-clearing operations, was the first through the door. Immediately he dropped down on one knee and fanned the hall with the submachine-gun. It was deserted. Franke and Hausser slipped into the house behind him. Then, together with Meisner and Brandt, who'd broken in through a kitchen window, they set about securing the house. A thorough room-by-room search was undertaken; quickly it became apparent that there was nobody there. Franke's relief that the house had been secured without the loss of any of his men was tempered by the knowledge that he was still no closer to locating Ravallo's team. Where had they gone? More to the point, though, had they even been in the house? His men had uncovered nothing to indicate that they had ever been there. Had Riedler been too quick in jumping to the wrong conclusions about the occupants of the command car? Was there actually a perfectly simple explanation for what Verga had seen? It was no secret that disillusioned Italian soldiers were defecting to the Resistance every week. And it wasn't even as if Verga had positively identified Ravallo from the artist's drawing Kuhn had shown him earlier in the alley. Just another assumption . . .

'Sir, we've found something,' Kuhn said from the doorway. 'I think you should take a look.'

Franke followed Kuhn to a door adjacent to the kitchen. Hausser, who was standing by the bed, looked round when they entered the room. 'I found these in the wardrobe, sir. They were in a suitcase.'

'What are they?' Franke demanded as he crossed to the bed.

'*Wehrmacht* uniforms, sir,' Hausser replied, gesturing to the pile of clothes he'd emptied out on to the bed. 'And two Gestapo uniforms as well.'

'Let me see,' Franke said. He pushed Hausser aside and picked up one of the Gestapo tunics. An officer's tunic. Hausser shone his torch on to the tunic as Franke held it up for closer inspection. The buttons were missing. Franke now had his proof to link Ravallo with the safe house, and to the Italian soldiers Verga had seen in the command car. Suddenly it all seemed to make sense. They'd discarded the incriminating German uniforms in favour of Italian uniforms so they would be able to blend in more easily with their surroundings. Who would give a group of Italian soldiers a second glance? Ravallo would have realized an artist's drawing of him would be circulated to all the roadblocks, ports and railway stations across the island, so what better way of disguising himself than by feigning a facial injury which would help to conceal his features? What soldier would dare to question a wounded officer about his injury?

'We know they were here, sir,' Kuhn said. 'What now?'

'Fix the front door,' Franke replied, tossing the tunic back on to the bed.

Kuhn and Hausser exchanged puzzled looks. 'Why do you want it fixed?' Kuhn asked.

'Because, according to Verga, the vehicle was driven by a member of the Resistance,' Franke replied. 'And if he's taken them to the station, or to another safe house somewhere in the city, then there is every chance he's going to come back here once he's dropped them off. And if that is the case,

I don't want him to suspect a thing when he gets back. The house must look exactly as it did when he left.'

'What about the window we broke to get into the kitchen?' Hausser asked.

'That's not important,' Franke replied. 'All we need to do is lure him into the grounds. Meisner and Brandt will be concealed in the garden. So, as soon as he pulls into the driveway and switches off the engine, he'll be trapped.'

'That's assuming he's dropped them off in the city, sir. What if he's driving them to a rendezvous somewhere outside of Palermo? He may not be back for hours yet.'

'Do you have a pressing engagement elsewhere, Hausser?' Franke retorted facetiously.

'No, sir,' Hausser replied, staring uncomfortably at the carpet.

'Then go and fix the door before the driver gets back. Kuhn, help him. Now move, both of you!'

'Sir, I can see headlights approaching the house,' Kuhn announced from the window. 'The vehicle's coming into view now. It's an Italian army command car. One occupant – male . . . wait . . . there's a second pair of headlights behind the command car. They appear to be slowing as well.'

'One or two vehicles, it doesn't matter,' Franke replied. 'Nobody makes a move until both vehicles have switched off their engines.'

'The command car's turned into the driveway,' Kuhn said. 'It's pulling up on the lawn in front of the house. Engine off. The second vehicle's also in view. It's a small car . . . a Fiat. Also one occupant – female. It's pulled up behind the command car. Engine off. She's getting out and crossing to the command car. Male occupant still in the command car . . . Meisner and Brandt have broken cover and are moving in to intercept them, sir.'

'Let's go,' Franke ordered. He drew his holstered pistol as he followed Hausser to the front door. Hausser and Kuhn had earlier wedged the door back into place. Now Hausser found it was jammed. 'Open it!' Franke yelled in frustration, then he brushed Hausser aside with his arm and yanked savagely on the handle. The door opened but one of the hinges broke free, and Franke had to clamp both hands around the edges and drag it across the carpet. He emerged out on to the pathway, his pistol levelled at Venucci and Gina who were now standing by the command car, their hands on their heads. Both had already been frisked, and Venucci's rifle confiscated from the back of the vehicle. Meisner stood in front of them, Brandt behind them to block off any escape. Venucci spoke to Franke in Italian, then gestured to Gina beside him. 'Kuhn, get out here,' Franke barked irritably over his shoulder.

Venucci understood enough German to be able to communicate with the soldiers in their own language. But it was imperative that he keep up the pretence of being an Italian soldier. It was all they had going for them now. He had to be strong, if only for Gina's sake. She was still little more than a child in his eyes, and he was determined to protect her, even at the expense of his own life if necessary . . .

'Name?' Kuhn snapped at Venucci.

'Tessoti, Lino Tessoti,' Venucci replied and reached a hand towards his tunic pocket. Franke knocked his hand away with the barrel of his pistol. 'I was just going to show you my papers, sir,' Venucci assured him, his hands raised defensively in front of him.

Kuhn unbuttoned Venucci's tunic pocket and removed the documents. He paged through them, then offered them to Franke. 'They're sure to be forged,' Franke said without even looking at them. 'Get them inside.'

'Sir, there must be some misunderstanding here. I'm sure we – '

'Shut up!' Kuhn grabbed Venucci by the arm and propelled him towards the house. Hausser had removed the door from its hinges; it was now propped up against the corridor wall. Venucci and Gina were taken into the lounge and the light was switched on for the first time since the Germans had arrived at the house. Brandt and Hausser took up positions on either side of the window. Meisner brought up the rear and closed the lounge door behind him. He stood guard in front of it.

'Where did you take Ravallo?' Franke demanded.

Venucci shook his head in puzzlement when Kuhn translated for him. 'I have been out with my girlfriend tonight,' he said, indicating Gina beside him.

'In two cars?' Kuhn challenged.

'She has to leave for work early in the morning. We thought – '

'Enough of this charade,' Kuhn cut in angrily. 'Is this your house?'

'Yes, sir,' Venucci replied.

'Then perhaps you can explain the German military uniforms we found in the bedroom. Two of them have been positively identified as being the ones worn by enemy agents who attempted to penetrate the security cordon at the Grand Hotel yesterday afternoon.'

'Uniforms?' Venucci replied in genuine bewilderment. The pretence was over. Massimo had contacted him over the radio shortly before they'd left for the station to assure him that he'd arrange for the German uniforms to be removed while they were out. So why hadn't it been done? Had the courier been scared off after witnessing the arrival of the German soldiers at the house? It seemed the only logical explanation. But then why hadn't they been warned as well? Why had they been allowed to walk straight into a trap? Were they really that expendable? He knew that not only did the uniforms tie them in with Ravallo's team, but it also linked them to the Partisan ambush the previous day. He could feel the net tightening around them, and there wasn't a thing he could do to save either of them.

He suddenly felt a deep sense of betrayal. They'd been left to the mercy of the Germans. After all he'd done for the

Partisans since the German occupation, was this how they repaid his loyalty? And what of Gina? Eighteen years old. She should have had her whole life ahead of her. What future now?

'I'll make a deal with you,' Kuhn said to them. 'Tell us what we want to know, and you have my word that you won't be handed over to the Gestapo for further interrogation.'

'Go to hell,' Venucci snarled.

Franke grabbed Kuhn by the arm and led him away from the prisoners. 'What did you just say to them?' Kuhn told him. 'Did I give you the authority to make deals with them?' Franke asked angrily. 'You're here as my interpreter, and if you can't carry out that duty properly then I'll have you replaced with someone who can. Is that clear, Sergeant?'

'Yes, sir,' Kuhn replied tersely.

'Brandt, go and find me some rope,' Franke ordered.

'Sir, if I can get them into our confidence, I think I can get a lot more out of them than just the whereabouts of the enemy agents,' Kuhn said once Brandt had left the room.

'I'm not interested in anything else, Kuhn,' Franke replied.

'So you intend to hand them over to the Gestapo afterwards?' Kuhn asked.

'We'll see,' was all Franke would venture on the subject.

When Brandt returned with a length of rope he had found in the kitchen, Franke ordered the prisoners to kneel, then had their hands bound behind their backs and the excess rope used to secure their ankles, effectively immobilizing them. Franke crouched down behind the trembling Gina and placed the barrel of his pistol lightly against her elbow. He looked at Venucci, who was watching him with a growing sense of apprehension. 'Kuhn, ask him where he took Ravallo and his colleagues tonight. If he refuses to answer, I'll put the first bullet through her elbow. The next wrong answer, and I'll shatter her kneecap. I've got a whole magazine to experiment on different parts of her body. That's eight bullets in all. And only the last bullet will kill her. Then, when she's dead, I'll start on him. Tell him.'

'He doesn't have to tell me, I understood what you said,' Venucci said in German. 'What kind of animal are you? She's only a child.'

'You should have thought about that before you recruited her,' Franke retorted contemptuously. 'But then all the so-called "Resistance movements" are the same, aren't they? You don't care how old they are, just as long as they can point a gun and kill another German soldier. That's all you care about, isn't it? I'm not the one with their blood on my hands. You are. And all those like you who continue to advocate this futile war of resistance. The guilt is yours, not mine.'

Venucci looked in desperation at Gina. Her doe-eyes were wide and fearful and brimming with tears. They were going to die, of that he was certain. It was now just a question of degrees. Slowly and agonizingly or quickly and painlessly. If he held out, Gina would die in the most excruciating agony imaginable. How could he possibly do that to her? Yet at the same time he knew that if he told the Germans what they wanted to know, Ravallo and his team would never leave the island alive. They'd be arrested on the train, then handed over to the Gestapo for interrogation. He had no doubt that at least one of them would eventually break under the Gestapo's merciless torture and, with the sensitive information they had between them about both the Italian and Sicilian Resistance, it would lead to mass arrests which would undoubtedly set both organizations back considerably in their ongoing struggle against their fascist oppressors. What to do? He saw the first tear escape from the corner of Gina's eye as she shook her head resolutely at him, almost as if she knew what he was thinking.

'Answer the question!' Franke yelled, and Gina cried out in pain when he jerked her arm back sharply and pressed the barrel harder into her skin.

Venucci had been so caught up in his own thoughts that he hadn't even heard the question put to him. Not that it mattered. 'Go to hell,' he snarled at Franke.

Franke squeezed the trigger and Gina screamed in agony as the bullet shattered her elbow in an explosion of blood and bone which sprayed across the wall behind her. She fell sideways on to the carpet, where she lay whimpering as she cradled her bloodied, disfigured arm next to her body. Venucci turned his head away from her, struggling to fight back the rising bile in his throat. When he did finally look up, it was at the soldiers who were now congregated together by the door. He'd fully expected to see a look of supercilious triumph in their eyes. Instead there was only disgust. Gina screamed as Franke grabbed her shattered arm and yanked her roughly to her knees again. Venucci noticed Brandt, the soldier who had gone to fetch the rope, take a determined step towards Franke, the look on his face suggesting that he wanted to intervene, but the one called Kuhn put a restraining hand on his arm and shook his head.

'The second bullet will cripple her,' Franke announced as he pressed the barrel against Gina's kneecap. 'Do you really want me to do this to her? Do you?'

'He won't tell you anything,' she hissed through gritted teeth, then spat contemptuously in Franke's face.

Franke smiled coldly at her as he slowly wiped the saliva from his cheek. 'What's it going to be?'

Venucci lowered his eyes and shook his head. His body jerked instinctively as the second shot rang out and Gina's anguished howl of tortured agony seemed to penetrate the very depths of his soul, reverberating like an accusing echo within the walls of his subconscious mind. A voice – it sounded so distant to him – broke the lingering silence, and he saw two of the soldiers restrain Brandt who was now pleading with Franke to stop the horrific mutilation. Gina had mercifully passed out from the sheer intensity of the pain, and she lay motionless on the floor, the pale carpet around her shattered limbs now drenched in a thick red syrup of blood.

'You think I'm enjoying this?' Franke shouted at Brandt.

Kuhn opened the door and shoved Brandt out roughly into the hallway before he could reply.

Franke stared at the broken figure of Gina Roetta lying at his feet. 'Somebody has to do it. Someone has to make them talk. Kuhn, do you want to do it?' Kuhn lowered his eyes but didn't say anything. Franke held out the pistol towards the other two soldiers. 'Meisner, take the gun. Go on, take it! Hausser, do you want it?' Neither man moved. 'No, it's always left to me. I always get the dirty work that nobody else wants to do.' He laughed disparagingly to himself, then prodded Gina with the tip of his blood-streaked shoe. 'Kuhn, get me some water. We need to revive the bitch. The fun's just beginning.'

Kuhn stared helplessly at her, fighting back the rising anger inside him. As he wrenched open the door, he heard the sound of an approaching engine outside in the street. Seconds later the *Kübelwagen* pulled up outside the house.

'It's Hoffman, sir,' Meisner said from the window.

Moments later Hoffman entered the house and saluted Franke when he emerged from the lounge. 'I've just had Major Riedler on the radio, sir. Ravallo was seen earlier at the railway station. Major Riedler's on his way there now. He wants you to meet him there as soon as possible.'

'Is Verga still in the *Kübelwagen*?' Franke demanded.

'No, sir, I threw him out before I drove over here. He was complaining about not having been paid for the information he gave you about the safe house but I told him to take it up with the Gestapo.'

'You did well,' Franke said, then returned to the lounge. 'We're moving out.'

'What about them?' Kuhn asked, gesturing to Gina and Venucci.

Franke's reply was to shoot Gina through the back of the head. Her body jerked, then she lay still. Venucci raised his eyes and looked Franke defiantly in the face. Franke showed no emotion as he levelled the pistol at Venucci's forehead and squeezed the trigger. The force of the bullet rocked Venucci back on his bound legs, then he toppled lifelessly on top of Gina's body. Franke slipped the pistol back into its holster and moved to the door. 'The show's over, gentlemen. Let's go.'

'Where are the men?' Riedler asked after he'd returned Franke's salute.

'I told them to wait outside in the *Kübelwagen*, sir. Do you want me to get them?'

'No, they'll be briefed later, along with the rest of the unit,' Riedler replied. He muttered irritably under his breath as a large woman with two bickering children in tow shoved past him on her way to join the queue at the ticket barrier. He led Franke to a quieter area of the concourse, then took a packet of cigarettes from his pocket and lit one. 'Ravallo was positively identified from the artist's drawing by a policeman who was on duty here earlier tonight. The policeman noticed an army command car pull up in a no-parking area. Four men got out. All were dressed as Italian soldiers. Three of them came in here before he reached the vehicle, so he wasn't able to provide any descriptions of them. When he challenged the driver about ignoring the no-parking sign, Ravallo turned on him and gave him some story about having been injured in North Africa and that he was on his way home to see his family. The policeman backed down, not wanting a confrontation, and the last he saw of Ravallo was when he came in here.'

'Do you know which train they caught?'

Riedler nodded triumphantly. 'A soldier on duty at the ticket barrier also remembers Ravallo. According to him, they took the train to Catánia.'

'That doesn't necessarily mean that will be their final destination,' Franke pointed out.

'Agreed. I'd say it was their intention to get as far away from Palermo as possible before we could secure the city. The tickets weren't bought in advance, we know that much, so it could even be a case of getting on the first available train out of the city, irrespective of its destination. It's unlikely they'd get off at one of the smaller stations along the way. These are tiny villages with very basic means of transport. Strangers would always be very noticeable in that sort of environment.'

'And they wouldn't want to draw any unnecessary attention to themselves,' Franke concluded. 'What's the plan, sir? Are we going to intercept the train and arrest them?'

'We can't risk wasting any more time than's absolutely necessary,' Riedler told him. 'I've already arranged for a detachment of soldiers to meet the train at Valledolmo – it's one of the many smaller stations along the way. They'll arrest Ravallo and the others, then bring them back to Palermo for further questioning.'

'Assuming they haven't already left the train.'

'We know they're still on the train,' Riedler replied to Franke's surprise. 'At least they were the last time the Gestapo were in contact with their operative on the train. I'm told they have teams of these operatives working incognito in all the occupied territories. They speak the native language fluently, and their job is to mingle with the other passengers and try to establish whether there are any members of the Resistance, or Resistance sympathizers, on the train. Then they pass this information back to their headquarters via the small radio-transmitter they carry with them.'

'So it looks as if our work will be finished here after Field-Marshal Kesselring and his chiefs-of-staff leave Sicily in the morning,' Franke said. 'Do you know where we'll be posted after this? Will we be returning to the Eastern Front?'

'Having received no orders to the contrary, I can only assume we'll be sent back there,' Riedler said. He dropped his cigarette butt and ground it underfoot. 'But this isn't over yet. Not until Ravallo and the others are safely under lock and key.'

'That should just be a formality now.'

'Don't make the mistake of underestimating them. They almost pulled off a very audacious coup at the hotel yesterday. It was only by a stroke of good fortune that they didn't succeed.' Riedler took the packet of cigarettes from his pocket again and cursed when he discovered he'd just smoked the last cigarette. He crumpled the packet into a ball and tossed it on to the floor. 'You never told me what happened after you'd met with the Gestapo's informer tonight?'

'I thought Hoffman would have told you, sir,' Franke replied.

'He told me what he knew but, considering that he was sitting in the *Kübelwagen* when you and the others went to the house, it wasn't very much.'

Franke briefed him, careful to omit any reference to his brutal treatment of Gina Roetta before he'd killed her. He knew Riedler wouldn't have approved of his methods.

'You shot them?' Riedler said incredulously. A look of anger flashed through his eyes. 'Why does everything with you have to be resolved through the barrel of a gun? They could have been handed over to the Gestapo for further interrogation.'

'I didn't see the point, sir. They wouldn't have talked, not even if they'd been tortured.'

'And how can you be so sure of that?' Riedler asked.

'You tend to get an instinct for these things when you're with the Special Forces, sir,' Franke replied. 'I interrogated a lot of prisoners when I was in North Africa. You quickly learn to identify those who'll crack under pressure and those who can hold out under any amount of torture.'

'For God's sake, we're talking about a young girl here. Are you telling me that, with all the barbaric equipment at their disposal, the Gestapo couldn't have broken her?'

'It's not always the age that's the important factor, sir, it's what they've got here,' Franke said, pressing his clenched fist against his chest.

'I want a written report of what happened tonight,' Riedler told him. 'And I want it by the morning.'

'You'll have it, sir,' Franke assured him. 'Do you need me for anything else here tonight, sir?'

'No, go on back to the hotel,' Riedler said. 'And take the men with you. I'll be along shortly.'

Franke saluted him, then disappeared out through the main doors. Riedler looked at his watch. It was one o'clock. He stifled a yawn, then rubbed his hands slowly over his face. When he finally let his arms drop to his sides, he was startled to find Kuhn standing in front of him. 'What are you doing here? I thought you'd be on your way back to the hotel by now.'

Kuhn glanced anxiously towards the main doors, then shook his head. 'The others have gone back to the hotel with Captain Franke, sir. I chose to remain behind. I had to speak to you. Alone.'

Riedler had always regarded Kuhn as one of his most trusted colleagues in the Parachute Regiment. A like-minded liberal and career soldier, with no interest in the politics of his country, Kuhn had been at the head of the guard of honour at Riedler's wedding. The previous year he'd also unselfishly risked his own life to drag the injured Riedler to safety during the airborne assault on Crete. Yet, in all the time he'd known Kuhn, Riedler had never seen him so agitated. He appeared nervous and ill at ease with his surroundings, almost as if he were expecting something to happen to him.

'What's wrong?' Riedler asked, but when he tried to put a comforting hand on Kuhn's arm, Kuhn jerked his arm away. Kuhn took a packet of cigarettes from his pocket and lit one with trembling fingers. 'I think you'd better give me one of those as well,' Riedler said. He lit it himself and discarded the spent match. 'Now tell me what's going on.'

'It's Captain Franke, sir.'

'Why am I not surprised to hear that?' Riedler said. 'What's he done now?'

Kuhn took a long drag on his cigarette, then exhaled the smoke out slowly through his mouth. 'I don't even know if I should be telling you this, sir. I feel no better than Verga. A cheap informer.'

'He's not cheap from what I've heard,' Riedler replied with a wry smile. There was no reaction from Kuhn. 'I've never seen you like this before,' Riedler said. 'Something's clearly bothering you. You know whatever you say to me will be treated in the strictest confidence.'

'With all due respect, sir, I don't think it will be too difficult for Captain Franke to work out who pointed the finger at him.' Kuhn tossed the cigarette on to the floor and ground it savagely underfoot. 'To hell with him. I've got to tell you, sir. A communiqué came over the radio when we were on our way here. There's a fire raging out of control in the Capo quarter. But what caught my attention was the fact that it had originated in the house we'd left not half an hour earlier. I believe Captain Franke's behind the fire, sir. It was the only way he could cover his tracks.'

'Cover his tracks?' Riedler replied with a frown. 'What are you talking about?'

'Did he tell you about the two prisoners we took at the house?'

'That he executed them, yes,' Riedler replied grim-faced.

'Did he tell you that he'd mutilated the girl first?' Kuhn asked.

Riedler slowly lowered the cigarette from his mouth. 'Tell me what happened.'

Kuhn described the events in explicit detail. 'We were all sickened by what he did to her, sir. Yet what disgusted me most of all was that he actually seemed to be enjoying himself. We're paratroopers, sir, not the Gestapo. He disgraced the regiment's name by his actions tonight.'

'And you think he arranged to have the house razed to the ground to destroy the evidence of what he'd done?' Riedler asked.

'Yes, sir, I do.'

'But there's still Hausser, Brandt and Meisner who'll back up your story,' Riedler said.

'I'm not so sure about that, sir. Captain Franke gave us this long spiel on the way over here, trying to justify what he'd done at the house. I have to admit it was a very impressive speech. Impassioned. Jingoistic. And frighteningly believable, especially to young, impressionable minds. I think they were taken in by it all. Brandt certainly was, and he was the most affected by what he saw at the house. I don't believe they'd turn on him. I was the only one who saw through him. And he knows that as well. He also knows that if I tried to publicly rake up the dirt on him, it would only reflect badly on the regiment. And I can't do that. The regiment's my whole life. That's why I felt I had to unburden myself on you, sir. I know you'll take the necessary steps to bring Captain Franke to task for what he did, without damaging the credibility of the regiment.'

'There are times when being an officer is a damn curse,' Riedler said after a thoughtful pause. 'We go back a long way, Manfred. What I'm going to tell you is not to be repeated to anyone.'

'You know it won't be, sir,' Kuhn assured him.

'A contact of mine in Brandenburg sent me a confidential copy of Captain Franke's personnel file shortly after he joined us. He was regarded by his superiors as one of the top recruits in the history of the unit. Intelligent. Dedicated. Fearless. A brilliant tactician – and also an excellent communicator, as you saw for yourself tonight. But there is one serious flaw in his character. He's a psychopath with what psychiatrists call an "authoritarian personality". That means he has extreme respect for authority, but an intense hatred towards those he regards as nonconformists. In this case, the two Partisans. Yet the psychiatrists at Brandenburg, in their infinite wisdom, decided that because these bouts of psychoses only surface at irregular intervals, they weren't reason enough to discharge him from the army. So instead he was promoted to the rank of captain and bundled off to us with their best wishes.'

'Does General Student know about this, sir?' Kuhn asked.

'I can only assume he does. He's never mentioned it, and I've certainly never raised the subject with him. To be honest, I've never witnessed Captain Franke's psychoses at first hand, so it's not even as if I could go to General Student with anything solid.'

'But if General Student knows, why did he allow Brandenburg to offload Captain Franke on to us?' Kuhn asked.

'All I know is that Captain Franke has many admirers in Berlin. And if the order did originate from there for him to be transferred to our unit, then there wouldn't have been much that General Student could have done to have prevented it.'

'Are you going to report the incident at the house tonight to General Student, sir?' Kuhn asked.

'Even if I did and the subsequent enquiry were to go against him, I can guarantee you now that any disciplinary action would be blocked by Berlin. How could they possibly justify disciplining him when the Gestapo and the SS are committing atrocities like this every day in the occupied territories? No, we'd just be spitting into the wind on this one, Manfred.'

'So, in other words, you're not going to do anything about it?' Kuhn said bitterly. 'By turning a blind eye to his behaviour, you're just giving him a licence to do what he wants in this unit, sir. We'll become no better than the Gestapo.'

'Don't ever raise your voice to me like that again,' Riedler chastised him angrily. He looked around him as he slowly regained his composure. 'I'm just as sickened as you are by what he did tonight. But, as I said just now, Captain Franke has a lot of admirers back in Berlin. I've even heard it said that some of them want me ousted and for him to take charge of the regiment. And if I were to start making waves now, it might just be the excuse they need to have me replaced. I've got to tread carefully at the moment. But that doesn't mean that I'm going to just stand by and let Captain Franke drag this unit down to his level.'

'What are you going to do?' Kuhn asked as he took the packet of cigarettes out of his breast pocket once again.

'You let me worry about that,' Riedler replied. He gestured to the packet of cigarettes in Kuhn's hand. 'Thanks, I will if you're offering.'

Kuhn opened the packet. 'I've only got one left, sir.'

'I only want one,' Riedler replied, plucking the cigarette from the packet.

Kuhn exhaled exasperatedly, tossing the empty packet into a rubbish bin as he went after Riedler who was already making his way towards the main exit.

TWELVE

Hillyard threw open the sliding door and tumbled excitedly into the compartment. 'The Germans are on to us,' he announced breathlessly. 'They know we're on the train.'

Evans was quick to close the door behind him. 'How?' he demanded. 'We've been careful to keep a low profile ever since we boarded the train. The blinds have been drawn at all times and, apart from you, none of us has left the compartment. How could the Gestapo agent have possibly known we were in here?'

'He didn't,' Hillyard replied, easing himself down on to the banquette beside Evans, still struggling to catch his breath after his desperate run from the guard's van. 'A policeman and a soldier who were on duty at the station tonight identified Nicky from an artist's drawing. It also seems the Germans know there are four of us travelling together. I don't know how they found that out, but that's what the Gestapo told their agent when they contacted him over the radio. He's been ordered to keep an eye on us until the train reaches Valledolmo.'

'And what happens at Valledolmo?' McIndoe asked.

'A detachment of troops have been dispatched from a garrison near Valledolmo to meet the train at the station,' Hillyard replied. 'The plan is that we'd be arrested at the station, then taken back to Palermo and handed over to the Gestapo.'

'Where is this Valledolmo?' Ravallo asked.

'It's the next scheduled stop,' Hillyard told him.

'What!' Ravallo exclaimed in disbelief. 'Why didn't you tell us that before?'

'The situation's under control,' Hillyard was quick to assure him. 'I've already spoken to the conductor and he assured me that he's got a plan in mind to get us off the train before it reaches there.'

'And what is this brilliant plan?' Ravallo demanded.

'He didn't exactly say,' Hillyard muttered uncomfortably.

McIndoe raised a hand to silence Ravallo. 'This isn't getting us anywhere. First things first. Bruce, have you told Stella and Neville about this?'

'No,' Hillyard replied. 'I came straight here from the guard's van.'

McIndoe turned to Evans. 'You said earlier that you know which carriage they're in. Go and get them.'

'The Gestapo obviously don't know about Neville and Stella, otherwise they'd have mentioned it over the radio,' Hillyard said after Evans had left the compartment. 'They could continue on to Catánia by themselves. The Resistance would be on hand there to take them on to the boat.'

'We need to get off this island as quickly as possible. If we were to fragment the team now, we'd have two separate units trying to make their way back to the boat through hostile territory. That would only work against us.' McIndoe shook his head. 'No, it's imperative that we stick together. If we jump train, they come with us.'

'It's going to be a calculated risk jumping off the train, even at this reduced speed,' Ravallo said as he pulled back the corner of the blind and peered out into the darkness. 'All it will take is for one of us to land awkwardly and sprain an ankle – or worse still, break a bone – to slow us down considerably. And you can bet the Germans will be coming after us in numbers when they discover we're not on the train when it reaches Valledolmo.'

'I don't see it being a problem,' McIndoe told him. 'Anyone unable to walk by themselves will be left behind. It's as simple as that.'

'That's a bit drastic, isn't it?' Ravallo said.

'I'm just being pragmatic, that's all,' McIndoe replied. 'Under any other circumstances we'd do our utmost to accommodate the wounded, but not only will we have the Germans breathing down our necks, we also need to get back to the boat before it's discovered. You know as well as I do that, without the boat, we'll be stranded here on the island. And then it would only be a matter of time before the Germans found us. Speed and manoeuvrability have to be of the essence here. At least that's how I would handle the situation if I were in command. But then it's not up to me, is it? You're the senior officer here, Nicky, and you'd have to make the final decision as to whether or not you'd be prepared to sacrifice a player if it came down to it.'

Ravallo let the blind fall back over the window. 'Then let's just hope it doesn't come to that,' he said.

The door opened and Evans led Stella and Johnson into the compartment. 'We bumped into the conductor on the way over here,' Evans announced as he closed the door behind him. 'He said he'd be along shortly.'

'Has Taffy told you what's happened?' McIndoe asked Stella as she sat down on the opposite banquette.

'Yes,' she replied.

'It's not good, but at least we've been forewarned,' McIndoe said. 'And that gives us the edge.'

'As long as the conductor comes up with a viable plan to get us off the train before it reaches Valledolmo,' Ravallo said.

There was a knock on the door and Evans lifted back the blind to see who was in the corridor. He opened the door and gestured for the conductor to enter the cramped compartment.

'Well?' Ravallo demanded of the conductor after Evans had closed the door behind him.

'There's a river about five kilometres further on up the line,' the conductor told him. 'It's the only stretch of water between here and Valledolmo. Your best bet would be to jump off the train there. The river's quite deep and the undercurrents aren't very strong. You won't have any trouble swimming to the bank. The bridge itself is a narrow single track. It's about a twenty-metre drop to the water. If you jump in quick succession on reaching the bridge, you'll all land safely in the water.'

'How do you know so much about the river?' McIndoe asked.

'I grew up around here,' the conductor replied. 'As a child I jumped off that bridge dozens of times. Believe me, I know that river well.'

'It seems to be our only chance,' Ravallo said, looking at the faces around him. There was a general murmur of agreement. His eyes settled on the conductor again. 'Where's the best place for us to jump from the train?'

'The guard's van,' the conductor replied.

'Is there any chance that our Gestapo friend will see us when we jump?' McIndoe asked.

'Not if you jump from the opposite side of the train to where he's sitting,' the conductor said. 'There are two doors, one on either side of the guard's van. I'll show you which one to use.'

The conductor waited until everyone had gathered together their belongings, then led them to the guard's van at the rear of the train. He unlatched the door on the left-hand side of the carriage, then gripping the handle tightly in both hands, he pulled open the door. A raw, icy wind whipped through the carriage, and McIndoe, who was standing directly behind the conductor, clamped his hand on top of his peaked cap when it threatened to fly off his head. The conductor tossed his own cap on to a sack of mail, then grabbed the metal rail at the side of the door and leaned precariously out of the doorway, his eyes screwed up against the biting wind as he sought to get his bearings. For a horrifying moment, McIndoe thought he'd actually lost his balance, and instinctively he reached out a hand to pull the man back inside, but he quickly checked himself and stopped short of touching him.

The conductor finally hauled himself back into the carriage, then retrieved his cap and tugged it back on his head. 'I know where we are now. The river's about three kilometres away. It's a relatively cloudless night, so you won't have any trouble seeing it before the train reaches the bridge. Well, I think it's time I paid a visit to a certain Gestapo officer to make sure he doesn't get the urge to look out of the corridor window while we're crossing the bridge.' He gave them a knowing smile. 'I'm sure I can find a way of keeping him occupied until we're clear of the river.'

Ravallo shook the conductor's hand. 'Thank you for all your help.'

'Good luck,' the conductor said. He left the van and they heard the sound of a key being inserted into the lock as he secured the interconnecting door behind him.

Ravallo discarded his officer's cap and tore the bandage from his face before moving to the open door, but when he peered out into the night he was struck by an overwhelming sense of forlornness. Apart from the occasional light from some isolated homestead in the distance, the veil of darkness was ubiquitous across the countryside. Even the half-moon seemed reluctant to intrude on its nigrescent domain, having retreated momentarily behind one of the few clouds visible in the night sky.

'Can you see the river yet?' Stella asked behind him.

'I can't see a damn thing,' Ravallo replied irritably. 'It's pitch-black out there.'

'Nicky, the bridge can't be far away now. If we miss it – '

'The only way we'll miss it is if I'm being constantly distracted by someone shouting in my ear,' Ravallo told her.

Stella threw up her hands in despair, then slumped down on to the nearest crate. She unfastened the nun's wimple from around her throat, pulled it off her head and tossed it on to the floor. She moved her head from side to side as she massaged the back of her neck, then uncoiled her raven hair and flicked it out on to her shoulders. She sat back against the side of the carriage, closed her eyes, and began to slowly tease her fingers through her hair to help give it back its shape.

'Is everyone ready?' Ravallo shouted, jarring her guiltily out of her fleeting moment of self-absorption. She got to her feet, backing into McIndoe, who had to grab her arm to prevent her from losing her balance. 'Sorry,' she muttered.

'Is everyone ready?' Ravallo called out again.

'Ready,' McIndoe shouted back above the monotonous chattering of the wheels beneath them. 'We've transferred the radio-transmitter, a couple of flashlights and all the medical supplies into one kit-bag.'

'The radio could get damaged when it hits the water,' Ravallo pointed out.

'It's a chance we've got to take,' McIndoe replied. 'It's already secured inside a lightweight watertight case, and we've taken the added precaution of wrapping the case in several layers of army tunics to help cushion the blow when it hits the water. There isn't much else we can do to protect it.'

'What about the other kit-bags?' Ravallo asked. 'The Germans will have tracker dogs who could pick up our scent from our clothes if we leave them behind on the train.'

'We'll take them with us,' McIndoe told him. 'We can weight them down later with stones and sink them in the river.'

Although Ravallo couldn't make out the bridge, he estimated that they must be fast approaching the river. 'Who's going to jump first? You sort out the order, Mac.'

'You go first, Nicky,' McIndoe said, patting him lightly on the shoulder. Ravallo looked round sharply at McIndoe, as if he was about to object, then gave a quick shrug and nodded in agreement.

McIndoe pointed to Evans. 'You'll follow Nicky. Bruce, you'll go third. Stella will go fourth. I'll jump last.' He noticed Stella wipe her hand nervously across her mouth and put a hand on her arm to get her attention. 'Don't tell me this is the first time you've ever had to jump out of a moving train into a cold river in the middle of the night?'

'Of course it's the first . . .' She trailed off with a sheepish grin when she saw the teasing smile on McIndoe's face.

'If it's any consolation, we're all just as nervous as you are about this,' McIndoe said, then gestured to Hillyard beside him. 'Even Bruce isn't exactly relishing the thought of jumping blind from a moving train, and he's an experienced acrobat.'

'Exactly. An acrobat, not a stunt-man,' Hillyard said, and his expression softened as he gave Stella a reassuring smile. 'All you have to worry about is clearing the bridge when you jump. And that won't be a problem if you make sure you launch yourself positively from the train. But, whatever you do, don't stop to think about what you're going to do. Hesitate, and you could make a mistake. You've got to be positive when you make that jump. After that it'll just be like a parachute drop. The water will absorb the impact of your fall.'

'We're coming up to the bridge,' Ravallo shouted to them. He could clearly see the ghostly pale reflection of the moon shimmering across the dark waters ahead. 'Get into a formation behind me.'

McIndoe knelt down beside the four kit-bags which were piled up beside the open door. He would throw them over the bridge in quick succession as the others jumped from the train. Not only would he have to be quick, but also precise in his accuracy. All it would take would be for one kit-bag to end up beside the track for the whole plan to backfire on them. The Germans would find it soon enough, and their sniffer dogs would be given a scent to follow. He grabbed the first kit-bag by its handles and placed it in front of him, ready to be dispatched the moment they reached the bridge. Even if the kit-bags landed on the riverbank, it didn't matter, as long as they could be retrieved afterwards and submerged in the water.

Ravallo drew back into the van, his body now braced to jump. They were passing over the bridge. A low wooden guardrail was all that separated the track from the drop to the river beneath them. It was roughly the same height as the floor of the guard's van. Ravallo had been psyching himself up for the jump, and let out a confident roar as he launched himself through the door and disappeared over the side of the bridge. McIndoe hurled the first kit-bag after him. It cleared the bridge. As did the second. And the third. He was so preoccupied with what he was doing that it was only when he hauled the last kit-bag towards him that he realized both Hillyard and Evans had already jumped. He looked up at Stella and saw the hesitancy in her eyes as she stood in the doorway, her hand clamped tightly around the rail, her knuckles white with fear. He knew he'd have to help her. But first he had to get rid of the kit-bag. He flung the kit-bag through the open door, his heart missing a beat as it struck the top of the wooden rail. After what seemed an eternity it finally toppled over into the river. Now his only concern was to get Stella off the train. He got to his feet and approached her.

'I can't do it,' she whispered fearfully as she stared, transfixed in fear, at the dark water below them.

McIndoe could see that the front portion of the train had already cleared the bridge and he estimated that they had, at most, five seconds to jump. Then it would be too late. 'Take my hand.'

'Sam, I can't – '

'Take my hand!' he repeated more forcefully, then grabbed her free hand in his. Her palm was clammy with sweat. He knew he was going to be taking one hell of a risk, but there was no other way to do it. If she didn't let go of the handrail when he jumped, he'd be yanked back in mid-air and could land heavily at the side of the track or even worse, he could be dragged under the wheels of the train. It was something that didn't bear thinking about. He remembered what Hillyard had said to her about being positive. Now was the time to find out whether she believed enough in herself to go through with it. 'We're going to jump together,' he told her, tightening his grip on her hand. 'Trust me on this, Stella. Just trust me. Jump . . .'

He launched himself through the doorway, his hand still locked in hers. There was no sudden jolt. No being pulled back. She'd trusted him. She'd jumped with him.

He remembered feeling the hammering blow to the side of his head as he hit the water. A fleeting moment of searing pain which ricocheted agonizingly through his head as if he'd been punched by a metal fist. Then, mercifully, he blacked out.

'Sam?'

He was vaguely aware of a voice. Distant. Distorted. Vague.

'Sam?'

Again the voice. Closer. Clearer. Familiar.

'Sam?'

A female voice. Anxious. Husky. Intense.

'Stella?' he muttered absently. He was suddenly aware of the dull, methodic pounding which was echoing deep within the recesses of his mind. He opened his eyes slowly, but everything appeared hazy and distorted in the darkness and he instinctively raised a hand to wipe across his face, as if to brush away the opaque veil which seemed to be covering his eyes. He first felt it when his fingers brushed against his forehead. He investigated further by tracing his hand gingerly over his forehead. It appeared to be a bandage. Then it all came back to him. The bridge. The fall. The concussion. Then nothing.

'Sam?'

He squinted up at Stella who was crouched over him as he lay on the riverbank, his head cushioned by a wet kitbag. She was no longer dressed in her nun's habit; she was now wearing an Italian army uniform. He screwed up his eyes against the incessant hammering inside his head, and at that moment all he wanted was for the pain to go away. She smiled gently at him. 'How are you feeling?'

'You don't want to know,' he replied with a grimace.

'Sam, I'm sorry,' she said in a soft, emotional voice. She put a hand lightly against his cheek. 'This is all my fault. If I'd jumped when I was supposed to, none of this would have happened.'

'You jumped, that's all that matters,' McIndoe told her, touching her hand reassuringly. 'Anyway, what did happen? All I remember is hitting my head on something as I hit the water. Then I must have passed out.'

'You hit your head on a submerged log,' she told him.

'How bad is it?' he asked, gingerly touching the section of bloodstained bandage over his left temple.

'It's a deep cut, Sam,' she replied truthfully. 'I've patched you up as best I can, but obviously you'll need it seen to by a doctor when we get back to Malta. But at least the dressing seems to have stemmed the bleeding. You were bleeding pretty badly for a while after we got you out of the water.'

'Who pulled me out of the water?'

'Nicky,' she replied.

'But it was Stella who saved your life,' a voice said behind her. Ravallo came into view. Like her, he'd also changed out of his wet clothes and was wearing the spare officer's uniform which had been packed in one of the kit-bags. 'You ended up face down in the water. She turned you over on to your back and kept your head above the water until I could get to you and bring you over to the bank. If she hadn't acted so quickly, we wouldn't be having this conversation right now. Another few seconds and you'd have drowned.'

'What do you say to someone who's just saved your life?' McIndoe said to her.

'I've been thinking the same thing,' she said softly. 'If you hadn't been there for me on the train, I'd never have jumped. You believed in me when I didn't even believe in myself.'

'But I didn't save your life,' McIndoe pointed out.

'Do you honestly think I'd have let the Germans take me alive once the train reached Valledolmo?' she countered.

'Then I guess we're even,' McIndoe said.

'Hardly. It was my fault that you were injured in the first place,' she replied. The disdain she felt towards herself was evident in her voice.

'You can discuss this later,' Ravallo said before McIndoe could reply. 'The train will have already reached Valledolmo, which means the Germans will know by now that we're not on board any more. It won't be long before they start doubling back on the route the train took in their search for us. We need to get the hell out of here before they descend on the area. Mac, are you up to it?'

'I'll manage,' McIndoe replied, but when he tried to sit up the pain increased sharply in his head.

'Here, take these,' Stella said, extending the tablets in her upturned palm.

'What are they?' McIndoe asked suspiciously.

'Painkillers,' she replied. 'I found them amongst the medical supplies.'

McIndoe picked them off her palm and swallowed them in quick succession, then allowed Ravallo to help him to his feet. He suddenly felt very light-headed and Ravallo had to grab his arm when his legs threatened to buckle underneath him. 'I think you'd better sit down again, Mac,' Ravallo suggested.

'I'm only going to slow you down,' McIndoe said once the dizziness had subsided. 'You go on with the others. Just leave me a gun and a couple of spare ammo clips.'

'We don't need martyrs. You're coming with us, Mac, and that's an end to it,' Ravallo replied firmly.

'Remember what I said to you on the train. Anyone unable to walk by themselves should be left behind. You know it makes sense.'

'I remember what you said on the train,' Ravallo said. 'And if I recall properly, you also said that, as the senior officer, it was my decision whether to sacrifice a player if it came down to it. Well, it has come down to it, and I'm not prepared to make that sacrifice. You're coming with us, even if it means I have to carry you over my shoulder. And that, Lieutenant McIndoe, is an order.'

McIndoe noticed Stella nodding in agreement. He looked past her at the approaching figure of Taffy Evans.

'Did you get through to the Partisans on the radio?' Ravallo asked Evans.

Evans shook his head. 'No, sir. The radio's dead. It looks like both the transmitting valves have blown simultaneously.'

'So replace them with the valves from the spare kit,' Ravallo said with a hint of irritation in his voice.

'The spare kit's missing,' Evans replied softly.

'Missing?' McIndoe said, wincing as a sharp pain shot through his head. 'You were supposed to have checked the set before we left the boat.'

'I did check it, sir,' came the defensive reply. 'The spare kit was there. Now when I looked in the panel to replace the valves, it was empty. But it was there on the boat. I know it was.'

'You didn't check it, did you?' Ravallo snapped.

'Yes, sir, I did,' Evans replied firmly.

'If Taffy said he checked it, then that's good enough for me,' McIndoe said, coming to Evans's defence.

Ravallo struggled to contain his rising temper. 'Bring it here. I want to see for myself.'

McIndoe eased himself down on to the kit-bag and waited until Evans was out of earshot before speaking. 'Both the transmission valves burning out at the same time? That's

314

stretching coincidence too far. Then, on top of that, the spare kit just happens to be missing as well. Very convenient.'

'In other words, sabotage,' Stella concluded.

'Of course it's sabotage.' McIndoe cursed under his breath as another bolt of pain speared through his head. 'Damn this headache.'

'And Higgins has orders to abort the operation if we miss a transmission,' Ravallo said. 'How long before you're due to radio through to Passiere again?'

'The next transmission's due in about three-and-a-half hours' time,' McIndoe said, checking his watch. He clamped his hands around himself and rubbed his arms. 'Christ, I'm freezing to death out here.'

'We changed into our dry clothes as soon as we got out of the river,' Stella said. 'Your uniform's over by the trees.'

'We'll talk more about this when I get back, but right now I'm going to get changed before I die of pneumonia,' McIndoe said. He struggled to his feet and made his way towards the trees.

'No radio. No transport. No chance. I think I'll have that carved on my headstone.'

'We're not dead yet, Nicky,' Stella said softly.

'That's rich coming from someone who nearly blew the whole operation back there. You said yourself that Mac had to hold your hand to get you to jump off the train. You're supposed to be an experienced field operative, not some child who constantly needs reassuring. If you can't handle this kind of pressure, Stella, then maybe you should apply for a desk job *if* we ever do get back to Washington.'

'At least I'm prepared to admit I've got faults,' she retorted, stung by his sarcasm. 'But then why am I bothering telling you this? You're Major Nicky Ravallo. You don't have any faults. You never make mistakes. You're the perfect officer in Military Intelligence.'

Before Ravallo could say anything he noticed Evans standing hesitantly in the background, the radio in his hands. 'Bring it here,' Ravallo said tersely, gesturing Evans towards them.

Evans handed the radio to him then pointed to the kit-bag on the ground. 'I'll get rid of this, shall I?' he said, sensing the tension between Ravallo and Stella. It made him feel distinctly uncomfortable, and he wanted no part of their personal quarrel.

'You do that,' Ravallo replied, waiting until Evans had retreated with the kit-bag before placing the radio on the ground and crouching down beside it. He tested the transmission frequency. Nothing. He tried boosting the signal. Still nothing. 'It's dead all right.'

'What I don't understand is how the saboteur could have rigged it in such a way that it would break down after the first couple of transmissions,' Stella said.

'I can think of at least two ways,' McIndoe said, fastening the top button on his dry officer's tunic. 'If he – ' his eyes went to Stella – 'or she knew in advance the lifespan of the transmission valves, they could have been set at a higher voltage to the voltage of the power heater so that they would burn out after a certain period of time. But that would have meant the mains transformer would have had to be altered to ensure the transmission valves would run at this higher voltage. The question then arises: when did the saboteur have the opportunity to carry out these modifications when we were only issued with the radio shortly before we left Malta? It would be too dangerous for them to start fiddling about inside the radio when they were already on the boat in case they were disturbed. How could they explain away what they were doing? No, I'm more inclined to believe the saboteur already had another set of transmission valves on them when they boarded the boat. Valves which contained a different filament material. One with a much lower resistance to the radio's voltage output. All they would have had to do is open the radio and switch the valves. It could have been done within seconds, and nobody would have been any the wiser.'

'You seem to be particularly well informed,' Ravallo said, his eyes riveted on McIndoe.

'We're back to the accusations again, are we?' McIndoe said contemptuously.

'We're all agreed the radio's been sabotaged,' Ravallo said. 'Question is: by whom?'

'Do you honestly think I'd have told you how I did it if I were the saboteur?' McIndoe countered. 'Credit me with a little intelligence, Nicky.'

'Oh I do, Mac,' Ravallo replied. 'It's a perfect example of the counter-bluff, isn't it? The saboteur explains exactly what they did and, in doing so, hopes to divert any suspicion away from themselves. After all, who would believe that they'd be foolish enough to admit to their own crime?'

'If you think I'm the saboteur, then why don't you kill me before I can do any more damage to this operation?' McIndoe said. He gestured to the holstered Beretta on Ravallo's belt. 'Go on, kill me if you're so sure of yourself.'

'That's enough, both of you,' Stella said, stepping between the two men. 'We've got three-and-a-half hours left to either find another radio, or to get back to the boat. Otherwise we're going to be stuck here on the island to fend for ourselves.'

'Stella's right,' McIndoe said. 'We've got to move out. Our best bet would be to try and find a village where we can make contact with the Partisans. They're our only realistic chance now of reaching the boat. We certainly won't make it on foot.'

'Tell your men to prepare to move out,' Ravallo said to McIndoe.

'What about that?' McIndoe asked, gesturing to the radio at Ravallo's feet.

'It's no use any more,' Ravallo replied. He picked up the radio and carried it to the edge of the river. He hesitated a moment, as if questioning his own judgement, then waded ankle-deep into the river and tossed the radio as far as he could into the water.

McIndoe crossed to where Evans, Hillyard and Johnson were standing by the trees. 'How are you feeling, sir?' Evans said, indicating the bloodstained bandage around McIndoe's head.

'It feels as if I've got Joe Louis shadow-boxing in my head, but hopefully the painkillers Stella gave me should start working pretty soon,' McIndoe replied.

'The radio was sabotaged, wasn't it?' Hillyard said.

'Two transmitting valves just happen to blow at the same time and there's no spare valves to replace them,' McIndoe replied. 'What do you think?'

'Which would imply that we have a saboteur in our midst,' Johnson concluded.

'It certainly looks that way,' McIndoe answered, knowing exactly where the conversation was leading. Only this time he didn't try to block it. He'd deceived them long enough. Yet he still believed he'd been right to do so. It had been to protect them – though judging by their faces they didn't see it the same way.

'So the story Starr gave us about the German spy being that Partisan, Sciarro, was actually a load of old bollocks,' Hillyard said angrily in English when McIndoe had finished his explanation.

'Stick to Italian!' Evans chided him sharply.

'Well, was it?' Hillyard demanded, reverting back to Italian.

'At the time there was a lot of evidence to point to Sciarro being the traitor,' McIndoe replied. 'Now it appears as if the Gestapo went to a lot of trouble to frame him as the traitor to draw any suspicion away from their man . . . or woman.'

'You think that Lieutenant di Mauro could be the German spy?' Johnson asked.

'Me. You. Her. Any one of us could be the spy. It could even be Charlie Higgins or Georges Passiere. Whoever sabotaged the radio could have done it either on the boat or after we'd come ashore. It's impossible to know when it happened.'

'How long have you known that Sciarro was framed?' Hillyard asked.

'I don't know that he definitely *was* framed,' McIndoe told him. 'Stella was adamant from the outset that he was innocent. I couldn't take the chance that she was wrong. That's when the three of us – Nicky included – decided it would be best to keep the operation on a need-to-know basis only, in case one of you was the traitor. It had nothing to do with Starr. I just used his name to make sure you didn't question my orders.'

'We should have been told the truth, sir,' Johnson said.

'And what good would that have done?' McIndoe countered. 'Could you honestly have worked together as a team, knowing there was the possibility that one of us was a German spy? No, and you know that. You'd have been constantly suspicious of each other. The distrust would have jeopardized the whole operation. That's why we chose not to tell you.'

'Why automatically assume the traitor is one of us? Why can't the traitor be one of the officers?' Hillyard said. 'Are you really so sure it's not one of the Yanks?'

'I told you, it could be any member of the team. But the three of us had already been briefed on the operation. It was a case of trying to limit the damage in case the traitor was someone from the ranks.'

'I'd say you've allowed yourself to be swayed by the Yanks,' Hillyard said.

'I wasn't swayed by anyone. I only did what I thought was in your best interests, and those of the operation as a whole.' McIndoe raised a hand to silence Hillyard before he could say any more. 'This isn't either the time or the place to be airing your grievances, but if you want to take the matter further with Vice-Admiral Starr when we get back to Malta, that's fine by me.'

'What for?' Hillyard snorted. 'He'll only take your side. He always backs his officers in any kind of dispute.'

'Starr never takes sides,' Evans said to Hillyard. 'If he backs an officer in a dispute, then it's because he thinks he's right, and not because he's trying to protect that officer's integrity.'

'I should have known you'd take the officer's side,' Hillyard said contemptuously. 'But then you always were good at that, weren't you?'

'That's enough!' McIndoe warned Hillyard. He turned to Evans. 'Get a bearing south-by-south-west on your compass. At least that way we'll know we're heading in the general direction of the boat.'

'What's going on?' Ravallo demanded as he and Stella approached them.

'The truth's finally come out,' Hillyard told him. 'We know we've got a traitor amongst us.'

'You certainly chose a hell of a time to drop the bombshell, Mac,' Ravallo said caustically to McIndoe.

'It was bound to come out sooner or later,' McIndoe replied. 'How was I supposed to explain away the disabled radio? Coincidence? I credit my men with a little more intelligence than that.'

'We might not be able to use the radio to contact the boat, but at least he can't use it either to contact the Germans,' Stella said in an attempt to diffuse the tension between her two fellow officers.

'"He"?' Hillyard said, looking straight at her. 'It could just as easily be "she".'

'I'm not the spy,' she was quick to tell him.

'But we don't know that, do we?' Hillyard replied.

'I've got the bearing on the compass,' Evans announced.

'Then let's move out,' Ravallo said.

Stella put a hand on McIndoe's arm as he was about to follow Ravallo towards the trees. 'How's the head?'

'Those painkillers seem to be doing the trick. The sledgehammer headache's gone, thank God. Now there's a dull throbbing in my temple, but I think I can just about live with that,' he replied.

'Are you two coming?' Ravallo called out to them.

'Yeah, yeah,' Stella muttered as they hurried after him.

'They weren't on the train, sir.'

Student stared at Riedler from the doorway, then entered the office and sat down in the armchair against the wall. He'd been woken from a listless sleep minutes earlier when Riedler had rung through to his room with the latest developments which had been radioed through to him from Valledolmo. Student had guessed it was bad news from the tone of Riedler's voice on the telephone. Now his worst fears had been confirmed. 'The Gestapo had a man on the train, didn't they?'

'Yes, sir. He's positive they didn't disembark at any of the stations along the way,' Riedler said.

'Which means they must have jumped from the train,' Student concluded.

'It certainly looks that way, sir. Question is: where did they jump off?'

'And why?' Student added. 'They must have been tipped off about the troops at Valledolmo.'

'A radio-transmitter was found concealed in the guard's van. It could have been used to listen in to the communiqués between the Gestapo and their man on the train. The senior conductor's already been taken away for questioning by the Gestapo.'

'Have they got anything out of him yet?' Student asked.

'Not as yet, sir. From what I could gather from the officer I spoke to at Valledolmo, the conductor seemed genuinely surprised by the discovery of the radio in the guard's van. Whether he is innocent, or whether it's just a bluff, we don't know yet.'

'What steps have been taken to track down the enemy agents since they bailed out from the train?' Student asked.

'I've had more troops dispatched to several key areas along the track where the enemy agents would have been most likely to have jumped. Rivers, lakes, marshes; places like that. I realize it's a long shot, sir, but it's all we can do until we've got more information to go on. I don't believe this was part of their plan, which means they'll have to improvise from now on. It's unlikely they'd want to proceed for too long on foot, knowing our troops will already be searching for them, so it's my guess they'll try and make contact with the Resistance to get them some transport. With that in mind, I've already spoken to the Gestapo, and they're getting in touch with as many of their informers as they possibly can, with instructions to keep an eye out for any unusual activity in their areas. Strangers would certainly stand out in a village at this time of night. I believe these informers are our best bet right now of finding them.'

'You seem to have the situation well in hand,' Student said, nodding to himself. 'I want you to establish a new base at the garrison near Valledolmo. You'll only need to leave a skeleton crew behind here at the hotel. They can join you as soon as Field-Marshal Kesselring and his chiefs-of-staff have left for Rome in the morning.'

'I'm glad you said that, sir,' Riedler replied. 'I've already contacted the *Luftwaffe* at the air-field to have a transport plane refuelled and ready to leave for Valledolmo within the hour.'

'It's obvious you don't need my input, so I'll get back to my bed,' Student said as he got to his feet. 'Keep me posted on any new developments.'

'That goes without question, sir,' Riedler told him.

'Why do I get the feeling neither of us is going to get much sleep tonight?' Student said.

THIRTEEN

'I can see a light over there.'

McIndoe hurried across to where Evans was crouched at the edge of the clearing and squatted down beside him. An isolated farmhouse. A single light. Not that he could see anything behind the net curtain which had been hung discreetly across the window. The yard, which was littered with rusted farm implements, and the crumbling stone wall which bordered the property, seemed only to add to its forlorn, unkempt appearance. 'What do you make of it?' McIndoe asked.

Stella, who appeared behind them, dropped to her haunches beside McIndoe and leaned her arm on his shoulder as she took in the isolated building. 'If nothing else, it's the first hint of civilization we've come across since we jumped from the train. And that was over an hour ago.'

'True enough,' McIndoe said. 'If the owners are sympathetic to the Partisan cause, we could be on our way to the boat within the hour.'

'And if they're not, we could be on our way to Gestapo headquarters within the hour,' Ravallo said behind them.

'Not necessarily, sir,' Johnson chipped in. 'If they aren't sympathizers, we could still pass ourselves off as a group of Italian soldiers who've become separated from our unit.'

'Either way, it's worth a closer look,' Stella said. 'We may not come across another living soul for the rest of the night.'

'It could be a trap,' Hillyard said. 'Countryside like this is typical Resistance heartland. They've got eyes and ears everywhere. How do we know the Partisans haven't been shadowing us for the last hour? They can't know who we are. We look like Italian soldiers and they despise them even more than they do the Germans.'

'If it is a trap, we're pretty exposed out here,' McIndoe said. 'Our best bet would be to take cover behind the stone wall. Admittedly it's not very high, nor is it exactly in pristine condition, but at least it would give us some protection in the event of any gunfire.'

'I'll do a recce of the farmhouse once we reach the wall,' Hillyard offered.

McIndoe nodded his approval. Hillyard was the best man for such a task. Silent, stealthy and deadly with a knife. They all still had the sleeve daggers strapped securely to their forearms, apart from Ravallo and Johnson who'd had theirs confiscated at the hotel.

'You make it sound as if you're expecting trouble,' Stella said.

'Just being cautious, that's all,' McIndoe said as he stared at the farmhouse. 'We Scots are renowned for that.'

Stella thought she sensed a hesitation in his voice. Unease? She followed his gaze. What was out there? Was he just overreacting? She looked at the others. They hadn't seemed to notice the flutter in his voice. She pushed the thought from her mind and wiped her clammy hands down the front of her tunic before tightening her grip on her rifle.

McIndoe was the first to break cover. His hands were sweating, making it difficult for him to keep a firm grasp on his pistol. All the time his eyes darted from side to side, watching for the slightest movement which would confirm his inner fears. There was something wrong about this place. Only he didn't know what. But how could he justify to his colleagues the uneasy feeling which was gnawing away at his stomach when he had nothing tangible to back up his doubts? God, how he hoped he was wrong . . .

The explosion was as sudden as it was deafening. He flung himself to the ground, winding himself in the process; as he struggled to catch his breath he became aware of a silence which seemed to have enveloped him. A silence he'd never imagined could exist. It was as if he were trapped in a vacuum. Then he heard a noise. Barely a whisper – yet to him it sounded like a roar as it shattered his fragile cocoon. Again he heard the noise, but by then he'd identified it as a voice – calling out his name. Slowly, almost reluctantly, he turned his head to investigate the voice, and what he saw in the shadowy moonlight would come back to haunt him in the innocence of sleep for the rest of his life.

Evans had stepped on an anti-personnel land-mine. Only he wasn't whispering. He was screaming. The anguished screams of a man in the grip of an agonizing death. Evans lay on his side, his left arm stretched out pitifully towards McIndoe as if in a desperate plea for help. Or at least what remained of his left arm. A stump of shattered bone and shredded flesh, severed below the elbow, covered in a thick coat of blood which pumped from the wound. McIndoe fought back the bile which surged up into his throat and tried to force itself into his mouth, as he stared in horror at the grotesque remains of the dismembered leg which lay close to Evans's mangled torso. Then his eyes went to Evans's stomach which had been laid open as if by the vengeful strike of a huge metal talon.

It was then he became aware of other voices. All around him. He looked at Ravallo who was lying flat on his stomach to his left. Ravallo was yelling at him, but it also sounded to him like a whisper. A distant whisper. It was only then McIndoe realized his encapsulated vacuum was an illusion of the mind. A pseudo-silence brought on as a direct result of the ear-splitting explosion when the land-mine had detonated within a few feet of him. He turned back to Evans and saw he was still screaming in tortured agony. His only concern at that moment was to reach his fallen colleague. To comfort him and be with him in those last, precious seconds of life. It was impossible to know whether they had blundered into an anti-personnel minefield, or whether it was an isolated mine which had been left behind by a retreating soldier. With that in mind he reholstered his fallen pistol and removed his sleeve dagger from the leather scabbard attached to the inside of his forearm. He then began the slow, laborious task of delicately inserting the tip of the dagger into the soil, ever fearful it would touch something solid beneath the surface. Soon the sweat was streaming down his face, but when he reached up to wipe it from his eyes, his fingers inadvertently brushed against his bandaged forehead. He felt the sticky texture of blood on his fingers. The wound was bleeding again. Not that it was important.

Evans was lying on his back when McIndoe finally reached him. His eyes were closed. No sound came from his bloodied lips. For a moment McIndoe thought he was dead. Then Evans let out an anguished scream. McIndoe drew his head back sharply. His hearing had returned. He took Evans's hand gently in his.

Evans opened his eyes when he felt the pressure on his hand. 'I . . . I knew you'd . . . come, boss,' he said through gritted teeth, then he coughed violently and the blood seeped from the corner of his mouth and down the side of his cheek. 'Boss, promise me . . . something,' he said between gasps of breath.

'Name it,' McIndoe replied.

'You'll . . . get them safely . . . safely off the island. Promise me . . . you will, boss.'

'You can count on it, Taffy,' McIndoe replied softly.

Evans dug his fingernails into McIndoe's palm as the excruciating pain racked his whole body. McIndoe removed the pistol from his holster and cupped his free hand under the back of Evans's head, placing the barrel lightly against his temple. The lone shot echoed across the silent country-side. McIndoe placed Evans's head on the ground and checked the carotid artery for any sign of life. Mercifully, there was no pulse. Only then did he notice that the others had formed a line behind Hillyard who, with the aid of his sleeve dagger, was now leading them slowly towards him. Nobody spoke. There was nothing to say.

McIndoe stripped off his tunic and placed it respectfully over Evans's face, then used his sleeve dagger to test the ground as he crawled carefully towards the approaching Hillyard. He knew he could have waited beside the body for them to reach him, but he didn't want them – and in par-ticular Hillyard and Johnson – to see the extent of Evans's horrific wounds. Their memories of Taffy Evans should be of the man he was in life, not a disfigured corpse lying in some foreign land. What really distressed him was the thought that there wouldn't be the time to retrieve the body and give it a decent burial. Not that Taffy was particularly reli-gious, but that was irrelevant under the circumstances. He deserved better than to be left to the mercy of the repug-nant vultures which constantly swept the skies in search of carrion. But it was out of his hands now . . .

The bullet slammed into the ground directly in front of him, and he jerked his body back with such force that he almost lost his balance. Without thinking, he stamped his hand down hard on to the untested ground beside him to steady himself. A second bullet struck the ground behind him. Then a volley of shots peppered the ground close to where the others lay, and Ravallo had to grab Johnson's arm to prevent him from scrambling to his feet. Johnson instantly regretted his panicky reaction and nodded ruefully to Ravallo, acknowledging his mistake.

'Don't move!' McIndoe shouted as more bullets spattered the ground around them. He'd established from the sound of the gunfire that there was more than one sniper and that they were concealed behind the stone wall. How long had they been there? He quickly pushed the question from his mind. There would be time for answers later, assuming they got out of the minefield alive. It was obvious to him the snipers weren't out to kill them. At least not straight away. They could easily have dispatched them with their first shots. Were they just toying with them, like a cat with a helpless bird, before going for the kill? Or were they trying to panic them into scattering for cover and possibly blowing themselves up in the process?

'Throw down your weapons.' The voice had come from the direction of the farmhouse. Although he still couldn't see anyone, McIndoe felt some relief that the order had been given in Italian. How he hoped these were Partisans, and not a unit of German soldiers with their customary Italian interpreter. 'I won't tell you again. Throw down your weapons.'

McIndoe and Ravallo exchanged glances. If these were Partisans, the last thing they wanted to do was antagonize them. Even if they weren't, what choice did they have? Ravallo gave the order for them to discard their weapons. McIndoe reluctantly placed his pistol on the ground at his feet, then slowly straightened up, careful not to move off the spot he was standing on, and clamped his hands on top of his head. The others all did the same. Only then did the shadowy silhouettes rise up from behind the stone wall. McIndoe counted six in all, although he was sure there would be others concealed in strategic positions around the farmhouse. They were all armed with submachine-guns. He could see that the silhouettes were dressed in an assortment of civilian clothes. Some wore jackets. Others were in their shirt-sleeves. Two were wearing flat caps. These had to be Partisans.

One of them stepped away from the others and lit a cigarette. The match momentarily illuminated his face. A middle-aged man with black hair and a black moustache which arched over the corners of his mouth. He shook the match out in his fingers, then flicked it over the wall. 'Some of my colleagues wanted to wager bets to see how many of you could get out of the minefield alive,' he announced, then took a long drag on the cigarette. 'But you're more useful to us alive. At least until we've had a chance to interrogate you.'

'Are you with the Partisans?' McIndoe called out.

'Do we look like German soldiers?' came the facetious reply. There were a few sniggers from those around him. 'We are Partisans. And you are traitors.'

'We're not Italian soldiers,' McIndoe told him.

'You can deny it now if you want, but we'll see how long you hold out under interrogation,' the man said.

McIndoe was loath to reveal their true identities, but at that moment they were running on empty. He had to play his hand – and there was no time to consult with Ravallo on what he was about to say. 'Three of us are British SOE. The other two are American Military Intelligence. I'm surprised that Giani Massimo hasn't told you about us or what we're doing here on Sicily.'

The man raised a hand to silence the others when they started to laugh again. 'There is a woman with you?' he asked.

'Yes,' Stella shouted, peering out from behind Ravallo.

The man gestured to the figure nearest him. 'Put a light on her.'

Stella shielded her eyes, dazzled by the intensity of the torch beam, then she lowered her hand and screwed up her eyes to let them see her features properly. 'I know you,' the man announced, wagging a finger at her. 'You are "Starling".'

Stella nodded. 'Yes. Have we worked together before?'

'Catánia harbour, three months ago,' the man told her. 'I was part of the unit who helped you to sink those two German torpedo-boats. You remember?'

'I remember,' Stella replied.

'I am Stefano,' he said, patting his chest with his hand, then he grabbed the torch from the man beside him and trained the light on his own face. 'You recognize me, Starling?'

Stella stared at him but, much as she tried, she just couldn't place his face. Then she realized what was different about him. 'Now I remember you. Only you didn't have a moustache then.'

'I had to grow it after my face appeared on wanted posters all over Catánia,' the man told her.

'I hate to break up this little reunion, but could you get us out of here?' Ravallo snapped at the man.

Stefano pointed to one of his men, who switched on his torch, then moved to the end of the stone wall where he carefully paced out ten steps. He stopped, then clambered over the wall and proceeded to walk another five paces, changed direction, and continued for another eight paces before changing direction yet again and pacing out another seven steps. When he stopped he was standing a couple of yards away from McIndoe. 'Come over to me,' he said to McIndoe. 'But not in a straight line. There is a mine buried in the ground directly in front of me.' He looked across at Hillyard and made a quick mental calculation in his head, then nodded to himself. 'There are no mines between us. You can walk straight over to me.'

McIndoe and Hillyard exchanged suspicious glances. The man seemed confident enough about where exactly the mines were planted. But what if he were wrong? Were they prepared to put their lives in his hands?

'I think I'll use the dagger to feel my way to you,' McIndoe decided.

The man smiled. 'You are safe, my friend. I will direct you. I would come over to get you, but I must stay here so that I can pace our way back to the wall.'

McIndoe wiped the sweat from his forehead. 'I just hope you know the position of the mines as well as you claim to do.'

'I should. I helped lay them.' He beckoned McIndoe towards him. 'Now, take one step towards me. Just one.'

There was a distinct reluctance in his movements when McIndoe stepped off the mark, and he gritted his teeth as he gingerly placed his foot on to the fresh patch of soil. He exhaled deeply as he brought his other foot through and carefully lowered it on to the ground. On the man's instructions, McIndoe then turned in a forty-five-degree angle and took another tentative step towards him. The sweat was biting into his eyes and he paused to wipe it away with his fingers. He wasn't surprised to find that his hand was trembling. Another step brought him alongside the man, who then made a cross in the soil with the tip of his shoe before taking a step backwards. He indicated the cross and told McIndoe to step directly on to it. McIndoe didn't even turn to face the man. Instead he stepped sideways on to the cross where he crouched down in sheer relief and wiped his hands over his sweating face. The man then went through the motions with Hillyard, instructing those lined up behind him to follow directly in his footsteps. Then, as each member of the team reached the cross he'd marked in the soil, the others would take a pace backwards until everyone was safely inside the secured passage. The caravan followed in the man's footsteps as if they were the hallowed footprints of a venerated saint. There was no margin for even the slightest error.

When they finally reached the stone wall, willing hands were waiting to help them out of the perilous minefield. Ravallo and Hillyard slumped down on to the grass on the other side of the wall, the obvious relief evident on their faces. Johnson leaned back against the wall, hands on knees like an exhausted runner after a particularly gruelling race. McIndoe walked the short distance until he was in line with where Evans's body lay in the minefield. He didn't know how long he'd been standing there when he became aware of someone beside him. It was Stella. 'I'm sorry about Taffy. I know you thought a lot of him.'

'Yes, I did,' McIndoe replied. 'He was a good man to have in your corner. He always stood up for what he thought was right, even if it meant taking an officer to one side and having a quiet word with him when he thought a particular plan of action would put lives in unnecessary danger. What's more, he was invariably right, which meant the officer then had to go off and rethink his strategy again. It happened to me when I first worked with him. I'm not ashamed to admit that. I'm going to miss him. I really am.'

They lapsed into silence, each caught up in their own thoughts, until Stefano approached them. 'I am very sorry about what happened to your friend. Had I known who you were . . .' He trailed off with a dejected shrug, knowing that no amount of words could compensate for what had happened.

'It's a bit late for apologies now, isn't it?' McIndoe turned on him, his pent-up anger and frustration bursting to the surface. 'You let us walk into the minefield, knowing full well there was every possibility that one or more of us could be killed. And if that wasn't enough, you then opened fire, hoping we'd scatter in panic and set off more mines. I don't care whether you thought we were Italian soldiers, that still doesn't justify what you did.'

'If you'd been forced to watch at gunpoint while your wife and daughter were raped by a succession of Italian soldiers, then maybe you could understand my motives,' came the embittered reply. 'We'd been following you for some time before you got here, and you never once gave us the impression that you were anything other than a group of Italian soldiers. That's why I gave the order to remove the warning sign from the edge of the minefield, and for a light to be left on in the farmhouse. I knew you wouldn't be able to resist going to the farmhouse when you saw the light.'

'I'm sorry about what happened to your wife and daughter, but you can't hold every Italian soldier responsible for the actions of a handful of their wayward colleagues,' McIndoe said in a calm, reflective voice. 'The Partisans' greatest strength has always been their ability to work as a collective unit. These kind of personal vendettas can only serve to undermine and ultimately fragment that strength.'

'You speak like a politician,' Stefano said disdainfully. 'But then I don't expect you to understand the revenge that burns inside me. You are not Sicilian.'

'She's Sicilian,' McIndoe said, gesturing to Stella beside him. 'Try and convince her that your vendetta's justified.'

'If she is truly Sicilian, then she already knows in her heart it's justified.'

McIndoe looked at Stella, expecting her to support him. Instead she walked off in the direction of the farmhouse. He hurried after her. 'Jesus, you actually agree with him, don't you?' he said in amazement, grabbing her arm when he caught up with her.

'Like you said, Sam. I'm Sicilian,' Stella replied coldly.

'Why don't you go and tell that to Taffy's widow back in Swansea?'

'It's got nothing to do with Taffy!' came the exasperated reply. 'Don't you see that? Just let it go, Sam.' She broke free from his grip. 'Just let it go.'

'What's going on?' Ravallo demanded, having been alerted by the sound of their raised voices.

'Nothing that need concern you,' Stella replied, disappearing into the farmhouse.

'Whatever you said to her obviously touched a nerve,' Ravallo said.

'It seems I've still got a bit to learn about the Sicilians,' McIndoe replied.

Ravallo's eyes flickered past McIndoe to the figure approaching them. 'Stefano's coming over. Do you want me to speak to him?'

'No, I'm OK now.'

'We'll remove the body from the minefield at first light and I'll see to it personally that he's given a proper funeral within the next few days,' Stefano told them.

'Thank you,' McIndoe said.

Stefano removed a packet of cigarettes from his shirt pocket. 'Do either of you smoke?'

McIndoe plucked a cigarette from the packet.

'We only had a few left when we left Palermo, but they were ruined when we jumped from the train,' Ravallo said, deftly taking the packet from Stefano's hand.

'I don't understand. You jumped from a train?' Stefano said with a puzzled frown.

'Forget it, it's a long story,' Ravallo replied, then held up the packet. 'You don't mind if I keep these, do you? God knows when we'll get any more.'

'You keep them,' Stefano said. He handed Ravallo a box of matches as well, then noticed one of his colleagues hovering in the background, trying to attract his attention. 'Please excuse me.'

Ravallo lit his cigarette and slipped a couple into his tunic pocket, then tossed the packet and the matches to McIndoe. 'Why don't you go and see if Stella would like one?'

McIndoe knew what Ravallo was implying – and he was right. McIndoe made his way to the back door and peered tentatively into the kitchen. Stella was sitting at the table, the previous day's edition of *La Sicilia* spread out in front of her. She glanced up at him when he entered the room, then returned her attention to the newspaper. 'I just came to say I'm sorry about what happened just now,' he said, the discomfort of the apology evident in his voice. He'd never been comfortable admitting to his mistakes. What made it worse was that he didn't believe he was in the wrong. 'I realize now I shouldn't have put you on the spot like that. I guess I just wasn't thinking at the time.'

'Are those cigarettes you've got there?' she asked without looking up at him.

'Yes. One of the Partisans gave them to us. I thought you might like one.' He opened the packet and extended it towards her.

She took one and he lit it for her. 'There's no need to apologize for what you said out there, Sam. After all, you only said what you thought was right. And you would be, if

334

we weren't in Sicily. Whether you agree with them or not, vendettas are an integral part of Sicilian life. Even the hot-blooded Italians don't share the same passion for revenge that the Sicilians do. I should know, it was the way my father raised me. He once killed a man who tried to cheat him on a deal. His honour was at stake. If he'd let the man get away, he'd have dishonoured his family's name. It might have been extreme, but at least nobody ever tried to cheat him again.'

'I can believe it,' McIndoe said, whistling softly to himself. 'Didn't the police do anything about it?'

'I remember they came to the house and took him away for questioning after the man disappeared. His body was never found so the police had to let my father go. I'm sure they knew he did it, but there wasn't enough evidence to prove it. It also helped that the man he killed was a petty criminal. They weren't exactly falling over themselves to solve the case.'

'What did happen to the body?' McIndoe asked, now hooked by the story.

'As you know, my father used to loot shipwrecks and sell anything of any value he found down there. The competition was pretty intense at times, especially if an old wreck was discovered that might have been carrying some kind of treasure. It was a case of whoever could reach it first and mark their territory ended up with the bounty. A boat could sit over the site of the wreck for days before its crew was ready to make the dive. In that time other boats would invariably lie at anchor a short distance away, and one way of deterring them from sending down divers was to throw buckets of blood and animal off-cuts into the water to attract any sharks that may be in the area. It's not often that you find sharks in the Mediterranean, but my father swore that there were Great Whites off the coast of Sicily. What better way of getting rid of the incriminating evidence than by feeding it to the sharks?' She carefully folded over the newspaper and placed it in the middle of the table, then smiled at McIndoe's horrified expression. 'That's what my mother told me some years later. Whether he actually admitted that to her, or whether it was just a story, I don't know. But it does make sense when you think about it.'

'I suppose it does,' McIndoe replied with a grimace of disgust. 'You certainly come from an . . . *interesting* family.'

She laughed. 'I guess that's one way of putting it.'

'It's a hell of a story to break the ice at parties,' Ravallo said from the doorway. 'And my guess is that's exactly how it began. At some party where your father was trying to impress one of the local girls.'

'He's seen all the newspaper cuttings my mother kept about the case and he still doesn't believe a word of it,' Stella told McIndoe, then she got to her feet and slapped the newspaper against Ravallo's chest. 'Ever the sceptic, eh, Nicky?' she said before disappearing out into the night.

Ravallo tossed the newspaper back on to the table and sat down opposite McIndoe. His eyes went to the open door before he spoke. 'I've never told Stella this, but I made a few discreet enquiries of my own about her parents when I took over as her controller. In particular her father. He certainly wasn't the person she liked to think he was. He was a small-time crook with heavy debts and a drink problem. He did have his own boat, but by all accounts it was a piece of junk held together with gum and glue. What he did have going for him was his family. His wife was crazy about him. As for Stella, she hero-worshipped him. And to give credit where it's due, he treated them both really well. Especially Stella. He absolutely doted on her. There wasn't anything he wouldn't have done for her.'

'You think she's invented this alter-ego because she didn't want to face the truth about what her father really was?' McIndoe asked.

'No, I don't,' Ravallo replied. 'You know Stella by now. She always speaks her mind. She's straight down the line like that. I honestly think she believes he was this roguish character who sailed the high seas in search of sunken treasure. I reckon that's the image he put over to her when she was a child. Why would she have any reason to doubt it? As I said, I've never told her any of this. Who am I to shatter the illusion for her?'

'What about the man her father was supposed to have killed?'

'A small-time crook did disappear at the time, and her father was one of those questioned about it. That much was obvious from the newspaper cuttings Stella's got at home. I guess he could have been murdered. Nobody was ever charged with the murder and the case was never officially closed. He could have done it, I suppose.'

'I'm not sure I'd be too quick to tell anyone if my father had murdered someone and then chopped them up into shark-bait,' McIndoe said.

'You might if you were Sicilian,' Ravallo replied wryly.

They heard the approaching footsteps on the narrow pathway leading up to the kitchen door. It was Stefano. 'I have news for you,' he told them, then pulled out a chair and sat down. 'I have just spoken to Giani Massimo on the radio. Starling also spoke to him and told him what happened on the train. He's told us to help you in any way we can. Tell us what you need.'

'For a start, transport back to our boat,' McIndoe told him.

'Yes, she mentioned the boat to me. Transport can be arranged. The only problem I can foresee are the German roadblocks. The Germans will be concentrating on this area now that they know you're no longer on the train, but if you give me the location of your boat, I can contact other Partisan units and find out exactly where these roadblocks have been set up. That way we'll be able to avoid them.'

'You seem very confident about that,' McIndoe said.

'This is our country. We have people in every sector who know all the back roads and all the short-cuts. How else do you think we're able to transport weaponry across the country with such ease? Even with their spies, the Germans can't hope to match our knowledge of the country.'

'How soon can we leave?' Ravallo asked.

'A truck is already on its way over here. It should arrive within the next few minutes. I've arranged for it to bring a fresh change of clothing for you all. I thought it best if you were dressed as migrant workers. That way you're less likely to arouse suspicion.'

'Good thinking,' Ravallo said. 'We'll also need the use of your radio-transmitter. If we don't contact our boat at a pre-arranged time, the captain has orders to abort the operation and return to Malta.'

'We'll take the radio with us in the truck.'

'What about new identity papers?' McIndoe asked. 'All we've got on us are our forged Italian army papers. They're not going to be of much use to us if we're going to be migrant workers.'

'You won't need any papers,' Stefano said. 'I told you, we'll work out the route in advance to bypass the roadblocks.'

'It's not as if we could do much about new papers anyway, not at this late stage,' Ravallo added. He noticed the frown linger on McIndoe's face. 'There you go again. Worrying. You've got to be more positive.'

'I'll be sure to bear it in mind,' McIndoe replied with a touch of sarcasm in his voice.

Stella hurried into the kitchen and jabbed her thumb over her shoulder. 'The truck's just arrived.'

Stefano got to his feet. 'We can leave as soon as you've changed out of those uniforms.'

'What are we waiting for?' Ravallo said as he pushed back his chair and followed Stefano from the room.

'Have you been able to make a positive identification yet?' Riedler asked as he stared at the body from behind the safety of the stone wall.

Franke switched on his torch and played the powerful light over the body. 'The face is hidden under the tunic but, even if we could see it, chances are we wouldn't recognize him. It's the tunic that interests me, sir. It carries the rank of captain. The man seen with Ravallo at the station earlier tonight was wearing the uniform of an Italian captain. Also, the scouting party who came across the body have already made some enquiries about troop movements in the area. There haven't been any Italian troops in this area for the past three days.'

'Where's their senior officer?' Riedler asked.

'When I last spoke with him, sir, he was with the radio operator,' Franke replied.

'I want to see him now!'

'I'll have him sent to you right away, sir.'

Riedler crossed to the farmhouse and entered the kitchen. He sat down, then pulled off his black leather gloves and tossed them on to the table. He stifled a yawn and rubbed his eyes wearily. What he'd give for a few hours' sleep. He knew most of the men felt the same way, and that they had gratefully put their heads down for the duration of the hour-long flight from Palermo to the air-base at Valledolmo. He hadn't been afforded the same luxury. Shortly before leaving Palermo, he'd been given the news that a total of eighteen civilians had been killed in the fire which had ravaged a section of the Capo quarter of the city earlier that evening. Another thirty civilians had ended up in hospital. He'd spent most of the flight listening to Franke's version of the events at the safe house.

Franke had tried to wash his hands of any guilt by churning out the same propaganda speech which had been so successful in winning over the younger soldiers who'd been with him at the safe house. As with Kuhn, it had left Riedler totally unmoved. Riedler had then questioned him at length about the fire, but Franke was adamant that he'd had nothing to do with it. By the time he'd finished questioning

339

Franke, Riedler was certain he was behind it, but he also knew he didn't have any evidence to substantiate these allegations. What's more, he realized Franke knew this as well. This only increased Riedler's determination to come up with a way to rid the Third Parachute Regiment once and for all of Captain Jürgen Franke . . .

The transport plane had barely touched down at the *Luftwaffe* airfield on the outskirts of Valledolmo, when word reached them that a scouting party had discovered a body, thought to be one of the enemy agents, in a minefield about fifteen miles south-east of the air-base. Two *Kübelwagens* and a troop-carrier were immediately laid on for their use. The *Kübelwagens* had sped on ahead of the more ponderous troop-carrier, arriving at the farmhouse in the past few minutes.

Franke knocked on the open door, then entered the kitchen with a young lieutenant following closely behind him. The lieutenant snapped to attention in front of Riedler. 'It is an honour to meet you, sir,' the lieutenant said in awe. 'I have heard so much about you – '

'I'm sure you have,' Riedler cut in. 'Are you in charge of the scouting party?'

'Yes, sir,' came the reply.

'What exactly did you find when you got here?' Riedler asked.

'The farmhouse was completely deserted, sir. But it was obvious that whoever had been here had only left minutes before we arrived.'

'Why was it so obvious?' Riedler queried.

'We found two mugs of coffee in the lounge. Both had only been partly consumed. The coffee in both mugs was still warm.'

'Tell Major Riedler about the truck,' Franke prompted the nervous officer.

'Yes, sir. The truck. We – our radio operator, that is – received word from our garrison shortly after we got here that an informer had telephoned to say he'd seen a truck leaving a village in this area shortly after two-thirty this morning. It was headed in this direction.'

'Did he get the licence number?' Riedler asked.

'No, sir.'

'What about a description of the vehicle?'

'He thought it looked like an SPA Dovunque light truck, sir.'

'What's that supposed to mean?' Riedler replied in exasperation.

'He said that by the time he got out of bed and went to the window, the truck was already some distance from his house, sir.'

'So why didn't he follow it?' Riedler demanded. 'I was under the impression all our informers in this area had been told to be on the lookout for anything suspicious. In my book, a truck driving through a quiet village at that time of night is definitely suspicious.'

'He had been contacted, sir,' the lieutenant said, 'but he can't drive.'

'What kind of clowns are they recruiting as informers over here?' Riedler hissed angrily.

'An alert has already been put out across the country, sir,' Franke told him. 'Chances are it would have been a Dovunque. From what I understand, they're very popular with the Resistance because of their excellent cross-country performance.'

'I don't care if it can sprout wings and fly, I just want it found!' Riedler yelled, then stabbed a finger in the lieutenant's direction. 'You get back on the radio and tell every officer at every roadblock that if the enemy agents do manage to escape, I'll see to it personally that they're on the next flight out to the Eastern Front. And that includes you. Now get to it!'

The lieutenant's hand was trembling so badly that he nearly knocked his cap off his head when he saluted Riedler. Then he hurried from the room and almost collided with a soldier who was approaching the kitchen. The lieutenant shoved the soldier aside roughly before he had a chance to apologize. The soldier stared after the retreating officer, then moved tentatively to the kitchen door.

'What do you want?' Franke demanded.

The soldier saluted him. 'We've found something, sir. In the woods.'

'Are you going to tell us what it is, or do we have to guess?' Franke demanded sarcastically.

'Clothes, sir. We found some clothes. They've been burnt.'

Riedler pulled on his gloves and tugged his peaked cap over his head before getting to his feet. 'Show us.'

The soldier led them to the glowing embers of a man-made fire at the edge of the thick woodland which bordered one side of the farmhouse. The pieces of burnt fabric which had been retrieved from the ashes were now lying on the grass. Franke directed his torch beam on to the smouldering remains, while Riedler used a fallen branch to sift carefully through them. 'Yes, they were here all right,' Riedler said as he stared into the darkened woods.

'They've only got a forty-minute head-start on us, sir,' Franke said, switching off his torch and falling in line with Riedler as he walked back towards the farmhouse.

'What are you suggesting?' Riedler said. 'That we go after them?'

'It would be better than just sitting around here, sir,' Franke replied.

'We don't know where they're headed. We could end up chasing our own shadows. No, we'll remain here and wait until there's a positive sighting of them. Then we can make our move.'

'What if they manage to evade the roadblocks?' Franke asked, pausing outside the kitchen door. 'The Resistance know this terrain much better than we do.'

'Granted. But when it comes down to it, there's only one way they can get off this island. By sea. They certainly couldn't do it by air. They'd be shot down within minutes of getting airborne. That's why I made contingency plans to cover for just such an eventuality before I left Palermo.'

'Which are?' Franke prompted when Riedler fell silent.

'That all operational *Schnellbooten* were to be put to sea to cover as much of the coastline as possible, and that two Messerschmitts at every air-base on the island were to be refuelled and ready for take-off should we need them. There are already three spotter planes in the air to help patrol the coastline. So whatever way they turn, they'll find there is no escape.'

'You know as well as I do, sir, that if they were cornered they would never let themselves be taken alive,' Franke said. 'That's standard procedure for covert operatives.'

'Then they'll die,' Riedler said coldly. 'It's as simple as that.'

'How far to go now?' Ravallo asked.

Stefano switched on his torch and focused the beam on the battered map which was spread out over his knees. 'We're about twelve miles from the coast. If we stay on this road we should reach the caves within the next thirty minutes.'

'All being well,' Johnson muttered from where he was seated on the wooden bench opposite them.

'I reckon we've made excellent progress, considering the amount of back roads we've had to take to avoid the German roadblocks,' Ravallo said. 'I've got to hand it to you, you've certainly got a fine communications network here on the island.'

'We have to, if we're to stay ahead of the Germans,' Stefano replied.

McIndoe looked at the two men, then dropped his cigarette butt on the floor and ground it out underfoot. He estimated they'd covered about thirty miles in the space of two hours. Ravallo was right. They'd made excellent progress, considering the numerous detours they'd had to take along the way to bypass the succession of roadblocks which had sprung up across the island in the last few hours. It was then that his eyes went to the radio-transmitter in the corner. He'd already contacted Passiere at the prearranged time to let him know they were on their way back to the boat. At least now he knew Charlie Higgins wouldn't leave without them. One less problem to worry about. But there was still a far more menacing problem for him to confront. The identity of the traitor. It was all he'd thought about since leaving the farmhouse and he'd studied each of the faces in the back of the truck, trying to decide which of them was hiding their true colours behind a mask of deceit. Yet in the end it had been a mixture of elementary logic and deductive reasoning which had finally thrown up a name. He now believed he knew the identity of the traitor . . .

'Roadblock ahead!'

The driver's shouted warning brought McIndoe back sharply to the reality of the moment, and he quickly concealed his Beretta submachine-gun under the wooden bench. Everyone did the same with their weapons.

'You said there weren't any roadblocks on this stretch of road,' Hillyard said to Stefano.

'It must have been erected within the last few minutes,' came the reply. 'It wasn't there twenty minutes ago when my colleagues checked the area.'

'How it got there isn't important right now,' McIndoe said. 'We follow the drill we agreed earlier.' He looked at Hillyard seated opposite him. They were both nearest the opening at the rear of the truck. 'You know what to do?'

'Leave it to me,' Hillyard assured him, deftly palming his sleeve dagger from its sheath on his forearm. He rested his hand lightly on his knee, the dagger hidden under his palm with the blade nestled between his middle and index finger.

McIndoe removed his own sleeve dagger, then leaned forward to peer through the windscreen when the driver slowed the truck as it neared the tangled roll of barbed wire which had been strung out across the road. A covered Opel Blitz truck was parked at the side of the road. There were only two German soldiers illuminated in the headlights, but he was sure there would be others sitting in the back of the truck. The two soldiers approached the driver's window, and the cab was suddenly flooded with the blinding light from a powerful torch. The driver put his hand to his face to shield his eyes, but his hand was batted aside and he was ordered to produce his papers for inspection. The second soldier moved to the back of the truck where he picked out each face with his torch. The beam lingered on Stella, then continued to sweep the rest of their faces before it finally settled again on Hillyard. 'Papers,' he snapped in Italian.

'I've got them right here,' Hillyard said, and his hand shot forward with such speed that the soldier didn't have time to react before the blade was embedded in his throat. Hillyard clamped his other hand over the soldier's mouth and slashed the blade sideways, slicing effortlessly through the windpipe. McIndoe jumped silently from the truck and grabbed the soldier's lifeless body before lowering it to the ground. Ravallo passed him down his submachine-gun, and McIndoe pressed himself up against the lowered flap before swinging round on the soldier who was still examining the driver's papers. The papers dropped from the startled soldier's hand, and he was still bringing up his MP.38 submachine-gun to fire when McIndoe cut him down with a burst from the Beretta. The soldier was dead before he hit the ground.

The others had already spilled on to the road before the flap at the back of the Opel Blitz was flung open. A soldier appeared and managed to get off a salvo in the direction of the Dovunque before Hillyard and Johnson opened fire. His body jerked grotesquely as a scythe of bullets found their mark and he was punched back into the truck. With Johnson and Hillyard firing into the back of the truck from their concealed positions at the back of the Dovunque,

McIndoe and Ravallo broke cover and sprayed the side of the tarpaulin. The soldiers trapped inside didn't stand a chance in the deadly crossfire. The firefight was over in a matter of seconds.

McIndoe saw the barrel of a submachine-gun poke through the driver's window, and he swung his Beretta on the cab and raked the door and window with a fusillade of bullets. An agonized scream emanated from inside the cab, and the submachine-gun fell to the ground. He ran to the driver's door and, with heart pounding, pulled the pin from a grenade he'd been carrying and dropped it through the shattered window. He flung himself to the ground; seconds later the shuddering explosion tore off the driver's door and hurled it into the middle of the road. McIndoe leapt to his feet and ran to the cab. The only body inside was that of the driver. The gunfire had already ceased as he made his way cautiously to the front of the truck. He swivelled round, his submachine-gun at the ready. There was nobody on the other side. He moved to the back of the Opel Blitz where Ravallo and Hillyard were standing, their submachine-guns now hanging limply at their sides. He counted a further five bodies in the back of the truck. The radio operator, who'd obviously been trying to send out a distress call when the firing had started, was slumped over the radio-transmitter, the handset still clenched in his bloodied hand. An anxious German voice could be heard trying to raise him from the other end. Ravallo jumped up into the back of the truck and checked the soldiers for any sign of life. Not surprisingly, there was none. He used his foot to push the radio operator away from the set, then he aimed his submachine-gun at the array of dials and instantly silenced the voice with a short burst of gunfire.

McIndoe went to assist Johnson and Stella who were busy trying to move the convoluted tangle of barbed wire and, between the three of them, they managed to create a gap wide enough in the road for the Dovunque to pass through. McIndoe retrieved the driver's papers and handed them back to him through the open window. 'Are you all right?' he asked.

'Yes. I just kept my head down until the firing stopped.'

'You're going to have to push this little beauty to the very limit,' McIndoe said, patting the side of the truck, 'because it won't be long before the Germans are swarming all over this place. And I, for one, don't want to be around when they get here.'

'Fortunately this is an isolated area of coastline. By the time the Germans find out what's happened, we'll be long gone. Hopefully you and your colleagues will already be at sea and out of range of their tentacles.'

'Sam?' Stella called out to him.

'I'll get everyone back into the truck, then we can move out,' McIndoe told the driver, then he walked over to where Stella was standing with the others at the back of the vehicle. Ravallo was crouched over a body which was sprawled out on the road. It was Stefano. The front of his shirt was drenched in blood. He'd been shot once in the chest.

'There are a couple of bullet-holes in the side of the tarpaulin,' Ravallo said. 'From the position of the body, it's my guess he was hit by a stray German bullet just as he was about to alight from the back of the truck.'

'Get him into the back,' McIndoe said. 'We've got to get out of here before the Germans send in reinforcements.'

Johnson and Hillyard lifted the body into the back of the truck. The driver pulled an old woollen rug out from under the passenger seat, and handed it to Hillyard to place over the body. McIndoe was the last to board and, after grabbing Ravallo's extended hand to haul himself into the truck, he nodded to the driver who started up the engine and pulled away from the roadblock.

'Excuse me, sir,' Kuhn said from the doorway. 'We've just been sent a communiqué from the army garrison at Gela.'

'What is it?' Riedler demanded.

'They received a Mayday call from one of the roadblocks. The radio operator at Gela thought he heard gunfire in the background. Then the contact was broken and shortly after that the line went dead.'

'Did they get the exact location of the roadblock?' Riedler asked.

'Yes, sir,' Kuhn replied.

'Show me,' Riedler said, spreading out a map of the area on the kitchen table. Franke used a couple of mugs to hold down the top edges. Kuhn removed a notebook from his tunic pocket, opened it at the relevant page, and placed it beside the map. The area was quickly located. An isolated stretch of coastline about fifteen miles south of Gela.

'We don't know that it was the enemy agents, sir,' Kuhn said. 'It could have been the Resistance. They target isolated roadblocks like that every day.'

'It could also be a ruse, sir, to try and draw us away from their intended rendezvous,' Franke added.

'I don't buy that,' Riedler said, staring at the map. 'If I was Ravallo, the last thing I'd want to do was draw any unnecessary attention on my team. Not even a diversion. I'd want to slip away as quietly as possible. If they were forced into a shootout, it means there wasn't any other way out for them. That's how I see it.'

'What do we do now, sir?' Kuhn asked.

'Captain Franke, radio through to the air-base at Gela and speak personally to the base commander,' Riedler said. 'I want the two Messerschmitts that are on standby scrambled and sent to those coordinates,' Riedler said, tapping the notebook. 'Kuhn, I want any *Schnellbooten* in that vicinity dispatched to the stretch of coastline bordering those coordinates.'

'So you think it is them, sir?' Kuhn said.

'I'm sure of it,' Riedler replied, tossing the notebook to Kuhn. He got to his feet, then crossed to the window and clasped his hands tightly behind his back. 'They've certainly proved themselves worthy adversaries. They've managed to stay one step ahead of us at every turn. But I've got a feeling their luck's about to run out.'

'I can't believe we've finally made it,' Stella said after she'd climbed from the back of the truck once it had come to a halt on a ridge overlooking the sea.

'We haven't made it yet,' McIndoe reminded her as he stared out across the magnificence of the dark, forbidding waters spread out before them. A final obstacle to challenge their freedom. And because of the notorious unpredictability of the world's great oceans, in many ways the most demanding obstacle of all.

'If I didn't know better, I'd swear you two didn't want to leave,' Ravallo said behind them.

'I could stand here forever and never tire of the view,' McIndoe replied as he gazed out over the silent waters.

'You stay there if you want, buddy, but the rest of us have got a boat to catch,' Ravallo said, patting McIndoe on the shoulder.

'You've got no soul, Nicky,' McIndoe said.

'And neither will you if the Jerries get hold of you,' Ravallo replied.

McIndoe fell in line behind Stella as they followed a Partisan down to the beach where two rowing boats were wallowing gently in the shallows, ready to take them back to the waiting MTB. McIndoe recognized the man who was seated in the nearest rowing boat as the same one who'd transported him from the MTB when they'd first arrived on the island. He greeted the man as he climbed into the boat, but there was no response. Not that it bothered McIndoe. The man was a fine oarsman. That was all that mattered. Hillyard and Johnson got into the boat with him, while Stella and Ravallo took to the other one. Willing hands pushed them away from the beach and the two oarsmen began the slow and arduous task of rowing them out to the nest of caves where the MTB was anchored.

McIndoe quickly found himself scanning the night sky for any sign of approaching enemy aircraft, the incident with the *Luftwaffe* bombers and their escort fighters still very fresh in his mind. The operation had almost been compromised before it had begun. It was with a great sense of relief that they finally reached the caves, which loomed up like ghostly sentinels silhouetted against the misty backdrop of the rugged Sicilian coastline. Their boat was the first to enter the cave, and McIndoe gave the order for Johnson to switch on his torch to aid the vision of the oarsmen. The beam cast teasing shadows across the walls, flickering and flitting like a nightmare of spectral apparitions around them. A sudden movement from within the optical illusion had McIndoe grabbing for the submachine-gun at his feet. A lone bat, disturbed by the approaching light had broken free from its perch on the arched cavern roof high above them, and had dived towards the boat before levelling out and disappearing into the darkness behind them. McIndoe cursed under his breath for having let his nerves get the better of him, then replaced the submachine-gun under his seat again. He was desperately tired. He'd gone without sleep for much longer periods than this on previous assignments, but the very nature of this operation had left him both mentally and physically drained. Normally not in need of much sleep, he welcomed the thought of the warm bed which would be awaiting him when they got back to Malta. He found himself subconsciously yawning, and quickly shut out any self-indulgent thoughts of sleep. There would be time for that later . . .

'Mine ahead!' Hillyard yelled as the rowing boat turned into a sharp bend in the tunnel.

McIndoe stared in horror at the German mine which was bobbing menacingly in the water not twenty feet in front of them. A wave gently buffeted the mine, pushing it closer to the boat. The Partisan was desperately trying to propel the boat away from the encroaching danger, his arms shuddering with the sheer effort of his task as he dug the oars deep into the water, when the sound of laughter came from the darkness further down the tunnel. McIndoe's first thought as he grabbed his submachine-gun was that the Germans had somehow managed to get past the Partisans on the surrounding cliffs and overrun the cave.

More laughter. Then a voice – echoing around the hollow confines of the cavernous tunnel. A distinctly familiar voice. The English was spoken with a lilting French accent. 'Welcome back, *patron*. Do not worry about the mine. It is quite harmless.'

'Passiere, is that you, you bastard?' Hillyard shouted back.

'And I love you too, *mon ami*,' came the chuckled reply.

'Mac, it's Charlie Higgins,' another voice called out from the darkness. 'I'll switch on the bow light so you can see where the boat's moored. Don't worry about the mine. It's only a replica. I'll explain everything to you when you come aboard.'

A worrying thought flashed through McIndoe's mind. What if he'd been wrong about the traitor? It wasn't even as if he had any real evidence, just his own gut feelings. What if it were Higgins? Or Passiere? Or worse still, both? No, it made no sense, he told himself. If this was a trap, they would be far more useful to the Germans alive. Why kill them now when all the Germans had to do was wait until they reached the boat to capture them? What Germans, he chided himself? He was overreacting. So why was there still a lingering doubt in the back of his mind?

The Partisan had already stopped rowing, despite having been assured by Hillyard that there was no danger to them, but he still kept an eye anxiously on the mine as it bobbed in the illuminated water. A light appeared in the darkness further down the cave, and for the first time the silhouetted outline of the MTB's bow became visible to them. The

Partisan made no move to pick up the oars and row towards the light. 'Those are my colleagues. I trust them implicitly,' McIndoe told him, as if he were trying to convince himself of that fact as well. 'If they say the mine's harmless, that's good enough for me. But I can understand if you don't want to go any further. We can transfer you to the other boat and I'll row – '

'I will row,' the Partisan interceded, a finger raised as if to signal the termination of any further discussion on the subject. He slipped the oars back into the water and began to row with determined strokes towards the light. Even so, he was obviously still not convinced the mine was harmless, and steered as wide a berth around it as he possibly could. In doing so he scraped the side of the boat against the side of the cave. Not surprisingly, the same manoeuvre was repeated by his colleagues in the boat following behind them.

A Jacob's ladder had already been dropped over the side of the MTB by the time the rowing boat came alongside the hull, and Hillyard reached out and grabbed one of the rungs. He hoisted himself up effortlessly on to the rope ladder, quickly climbing to the top, where Passiere was waiting to help him aboard. Johnson was the next to go. Then McIndoe. There was a broad grin on Passiere's face as he grabbed McIndoe's hand and helped him up on deck. 'It is good to see you again, *patron*.'

'It's good to be back,' McIndoe replied.

'Where's Taffy?' Higgins asked behind McIndoe.

'He didn't make it,' McIndoe replied grimly. 'How soon can we leave?'

'As soon as everyone's on board,' Higgins replied in a hollow voice, still numbed by the news of Evans's death. 'Are you expecting trouble?'

'You could say that. We had an unexpected run-in with a German patrol shortly before we got here. We managed to kill them, but not before their radio operator put out a distress call.'

'In other words, we could be getting some company before long,' Higgins said, then gestured to the wheelhouse. 'Come on up. We can talk more on the bridge while I get her started.'

McIndoe followed him up the metal steps and into the wheelhouse. 'So, what's the story with the mine?'

'There was a *Schnellboote* in the area earlier this evening. They were checking the caves. Fortunately for us the Resistance had already intercepted the radio transmissions between the boat and Gela harbour. So we knew they were coming. That's when the Resistance came up with the idea of the mine. It turns out they've got several replica mines which have been used to protect the contraband they've got stored in caves and grottoes all along the Sicilian coast. It has a small anchor to prevent it from moving more than a few feet in any direction. We knew the *Schnellboote* had orders to check every cave in this area, which is why the Resistance didn't place the mine at the mouth of the cave, as they normally do to deter unauthorized entry, because there was every chance the Germans might try and detonate it. So by placing it beyond the first bend inside the cave, it wouldn't be visible from the entrance. They couldn't risk blowing it up in such a confined area – it could have triggered a rock fall. So after the mine had been laid, I took the MTB into a tunnel further back there.' Higgins gestured into the darkness behind them. 'As it turned out, they reacted exactly as we anticipated they would. Judging by what I could hear, they reversed engines as soon as they saw the mine and high-tailed it out of the cave. We haven't had another patrol boat in this area since it left.'

'Ingenious,' McIndoe said. 'But why weren't we warned about it? Even the Partisans who rowed out here didn't know anything about it.'

'I thought it best for security reasons to play it close to the chest. Only the Partisans who laid the mine knew about it.'

The door opened and Ravallo entered the wheelhouse. He shook hands with Higgins. 'We're all aboard. Time to get us the hell out of here, Charlie boy.'

'You can count on it,' Higgins replied. He called down to Hillyard to weigh anchor.

'I'm going below to get changed out of these borrowed clothes. I'll see you guys just now,' Ravallo said as he left the bridge.

McIndoe watched as Johnson switched off the bow light, plunging the vessel back into darkness. Hillyard called out to the bridge that the anchor had been raised, and Higgins started up the engine and edged the boat towards the mouth of the cave.

Kuhn burst through the open kitchen door. 'We've got them, sir,' he announced breathlessly.

'What are you talking about?' Riedler demanded.

'A communiqué's come through from Gestapo headquarters in Palermo, sir, with the exact coordinates of the enemy boat. An alert has been sent out to all craft in the area, and we've already received confirmation that the two Messerschmitts which were scrambled from Gela should intercept the enemy vessel within the next few minutes. A *Schnellboote* has also been despatched to the area. ETA is five minutes.'

'How did the Gestapo manage to get these coordinates?' Riedler asked.

'You're not going to like this, sir,' Kuhn replied.

'Just tell me!'

'The coordinates were relayed to them from the enemy boat,' Kuhn said.

'That doesn't make any sense,' Riedler retorted, then his eyes narrowed as a look of disbelief slowly crossed his face. 'Unless . . .'

'That's right, sir,' Kuhn said when Riedler's voice trailed off. 'They've got an agent on board the enemy vessel.'

'We've been breaking our backs trying to track them down, and all the time they had their own agent on the inside. What the hell are they playing at, Kuhn?'

'I don't know, sir,' Kuhn replied. 'I asked them who the agent was, but they refused to say.'

'We'll see about that.' Riedler pushed back his chair with such force that it toppled backwards and clattered noisily to the floor.

'Do you want me to get Gestapo headquarters on the radio for you, sir?' Kuhn asked.

'No. I want all radio channels kept open for the time being. It's imperative that I'm able to stay in touch with the Messerschmitts and any of the *Schnellbooten* once they make contact with the enemy vessel.' Riedler picked up the chair and placed it back on its feet. 'But when this is over, someone at Gestapo headquarters is going to have to come up with some answers. That I can promise you.'

FOURTEEN

McIndoe heard the sound of scuffed footsteps on the metal steps outside, but before he could investigate further, the door was flung open with such force that it slammed against the adjacent wall and Georges Passiere lurched unsteadily into the unlit wheelhouse. His face was twisted in pain and his hand clamped tightly against the back of his head. '*Patron*, help me,' Passiere pleaded as he stumbled forward and fell to his knees.

Quickly McIndoe helped him to his feet and led him to the wall-mounted bench. Passiere slumped down on to the bench; only then did McIndoe see the blood seeping out from between the Frenchman's fingers. 'My God, what happened?' he asked anxiously.

'I was in the radio room, listening in to the German radio traffic, when I felt a sharp blow on the back of my head. I had my back to the door so I never saw who hit me. I must have passed out, because the next thing I remember is coming round and finding myself lying on the floor.'

'What happened when you came round?' McIndoe pressed him, already fearing the worst.

'I noticed the dial had been switched to another frequency. One I have never used before. The line was dead. I realized that whoever hit me was probably the same person who sabotaged your radio. I came up here as quickly as I could. I had to warn you, *patron*.'

'You did well, Georges,' McIndoe told him. There was no doubt in his mind that whoever attacked Passiere had purposely waited until the boat was clear of the cave, knowing there would have been too much interference inside the cave to either transmit or receive a signal, before using the radio to make contact with the Germans. It seemed the only logical explanation. If the Germans knew where they were, it would only be a matter of time before they were intercepted. He had to act fast if they were to have any chance of escape. 'Did you tell anyone else about this?' he asked Passiere.

'No, *patron*.'

'Let's keep it that way, shall we?' McIndoe said.

'I did not see anyone when I came up here.' A look of horror spread across Passiere's face. 'What if whoever hit me has already – ' he paused as he struggled to find the right words – ' dealt with the others?'

McIndoe and Higgins exchanged anxious glances. It was obvious that Passiere's words had struck the same chord of fear in both of them. What if he was right? It would be that much easier for the Germans to board the boat if the saboteur had already immobilized most of the crew. McIndoe shouldered his Sten gun, then removed the first-aid box from the cupboard where Higgins stored his charts and handed it to Passiere. 'You'll have to patch yourself up.'

'Let me come with you, *patron*,' Passiere said as he tried to get to his feet.

McIndoe put a hand on Passiere's shoulder and pushed him back down on to the bench. 'You're in no condition to go anywhere. Stay here.'

'*Patron*, you could use another gun.'

'That's an order, Georges,' McIndoe told him.

Passiere slumped back against the wall. McIndoe opened the door and slipped out on to the metal stairs. He scanned the bow deck. Deserted. This only increased the wretched unease which pulsed through his body. He descended the steps and was about to make his way towards the aft deck when he heard a scraping noise below. He reached the top of the stairs and fanned the area with the Sten gun. Nobody there. He moved slowly down the stairs, step by step, his back pressed up against the wall as he went. When he reached the bottom of the stairs he wiped the sweat from his forehead, then pivoted round, the Sten gun trained on the corridor. It was deserted. Then he heard the noise again. It was coming from the wireless room. He made his way stealthily along the corridor, and took up a position adjacent to the open door. Tightening his grip on the submachine-gun, he swung round, the barrel trained on the figure in the centre of the cabin. It was Nicky Ravallo.

Ravallo stumbled backwards in surprise, then clasped his hand to his chest and let out a deep sigh of relief when he saw who it was. 'Jesus, Mac, you scared the hell out of me.'

'What are you doing in here?' McIndoe asked coldly, without lowering the Sten gun.

Ravallo's eyes went to the weapon in McIndoe's hand. 'I was on my way up to see you guys on the bridge when I noticed the blood on the floor in here. There was no sign of Passiere, so naturally I came in to see if everything was all right. Obviously it isn't, otherwise you wouldn't be creeping around with that Sten gun. And would you mind not pointing it at me?'

'Where are the others?' McIndoe demanded.

'Stella's getting changed in one of the cabins. Like me, she wasn't too thrilled about wearing someone else's cast-offs.' Ravallo was now wearing his own black polo-necked jersey and black trousers. 'The last I saw of Hillyard and Johnson, they were up on deck, checking the anchor chain. Hillyard reckoned the chain was playing up when he pulled it in before we left the cave.'

McIndoe heard the sound of a door opening, and turned the submachine-gun on the figure who emerged from a cabin further down the corridor. Stella's eyes widened in disbelief, and she instinctively raised her hands. He let the submachine-gun fall to his side.

'What the hell's got you so spooked, Mac?' Ravallo demanded. McIndoe told them about the incident with Passiere.

'So whoever hit him has used the radio to give our position away to the Germans,' Stella said.

'That's how I see it,' McIndoe said.

'And you thought it was me?' Ravallo said in amazement.

'All I know is that it wasn't Charlie Higgins or me, because we've been on the bridge together ever since we left the cave,' McIndoe said.

'Unless you're both working for the Jerries,' Ravallo suggested, but there was no strength of accusation in his voice.

Their attention was drawn to the sound of the toilet being flushed. Hillyard emerged from the bathroom and froze mid-step when he found them staring suspiciously at him. 'Have I done something wrong?' he asked hesitantly.

'Nicky said you and Neville were up on deck checking the anchor chain,' McIndoe told him.

'We were, but it was too bloody dark to see what was making it snag,' Hillyard replied as he tucked his shirt into his trousers. 'We gave it up as a bad job after a few minutes.'

'Where's Neville now?' McIndoe asked.

'He's probably still up there. At least he was when I last saw him. Why, what's going on?'

'How long have you been in the Head?' Ravallo asked.

'Jesus, what is this?' Hillyard demanded.

'Just answer the question!' McIndoe ordered.

'I wasn't exactly timing myself,' Hillyard replied contemptuously. 'Five minutes. Perhaps a bit more. I don't know. My stomach's been playing up ever since we came aboard. I reckon it's that food we had at the farmhouse. Look, will someone tell me what the hell's going – '

'Listen!' McIndoe cut in, his finger raised to silence Hillyard. 'Do you hear that?'

Ravallo looked apprehensively at Stella and Hillyard but, like him, they couldn't hear anything other than the monotonous hum of the MTB's engines. Ravallo was about to speak when he heard it: the distant droning of an aircraft engine.

'Enemy aircraft approaching!' came Johnson's shouted warning from the deck.

'Man your stations,' Ravallo ordered. They hurried up on to the deck, where Johnson was already in position behind the stern-mounted twenty-millimetre Oerlikon gun. Hillyard took up a similar position behind the starboard Vickers machine-gun. Ravallo and McIndoe exchanged glances; both had had the same thought. There was no Taffy Evans to man the Vickers on the port side. 'I'll take it,' Ravallo said.

'No,' McIndoe replied, grabbing Ravallo's arm as he was about to make for the gun. 'I've trained on those things. I know them a lot better than you do. Go up to the bridge and tell Passiere to contact Valletta and find out if they've got any aircraft in the area. I've got a feeling we're going to need all the help we can get.'

'I'm on my way,' Ravallo said, and sprinted towards the wheelhouse steps.

The burst of gunfire from the Messerschmitt's wing-mounted cannons raked the water close to the boat. All three deck guns opened up on the plane as it zoomed low over the boat. Both McIndoe and Hillyard swivelled the Vickers on their portable axes and continued firing after the retreating Messerschmitt, but without success.

'Enemy aircraft approaching!' Johnson yelled from the stern. He opened fire on a second Messerschmitt, which had approached the boat undetected, the sound of its engines drowned out by the first plane. The second Messerschmitt also fired wide of the boat. McIndoe swung the Vickers on the aircraft, but it was already out of range. Passiere and Ravallo waited until the deck guns fell silent, then scurried down the wheelhouse steps and Passiere disappeared below deck to make contact with HQ in Valletta. Ravallo ran to where McIndoe was watching the second Messerschmitt turn slowly to make another run in on the boat. 'Get your head down, Nicky. The bastard's coming back.'

'Mac, look out,' Ravallo shouted. He gestured to the second Messerschmitt which was fast approaching the boat from a different direction.

'That's Hillyard's problem,' McIndoe shouted back, then he opened up on the menacing silhouette of the first Messerschmitt as it swooped down towards the boat. Johnson was following the fighter in the sights of the Oerlikon gun, and he pounded the night sky with a barrage of rounds as soon as it came within range. Hillyard engaged the first Messerschmitt, and both fighters opened fire within seconds of each other. McIndoe threw himself to the deck as the first Messerschmitt passed overhead, the bullets raking across the wooden deck. Johnson swung the barrel of the Oerlikon gun on the other Messerschmitt as it homed in on the boat.

'Get down!' McIndoe screamed at Johnson as a second fusillade of bullets raked across the superstructure. Johnson stood his ground defiantly, returning fire as the bullets chewed into the aft deck around him. He suddenly cried out in pain and stumbled away from the gun, dropping to his knees, his hands clutched tightly to his stomach.

Stella and Ravallo broke cover and ran to where Johnson was now doubled over on the deck. She gently prised his hands away from his stomach, and immediately feared the worst when she saw the dark stain of blood on the front of his shirt. 'I'm all right,' Johnson said through gritted teeth and held up his right hand. The blood streamed down his forearm from a flesh-wound on his palm. 'The bullet went straight through. Help me up, will you? I've got to get back to my post. Those Messers are going to be back and I'm damned if I'm going to let them finish me off next time.'

'You're in no condition to take them on again,' Ravallo said. He turned to Stella. 'Take him below and dress the wound.'

'I can't leave my post now, sir,' Johnson replied.

'I'll take over,' Ravallo told him. 'You get that hand treated. That's an order!'

'Yes, sir,' Johnson reluctantly agreed. 'But when I've been patched up, I'm coming right back up here again. No disrespect, sir, but I'll want my gun back when I do. I haven't finished with those Boche. Not by a long way.'

It was a side of Johnson that Ravallo had never seen before. Defiant. Determined. Resolute. But, more than that, the guy had shown incredible courage by staying at his post, knowing full well there was every chance he could have been killed as a result of his selfless actions. Johnson had gone up a hell of a lot in his estimation.

'Two Messers incoming,' Hillyard yelled from the starboard side.

'*Schnellboote* approaching fast to starboard!' McIndoe called out before Ravallo could turn the Oerlikon gun on the approaching Messerschmitts. There wasn't time to react to McIndoe's warning, as both fighters opened fire simultaneously on the boat, and Ravallo had to take desperate evasive action as a fusillade of bullets ripped into the deck around him. He wiped the blood from his chin where a splinter had nicked his skin, and he was still getting to his feet when their boat was illuminated by the powerful spotlight which was mounted on the deck of the German *Schnellboote*. McIndoe tried to take out the light with a concentrated burst from the Vickers, but was forced to take cover when the Germans returned fire with their powerful deck guns.

'*You have exactly one minute to switch off your engines and surrender,*' an amplified voice boomed out in German from aboard the *Schnellboote*. '*If you refuse, your boat will be sunk.*'

'We've got the faster boat,' Ravallo called out to McIndoe. 'We can outrun them.'

'Not before they launch a torpedo,' McIndoe replied. 'And even if we were able to evade the torpedo, we'd still have to deal with the Messers.'

Ravallo looked up anxiously for any sign of the Messerschmitts. He couldn't see them. One small mercy. But he knew it would only be a matter of time before they were back. 'So what do we do?'

'You tell me, you're the commanding officer,' McIndoe called back.

'Right now, I'm open to suggestions,' Ravallo replied.

'If we surrender to them, we'll be taken ashore and handed over to the Gestapo,' Stella shouted from her crouched position beside Johnson at the top of the stairs. 'I say we stand and fight it out with them. At least that way we'd have a better chance of survival than we'd have at the hands of the Gestapo.'

'I'm going to have a word with Charlie,' McIndoe said.

'I'll come with you,' Ravallo said, and they ran doubled over to the metal steps on the starboard side of the wheelhouse. At least now they were on the *Schnellboote*'s blind side. A brief respite.

'What are we going to do, boss?' Hillyard asked from behind the Vickers gun.

'That's what we're going to find out,' McIndoe replied, following Ravallo up the steps and into the wheelhouse.

Higgins looked round sharply at them, his face streaked with sweat. 'Thank God you're here,' he exclaimed. 'We've got big problems.'

'You think we haven't noticed?' McIndoe retorted tersely.

'I'm not talking about the Jerries out there. The Messers must have been ordered to target the engine room. One of our engines has taken a direct hit. It's still working, but at a greatly reduced capacity. To be honest, I'm surprised it's still working. It could go at any time.'

'Would that cripple us?' Ravallo asked.

'No, but it would slow us down considerably. We'd never be able to outrun the *Schnellboote*,' Higgins said. 'That's not all though. We've lost Graves – the chief engineer. He was killed when the Messers made their first run on the boat. There's only Baines down there now. He can't possibly run the show by himself, not with the engine in such bad shape.'

'In other words, you think that we should cut the engines and surrender?' McIndoe said.

'Fortunately that decision's not up to me,' Higgins replied, his eyes going to Ravallo. 'I can only report on the facts as I know them.'

'*Your time is up,*' the amplified voice echoed across the waters. '*This is your last warning. Switch off your engines or else you will be sunk.*'

McIndoe and Higgins looked to Ravallo, who was weighing up the situation as he stared out across the ocean through the bullet-scarred window. 'Cut the engines,' he said reluctantly. Higgins immediately powered down the boat and radioed Ravallo's order through to Baines in the engine room.

'What now?' McIndoe asked.

'I say we make a stand and fight,' Higgins said. 'If we surrender, we'd be handed over to the Gestapo. And we all know about their methods of interrogation.'

'That's what Stella said.' Ravallo looked at McIndoe. 'Mac, what do you think?'

'I agree with Charlie,' McIndoe said. 'How about you?'

'Personally, I'd be prepared to take my chances as a prisoner,' Ravallo replied as the boat came to a full stop. 'They would still have to get us back to Palermo. A lot of things could happen between here and there, especially as the Resistance would know we'd been captured by the Germans.'

'You're the senior officer on board, Nicky,' McIndoe said. 'It's up to you to make the final decision.'

'*You will all assemble on the bow deck and wait to be boarded. Anyone who attempts to resist will be shot.*'

'You know as well as I do that none of us would get off this boat alive if we tried to make a stand against the kind of firepower they've got out there,' Ravallo said. 'Not only are we outmanned and outgunned, but any attempt to outrun them would be suicidal with one of the engines out of action. My first responsibility has to be to the safety of the crew. I say we lay down our arms and surrender. At least this way we'd still be in with a chance of coming out of this in one piece.'

McIndoe placed his Sten gun on the bench, then nodded to Higgins, who tugged the Webley pistol from his belt and tossed it on to the floor at Ravallo's feet. 'I hope you remember this moment when the Gestapo are ripping out your fingernails with a pair of pliers,' Higgins said bitterly.

'*You, on the bridge. Make your way down on to the deck. Do it now!*'

'It could also be the moment I saved your life,' Ravallo replied with equal acerbity. He crossed to the door and pulled it open. They filed down the steps and on to the deck.

'What's going on?' Hillyard demanded, still in position behind his Vickers gun.

'Stand away from the gun and proceed to the bow deck,' Ravallo replied.

Hillyard's eyes widened in disbelief. 'We're not going to . . .' He trailed off and looked in horror at McIndoe. 'Boss, if we surrender – '

'You heard the officer!' McIndoe cut in, the fury in his voice directed not only at Ravallo, but also at himself. Ravallo was right: they'd never get off the boat alive if they tried to fight it out. The alternative was to be handed over to an implacable Gestapo out to avenge the death of Ernst Brausch. Days of slow, excruciating torture before the merciful release of death finally freed them from what would be left of their shattered existence. Ravallo's argument in favour of some Partisan operation to free them en route to Palermo was, in McIndoe's view, hopeful in the extreme. He believed that

Ravallo had made the wrong decision and, as his second-in-charge, he'd already made up his mind to relieve Ravallo of command at some point within the next few minutes. He'd contemplated taking command of the boat while they were still on the bridge, but had quickly discounted the idea as rash and illogical. There would have been nothing to gain by playing his hand too quickly. He didn't have a specific plan in mind; he'd bide his time and let the Germans unwittingly dictate the right moment by their actions. There was no doubt in his mind that the whole crew would die making a last, defiant stand against the Germans, but at least this way they would die with honour . . .

He waited until Ravallo had disappeared around the side of the wheelhouse, then turned to Higgins and Hillyard who were following behind him. 'I'm going to make a move against the Germans,' he whispered as a matter of urgency. 'I don't know exactly what I'm going to do, but you'll know when it happens. When I do make a move, go for the deck guns and give them hell. It's our only chance. We may not make it off the boat, but at least we'll have the satisfaction of taking as many of them with us as we can before they get us.'

'Yes, sir,' Hillyard replied with a broad grin.

A volley of bullets scythed over the top of the wheelhouse. *'You were told to come out with your hands on your heads. Do it now.'*

McIndoe led the way on to the bow deck. Stella and Johnson were standing beside Ravallo. There was no sign of Passiere. McIndoe noticed that the two Messerschmitts were now circling slowly in a wide circumference above them like giant metallic predators, watching with detached disdain as their prey floundered helplessly below them. He screwed up his eyes against the piercing light as he looked across at the *Schnellboote* which rocked gently in the water off the starboard bow. They had one spotlight trained on the MTB's bow and another constantly sweeping the rest of the craft for any sign of further movement.

'*Patron*, it is Georges. Can you hear me?' a voice called out behind them.

'Don't look round!' McIndoe hissed when Johnson turned his head towards Passiere. 'I can hear you, Georges. Where are you?'

'I am on the stairs, *patron*,' Passiere replied. 'They cannot see me from their boat.'

'Did you manage to contact Valletta HQ?' McIndoe asked.

'*Oui, patron*. They have put out a Mayday to any Allied craft in the area, but there has been no response to their broadcast so far. Do you want me to come out or go back to the radio room?'

'Come out, Passiere,' Ravallo told him. 'The longer you hold out down there, the worse it will be for you when the Germans board the boat.'

'Ignore that order, Georges,' McIndoe replied. 'Stay where you are. You'll be more useful to us as a loose cannon below deck.'

'What the hell's going on?' Ravallo asked, glaring at McIndoe. 'How dare you countermand my orders?'

'It's my opinion that you're not fit to continue as the senior officer on board this vessel so, as your second-in-charge, I'm formally relieving you of your command,' McIndoe told him. 'I know that Charlie and my boys will stand by me.'

'This is tantamount to mutiny,' Ravallo said furiously.

'You can have me court-martialled if we ever get out of this alive,' McIndoe replied. His eyes turned to Stella. 'Are you with the rest of us?'

'Of course she's not,' Ravallo said indignantly.

'What are you going to do?' she asked McIndoe.

'Make a stand and fight,' McIndoe replied. 'You know as well as I do that if we were to surrender to the Germans we'd end up in the hands of the Gestapo. I for one would rather die here and now than at the hands of those butchers.'

'I've already told you, Stella's not – '

'Shut up, Nicky!' she cut in savagely. 'I'm not some ventriloquist's dummy that you can constantly manipulate to suit your own ends. I'll speak for myself. You've never witnessed the brutality of the Gestapo at first hand, have you? Well, I have. Too many times. No, Nicky, I'm with Sam this time. I'd rather die now than let the Gestapo get hold of me.'

Ravallo managed to mask his shredded dignity behind a veil of silence. What was there to say? Not only had he lost the respect of McIndoe and his SOE colleagues which had been so important to him, but even Stella had turned against him. The one person he thought he could have counted on to stand by him in the face of such adversity. Yet what was so galling was that he'd genuinely believed he was only acting in the best interests of the crew when he'd made his decision to surrender to the Germans. At least they would have had a chance, however slim, of survival once they'd reached the mainland. What chance of survival now?

'They're lowering a rowing boat from the *Schnellboote*,' Hillyard said, breaking the silence.

'We'll wait until it's clear of the *Schnellboote*. That will make it an easy target,' McIndoe said. 'Wait for my signal, then go to your stations. We've got to assume they've already got a torpedo in the tube so I'll go for the *Schnellboote*'s engine room with the other Vickers. Neville, you and Bruce concentrate your fire on the Messers.

'Charlie, I realize the damaged engine could go at any time, but once the firing starts I want you back on the bridge. Any kind of movement will be preferable to us sitting out here like lame ducks. Stella, you'll be with me. You'll take out the spotlights, then concentrate your fire on the deck area, and in particular the crew manning the deck guns.'

'You're asking a hell of a lot here, Mac,' Higgins said.

'What have we got to lose?' McIndoe replied. 'Chances are they'll launch a torpedo as soon as we open fire on them. But at least we'll have gone down fighting. And isn't that what we agreed?'

'What do you want me to do?' Ravallo asked, his eyes fixed on the rowing boat as its hull touched the water. He looked at McIndoe on receiving no reply. 'I can help, God dammit. Tell me where you want me.'

'With Stella. You two can – '

The rest of his sentence was lost forever in the deafening explosion which tore the *Schnellboote* apart with such dissilient ferocity that it disintegrated in a searing ball of fire before their very eyes. Stella and Johnson, who'd been standing closest to the railing, were both knocked off their feet by the sheer force of the shuddering blast. The others dropped to the deck and wrapped their arms protectively over their heads as the flaming debris rained down over the boat.

Ravallo felt a searing pain shoot up the back of his leg as a finger-length sliver of smouldering metal sliced through his trousers and embedded itself deep in his flesh. He instinctively reached down to pull it out, but jerked his hand away sharply when his fingers touched the red-hot fragment. With the pain now almost unbearable, he improvised by ripping the sleeve off his polo-neck jersey and wrapping it tightly around his hand, then he reached down again and, gritting his teeth in agony, he clasped his thumb and forefinger around the fragment, gingerly extracting it from his flesh. He was the first to his feet and stared at where the *Schnellboote* had once been anchored. There was now nothing left of the boat, apart from the charred driftwood which was floating forlornly on the surface of moonlit water. There was no movement in the water to indicate any survivors amongst the wreckage. Not that it surprised him. He knew it would have been nothing short of a miracle for anyone to have survived the explosion.

He'd already come to the conclusion that the *Schnellboote* had been destroyed by a torpedo fired from a submarine. There was no other explanation which could account for such destruction. Not that he'd seen the sub. But that was hardly surprising with the Messerschmitt still in the area.

Whether it had been a conscious realization of their presence, or subconsciously hearing that familiar droning noise in the back of his mind, he didn't know, but his worst fears were realized when he looked up and saw the two Messerschmitts in a close parallel formation as they dived menacingly towards the boat. 'Messerschmitts incoming, man your stations,' he yelled as he ran towards the Oerlikon gun, each jarring step sending a shooting pain up the back of his leg.

Higgins ran to the wheelhouse to restart the engines. McIndoe and Hillyard had already started running towards the Vickers gun by the time Ravallo reached the Oerlikon gun. One of the Messerschmitts peeled away to attack the boat from a different direction. Ravallo ignored it as he lined up the remaining fighter in the gun's sights. 'Come on, you bastard, closer,' Ravallo shouted at the approaching fighter. 'Closer . . . closer.'

The fixed twenty-millimetre cannons on the Messerschmitt's wings crackled into life, strafing the water as it homed in on the boat. Ravallo didn't flinch as the bullets came ever closer to him. He heard one of the Vickers fired behind him, but he didn't take his eyes off the approaching fighter; his only concern was to keep it centred in his sights, as if it were a fly being inextricably drawn into the centre of a spider's web. The roar of the plane's engines resounded like thunder in his ears and he opened his mouth and let out a sustained yell – a furious war cry of pent-up adrenaline – and finally opened up on the fighter, directing his fire on the figure silhouetted behind the cockpit window. The pilot was still frantically trying to pull the plane out of its dive when a row of bullets scythed across the window. He was hit several times and his harnessed body jerked grotesquely in the seat before slumping forward over the controls. Ravallo punched the air in delight when the stricken Messerschmitt veered out of control and tumbled helplessly towards the ocean. Then, just when it seemed as if the Messerschmitt would plunge into the sea, it suddenly levelled out. For one horrifying moment, Ravallo thought that the pilot had somehow managed to regain control of it. His fears were quickly allayed, however, when the plane twisted violently in its final death throes and the tip of the wing was sheared off as it struck the water. The imbalance threw the plane out of kilter, and it cartwheeled spectacularly across the surface of the water, spitting out more debris from the wings and the tail. It landed belly-down in the sea, sending up a surge of water from beneath its shattered body. Water poured in through the broken fuselage, and within seconds the plane had disappeared beneath the waves.

Ravallo was jolted out of his premature celebration when the remaining Messerschmitt made another attack on the boat. Bullets sprayed across the deck as both Vickers guns fired mercilessly at the plane, but by the time he'd managed to turn the Oerlikon gun towards the retreating fighter, it was already out of range. It was then Ravallo heard the sound of more aircraft engines in the distance, sending a shudder of despair through his whole body. They couldn't hold out against any more enemy fighters. They'd been stretched to the limit just dealing with two. He located the remaining Messerschmitt and, satisfied it would still be some time before it made another dive on the boat, he set about scanning the sky for the aircraft. He wasn't surprised when he couldn't see them. He looked across at McIndoe and could see by his grim expression that he'd also heard the approaching engines.

Johnson ventured out from where he and Stella had taken cover at the top of the stairs. He pressed a finger to his left ear to block out the sound of the Messerschmitt as he concentrated his attention on the pitch of the other engines. Ravallo watched him closely and he became intrigued when a faint smile flickered across his lips. 'What is it?' he called out to Johnson.

Johnson looked across at Ravallo and the smile broadened into a grin. 'To use one of your country's analogies, sir, the cavalry's on its way.'

'What are you talking about?' Ravallo replied, his frustration only heightened when he noticed that McIndoe was now also smiling to himself.

'Those aren't Boche fighters, sir, they're Hurribirds,' Johnson told him.

'RAF Hawker-Hurricanes,' McIndoe said.

'How can you be so sure?' Ravallo asked Johnson.

'The pitch of the engine, sir. It's different to any of the Boche engines. In fact, it's totally different from, say, a Spitfire or a – '

'I think Major Ravallo gets the picture, Neville,' McIndoe cut in wryly.

'Four Hurris approaching,' Higgins shouted excitedly from the wheelhouse.

Two of the Hurricanes broke formation and went after the lone Messerschmitt which had already turned in for another attack on the boat. Both Hurricanes engaged the German fighter with machine-gun fire, and the Messerschmitt had to take evasive action as it wheeled away from the approaching planes. The two Hurricanes went in pursuit, and a great cheer went up from those on the deck when a thick pall of smoke erupted from the side of the Messerschmitt's fuselage. The doomed plane began to spiral out of control and plunged helplessly towards the sea. One of the Hurricanes followed it down, and pulled out of its steep dive only when the Messerschmitt ploughed into the ocean. Another cheer went up when the Hurricane returned and did a victory roll above the boat before taking up its position in the tight formation to starboard.

Stella hurried across to where Ravallo was slumped against the railing, his face twisted in pain as he clasped his hand to his injured leg. 'Nicky's hurt,' she called out as she crouched down beside him.

'I'm all right,' he hissed irritably. 'It's just a flesh wound, that's all.'

McIndoe was the first to reach them, the concern evident on his face. 'What happened?'

'I'm fine, thank you, *sir*,' Ravallo replied, spitting out the last word with venomous sarcasm.

'I can understand how you must be feeling right now, Nicky,' McIndoe said in an attempt to diffuse the tension between them. 'But I still believe I was justified in taking command when I did.'

'How the hell can you possibly know what I'm feeling right now?' Ravallo said bitterly.

'My first assignment as a team leader was to blow a railway bridge on the outskirts of Rome,' McIndoe told him. 'I'd just completed my officer's training, and of course I thought I could go out there and win the war single-handedly. Truth was I was a naïve greenhorn with no field experience whatsoever. That's why I'd been assigned an experienced second-in-command. Sergeant Taffy Evans. After the bridge was destroyed we had to rendezvous with the Partisans. There were two possible routes we could have taken to the rendezvous. I chose what I thought would be the safer bet. Taffy disagreed. He pointed out several possible blind spots where the Germans could lie in wait for us. I wasn't convinced, but Taffy was adamant that we should take the other route. When I tried to pull rank to enforce my orders, he announced that in the interests of the men he was going to assume command until we reached the rendezvous. The men trusted his judgement implicitly, so naturally they went along with him. We reached the rendezvous without incident, and Taffy then returned command of the operation to me. I remember only too well how I felt at the time. Anger. Resentment. Humiliation. The moment we arrived back in Blighty, I went straight to Starr and demanded Taffy's head on a plate.'

'What did he say?' Stella asked as she ripped the back of Ravallo's trousers to get at the wound.

'That I was very fortunate to have had a wise head like Taffy on my team, and that he had no intention of taking any action against him. It was only later I discovered the Germans had laid an ambush for us at one of those blind spots. So if Taffy hadn't stood up to me, I wouldn't be here now telling you any of this. It made me realize then just how much I still had to learn about field work.'

'I assume that last bit was aimed at me?' Ravallo said, and he winced as Stella gingerly wiped away the blood which coated the wound.

'As they say, if the cap fits . . .' McIndoe said.

'Too damn tightly for comfort . . .' He trailed off and inhaled sharply through his teeth as Stella dabbed disinfectant on to the wound. 'Will you take it easy with that stuff, for God's sake?'

'Would you rather I just left it and let you get an infection?'

Passiere appeared at the top of the stairs. '*Patron*, I've got the flight-lieutenant on the radio,' he announced, gesturing towards the formation of Hurricanes. 'He's asking to speak to one of the senior officers.'

'You take it,' Ravallo told McIndoe, then gritted his teeth as Stella dabbed more disinfectant on to the wound. This time he said nothing.

McIndoe followed Passiere to the wireless room, where he slipped the headphones over his ears, then introduced himself to the flight-lieutenant who was commanding the accompanying fighters. 'We appreciate you bailing us out of trouble back there, sir.'

'Glad we could be of help, Lieutenant, but it looked like you chaps had the situation pretty well under control, judging by the way you dealt with the other Messer,' came the reply. 'We saw it go down soon after we'd got a visual on your boat. Damn fine job. Was that your handiwork?'

'No, it was Major Ravallo,' McIndoe said as he helped himself to a cigarette from the packet on the table.

'The Yank? Yes, I've heard about him. A bit of a canteen cowboy by all accounts. I believe he was at the air-base a couple of days ago regaling the aces with tales of his Brooklyn childhood. Unfortunately I was airborne at the time, so I didn't get to hear any of them.'

'At Luqa, yes,' McIndoe said with a chuckle. 'Is that where you were scrambled from?'

'Initially, yes, but we were already in the air when your Mayday was picked up by ops in Valletta. We'd just finished fending off another Boche bombing raid on Grand Harbour, so we were able to fly straight out to assist you. Our orders are to stay with you until you reach Valletta. Not that I think the Germans will send up any more fighters. I think we've bloodied their noses enough for one night.'

'I certainly hope so, sir. I think we've all had quite enough excitement as it is,' McIndoe said. The signal was terminated and he discarded the headphones.

'This message came through for you from the commander of the sub which torpedoed the *Schnellboote*,' Passiere said, handing McIndoe a sheet of paper. 'He said you would understand it.'

McIndoe smiled to himself as he read the note: *Attention: Lieutenant Samuel McIndoe – Well, old boy, it seems like your fairy godmother has had to come to your rescue once again. Hope we didn't startle you too much with the little package we sent over to the* Schnellboote. *All part of the service. At least that's one less* Schnellboote *for you to worry about when you next find yourself on your travels out here in the Mediterranean. Good luck to you all, and God speed your return to friendly waters.*

Lieutenant-Commander Reginald Stockton-Jones
HMS Unbeaten

'Do you want me to contact *Unbeaten* on the radio for you, *patron*?' Passiere asked.

'No,' McIndoe said as he got to his feet. He indicated the protective gauze bandage which covered the laceration behind Passiere's ear. 'How's the head?'

'A lot better than yours by the look of it, *patron*,' Passiere replied.

With everything that had happened since returning to the boat, McIndoe had almost forgotten about the injury he'd sustained when he'd jumped from the train. He moved to a mirror which was mounted on the back of the door and screwed up his face in disgust when he saw that the bandage around his head was soiled with blood. 'I tell you, Georges, the first thing I'm going to do when I get back to Malta is soak in a long, hot bath and just forget about all my worries.'

'All of them, *patron*?' Passiere asked with a questioning look as he resumed his seat. When McIndoe didn't answer, Passiere leaned forward in the chair, his elbows resting on his knees. 'Do you know who the traitor is?'

'I've got a good idea, yes,' McIndoe replied.

'Does he know that you know?' Passiere asked.

McIndoe paused in the doorway. 'I doubt it. And who said it was necessarily a "he"?'

'I just assumed . . .' Passiere's voice trailed off as McIndoe left the cabin.

'Gela airfield have just confirmed that they've lost contact with the other Messerschmitt as well, sir,' the radio operator announced, slowly removing his headphones and placing them on the table in front of him. 'The last thing the pilot told them was that he'd been engaged by two RAF Hawker-Hurricanes. Then nothing.'

'Scramble the other Me109s that are still on standby, sir,' Franke said to Riedler who was standing at the window with his back to them, his hands clamped tightly behind his back. Riedler hadn't spoken since word reached them from Gela that first the *Schnellboote*, and then one of the Me109s, had been destroyed. When Riedler didn't answer, Franke got to his feet and crossed to the window. 'Sir, do you want me to give the order to scramble the rest of the Me109s?'

'I heard you the first time, Franke,' Riedler said softly, then fell silent again.

'Sir, I feel we should act – '

'To do what?' Riedler snapped as he rounded on Franke. 'It's over, can't you see that? You read the communiqué the Gestapo sent us listing the features of the enemy boat. A prototype which can easily outrun even the fastest *Schnellboote*. At that speed, it'll be well on its way back to Malta by now. So even if we were to scramble the Me109s, it's highly unlikely they'd catch up with it before it reached Grand Harbour. And even if they did, the boat's got an escort of at least four RAF fighters. That number may have increased by now, I don't know. I'm not prepared to sacrifice any more of our pilots.'

He perched on the edge of the nearest chair, his eyes fixed on an imaginary spot on the carpet. When he spoke again his voice was quieter, more thoughtful. 'I always knew there was a chance the British might have a submarine in the area, but when I asked for a U-boat to protect the *Schnellboote* I was told that all available U-boats had already been dispatched to intercept a British convoy off the Tunisian coast. Field-Marshal Kesselring's orders.' He looked up slowly at Franke, the bitterness of personal failure evident in his tired, bloodshot eyes. 'I'll no doubt be expected to shoulder the blame for this whole fiasco once it reaches Field-Marshal Kesselring's desk. And you know what that means, don't you? We'll all be sent back to the Eastern Front.'

'Are you going to radio through to General Student and tell him what's happened, sir?' Franke asked.

'It would take a brave man to wake the general now and tell him that the enemy boat's slipped through the net. No, I'll wait until we get back to Palermo and brief him in person.' Riedler rubbed his hands over his unshaven face, then slowly got to his feet. 'Tell the men to prepare to move out. There's nothing to keep us here now.'

FIFTEEN

'It's hardly the most satisfying outcome, is it?'

'No, sir, but the main thing is that the invasion plans didn't fall into the enemy's hands,' General Kurt Student replied. 'That would have been catastrophic. Those plans contained highly sensitive information relating to German troop and armour strengths here in Sicily and on the Italian mainland.'

Field-Marshal Albert Kesselring seemed nonplussed by Student's argument. They were sitting in the empty hotel dining room, where they'd both just eaten a sparing breakfast during which Student had briefed Kesselring on the events of the previous night. It was hardly the kind of news Kesselring had wanted to hear first thing in the morning.

Student helped himself to another cup of coffee from the fresh pot which had been left for them by the waiter after he'd finished clearing the table. 'I assume the invasion plans that were drawn up here yesterday will have to be scrapped?'

'That goes without saying,' Kesselring replied. 'We'll have to reschedule another meeting, probably in Rome. I don't know when it will be, though. It took long enough to get all the chiefs-of-staff together for yesterday's meeting.'

'If we leave it too long, we'll have lost the initiative,' Student told him.

'Don't you think I know that?' Kesselring replied. 'I've already received orders to return to Berlin at the end of the week to make a full report to the *Führer* concerning the events here yesterday. He's been opposed to an invasion of Malta from the very start. This could provide him with just the excuse he needs to terminate the project. I'm going to have my work cut out trying to convince him otherwise. I'll need detailed reports from both you and from Riedler so that I can prepare a strong case to present to the *Führer*.'

'You'll have them within twenty-four hours, sir,' Student assured him.

'Where is Riedler by the way? I haven't seen him since he got back to the hotel this morning.'

'I told him to get some sleep after he'd finished briefing me. He was exhausted. Do you want to see him before you fly back to Rome, sir?'

'No, let him sleep,' Kesselring replied. 'I want him at his best for when he writes up that report for me.'

'He was very concerned about how you'd react to what had happened last night,' Student said. 'He's already resigned himself to the fact that you'll be sending him and his men back to the Eastern Front as punishment for failing to capture the enemy agents.'

Kesselring smiled. 'You can tell him I've got no intention of sending him back to Russia. There's more than enough undistinguished officers doing the rounds to fill those dead-end vacancies. I thought of putting his name forward as a possible recruit for the Special Forces. He's proved himself more than capable over the past couple of days, even if the final outcome wasn't to our advantage. Considering what he was up against – including the Gestapo's obstructive tactics – he did remarkably well in getting that close to capturing the enemy.'

'I agree, sir,' Student replied.

Kesselring drained his cup, then picked up his attaché case from beside his chair and got to his feet. 'I assume you've already heard about the attack on the Allied convoy off the North African coast earlier this morning?'

'No, sir, I haven't,' Student replied hesitantly.

'I thought the news would have filtered through by now,' Kesselring said. 'No matter. It will soon enough. You'll recall I was concerned yesterday that the Allied High Command may have found a way of intercepting our Enigma transmissions, and that to test this theory I dispatched all available U-boats to the island of Cani to intercept an Allied convoy which was due to pass there in the early hours of this morning.'

'Yes, sir, I remember the conversation well,' Student said.

'Good news. The wolf-pack sunk seven of the nineteen-strong escort force: four destroyers and three cruisers; but more importantly, they also sunk five of the eight cargo ships which were taking desperately needed supplies to Malta. Another two destroyers and a battleship were badly damaged in the attack. We lost one U-boat, presumably as a result of a depth charge. The convoy was so badly crippled, it had to turn back for Gibraltar. There were no Allied submarines in the area to defend the convoy and, according to one Royal Navy officer who was picked up from the sea by one of our U-boats, the convoy wasn't given any prior warning of the intended ambush. The British would never have sacrificed such a vital convoy had they known in advance the exact time and coordinates of our intended attack. I'm now satisfied in my own mind that our Enigma programme is quite secure.' Kesselring looked at his watch. 'Well, if you'll excuse me. I've got an important ops meeting in Rome at two o'clock this afternoon. I'll hope to see you within the next twenty-four hours with those reports.'

Student saluted him. 'You can count on it, sir.'

'I'll see myself out, Kurt. You finish your coffee,' Kesselring said. He shook hands with Student, then strode from the room.

'Good afternoon, sir,' Sergeant Janet Cross said as she got to her feet to salute Ravallo when he entered the office.

Ravallo returned the salute. 'I have an appointment to see Vice-Admiral Starr.'

She reached for the telephone. 'I'll just let the Vice-Admiral know you're here.' When she replaced the handset she gestured to the closed door behind her. 'Please go through, sir.'

'Thank you,' Ravallo replied, and entered the inner chamber.

'Come in and close the door, Ravallo,' Starr instructed, then stabbed the well-chewed stem of his pipe at the chair which had been placed in front of his desk. 'I asked for you to be here at two o'clock,' he said as Ravallo was about to sit down. 'You're eight minutes late.'

Ravallo slowly straightened up. As he stood uncomfortably in front of Starr, he felt for all the world like some scampish schoolboy up in front of his obdurate headmaster. 'I'm sorry, sir. The driver who brought me here had to make several detours as many of the streets were still impassable after the air-raid last night.'

'Then why didn't you anticipate these problems in advance and arrange for him to pick you up from your lodgings that little bit earlier?' Starr queried.

'It would certainly have made more sense, sir,' Ravallo was quick to agree.

Starr opened the leather pouch at his elbow and tamped a fresh wad of tobacco into his pipe. 'I'm sure you'd be a lot more comfortable if you were to sit down,' he said before lighting his pipe.

'Yes, sir, of course,' Ravallo muttered as he sat down.

'How's the leg?' Starr asked.

'Just a few twinges when I put any weight on it. The doctor who treated the wound told me it would heal up just fine.'

'Yes, so he said in the report he forwarded me earlier this morning,' Starr said. He pushed a second ashtray across the desk towards Ravallo. 'Please feel free to smoke if you wish.'

'Thank you, sir,' Ravallo said. He took a packet of cigarettes from his tunic pocket and lit one.

'You know why I've asked to see you, don't you?' Starr asked.

'I assumed it was for a debriefing, sir,' came the cautious reply.

'Not exactly, no,' Starr replied as he sat back in his leather chair. 'I've already got a fairly broad picture of what happened in Sicily. Passiere may be a damned irritating foreigner at times but he's also the finest "ghost" – radio operator – that we have in the SOE. His reports are always concise and very factual.

'I won't actually be handling your debriefing, or that of any other member of your team for that matter. I've already assigned two of my senior aides to carry out that particular task. No, my only concern right now is to root out this traitor as quickly as possible before they can cause any further damage to the stability of this organization. I regard treason as the most heinous crime of all, and I've already assured Whitehall that I'll leave no stone unturned in my quest to track down the scoundrel.

'You and Lieutenant McIndoe were the two senior officers on this operation. I'll be speaking to McIndoe later this afternoon but, as the senior officer, I wanted to get your input first. Of course anything you say to me in this room will be treated in the strictest of confidence, but once we've apprehended the culprit, your full cooperation will be expected at any future trial.'

'That goes without saying, sir,' Ravallo replied.

'Do you know who the traitor is?'

'I have my suspicions, sir,' Ravallo said. 'It wasn't until after we'd jumped from the train that I first began to suspect him. I believe it's Bruce Hillyard.'

Starr's face remained impassive as he continued to suck on the stem of his pipe, a cloud of smoke gathering ominously above him. 'Please go on,' he said without removing the pipe from his mouth.

'The conductor – who was working for the Resistance – warned us when we boarded the train that there was a Gestapo officer on board who was equipped with a radio which he used to keep in touch with Gestapo headquarters. The Resistance have installed several similar radios – '

'I do know about these radios, Major,' Starr pointed out. 'The SOE was instrumental in smuggling them into the country in the first place. Just get to the point, will you?'

'Well, sir, the conductor told us he could only listen in to the radio when he was in the guard's van. And, with the train being so full, he wouldn't be able to spend much time there. He suggested we monitor the radio ourselves. We agreed and decided to break it down into hourly shifts. Hillyard was quick to volunteer for the first shift. He hadn't been gone very long when he came back to tell us the Gestapo knew we were on the train. It would have been a simple matter for him to have either made contact with his controller over the radio, or else to have spoken in person to the Gestapo agent who was travelling on the train.

'Then, when we jumped from the train, Hillyard offered to carry the kit-bag which contained our radio. He would have had more than enough time to sabotage it and discard the radio spares in the initial confusion when Mac – Lieutenant McIndoe – was concussed. Stella and I swam out to him, leaving Hillyard alone on the river-bank. In retrospect I realize that was a mistake, but to be honest the radio was the last thing on my mind. I know Evans was still in the water, albeit some distance downstream, because I remember him shouting to me that he wouldn't be able to reach the lieutenant before either Stella or I could get to him. I don't know where Johnson was – possibly he was also still in the water – but he definitely wasn't with Hillyard.

'Lieutenant McIndoe had this theory that the radio could have been sabotaged before we left Malta,' Ravallo continued. 'I'm not discounting his theory, sir, but the more I thought about it afterwards, the more I came to believe it was more likely to have been sabotaged after we'd already reached Sicily. And it wasn't as if there would have been much opportunity for anyone to have tampered with the radio after we'd landed, as both Lieutenant McIndoe and myself were exceptionally vigilant when it came to keeping an eye on it.'

'Except when Bruce Hillyard had it when he jumped from the train,' Starr said thoughtfully. 'Why did you let him take it?'

'Hillyard reckoned that because he was a trained acrobat, he could carry the extra weight when he jumped from the train. We didn't argue because – to be honest – we were all pretty much on edge at the time, as I'm sure you would be, sir, if you were waiting to jump out of a moving carriage.'

'I wouldn't know, Major, I've never tried it,' Starr said dryly. 'And that's the basis for your case against Hillyard, is it?'

'I realize it's all circumstantial evidence, sir, but I've got a gut feeling I'm right about him,' Ravallo said.

'You'll find that gut feelings don't generally hold much sway in our British legal system,' Starr told him bluntly. 'Having said that, though, you're a highly respected Intelligence officer with impeccable credentials, and I can assure you what you've told me today will certainly be investigated further.'

'I assume everyone on the team is being thoroughly investigated, sir?' Ravallo said.

'Would you expect it any other way?' Starr asked.

'No, sir, of course not.' Ravallo stubbed out his cigarette. 'Sir, may I ask you a question? It's not related directly to what we've been discussing. It concerns the operation itself.'

'Go ahead,' Starr replied.

'In your opinion, just how successful was it, considering it didn't exactly go according to plan?'

'It's still too early to assess the overall success of the operation but my . . . gut feeling, as you would call it, would suggest we achieved what we set out to do,' Starr said after a thoughtful pause. 'I find it inconceivable that a shrewd tactician like Field-Marshal Kesselring would even consider implementing the plan which was drawn up at the hotel, knowing it's now been compromised. No, he'll have to go back to the drawing board and start all over again, which will mean rearranging another conference for a time convenient to all concerned. That could take weeks. Perhaps even months. Then it would still have to be approved by Hitler, which means it could take even longer to finalize. By then Malta's air defences will have been strengthened considerably, with the addition of the fifteen Spitfires which are due to arrive here in the next few weeks. The War Office believes, as do I, that the arrival of these Spitfires will tilt the balance sufficiently in our favour and give us the edge in the air. And without total air superiority over Malta, the Germans would never risk a land invasion.'

'Then at least some good's come out of it,' Ravallo said.

'That remains to be seen,' Starr replied. He looked at his watch. 'Is your driver still here?'

'Yes, sir, I asked him to wait for me.'

'Good, because you're due at Fort Campbell for your debriefing at three o'clock. Your driver will know where to take you.'

'Yes, sir,' Ravallo said, getting to his feet and saluting Starr.

'Oh, and Major?' Starr called out to Ravallo as he crossed to the door, 'try not to be late, will you?'

Ravallo smiled to himself as he left the room.

'Hello, Janet.'

Sergeant Janet Cross looked up from her typewriter and smiled at the familiar figure of Sam McIndoe standing in the doorway. She got to her feet and saluted him. 'Good afternoon, sir.'

'Five o'clock? I guess it still is,' McIndoe replied, looking up at the wall clock as he removed his peaked cap and tucked it under his arm.

'My God, what happened?' she asked when she saw the swathe of white bandage wrapped around his head.

'I rather foolishly tried to head-butt a submerged log. Not advisable,' McIndoe replied with a wry smile, then gestured to the closed door behind her. 'Is he in?'

She nodded, and picked up the telephone to let Starr know that McIndoe had arrived. 'You're to go straight in, sir,' she told McIndoe as she replaced the handset.

McIndoe opened the door and stepped into the room. He coughed violently as he was instantly engulfed in a thick brume of foul-smelling tobacco smoke which hung ponderously in the air. As he waved it away from his face, he saw Starr seated behind his desk, oblivious to the odious haze as he puffed on his pipe. McIndoe knew that Starr was brooding: it was the only time he smoked that heavily. 'Afternoon, sir,' he said, and began to cough again as the smoke seeped insidiously into his throat the moment he opened his mouth.

'Pick up a bit of a cold when you were over in Sicily, did you, McIndoe?' Starr asked without taking his eyes off the document he was reading.

'No, sir,' McIndoe replied as he used his hand to fan the smoke away from his face. 'It's the smoke in here, sir. It's quite overpowering.'

'Smoke?' Starr mused absently, then he looked up at McIndoe. 'Ah, yes. Leave the connecting door open. That should help to disperse it. Janet will be leaving shortly anyway.' He activated the small fan on the steel cabinet behind him, then pointed to the chair in front of his desk. 'Sit down.'

'Thank you, sir,' McIndoe said.

'According to the doctor's report, that's a pretty nasty gash you've got there,' Starr said.

'Fifteen stitches and a bit of a headache. It could have been a lot worse, sir.'

'I've just finished reading the transcript of your debriefing earlier this afternoon,' Starr said, tapping the document in front of him. 'I noticed you were particularly critical of Major Ravallo's role in the operation. Don't you think you were perhaps being a bit harsh on him? It was his first field operation, after all.'

'I merely told it as it happened, sir,' McIndoe replied.

'I can still remember a certain raw young officer being sent on his first operation to blow up a bridge outside Rome,' Starr said. 'I specifically assigned him a good back-up man to steer him through any difficulties. If it hadn't been for the experience of Sergeant Evans, you'd never have made it back, would you?'

'No, sir,' McIndoe said.

'Let me tell you something off the record, McIndoe. You already know that much of this operation was masterminded by Military Intelligence in Washington, but what you won't know is that they wanted overall command from the start, and they'd even assigned one of their own field officers as Major Ravallo's second-in-command when the blueprint arrived on my desk in London. I've no doubt he would have served the team admirably but I was quite insistent that, if the SOE were to be involved, then I'd want my own officer as Major Ravallo's official back-up man. You were the obvious choice as far as I was concerned. Not only are you one of the finest serving officers in the SOE but, more importantly, you had the necessary field experience that Major Ravallo was lacking. He'll have learnt a lot from you, just as you learnt a lot from Evans on your first operation. We all have to start somewhere.'

'Yes, sir,' McIndoe said stiffly.

'Something on your mind, McIndoe?' Starr asked.

'The real reason why you asked to see me, sir,' McIndoe replied.

Starr's hand froze as he was about to slip the pipe back into his mouth. He jabbed the stem towards the open door. McIndoe crossed to the door and peered out into the outer office. Sergeant Janet Cross had already gone. He closed the door all the same, then returned to the chair and retook his seat. 'Do you know the identity of the traitor?' Starr asked.

'Yes, sir, I believe I do,' McIndoe replied. He took a packet of cigarettes from his pocket and lit one. 'I think it's Major Ravallo.'

'That hardly comes as any surprise, not after reading the notes taken at your debriefing. I'm sure the officer who debriefed you would have put that down to the animosity you were feeling towards Major Ravallo as a result of the way he handled certain aspects of the operation. But then he doesn't know all the facts.' Starr clenched the pipe tightly in the corner of his mouth. 'Do you have any proof to substantiate these allegations of treachery against Major Ravallo?'

'Nothing tangible that would stand up in a court of law, sir,' McIndoe replied. 'But if circumstantial evidence was all that was needed to convict him, then the bastard would be swinging from the gallows by now.'

'Let's keep this civil, shall we?' Starr said firmly.

'With all due respect, sir, you didn't see what happened to Taffy Evans,' McIndoe retorted sharply.

'Evans was killed by a Partisan land-mine,' Starr reminded him. 'His death was a tragic accident. Nothing more.'

'Except that we shouldn't have been anywhere near the minefield in the first place,' McIndoe said. 'It would never have happened if the Germans hadn't been on to us so quickly after we'd boarded the train.'

'And you blame Major Ravallo for that?' Starr said. 'According to your debriefing notes, you left the safe house together after Massimo arranged for you to take the train to Catánia. And apart from Hillyard, you all remained together in the compartment until you made your escape. How could Major Ravallo possibly have alerted the Germans in that time? I think you're letting your emotions get the better of you, McIndoe. I realize you were closer to Evans than anyone else in the SOE, and that his death has obviously affected you but, quite frankly, if this is an indication of your so-called "circumstantial" evidence against Major Ravallo, then it's pretty weak to say the least.'

'With all due respect, sir, I never said I believed Major Ravallo made contact with the Germans between the time we arrived at the safe house and the time we boarded the train,' McIndoe said in his defence. 'You just assumed I did. The only time he could have tipped-off the Germans would have been when he had that altercation with the police-man outside the train station. If he had, I hardly think the Germans would have let us leave Palermo when they could have arrested us at the station. What I was inferring was that I believe Evans's death was the result of a fateful chain of events which were triggered by Major Ravallo even before any of us had met him.'

'Then perhaps in future you would kindly refrain from making these inferences and just say exactly what you mean,' Starr said gruffly. 'Now let's hear this evidence you've got against Major Ravallo.'

'Firstly let me say I think he was solely a Gestapo agent, and that they probably kept his identity a secret from the rest of the *Wehrmacht*, certainly until after the incident at the hotel,' McIndoe said.

'Why do you say that?' Starr enquired.

'I spoke to Johnson at length after the ambush on the Gestapo convoy outside the church. He was adamant that General Student and the security team at the hotel were genuinely surprised when Major Ravallo was caught on the premises. That would suggest they had no previous know-ledge of the planned break-in. And if Student hadn't been forewarned, then it's safe to assume that neither had Field-Marshal Kesselring or any of his chiefs-of-staff. I don't believe for a moment they would have acted out a charade just for Johnson's benefit. Why bother? He'd already been appre-hended. No, I believe the Gestapo had a monopoly on this operation. It would have been some coup for them, and in particular Brausch, to have apprehended us all on the island.'

'It's certainly an interesting theory,' Starr replied. 'You said earlier you believed Major Ravallo was involved even before he arrived here on Malta. What makes you say that?'

'As you said just now, sir, most of this operation was planned by the Americans. We know Major Ravallo was, by his own admission, the one who came up with the idea of impersonating Schenk.'

'So you think Schenk was involved as well?' Starr asked.

'On the contrary, sir, I don't think he knew anything about it. If he did, he wouldn't have got involved in a gunfight with the Resistance when he was captured. He would have let them take him prisoner – perhaps with a bit of a struggle to make it look more authentic – knowing he'd be freed at some later stage. But from what Venucci told me afterwards, Schenk was fighting for his life. He would have killed them without a second thought. Those are hardly the actions of a man who wanted to be captured, are they?'

'So why wasn't he told?'

'You'd have to ask the Gestapo that, sir, but considering how feared and reviled these internal inspectors are within the organization, I wouldn't be surprised if they'd purposely chosen not to tell him anything. But then that's just speculation, and it doesn't really have any bearing on any of this. The point being, if Major Ravallo is working for the Gestapo, then the chances are they would have been in on the operation as well – calling the shots and constantly monitoring the events through him. Who knows, even the idea of impersonating Schenk could have been theirs. But again that's just speculation. They certainly knew we were due on the island – that much was obvious by the increased patrols along the coastline. That, of course, led to us being ambushed at the farmhouse by a German patrol shortly after we came ashore.'

'Except on that occasion Major Ravallo ended up saving the day, didn't he? If he hadn't showed up when he did, the operation would effectively have been over. Why would he have done that if he was working in league with the Germans?'

'The patrol, which we learnt had earlier become separated from their main unit, consisted only of five men. They didn't have any means of transport, nor did they have a radio to call in for reinforcements. By the time Major Ravallo made his entrance there were already a dozen armed Partisans outside the kitchen where we were being held. More were concealed in the surrounding undergrowth. Major Ravallo would have realized the Germans were in an impossible situation. The last thing he would have wanted would have been a shootout between the Germans and the Partisans in such a confined space. We'd have been the ones caught up in the middle of it all. Including himself. It was an act of self-preservation, nothing more. He would have known there would be other, more clear-cut, chances for the Gestapo to capture us.

'Then we come to the main thrust of the operation at the hotel in Palermo. When Major Ravallo first insisted on going in alone I thought it was a good idea – it would minimize the damage to the team as a whole if he were caught. But having reflected on it more carefully, I realize now the reasoning behind it was actually far more cunning than that. I think the Gestapo sanctioned the plan on the understanding they could protect his cover, and that's why I believe they agreed to let him impersonate Schenk. He would have led the Gestapo to the safe house where we'd all agreed to meet up afterwards. There they would have confiscated the camera and we'd all have been taken away for interrogation. Then they could have released details of our operation to Kesselring, claiming to have extracted it from us under torture. At least, that's the way I read it.'

'It's an intriguing theory, McIndoe, and a worrying one at that,' Starr said at length. 'There's still a couple of things that don't add up, though. Why did Ravallo shoot Brausch in cold blood if, as you claim, they were on the same side?'

'In my opinion, sir, that has to be one of the most damning pieces of evidence against him. When he was caught at the hotel, he knew we had orders to abort the operation and return to the safe house. He couldn't possibly have known we'd stage an ambush. He realized Brausch could be a serious liability. What if Brausch were sent back to England, as originally planned and, under interrogation, fingered Ravallo as a Gestapo spy? There was only one way for him to ensure his cover remained intact. Kill Brausch before he could talk. Dead men tell no tales. Isn't that what they say?

'The other damning piece of evidence as far as I'm concerned was when Brausch insisted on speaking to Major Ravallo alone after he was captured at the hotel. According to Johnson, Brausch wouldn't even let any of the senior security officers stay in the room with them. I asked Major Ravallo about that afterwards, and he claimed Brausch had tried first to reason with him to talk and, when that had failed, he'd gone on to explain in graphic detail what grisly delights awaited Johnson and himself, when they reached Gestapo headquarters. I wasn't convinced then and I'm not convinced now. I think they were plotting their next move, seeing as their original strategy hadn't gone according to plan.'

'If Major Ravallo is an enemy agent, why did he risk his life by shooting down that Messerschmitt?' Starr asked.

'Because the Messerschmitt was shooting at him!' McIndoe retorted with a bemused smile, as if that were patently obvious. 'As you already know from my debriefing notes, he tried his damnedest to get us all to surrender to the Germans but, when the *Schnellboote* was destroyed, the Messers must have been given orders to sink the boat. Major Ravallo would have realized that along with the rest of us. We go back again to basics of self-preservation. It's not a difficult choice, is it?'

'You certainly make a convincing argument except, as you so rightly said, there's not a shred of evidence that would hold up in a court of law. It would cast a shadow of doubt on Major Ravallo's credibility as an intelligence officer, but whether the Americans would suspend him is quite another matter altogether. I've already spoken to my opposite number in Military Intelligence about the operation, and he's prepared to put his career on the line if it means vouching for the integrity of both Major Ravallo and Lieutenant di Mauro. Do you think she could be involved as well?'

'No, sir, I don't,' came the resolute answer.

'Is that a professional or a personal view?' Starr asked.

'I don't know what you mean, sir,' McIndoe replied as he shifted uncomfortably in his chair.

'I know you're fond of her, lad,' Starr said in a surprisingly paternal voice. 'And who can blame you? She's an intelligent, strong-willed and very beautiful young lady. The perfect attributes for a female spy. The lure of seduction can be a very powerful weapon indeed.'

'I resent that, sir,' McIndoe retorted indignantly as he jumped to his feet.

'Oh, for goodness' sake, McIndoe, that wasn't aimed at you. Now sit down.' Starr took another puff on his pipe as McIndoe slowly retook his seat. 'I know nothing happened between you and the young lady. You may not be averse to a bit of foul play on the rugger field, as I was quite dismayed to witness when I last saw you play at Twickenham, but I know that off the field you've always been the perfect gentleman. All I'm saying is that, if Major Ravallo is a German spy, then there's always the chance that as her controller he could have recruited her as well.'

'No, sir, I don't buy that,' McIndoe said decisively. 'Why did she risk her career – not to mention her life – by blatantly disregarding orders to abort the operation after Major Ravallo was caught at the hotel? If they were in league together, she'd have known he would have been safe in the hands of the Gestapo.'

'It's certainly a valid point in her favour, I'll grant you that,' Starr mused, then tapped the debriefing notes in front of him. 'Why did you risk your career by going along with her? You never fully explained that to the debriefing officer.'

'I think I did, sir,' McIndoe replied. 'The others sided with her as well. What could I do? Order them at gunpoint to leave the church? Hardly practical.'

'Fair enough – and, for the record, I'm prepared to overlook your insubordination this one time due to the nature of the operation – but what I don't understand is why you helped Major Ravallo if you were so convinced that he was a German spy?'

'At the time I still wasn't convinced he was a Gestapo agent . . .' McIndoe trailed off and clamped his mouth shut, as if he were censoring himself before he said something he might regret.

'You were going to say something else? You should know by now you can talk quite freely in front of me. These conversations are always completely confidential. We've had enough of them in the past for you to know that.'

'I was going to say there's always a chance, however small, that I'm wrong about Major Ravallo and that he's not a Nazi spy. I could never have lived with myself if it were true and I'd let him die at the hands of the Gestapo.'

'At last, a glimmer of light in the darkness,' Starr said.

'Are you saying you think he's innocent, sir?' McIndoe asked in surprise.

'I never said any such thing,' Starr replied with a scowl. 'What I am saying is that it's good to keep an open mind in this business. It's very easy to accuse someone of treachery because certain circumstances seem to point to their guilt. What if you're wrong about Major Ravallo – I'm not saying you are, but what if a subsequent investigation were to exonerate him? You'd have to make reparations with your own conscience for having doubted him in the first place.'

'If he were cleared, then I'd be a lot more worried that there'd been some kind of conspiratorial cover-up to spare the blushes of Allied Intelligence.'

'That's well out of order, McIndoe!' Starr thundered. 'I'll be handling this investigation personally, and should I find against Major Ravallo – or anyone else for that matter – then by God I'll see to it that they face the full wrath of the law.'

'I'm sorry, sir, I didn't realize you'd be taking charge of the investigation,' McIndoe said contritely. 'I know you'll be totally impartial in your evaluation of the facts. I was just worried that perhaps the Yanks would have wanted to handle the investigation themselves so they could quietly brush the dirt under the carpet to save themselves any embarrassment.'

'There will be no cover-up,' Starr replied in a more equanimous tone of voice. He placed his pipe on the desk. 'That's all for now, McIndoe, but I want you to report back here with Sub-Lieutenant Higgins at exactly twenty hundred hours tonight. By then I hope to have instigated a plan which should prove once and for all whether Major Ravallo is working for the Germans. I'll brief you both then.'

McIndoe got to his feet, saluted Starr, then crossed to the door where he paused with his hand resting lightly on the handle. 'I never knew you were interested in rugby, sir.'

'What?' Starr replied absently, looking up from the document he'd started to read. He removed his reading glasses. 'Oh yes, I always try and get to the international matches at Twickenham whenever I can. Cricket's still my first love, though. Has been since I was a boy. I find nothing more relaxing than a warm afternoon at Lord's watching the likes of Hutton and Leyland knock the stuffing out of those damnable Australian bowlers.'

McIndoe smiled to himself, imagining the bulbous figure of Starr with his panama hat and pipe sitting in the pavilion at Lord's. 'When did you see me at Twickenham, sir?'

'In '38, when Scotland won the Triple Crown. You know as well as I do that the try you scored in the dying seconds of the match should never have been allowed to stand. I had an excellent vantage point close to the pitch and I saw you put your hands into the loose maul to retrieve the ball which had been released by one of your forwards after he'd been tackled. Only none of the players in the maul had played the ball with their foot before you picked it up. And that's a foul. That should have been a penalty to England. We'd have cleared our lines and held on to win the match. But you were clever. You made sure you were on the referee's blind side when you committed your indiscretion. He was totally unsighted. The damned cheek of it all.'

'Initiative, improvisation and just a touch of impertinence thrown in for good measure,' McIndoe said with a grin.

Starr's smile vanished as quickly as it had appeared, and he slipped on his reading glasses again. 'Eight o'clock, McIndoe. Don't be late.'

'What does he want to see us about?' Higgins asked after McIndoe had passed on Starr's orders.

'He's concocting some scheme to weed out the traitor,' McIndoe replied as he poured himself a shot of whisky from the bottle Starr had sent over to the house. 'Do you want a dram?'

'I'm not a whisky drinker, you know that,' Higgins replied.

'Of course, I was forgetting, you're a damn heathen when it comes to appreciating the finer points of alcohol,' McIndoe said good-humouredly.

'Give me an old-fashioned pint any time,' Higgins said.

'I rest my case, m'lord,' McIndoe said, taking a sip of whisky before placing the tumbler on the table beside him. 'Where is everybody, by the way?'

'They're catching up on their sleep,' Higgins replied, stifling a yawn as he got to his feet. 'Which is what I'm going to do. Even if it is only for an hour.'

'Do you want me to wake you around half-seven?' McIndoe asked.

'I'd appreciate that, Mac. I'm two doors down on the right.'

McIndoe watched Higgins leave the room, then he reached for his drink and cradled the tumbler between his hands. He was exhausted, but an hour's sleep wouldn't do him any good. If anything, it would only make him even more tired. He replaced the tumbler on the table – that certainly wasn't helping him any either. What he needed was a coffee. Black and unsweetened. If there was any in the house. He went through to the kitchen and checked the cupboards. All he could find was tea. Well, it had caffeine. It would have to do. He lit the stove, then filled the kettle from the tap in the sink and placed it on the plate.

'If you're making coffee, I'd love one,' Stella said from the doorway.

McIndoe looked round at her. She was wearing a cotton wrap tied tightly around her slender body and her unkempt raven hair hung loosely on her shoulders. It was obvious from her appearance she'd just woken up. 'Sorry, no coffee,' he said. 'Tea?'

'The British and their fixation with tea,' she said, pulling up a chair and sitting down at the wooden table in the middle of the kitchen. 'Frankly, I don't see the attraction myself.'

'Was that a yes or a no?'

'That was a roundabout way of saying yes, seeing you've got no coffee,' she said with a sheepish chuckle.

'Can't sleep?' he asked as he removed two cups from the cupboard.

'I slept for most of the afternoon, after I'd got back from my debriefing,' she replied, taking a packet of cigarettes from the pocket of her wrap. She lit one and left the packet on the table. 'I could have happily slept for another week, but when I woke up a few minutes ago, all I could hear was this loud snoring coming from the next room. I knew then I wouldn't be able to get back to sleep. I can't sleep if I can hear snoring. I've been like that since I was a child. I remember my father used to be a heavy snorer, and with my parents' room being next to mine, I used to lie awake for hours until I fell asleep from sheer exhaustion.'

'May I?' he asked, gesturing to the cigarettes on the table.

'You know you don't have to ask,' she said, pushing the packet towards him.

'Who's in the room next to you?' McIndoe said after he'd lit himself a cigarette. 'I'll see if I can get him to stop snoring.'

'Actually, I think it's Frenchy,' she replied with a grimace.

'Then I respectfully withdraw my offer,' McIndoe said. 'Nothing ever wakes him. He once slept through a *Luftwaffe* air-raid. Didn't so much as stir. Quite remarkable.'

'You think a lot of him, don't you?' she said.

'We've been through a lot together since he joined the Firm. He can be a bit of a character at times, but he's always been totally dependable in a crisis. A bit like Taffy really.' McIndoe clapped his hands together. 'Enough reminiscing. Let's talk about someone else, shall we?'

'OK. Who?' she enquired.

'You.'

'Me?' she replied in surprise. 'Why do you want to talk about me?'

'Not just you,' McIndoe said as he sat down opposite her. 'I realize that . . . well, we haven't exactly known each other very long, and even though we've had our differences . . . well, I think you know that I've come to like you . . . a lot. And I get the feeling – and I hope I'm not wrong – that, well . . . you kind of like me too . . .' This wasn't going at all well. In fact, it was going disastrously wrong. How come he could plan and execute dangerous military strategies with complete confidence, and yet when it came to something as simple as asking a woman to go out with him, he immediately became this tongue-tied buffoon stumbling hesitantly over his every word? What made it worse was he'd already worked out in his mind exactly how he was going to approach this moment. So why the hell didn't he recognize anything that had just tumbled embarrassingly out of his mouth? And, to make matters worse, he could now feel the droplets of sweat beginning to gather on his forehead. This was fast turning into a nightmare. Try *and salvage something out of this*, he said in desperation to himself. 'What I'm actually trying to say is . . . well . . .'

'That this is your roundabout way of asking me out on a date, right?' she said with a gentle smile. 'I'm flattered, Sam. I really am.'

'But?' McIndoe asked hesitantly, already anticipating the worst. *You've only got yourself to blame after the way you bungled it*, he chided himself furiously.

'I like you a lot, Sam, but not in that way. It would only send out the wrong signals if I were to agree to go out with you. I regard you as a friend. A good friend. And I hope we can continue to build on that friendship for many years to come.'

'Nicky told me you only regarded me as a friend. He warned me not to confuse friendship with something deeper. But of course I knew better, didn't I? I had to go and put my big foot in it.' McIndoe pushed back his chair and crossed to the stove where he tried to hide his discomfort by turning the kettle around absently over the open flame. 'Why didn't I listen to him? God, I feel such a fool now.'

'Well, don't,' she said, then moved her chair until she could see him. 'Believe me, most women would have jumped at the chance to go out with someone like you. You'd be regarded as quite a catch, you know that?'

'I'm not so sure about that. I seem to attract the kind of women who'd much rather unburden all their personal problems on to me, and as soon as I've managed to sort out their lives for them, they're off to find some handsome bloke to sweep them off their feet. It's just not fair.'

'You poor thing,' she said with gentle sarcasm.

'I bet Nicky never has that trouble,' he said good-humouredly. 'Not with his looks.'

'Sure, women are attracted to Nicky's looks. But looks fade. You'll always have that special knack of being able to unweave a woman's tangled emotions. That's quite a talent you've got there. Don't knock it.'

'If that's supposed to make me feel any better, it doesn't.'

Stella chuckled at his mock scowl. 'Now you know why I want to keep you as my friend. That way I can come to you with all my personal problems.'

'So that some handsome bloke can come along and sweep you off your feet?' McIndoe asked. 'Or has that happened already?'

The smile disappeared as her eyes turned to the kettle as it began to whistle. 'I think the water's boiling.'

'I can take a hint,' he said softly as he lifted the kettle off the stove. He prepared the tea then brought the teapot to the table.

'I'll pour,' she offered.

'I can manage,' he said tersely.

She could sense the tension as she watched him fill the two cups. He placed the teapot on the mat in the centre of the table and handed her one of the cups. She added a dash of milk to her cup. 'Sam, about what you asked me just now. You know, if there was already someone else in my life – '

'It wasn't my place to ask,' came the riposte.

'No, you were right to ask. I should have been straight with you from the start. I'm the one who was in the wrong. One minute I'm calling you a friend, and the next minute I'm brushing you off like some stranger. I can't have it both ways.'

'So what you're saying is there is someone else in your life?' he asked, much of the animosity now gone from his voice. In its place was a resigned acceptance of what he'd already perceived to be the inevitable.

'Yes, there is,' she said softly.

'I just hope he realizes what a lucky bugger he is, if you'll pardon my language,' McIndoe said with a sad smile. He pushed the cup away from him. 'I don't know why I'm bothering to drink that. It's absolutely ghastly. It tastes like recycled dishwater.'

'I didn't want to say anything; I thought perhaps that's the way you liked it,' Stella said, screwing up her face in agreement.

'God, no. It was probably bought on the black market. With such strict rationing here on Malta, the local racketeers can get away with murder.' He removed the lid from the teapot and sniffed the sodden pulp which lay in the cradle of the strainer. 'There's certainly tea leaves hidden in there somewhere, but you'd need the great Sherlock Holmes to find them.'

'Which begs the question, just what's it been mixed with?'

'Probably some cheap, inodorous herb.' He carried the teapot over to the sink and poured the contents down the drain. 'I'll make a deal with you. When you come to visit me in Scotland – which I hope you will do some day – I'll introduce you to Earl Grey tea. I guarantee you'll like it.'

'Deal,' she agreed.

McIndoe looked at his watch. 'I'd better go and have a shave and put on a clean shirt. I've got a meeting with Starr at eight o'clock.'

'What about?' she asked.

'What do you think?' he replied, stubbing out his cigarette in the sink and discarding it in the bin.

'The traitor?'

McIndoe nodded. 'Starr's taken charge of the investigation to find the traitor and, as I'm sure you've already gathered from having met him, he's the embodiment of the British bulldog. Once he gets his teeth into something, he just won't let go. I've got a feeling it won't be long now before we finally know the truth.'

'So you think he's already got an idea who it is?' she asked, reaching for another cigarette.

'Oh, I think so,' McIndoe replied with a knowing smile as he crossed to the door. 'A very good idea.'

* * *

401

McIndoe knocked on the door. No answer. He tried the handle. The door was unlocked. He pushed it open and stepped inside. The room was in darkness except for a thin sliver of light which was emanating from under the inner door leading into Starr's office. McIndoe gestured for Higgins to enter the room, and waited until he'd closed the door behind them before making his way silently towards the source of the light.

Higgins grabbed his arm as they neared the door. 'Why are we tiptoeing?'

'Why are you whispering?' McIndoe replied. They grinned at each other, then McIndoe rapped on the door.

'Come,' came the familiar boom. They entered the office and found Starr entrenched as usual behind his paper-strewn desk, with a thick haze of smoke hanging over him. 'Sit down,' Starr ordered without acknowledging them as he continued to rummage through the papers in front of him. He spent the next minute gathering together the loose sheets of paper before filing them in the open folder in front of him. He closed over the folder and placed it in his top drawer. 'Much better,' he announced, then looked at them for the first time since they'd entered the room. 'I've just spoken to the senior duty officer at the dockyard. The MTB's been given the all-clear to return to sea.'

'Are *we* returning to sea, sir?' Higgins said suspiciously.

'You're returning to Sicily, to be more precise,' Starr replied.

'You must be joking!' McIndoe exclaimed in disbelief.

'I beg your pardon?' Starr retorted sharply.

'Sir, with all due respect, we just made it out of there by the skin of our teeth,' McIndoe said, quickly assuming a more conciliatory tone of voice. 'The next time there's every chance we won't make it out of there at all.'

'Except that the last time you were compromised even before you reached Sicily. This time the Germans won't be forewarned that you're coming. That will give you the edge.'

Starr removed his glasses and rubbed his eyes. 'I realize you'll be taking a calculated risk by going back there again so soon, but it's the only way we're going to finally discover whether Major Ravallo is the German spy.'

'You think Nicky's the traitor?' Higgins asked.

'Lieutenant McIndoe seems to think so, and he certainly put across a strong argument to back up his allegations,' Starr replied.

'I guess it makes sense after the way he acted on the bridge,' Higgins said, casting a sidelong glance in McIndoe's direction.

'I asked you both here tonight because, quite frankly, you're the only two I know I can trust. You were both on the bridge when Passiere was attacked in the wireless room and, much as I'm inclined to believe you're right about Major Ravallo, McIndoe, I still can't take the chance of confiding in any of the others in case you are wrong. After all, none of them has proven alibis that would eliminate them as suspects.'

'Passiere's also in the clear, surely?' Higgins said.

'The wound he got in the radio room could have been self-inflicted to deflect the suspicion away from himself,' Starr replied. Noticing the look of scepticism on their faces, he added, 'I agree it seems highly unlikely, but it is a possibility which can't be discounted.'

'So what exactly is this plan of yours, sir?' McIndoe asked.

'It's very simple really. You will tell the others that Giancarlo Massimo contacted me earlier this evening to say he knows the real identity of the traitor. Obviously with all the *Abwehr* listening posts on Sicily, it would be too risky to transmit the name over the radio, so he's placed the name in a sealed envelope which you are to collect and bring back to me.'

'Is this true, sir?' Higgins asked.

'There is an envelope and there is a name inside it.' Starr sucked on his pipe, then allowed himself an ironic smile. 'Actually, it's your name.'

'What?' Higgins replied in horror.

'It's a bluff, for God's sake,' Starr was quick to assure him. 'As I said to you earlier, I know neither of you are implicated in this treachery. That's why I've used your name. You're above suspicion.'

'I don't understand what you hope to gain by this, sir,' McIndoe said.

'Just this: the sheet of paper inside the envelope has been treated with a special solution, invisible to the naked eye, but which will reveal any fingerprints under ultra-violet light. Major Ravallo and Lieutenant di Mauro will be sent ashore to collect the envelope from Massimo. He'll give them specific orders that the envelope's for my eyes only. Major Ravallo will be told to keep it on his person for the return journey, and not to open it under any circumstances. If, however, Major Ravallo is the traitor, then he won't be able to resist checking to see if it's his name inside the envelope. He wouldn't have any other reasons to disobey orders, would he? So if I were to subsequently find his fingerprints on the paper, then we'll have our traitor, won't we?'

'He'd need to replace the envelope, sir,' Higgins pointed out.

'There's writing paper and envelopes in one of the cabins on the MTB. I saw them when I went to inspect the damage to the boat shortly after you returned from Sicily. That's how I came by this idea in the first place. We need to make it easy for Major Ravallo to cover his tracks, but without him suspecting for one moment he's actually tightening the noose around his own neck.'

'Why does Stella have to go with him?' McIndoe asked, the thought having been lingering uncomfortably in his mind ever since Starr had first mentioned her.

'I have reason to believe they may be in this together,' Starr told him.

'That's absurd,' McIndoe replied sharply. 'We've been through this before, sir.'

'That was before I received a communiqué from my opposite number in Military Intelligence. It's classified information but let's just say he's not as convinced of their innocence as he was earlier today.'

'Sir, if there's something we should know – '

'Nothing whatsoever to concern you, McIndoe,' Starr interceded, his finger raised in admonishment. 'You know better than to question classified information. Now that's an end to it.'

'I don't believe a word of it,' McIndoe snapped. 'Not Stella.'

Higgins was quick to put a restraining hand on McIndoe's arm, knowing only too well his feelings for Stella. 'Sir, you said this time the Germans wouldn't know we were coming,' he said, directing Starr's attention away from McIndoe. 'How can we be sure of that unless the wireless room is sealed off?'

'It will be, at least until you arrive off the coast of Sicily. I'm told there's a key for the wireless-room door on the bridge. Lock the door before you leave port and keep the key on the bridge at all times.'

'Where are we due to rendezvous with the Resistance, sir?' Higgins asked.

'The same coordinates as before. Only this time you'll lay anchor off-shore and not retreat to one of those caves. You'll need to maintain radio contact with the Partisans once the two of them are ashore. That wouldn't be possible with all the interference inside those caves. I've arranged for two of our subs to take up positions close to where you'll be anchored. That should help to put your minds at rest.'

'When do we brief the others, sir?' Higgins asked.

'Once you're at sea. Not before. You'll leave at midnight.' Starr closed the folder in front of him. 'Thank you, gentlemen. That will be all. I'll speak to you again on your return.'

'Come on, Mac, let's go,' Higgins said, getting to his feet.

McIndoe remained seated, his eyes fixed on Starr. 'You're keeping something from us, sir, aren't you? We're laying our lives on the line here. I think it's only fair that you should level with us.'

'You've been given your orders, Lieutenant McIndoe.'

'If anything happens to Stella – '

'I will not be lectured to by a junior officer!' Starr thundered as he rose to his feet, his face flushed with rage. 'How dare you question my authority? You will do as you're told. I will not tolerate your insubordination.'

McIndoe jumped up, but Higgins grabbed his arm and pulled him away roughly from Starr's desk. 'Are you mad?' he hissed at McIndoe. 'Outside. Now.' McIndoe struggled to break free of the grip, but Higgins held firm as he jerked open the door, propelled McIndoe into the outer office, then followed him out and closed the door behind him. McIndoe looked back at Starr's door, then cursed angrily before storming out into the corridor. Higgins went after him. 'Jesus, Mac, what the bloody hell got into you back there?' he demanded.

'I don't buy what he said about Stella,' McIndoe replied. 'When I spoke to him earlier today he told me Military Intelligence were a hundred per cent behind them both. Now suddenly they're both expendable. It doesn't make sense, Charlie. It just doesn't make any sense.'

'You're letting your feelings for Stella cloud your professional judgement.'

'No,' McIndoe snapped. 'No, no I'm not,' he said in a quieter voice. 'I talked to her today. I know where I stand with her now. It can't ever be anything more than friendship. I accept that.'

'So what are you saying here, Mac? That Starr didn't receive any communiqué from Washington? That he's making it all up?'

'I don't know,' McIndoe said in desperation. 'It just doesn't seem right, that's all.'

'What would he have to gain by putting Stella's life in danger?'

'I don't know. I just feel uneasy about the whole thing.' McIndoe gestured to the steps at the end of the corridor. 'Come on, we've still got to wake the others and get them wide-eyed and ship-shape for another exciting midnight cruise.'

'I'll leave Frenchy to you,' Higgins said, putting an arm around McIndoe's shoulder as they climbed the steps which led up to the courtyard where their driver had parked the Bedford MW.

'Jesus, now I definitely know it's not my night,' McIndoe groaned as they emerged out into the courtyard.

'Sleep well?'

'Yes, sir, but I have been up for the past few hours. I've been working on my report for Field-Marshal Kesselring,' Riedler replied as he crossed the bare polished floorboards to the table where Student had just finished his dinner.

'Sit down, Hans,' Student said, gesturing to the chair opposite him. 'Coffee?'

'Please.'

'Two coffees,' Student instructed the waiter, who was busy clearing the table.

'Is Field-Marshal Kesselring still in the hotel, sir?' Riedler asked.

'No, he left this morning. About ten. And, contrary to what you thought, he was actually very impressed with the way you handled the operation. He told me so himself. He's even talking about putting your name forward for the Special Forces. I'm sure he will, and with his recommendation you'll have no trouble being accepted.'

'I thought he'd be ready to string me up after what had happened,' Riedler said, an overwhelming sense of relief evident in his voice.

'You've got to be more confident about yourself, Hans,' Student told him.

'Except that confidence comes from success, sir.'

'It also comes from learning from your mistakes,' Student told him.

Riedler waited until the waiter had poured out their coffees and retreated before speaking. 'Sir, did Field-Marshal Kesselring manage to find out anything about this Gestapo agent before he left the hotel? You said he was absolutely livid when he found out about their deception, and that he intended to ring *Reichsführer* Himmler personally for an explanation.'

Student glanced across at the waiter to satisfy himself that the man was out of earshot. Even so, he still sat forward, and when he spoke his voice was hushed. 'By all accounts, *Reichsführer* Himmler was furious when he found out that neither Brausch nor any of his senior officers here on the island had bothered to brief either Field-Marshal Kesselring or myself about the existence of their agent. And, knowing the *Reichsführer* as I do, you can be sure heads will roll at the Piazza Bologni before the week's out. He refused to divulge the name of their agent – which is understandable – but what he did say was that the local Gestapo had been given orders to pass on any information to us they received from their agent. It turns out, however, they didn't hear from their agent after the enemy boat left Malta, not until they received the coordinates of the boat when it was leaving Sicily. Whether the agent gave the Gestapo a reason for this enforced silence, I don't know. *Reichsführer* Himmler didn't offer any explanation to Field-Marshal Kesselring.'

'Do you think the *Reichsführer* was telling the truth?' Riedler asked.

'*Reichsführer* Himmler is a law unto himself, but I can't see what he'd have to gain by lying to Field-Marshal Kesselring. We may have our ideological differences with the Gestapo, but at the end of the day we're still fighting the same enemy. No, I'm inclined to believe him. I know Field-Marshal Kesselring did.'

'It's still a case of closing the stable door after the horse has already bolted,' Riedler said dejectedly.

'Not necessarily,' Student replied. 'What if I told you that you were going to get another chance to finish the job?'

'I don't understand, sir,' came the puzzled reply.

'I didn't call you down here to discuss Field-Marshal Kesselring's conversation with the *Reichsführer*. I've received information within the last hour that the same unit under the command of the American, Ravallo, is returning to Sicily later tonight. Why, I don't know. But then it doesn't really matter since we already know where the boat will be anchored. We also know when it will be leaving Malta, so that gives us a rough estimation of when it will reach Sicily. I haven't contacted the *Luftwaffe* or the *Kriegsmarine*. I thought you'd want to handle the welcoming party personally.'

'Thank you, sir,' Riedler said with a smile. 'I won't let you down.'

'It won't be me you'd be letting down if you fail this time, Hans. It'll be yourself; whatever happens tonight will reflect on any future application to join the Special Forces.' Student took a sip of coffee, then lowered the cup without taking his eyes off Riedler's face. 'But then I already know you won't let yourself down. I have every confidence in your ability.'

'What are the rules of engagement, sir?' Riedler asked.

'The same as they were before. If possible, capture them alive for interrogation. If not, kill them.'

'They'll never let themselves be taken alive, sir. They'll stand their ground and fight to the last man,' Riedler said.

'You admire them for that, don't you?'

'Don't you, sir?' Riedler countered.

'Yes, I do – although I'd still prefer it if they were captured alive. The knowledge they must have between them of the ongoing British and American covert operations here in the Mediterranean would prove invaluable to us.'

'I wouldn't count on any prisoners, sir,' Riedler said philosophically. 'Will they have any air or sea cover this time?'

'According to the communiqué, they'll be coming in completely unprotected.'

'You'd think they'd have some kind of cover, like they had the last time.'

'I can easily have a U-boat dispatched to the area if it would make you feel more comfortable,' Student offered. 'But you know how trigger-happy these U-boat captains are in those kind of situations. A stationary boat. It's the perfect target practice for them. He might just decide to torpedo the boat and claim the glory for himself. You wouldn't want that, would you?'

'I can always radio for backup should the need arise, sir,' Riedler replied.

'Of course you can,' Student said, then handed Riedler a sheet of paper. 'Those are the coordinates and the boat's estimated time of arrival off the Sicilian coast. The rest is up to you, Hans.'

'It would seem Field-Marshal Kesselring's call to the *Reichsführer* had the desired effect after all. The Gestapo certainly didn't lose any time passing on this information to you.'

'Oh, this didn't come from the Gestapo,' Student replied.

'It didn't?' Riedler said in surprise. 'Then how did you come by it?'

'It was picked up by one of the *Abwehr's* listening posts on the island. The transmission originated from Valletta. The *Abwehr* couldn't pinpoint its exact location, but they're almost certain it originated from St Elmo's Fort. That's the base of British Intelligence over there. So if you're right about these covert operatives fighting it out to the last man, then someone at the base has just sent them to their deaths.' Student gestured to Riedler's empty cup. 'More coffee?'

SIXTEEN

It could never be the same again. That much had become obvious to McIndoe at the briefing he'd held shortly after the MTB had left Grand Harbour. Suspicion and uncertainty had been branded on every face. He realized, in retrospect, that these feelings had been simmering insidiously beneath the surface ever since the noncommissioned men had discovered the officers had been holding the truth back from them. At the time – and to their lasting credit – they had managed to overcome their unsettled emotions and continued to work together as a team. But he already knew that, even if the traitor was brought to justice, there was already too much deep-rooted bitterness and resentment amongst that particular combination of men for them ever to serve together again as an effective operational unit. Even though there was now little communication between Hillyard, Johnson and Passiere, McIndoe knew much of their anger was directed at him for having concealed the truth from them for so long. He felt it was completely unjustified, still believing he'd acted in the best interests of his men by shielding the truth from them. What concerned him the most, however, was whether those actions would affect his future standing as an officer. If he were to lose the confidence of the non-commissioned men back home, he'd quickly become a liability in the field, and that would mean his career in the Firm would effectively be over.

He looked down from the bridge at Hillyard who was manning the starboard Vickers gun. Not surprisingly, Hillyard had reacted the most vociferously. As far as he was concerned, McIndoe had abused his position as an officer by deceiving them in the way he had. He'd already told McIndoe that to his face. Despite their differences, he still regarded Hillyard as a fine field operative, even if his attitude towards authority was distinctly questionable. And Hillyard would be the most likely agitator when it came to stirring up any kind of resentment against him when they got back to England.

His eyes went to the stern and the shadowy figure standing behind the Oerlikon gun. Johnson. He'd said little about it all, preferring to keep his thoughts to himself, as was his way, but it wasn't difficult to read the look of hurt in his eyes. Alienation. And for McIndoe that had cut the deepest.

He couldn't see Passiere on the port side. Even he'd changed dramatically over the last twenty-four hours. Gone was the chirpy, loquacious Frenchman he'd come to know so well over the last two years. Now he was quiet and withdrawn, as if reluctant to openly criticize an officer he'd come to regard as a friend. The situation hadn't been helped when he'd been informed shortly before they left Grand Harbour that the wireless room would remain locked until they reached Sicily. Not only was he being prevented from doing his job, but he was also being barred from what he regarded as his own sacred domain. The sacrilege of distrust was everywhere.

McIndoe knew that much of the acrimony currently being targeted at him was, in fact, their way of venting the frustration and anxiety they were feeling at not knowing who had betrayed them. There was a distinct reticency to talk about it amongst themselves and, in a perverse way, he felt strangely comforted that they could turn their anger on him.

The door opened and Ravallo entered the wheelhouse. 'We need to talk, Mac.' His eyes went to Higgins. 'Alone.'

Higgins shot Ravallo a disparaging look. 'You'll forgive me if I don't leave the bridge. Unless, of course, you'd care to take the wheel?'

'I'll be in the cabin where you held the briefing earlier tonight,' Ravallo said, then disappeared back out into the night.

'What the hell was all that about?' McIndoe demanded of Higgins. 'We agreed to keep our personal feelings for Nicky under wraps. The first time you see him you can't resist making some snide remark. He is still the senior officer on board, in case you'd forgotten.'

'He's also a bloody Nazi spy,' came the disdainful reply.

'Do you want everyone to hear you?' McIndoe hissed, quickly closing the door.

'They would already know if it were up to me.'

'Well it's not, is it?' McIndoe retorted.

'Why are you protecting him when you know he's guilty?'

'Because at the moment all I've got is a lot of unsubstantiated evidence,' McIndoe told him. 'And in case you've forgotten the cornerstone of British justice, he's innocent until proven guilty.'

'You've certainly changed your tune,' Higgins said.

'No, I think you'll find that *I* haven't,' McIndoe said.

He left the bridge and made his way to the cabin below deck. The door was open. Stella was sitting motionless at the table on the opposite side of the room, her eyes cast downwards as she stared at the smouldering cigarette which was balanced on the edge of the ashtray in front of her. Ravallo stood beside the table, arms folded, seemingly lost in thought. McIndoe was almost reluctant to venture into the cabin, not wanting to disturb the moment.

'He thinks I'm the traitor, doesn't he?' Ravallo said softly as McIndoe continued to hover in the doorway.

'Pardon?' McIndoe said in surprise.

Ravallo turned his head to look at McIndoe. 'Higgins thinks I'm the traitor.'

'Charlie?' McIndoe replied, horrified that Ravallo may have overheard Higgins's outburst after he'd left the bridge. 'Why do you say that?'

'It's true, isn't it?'

'No, of course not,' McIndoe replied as he entered the cabin.

'Then who's "the bloody Nazi spy"?' Ravallo asked. 'It's all I heard before you closed the door. He was talking about me, wasn't he?'

'You've got to understand that Charlie's under a lot of pressure – '

'It's OK, you don't have to defend him,' Ravallo said quickly. 'You also think it's me, don't you? In fact, I initially thought it was just you who suspected me. That's the reason why I wanted to speak to you down here. Away from the others.'

McIndoe realized there was little point in continuing the façade any longer. 'How did you know I suspected you?' he asked suspiciously.

'I told him,' Stella said, reaching for her cigarette.

'Stella and I had a long talk after the briefing earlier tonight. That's how we – or rather, Stella – came to the conclusion that you – and Starr for that matter – suspected me, or perhaps even both us, of working for the Germans.'

'I never thought Stella was involved,' McIndoe said, sitting down opposite her.

'That's something, I guess,' Ravallo said. He reached for the packet of cigarettes on the table, lit one, then tossed the packet back on to the table. He took a long drag and exhaled the smoke slowly before speaking again. 'I realize that there may have been . . . shall we say, certain events over the past few days which could have put me in the frame. But I'll tell you now, Mac, I'm not your man. I'm not a traitor, whatever you or anyone else may think.'

'And that's it?' McIndoe said.

'I can't undo what's happened. I'm the first to admit I made some bad decisions during the course of this operation, not least when I gave the order to surrender when the *Schnellboote* threatened to sink us.' Ravallo gestured to Stella. 'Even Stella refused to back me on that one. That says it all. But that was inexperience, pure and simple. At the time I honestly thought I was acting in the best interests of the crew, but now I realize I was wrong. But there's still a hell of a difference between inexperience and wilful treason.'

'How did you come to the conclusion that I suspected Nicky of being the spy?' McIndoe asked Stella.

'Why else would we be sent ashore to get this envelope from Massimo?' Ravallo answered for her. 'It's a test, isn't it, to see whether I'd take the chance of trying to make a break for it if I thought my name was in the envelope? What exactly was the plan? Were the Resistance going to kill me, is that it?' He took another drag on the cigarette. 'Sorry to disappoint you, Mac. I know I'm innocent. So it won't be my name in that envelope. And to prove just how confident I am of that, we've decided that I should remain on board while Stella goes ashore by herself to collect the envelope. I'll even hand my weapon over to you if that's what you want. I know Starr gave you specific orders for the envelope to be delivered to him unopened but under the circumstances I'm prepared to risk disciplinary action by disobeying those orders when Stella returns to the boat. I've got nothing to hide, so the sooner we get to the bottom of this, the sooner the real traitor can be brought to justice. And isn't that what this is all about?'

McIndoe's initial reaction was a mixture of surprise and suspicion. Why was Ravallo prepared to take the chance that it wasn't his name in the envelope if he was the traitor? Was it some kind of bluff ? It made no sense . . . unless he was wrong about Ravallo. That seemed inconceivable when all the evidence pointed to him being the spy. He'd already considered, then dismissed, the idea that Stella might be part of the conspiracy. Neither of them could possibly have known it wasn't Ravallo's name in the envelope so he'd have nothing to gain by sending her ashore by herself. Unless . . . no, McIndoe tried to push the thought from his mind, but it returned. He had to face up to the possibility: what if it was Stella who was working for the Germans?

He refused to believe it. But what about the incident when they'd picked her up off the Sicilian coast? The Germans hadn't been far behind her. Had she tipped them off in advance about the rendezvous? Why had she been so quick to want to stay behind at the church after Ravallo had been captured at the hotel, knowing the Germans would flood the area with troops? Why had she appeared so reluctant to jump from the train, knowing there was a unit of German soldiers waiting for them at the next station? No, he still refused to believe it. Not Stella. Yet what also worried him was that, if he could write off those incidents as mere coincidence, then why couldn't he do the same when it came to the evidence against Ravallo? Suddenly he was confused. He didn't know what to believe any more. All he knew was that he didn't have the authority to order Ravallo to go ashore with her – even though the whole operation depended on him going – nor could he refuse to let her go by herself without a damn good reason. And he didn't have one, not without revealing the truth behind the doctored paper in the envelope. All he did have was supposition, speculation, and a lot of worthless circumstantial evidence . . .

'I believe in Nicky,' Stella said softly. 'I know in my heart he's not a traitor and I'm prepared to stake my life on it by going ashore to get the envelope. That will prove once and for all that he's innocent.'

It wouldn't prove anything, and McIndoe knew it. He was on the verge of calling off the whole operation and having Higgins turn the boat round and return to Malta, but there was still a nagging doubt in the back of his mind that they could be working in league together. And if they were, they'd expect one of their names to be contained in the envelope. What if their plan was to substitute the sheet of paper for one with a different name? She could already have an envelope secreted somewhere on her person which she could use to reseal the new sheet of paper before she returned to the boat. Yet all his instincts told him she wasn't involved. But could he afford to take that chance?

'Well, Mac, what do you say?' Ravallo asked.

'We'll go with your plan,' McIndoe replied.

'Do you want me to hand over my gun?' Ravallo queried as he reached for his holstered Colt .45 automatic.

'Keep it,' McIndoe said tersely, then got to his feet and left the cabin.

The *Linse* had been Franke's idea. A radio-controlled motor-boat, seventeen foot long and fitted with a standard Ford V8 engine producing ninety-five horsepower, which could be packed with an explosive charge weighing anything up to a thousand pounds and guided with unerring accuracy by means of a built-in UKW receiver on to its intended target. It was only used at night to fully maximize the element of surprise, and required a trained pilot, or K-man as they were known in the *Kriegsmarine*'s élite Special Forces unit, K Flotilla, to manoeuvre it silently into position. The pilot would then open the throttle and direct the *Linse* towards the enemy ship at top speed before switching on the radio-receiver which would automatically pass control of the craft over to an operator on the command ship. This done, the pilot then bailed out into the sea, leaving the controller to guide the craft to its target. On impacting with the enemy ship, an initial explosion would break the *Linse* in half, and the aft section containing the main explosive charge would sink and detonate underneath the vessel with the force of a sea mine.

Brandenburg and K Flotilla had previously undertaken a series of successful *Linsen* night raids against the Russians in the Bosporus and the British in the North Atlantic, with the result that *Linsen* units had since been deployed in areas where they could continue to inflict the maximum amount of damage on Allied shipping. The Mediterranean was no exception.

All it had taken was one phone call to the relevant authorities for Riedler to secure the use of a *Linse*, as well as a *Schnellboote*, from the *Kriegsmarine* base at Gela harbour. He'd chosen twelve of his most experienced paratroopers to accompany him and Franke to Gela aboard a Junkers transport plane, which had been put on standby for them at the *Luftwaffe* air-base outside Palermo. On arriving at Gela harbour, Riedler discovered to his satisfaction that the instructions he passed on over the telephone had been carried out to the letter. The explosives had already been stored aboard the *Schnellboote*, and one of the lifeboats had been removed to make room for the *Linse*. He'd then dispensed with the *Schnellboote's* regular crew, save for the captain and two engineers, and replaced them with his own men before setting out for the grid coordinates he'd already consigned to memory.

An hour later and the unlit *Schnellboote* was now safely ensconced in the mouth of the largest of the caves which were sprawled out along the rugged coastline. The men had already packed the explosive charge into the *Linse*, which had then been lowered into the water and tethered to the side of the *Schnellboote* with a length of rope. It was now just a question of waiting for the enemy vessel to arrive . . .

'Excuse me, sir, but I've assembled the men on deck as you requested,' a voice announced behind Riedler, who was standing on the bow deck with his hands clamped tightly around the railing, a distant look in his eyes as he stared out across the dark, untroubled waters beyond the cave.

Riedler appeared startled by the voice, then his face softened and he smiled fleetingly at Kuhn. 'Thank you, Sergeant.'

The men came to attention when Riedler appeared. He told them to stand easy. 'I would estimate that the enemy vessel should get here within the next ten to fifteen minutes. If all goes according to plan, we should be able to monitor any traffic to and from the boat from inside the cave. It's imperative that we remain undetected in here. It's very quiet out there, so any noise is likely to travel a long way. For that reason I want complete silence from the moment the boat's first spotted. I'm going to keep a skeleton crew on deck with me – Lieutenant Franke, Sergeant Kuhn and two men to man the guns. The rest of you are to go below deck and await further orders. Be warned, though, if I hear so much as a cough you'll all be on report. Every last one of you. Dismissed.'

Kuhn selected two NCOs and posted them to the port and starboard guns, then waited until the rest of the men had disappeared below deck before closing the hatch door behind them. He then turned back to Riedler. 'Sir, who's going to pilot the *Linse?*'

'I discussed that earlier with Lieutenant Franke,' Riedler said. 'He suggested you.'

Franke smiled coldly at Kuhn, the disdain he felt for him reflected in his eyes. 'As far as I'm aware, apart from the Major and myself, you're the only other man on board who's actually piloted a *Linse.*'

'I did once, sir, in a training exercise,' Kuhn said, directing his reply to Riedler.

'So now's your chance to put that training to good use, Kuhn,' Franke said. 'There's a rubber suit for you on the bridge. Go on, you don't have much time.'

'Stand fast, Sergeant,' Riedler said when Kuhn made towards the steps leading up to the bridge. 'I need an experienced pilot. Someone who's served in a *Linsen* unit before.

And there's only one man on board who's done that.' He turned to Franke. 'Not so, Lieutenant?'

The sneer vanished from Franke's face. 'Me, sir?' he said hesitantly.

'Is there a problem?' Riedler demanded.

'No, sir,' came the immediate response.

'Good.' Riedler leaned on the railing and looked down at the silhouette of the *Linse* as it wallowed in the water.

'Kuhn could just as easy manoeuvre the *Linse* into position. This has got nothing to do with me being an experienced pilot, does it?' Franke said, staring at the back of Riedler's head.

'No, it hasn't,' Riedler replied. 'It has to do with your admirers amongst the Nazi hierarchy back in Berlin who'd like nothing more than to see you take over as my successor as the leader of this unit. But believe me, it's never going to happen. Even if I were to leave the regiment, I'd make damn sure my successor was someone I respected; someone who the men would regard not just as a commanding officer, but also as a friend. That's just not you, is it? You're far more concerned about political rhetoric and Nazi ideology than you'll ever be about the welfare of your men. You'd rule by fear and intimidation. That may go down well in your Brandenburg units, but it cuts no ice here. These men are professional soldiers who totally despise you and your kind. You wouldn't last a day in command before someone put a bullet in your back. But I'd never let it come to that. One way or the other, you're finished in this unit. At least this way you have a chance to leave with honour. If you survive, you'll no doubt be decorated personally by the *Führer*. If not, you'll have died for your country. Another martyr for the Nazis to toast at their next banquet in the halls of the Reichstag.'

'And if I refuse to go?' Franke said, his contempt for Riedler now openly evident in his voice.

'Then I'd have you shot for cowardice,' Riedler told him. 'Then all your precious medals would be taken back and your family would be ostracized, hurled from the bosom of your beloved Party. They'd be outcasts, no better than the Jews. Imagine their shame. Is that really what you want?'

In a blinding moment of surging rage brought on by the sheer humiliation of his own helplessness, Franke went for his bolstered pistol. His hand froze on the butt when he heard a staccato of metallic clicks and he found three FG.42 automatic rifles trained on him. Kuhn shook his head when Franke's eyes settled on his face. 'You draw your weapon on a senior officer, sir, and we'll kill you.'

Franke slowly fastened the clip over the mouth of his holster, then saluted Riedler stiffly before hurrying up the steps and on to the bridge. Riedler ordered the two NCOs to return to their posts. Kuhn looked up at the bridge, his hand still resting lightly on the stock of his rifle. 'Sir, with all due respect, was it wise to antagonize him like that? If he does come out of this alive, and there's no reason why he shouldn't, what's to stop him reporting what happened here tonight? It would only be his word against ours but, as you said, he's a lot of influential friends back in Berlin.'

'He's not going to survive – and he knows it. He knew with his history of mental instability, being transferred to this unit was his last real chance of saving his military career. I know they won't take him back at Brandenburg. Not with his track record. He'd be finished, and no amount of medals could make up for that kind of humiliation. But if he were killed tonight in the line of duty, I'd see to it he was buried with full military honours. That way his family name would remain intact, as would his reputation as a respected officer of the *Wehrmacht*.' Riedler nodded thoughtfully to himself. 'Dignity. That's all he's got going for him now.'

'Drop anchor,' McIndoe called down to Hillyard from the bridge after Higgins had cut the engines.

'I'm not happy about being exposed out here like this,' Higgins said.

'Neither am I, but we've got our orders,' McIndoe replied.

'The boat's a sitting target, Mac. One torpedo: that's all it would take to blow us all to hell.'

'That's why we've got the two subs to monitor for any U-boat activity in the area,' McIndoe reminded him.

'Why don't I feel reassured?' Higgins retorted.

'Look, the sooner we get this over with, the sooner we can get out of here.'

'That's another thing,' Higgins added. 'What's the use of Stella going ashore alone? The whole idea was that Ravallo would go with her.'

'We've got to give him as much slack as he wants and wait to see what happens.' McIndoe took the wireless-room key from the chart cupboard. 'I'm going to open up for business.'

'So you still think he's in this alone?' Higgins called out as McIndoe reached the door.

'Yes, I do,' McIndoe replied steadfastly. He left the bridge and made his way down to the starboard deck, where Hillyard and Johnson were using two lengths of rope to carefully lower an inflated dinghy over the side of the hull. Ravallo and Stella were hovering in the background, wanting to help but knowing at the same time they would only get in the way.

'*Patron*, you have the key for the radio room?' Passiere asked from the top of the stairs. 'I must contact the Partisans to make sure it is safe for Stella to go ashore.'

McIndoe handed him the key. 'Report back to me as soon as they've given you the all-clear.'

'*Oui, patron*,' Passiere said before disappearing down the stairs.

'Who's going to row Stella ashore?' Ravallo asked.

'Hillyard can do it,' McIndoe said, then turned to Stella. 'Are you armed?'

She patted the Colt .45 holstered on her belt. 'I'll take a Sten gun with me as well.'

'You know what to do once you get ashore?' McIndoe continued.

'Yes, I know,' came the terse reply. 'Now stop fussing, will you?'

Ravallo put a hand on her arm. 'Ease up, girl. Mac's only concerned about you. We all are.'

'There's no need,' she informed them. 'I can look after myself.'

McIndoe had no doubt of that. He was about to reach for his cigarettes when he checked himself. The boat was in complete darkness. It was imperative that it remained that way. A match, even if only alight for a brief moment and sheltered by a cupped hand, or the glowing tip of a smouldering cigarette, could be spotted from the shore. Even so, he could have killed for a cigarette. He pushed the thought from his mind.

'The dinghy's in the water, boss,' Hillyard said.

'Good. As soon as Georges gives us the green light, you two can get underway.'

'I'm going to wait in the dinghy,' Stella announced after she'd shouldered her Sten gun. She turned to Johnson. 'Drop the Jacob's ladder over the side for me, will you?'

'Look out for yourself,' Ravallo said softly beside her.

'I will,' she replied as she moved to the railing.

McIndoe touched her lightly on the arm as she passed him. 'Take care.'

Her delicately exquisite features were illuminated momentarily in the gentle reflection of the pale moonlight when she turned to him. She looked for all the world to him like an angel, caught in a luminous aura that simply took his breath away. In that instant she was the most beautiful woman he'd ever seen. Then the moment was gone. She clambered nimbly over the railing, grabbed hold of the rope ladder, then began to descend slowly towards the dinghy.

Passiere reappeared at the top of the stairs, 'It is a clear coast, *patron*.'

'What?' McIndoe replied in puzzlement, then he chuckled softly to himself when he realized what Passiere meant. 'You mean the coast is clear.'

'Is it not the same thing?' Passiere replied with a frown which quickly turned to a scowl when he saw the smiles on the faces around him. He muttered something under his breath and dismissed their amusement with a flick of his hand before disappearing back down the stairs.

'You're to drop Stella on the beach, then row back to the boat. She'll radio through when she's ready to be picked up again.'

'Sure, boss,' Hillyard said. He vaulted over the railing, grabbed the rope ladder, and scrambled down to the dinghy with the ease of a monkey descending a tree. Once inside the dinghy he grabbed an oar in each hand and began to propel the dinghy towards the deserted shore.

'Neville, keep watch on deck,' McIndoe told Johnson. 'Major Ravallo and I will be down in the wireless room monitoring the lieutenant's progress over the radio. Call us at the first sign of anything suspicious. And I mean anything.'

'You can count on it, sir,' Johnson told him, walking towards the stern.

Ravallo started down the stairs, but McIndoe paused on deck for a moment, looking around him slowly. That he couldn't see any movement in the dark beyond the boat gave him some comfort. But it was what he couldn't see beneath the water that left him with a distinctly uneasy feeling. He knew there were supposed to be two British subs in the area, guarding them like concealed hunters waiting for the predatory carnivore to approach the tethered goat. But how often was the goat killed before the hunter could bag his trophy? He tried to shrug it off, but the thought lingered uncomfortably with him as he went after Ravallo.

Riedler monitored the dinghy's progress through a pair of powerful binoculars. Why were only two of them going ashore? Were they an advanced reconnaissance team? They wouldn't find anything, even though the area was already saturated with troops of the seventy-sixth infantry Division who'd been drafted in from the garrison at Gela. The senior officer had been given strict orders to keep his men concealed until all the enemy personnel were safely ashore. Riedler had threatened the officer with an indefinite posting to the Eastern Front if he didn't follow those orders to the letter. It seemed to have had the desired effect.

The dinghy reached the shallows and one of the two dark-clothed figures jumped out nimbly into the water and waded the short distance to the beach. It was a woman. Riedler turned the binoculars back on the dinghy and saw that the lone figure was already rowing away from the shore. Why was he leaving? Why hadn't they both gone ashore? He focused on the woman again as she ran towards the thick undergrowth which bordered the beach. Then she was gone, swallowed up in the darkness.

He slowly lowered the binoculars and looked across at the silhouette of the unlit MTB as it rocked gently in the water. 'What's your game, Ravallo?' he muttered to himself.

'Pardon, sir?' Kuhn asked quietly beside him.

'I was just thinking out loud,' Riedler replied, then raised the binoculars to his eyes again.

'What do we do now, sir?'

'We wait, Sergeant,' Riedler said softly, watching as the dinghy headed back towards the mother craft. 'We wait.'

McIndoe was becoming increasingly worried. It had now been fifteen minutes since Hillyard had returned to the boat, and Passiere still hadn't received confirmation that Stella had made contact with the Partisans. The radio remained silent. Had something gone wrong? Had she been captured by a German patrol? He knew he was probably just being alarmist – but still the anxiety remained.

He'd spent much of the time pacing up and down the corridor outside the wireless room, constantly punching his fist into his palm like a perturbed father awaiting his daughter's return from a date he'd regarded as dubious from the start. When he wasn't pacing, he was hovering uncertainly in the doorway, his eyes moving between Passiere and Ravallo who were seated inside. How could they just sit there so calmly? It was a question he'd asked himself each time he stopped in the doorway. At least Passiere had an excuse. He couldn't move from the radio in case he missed something over the headphones. It was Ravallo who'd become the focus of his attention: hunched forward on his chair, elbows on his knees, hands clasped tightly together in front of him. He'd remained that way ever since he'd first arrived in the wireless room, occasionally moving his eyes to look across at Passiere as he rocked on the back legs of his chair. Yet what unnerved McIndoe most of all was the expressionless look on Ravallo's face. Once again that impenetrable mask was being used to conceal his true emotions. It was impossible to know what really lay behind the façade . . .

Suddenly Passiere sat forward, the front legs of his chair banging down loudly on to the wooden floor, and he grabbed the pen and pulled a block of transcript paper towards him.

'What is it, Georges?' McIndoe asked excitedly, hurrying across to where Passiere was seated. Passiere hadn't heard him with the headphones over his ears.

Ravallo tried to get Passiere's attention by tapping him on the shoulder, but the Frenchman raised a hand towards him, indicating for him to wait, then he touched his hand to one of the headphones, his face creased in a frown. The frown quickly became a look of apprehension as he tossed the pen aside and began to jab furiously at the transmitting key. He shook his head in desperation, tapped in another code, then tore the headphones off and leapt to his feet. 'They have got her!' he blurted out in a shaky voice. 'They have got Stella, *patron*. Just after she identified herself with her own code-sign she signalled MMR, MMR.' His eyes went to Ravallo. 'That is our code for danger.'

'What happened?' McIndoe demanded.

'She said something about an ambush. Then – finish.' Passiere's hand came down sharply in a gesture of finality.

'I'm going after her,' McIndoe announced.

'I'm coming with you,' Ravallo called out after McIndoe who was already heading for the door.

'No, you stay – '

'I don't want to hear it,' Ravallo cut in savagely. 'Now let's go!'

McIndoe wasn't going to argue. It would only waste valuable time. They ran up the steps and on to the deck.

'What's happened, boss?' Hillyard asked anxiously as he and Johnson hurried over to where Ravallo was already beginning to descend the Jacob's ladder.

'Stella's been caught in an ambush,' McIndoe said. 'We're going ashore.'

'I'll come with you, boss,' Hillyard volunteered.

'No, I want you two to stay here and guard the boat. It could be some kind of trick to lure us away and leave the boat unprotected.'

'Come on, Mac,' Ravallo shouted up to him.

McIndoe clambered over the railing, then paused to look at Hillyard. 'Give us fifteen minutes. If we haven't contacted you by then, tell Charlie to get out of here. And that's an order.'

Hillyard nodded grimly.

McIndoe barely had time to unfasten the rope which tethered the dinghy to the railing before Ravallo was pro-pelling the small craft away from the sanctuary of the boat with powerful strokes of the oars. McIndoe looked past Ravallo towards the beach. It appeared deserted. Then he looked at Ravallo face-on for the first time since they'd left the wireless room, and realized the mask had been ripped away, finally exposing the monster. The narrowed eyes were devoid of any fear or concern. All he could see was cold, impassive disdain as they looked back at him. McIndoe shuddered, as if caught in a sudden gust of icy wind.

It was at that moment it all made perfect sense to him. Why hadn't he seen it before? How could he have been so blind? The truth had been staring him in the face ever since Ravallo first put forward his contingency plan to recover the envelope. Ravallo had sent Stella ashore knowing she'd be walking straight into a German ambush. And if the Germans could capture her, together with Massimo, then nobody back at Allied HQ would ever know whose name had been in the envelope. Suddenly he felt sick inside. How could he have gone along with the plan? At that moment he despised himself even more than he did Ravallo. It was obviously Ravallo's intention to lead him into the ambush as well. The Gestapo would be falling over themselves with gratitude to have such a prize catch in their nets. But it wasn't going to happen that way . . .

McIndoe was the first out of the dinghy when it reached the shallows, and he steadied it to let Ravallo get out after him. They pulled it up on to the beach. McIndoe turned away from Ravallo and unholstered his Webley pistol. 'Nicky?' he called out softly, the barrel already trained on Ravallo's back.

'Come on, Mac, there's no time – ' Ravallo broke off abruptly when he turned to find the pistol aimed at him. 'What the hell's going on?'

'Take out the Colt very slowly and throw it to me,' McIndoe said, indicating the holstered pistol on Ravallo's belt. Ravallo hesitated. 'Do it, Nicky – now!'

Ravallo eased the Colt from its holster with his fingertips, and tossed it on to the sand at McIndoe's feet. 'Do you honestly think I'd have sent Stella in alone if I'd known this was going to happen?'

McIndoe picked up the fallen weapon without taking his eyes off Ravallo, and tossed it into the water behind him. 'It was all part of the plan, wasn't it? Only I didn't realize that until it was too late. Too late, that is, to have prevented Stella from being captured by the Germans. And, believe me, that oversight's going to haunt me for the rest of my life. But at least I'm not going to give you the satisfaction of seeing me walk into your finely spun web as easily as she did. This is as far as I go.'

'For God's sake, Mac, Stella's in trouble – '

'Stay where you are!' McIndoe snarled when Ravallo took a tentative step towards him. Even under duress, Ravallo's act didn't falter, he thought bitterly to himself. The uncertainty, the impatience, the puzzlement – it was all so perfectly orchestrated.

'If you think I'm a traitor, then why don't you pull the trigger and be done with it?'

'Don't think I'm not tempted,' McIndoe replied. 'I know I should take you back to Malta to face a court martial and a firing squad. Or perhaps I should have had you shot earlier and had your body dumped at sea. But I'm not a monster like you. That's why I'm going to give you what you never gave Stella. A chance. Go on back to Germany. I'm sure you'll get a hero's reception. But after you've finished soaking up their spurious accolades, you'll have plenty of time to reflect on what you've done. Your conscience will never let you forget.'

'You're wrong, Mac, you're so very wrong,' Ravallo said, his voice now barely a whisper.

'What really cuts me up inside is the way you let Stella walk into that ambush in a last-ditch attempt to save your own miserable skin. I honestly thought you cared about her. I thought you even loved her. I know she sure as hell loved you. She'd have done anything for you. And this is how you repaid her trust.' McIndoe moved backwards towards the dinghy without lowering the pistol. 'This is where we go our separate ways. Please pass on my apologies to your friends in the Gestapo for not accepting their hospitality. Now get out of here.'

Ravallo said nothing then, with shoulders hunched as if in defeat, he slowly trudged up the wet sand towards the undergrowth. He didn't look back. Then he was gone.

McIndoe pushed the dinghy out into the shallows then climbed inside. Only then did he lower the pistol and place it in the bottom of the dinghy. Picking up the two oars, he began to row the small vessel determinedly away from the deserted beach.

Riedler was puzzled by it all. Twice now the dinghy had gone to the beach, and on both occasions one person had remained behind while the other had returned to the boat. And as if that wasn't baffling enough, the scene he'd just witnessed between the two men on the beach had been bizarre to say the least. All his instincts told him it had something to do with the Gestapo agent. But if he was right, why had the agent been allowed to walk away? It made no sense to him. Not that it mattered. He had a more urgent problem to solve: whether to order the destruction of the boat while it still lay at anchor, or to hold back in case any more of the crew were transferred to the shore where they could be taken prisoner and turned over to the Gestapo for interrogation? The arguments for both cases were strong. These were covert Intelligence operatives who could provide vital information not only about current and future Allied operations in the Mediterranean, but also about the resistance both in Sicily and on the Italian mainland. Yet at the same time he knew from the technical data which the Gestapo had passed on to him about the enemy boat that, with its blistering speed and adroit manoeuvrability, it could easily outrun the *Linse*. Once the boat started up its engines, it would already be too late to despatch the *Linse* to intercept it.

He'd failed once to destroy the boat. Now he'd been given a second chance to redeem himself. A lifeline. He knew General Student had gone out on a limb for him by talking Field-Marshal Kesselring into giving him another chance. If he failed again, he knew he'd be back scouting for the Sixth Army on the Eastern Front. But, more importantly, it would also reflect badly on General Student's judgment. And he would never allow that to happen. He had to make the right decision. And quickly . . .

Franke was sweating. He'd put it down to the fact that the rubber suit he was wearing was too tight, and that the elasticated wrists and ankles dug uncomfortably into his skin. But he knew he was fooling himself. For the first time in his life he was genuinely scared as he sat tensed behind the controls of the *Linse*. His right hand rested lightly on the steering column, his left hand trailed in the cold dark water. Every few minutes, for the past fifteen minutes, he'd formed a cup-shape with his left hand to scoop up a little water to splash over his face. It was refreshingly cool, but only a temporary respite; soon the sweat had run down the side of his face again.

He'd always maintained that death didn't frighten him. But that boast had always been made with a contemptuous sneer when he had a weapon to defend himself and the chance to fall back on the defensive if the need arose. Even though the odds might have been stacked against him in those situations, at least he had had a percentage chance of surviving. Now he didn't. He was going to die. And it terrified him. He still had so much to do with his life. So many ambitions still unfulfilled. But it was too late now for regrets. He knew what he'd been letting himself in for when he agreed to leave Brandenburg and join the Third Parachute Regiment. His last chance to prove himself to his superiors. His orders had been simple. Oust the anti-Nazi, Riedler, in any way he could, though preferably by accruing enough evidence to publicly renounce him in a show trial in Berlin, and his reward would be the leadership of the Third Parachute Regiment. But he'd realized soon after his arrival on the Eastern Front to join Riedler's unit that it would be much harder than he'd anticipated.

He had had no trouble gathering the evidence against Riedler. Riedler openly denounced the Nazi Party hierarchy back in Germany, often in front of his men, and was particularly critical of *Reichsmarschall* Goering and the *Luftwaffe* for not supporting the ground troops in Russia. It was the men who were the problem. He'd never seen such overwhelming respect for a commanding officer. Not even at Brandenburg. It verged on idolatry. How could he ever have hoped to replace Riedler, especially as he'd be regarded as the Judas who'd been sent to betray him? The men would never follow him after that.

It had only been within the last couple of days that the first doubts about the real reason for his transfer to the paratroopers had begun to creep into Franke's mind. He'd first been diagnosed as psychotic at school. A mild psychosis, the family doctor had informed his parents. It had been overlooked when he joined the *Wehrmacht*, and then when he'd been transferred to Brandenburg. His file at Brandenburg headquarters was littered with references to his violent temper, often against recruits under his command, yet no action had ever been taken against him. He didn't regret any of the beatings he'd meted out to the youngsters because he knew it made them tougher soldiers. He also knew his superiors were turning a blind eye to his psychosis because of his bravery on the battlefield. He was an inspiration to every recruit who ever wanted to join Brandenburg.

Then he'd attacked a senior officer who'd taunted him about the history of mental instability in his family. Although the whole incident had been covered up and those present in the officers' mess that night sworn to silence, the following day he was on his way to the Third Parachute Regiment. He was told before he left that he would never again hold a command in any Brandenburg unit. It was obvious to him he was regarded now as a danger to those around him. So why transfer him to the paratroopers, unless he was only being used to discredit Riedler? Riedler had been right when he'd said his men would have put a bullet in his back within a day of his taking charge of the unit. Had his superiors at Brandenburg known all along that Riedler's men would never accept him? Had he been deliberately thrown to the wolves? Did they want him dead?

Franke closed his eyes tightly and clasped his hands despairingly over his face as the reality of these self-damning questions echoed accusingly inside his head. He just wanted them to stop. Make them stop. He slowly opened his eyes and, as he looked across at the MTB, he realized he didn't have to be scared of dying any more. Not if he was in control of his own destiny. He reached down and untied the rope which tethered the *Linse* to the side of the *Schnellboote*.

'Sir, look!' Kuhn said, directing Riedler's attention to the *Linse* as it coasted silently out of the cave. 'He was told to await your orders.'

Riedler focused the binoculars on the retreating *Linse* as it headed out slowly into the open sea.

'What do you want me to do, sir?' Kuhn asked anxiously.

'Give him covering fire once he gets into position and opens the throttle. But not before.' Riedler retrieved the radio control box from where he'd left it on the deck, then returned to the bow and scanned the length of the MTB with his binoculars. He could make out a figure behind the Vickers gun. Another member of the crew was seated behind the Oerlikon gun. Neither man had seen the *Linse*. Just another few seconds, then Franke could activate the switch on his helmet and pass command of the vessel to the radio control box. Then a worrying thought crossed his mind. What if Franke didn't pass control of the *Linse* over to him when the time came? What if, in a last gesture of defiance, he was going for glory himself? All it would take was for one bullet to incapacitate him and the *Linse* would go out of control. Riedler wet his dry lips nervously but, before he could think any more about it, he heard the sound of shouting coming from the deck of the enemy vessel. A moment later the Vickers gun opened up on the *Linse*.

'Cover fire!' Riedler yelled at Kuhn, who was already poised behind the twenty-millimetre machine-gun on the bow deck.

Kuhn sprayed a fusillade of bullets low across the deck of the enemy boat, and the Vickers fell silent as the crewman scrambled desperately for cover.

'Keep firing,' Riedler ordered as he continued to monitor the *Linse* through the binoculars. 'Come on, Franke, open the throttle and switch the controls over to me,' he muttered under his breath, his hand gripped tightly around the black control box. 'Switch over, God damn you.' Franke opened up the throttle and the *Linse* sped towards its target. 'OK, now give me control,' he shouted angrily, as if he were hoping Franke would somehow hear him.

A Sten gun opened fire from a concealed position on the deck, and Riedler watched in horror as Franke's body jerked as a scythe of bullets hit him. Franke slumped forward over the controls, and the *Linse* immediately began to veer off course. Riedler stared at the control box in his hand. The red light remained unlit. Franke hadn't passed over control of the *Linse*. The operation had failed. Again. All they could do now was to try to incapacitate the boat and radio through for reinforcements. It had all gone so horribly wrong . . .

'Sir,' Kuhn said excitedly. 'The light. It's on.'

Riedler looked at the box again. He blinked rapidly to make sure his eyes weren't deceiving him. They weren't.

The light had been activated. He now had control of the *Linse*. He immediately set about correcting its wayward course and homed it in on the enemy boat as Kuhn continued to rake the deck with gunfire.

Riedler directed the *Linse* into the side of the enemy boat. The force of the collision triggered off the initial charge in the *Linse's* bow, tearing it away from the rest of the vessel and ripping a small hole in the side of the MTB's hull. The aft section of the *Linse*, which contained the main explosive charge, flooded and sank beneath the water. Kuhn stopped firing, and for a couple of seconds there was an eerie silence before the explosives detonated directly beneath the MTB's damaged hull.

The MTB disintegrated in a fireball which breathtakingly illuminated the night sky like some brilliant pyrotechnic display as debris was hurled hundreds of feet into the air. Then, as quickly as it had appeared, the fireball was gone. It was almost as if it had never happened. All that remained were the burning embers of wood which rained down on to the cold dark water like a shower of dying meteors plunging helplessly to their obscurity. Seconds later, even these last fragments of life had been doused, and once more darkness prevailed. Nothing remained. Only silence, and death.

Riedler became aware that the rest of the men had hurried up on to the deck on hearing the explosion, and had collected behind him, their eyes as one staring at the spot where the MTB had once been at anchor. Nobody spoke.

Riedler pushed the control box into Kuhn's hands, then gestured to the captain on the bridge to take the *Schnellboote* out of the cave. One of the men reacted to the captain's order to weigh anchor and hurried towards the stern.

'Are we going to look for survivors, sir?' another asked.

'Survivors?' Riedler said in surprise. 'You're an optimist, if nothing else.'

'If anyone survived that, they deserve better than to be handed over to the Gestapo,' Kuhn said. Riedler nodded in agreement.

'Where to, Major?' the captain called down once the boat was clear of the cave.

'Back to Gela,' Riedler told him.

Riedler stared out across the dark water to where the MTB had been at anchor, and his hand came up to his head in a formal salute. Then, as if fêted by divine intervention, a distant roll of thunder rumbled in the distance. Riedler found that appropriate. A requiem for the dead . . .

SEVENTEEN

'You've got no right to be alive . . .'

Those had been the first words Sam McIndoe had heard on regaining consciousness at the Forty-fifth British Field Hospital on Malta nine years earlier, and there hadn't been a day since then that he hadn't given praise to the Lord for his life. But his gratitude was tinged with great sorrow. He'd been the only survivor. Charlie Higgins, Bruce Hillyard, Neville Johnson, Georges Passiere: all had died on that fateful night off the Sicilian coast.

How he'd managed to survive the explosion would always remain a mystery to him. He remembered getting off a burst from his Sten gun in the direction of the *Linse*, even though, like the others, he'd been pinned down by the raking gunfire which had emanated from one of the caves. He remembered the joy he'd felt when he saw his bullets hit the target – but it had been very short-lived joy. He remembered the *Linse* slamming into the side of the boat, and the initial explosion which had knocked him off his feet. He remembered cracking the back of his head on the railing as he fell. He remembered nothing else.

He discovered later that he'd been found in the water by a trawler and handed over to the Resistance. Within hours he'd been put aboard a British submarine and taken back to

Malta, where he'd remained in a coma for the next five days before regaining consciousness. A month later he'd been transferred to the Ballochmile Hospital in Glasgow, where he'd undergone successful plastic surgery on his shattered left leg. Never again would his darting runs and aggressive pack leadership grace a rugby field.

His career as a field operative over, he'd been given a mundane desk job at SOE headquarters in London until the end of the war. He'd returned to Glasgow in 1946 to take up a post as a lecturer in Classics at his old university . . .

The telegram had arrived at the house the previous day. Out of the blue and most unwelcome. He'd read it so many times he knew it by heart:

ONLY THE GOOD DIE YOUNG STOP HALLELUJAH STOP THE DEVIL DOES INDEED LOOK AFTER HIS OWN STOP NOW A SUCCESSFUL BREEDER OF OIL WELLS STOP STAYING SAVOY WITH ALL THE OTHER MILLIONAIRES STOP RRR

NICKY

RRR. The SOE code-sign for 'Where do we rendezvous?' He'd wired back the same day: SEE YOU SAVOY 7 P.M. WEDNESDAY.

He still had no idea why he'd sent a reply, let alone agreed to meet with Ravallo. It was just something that had to be done. A loose end of his life which needed to be cut off. For ever . . .

Well, here he was. Seven o'clock. The foyer of the Savoy Hotel. He felt decidedly uncomfortable surrounded by so much opulence. This wasn't for him. Too fashionable. Too glitzy. Too expensive.

'Can I help you, sir?'

The man was dressed in a pair of immaculately pressed pinstriped trousers and a sombre black jacket. Management. He eyed McIndoe's inexpensive, off-the-peg suit with obvious distaste. *Probably thinks I'm a bum*, McIndoe mused. Which was quite understandable considering the vast majority of the men in the foyer were dressed in evening suits.

'I'm here to see Nicky Ravallo,' McIndoe told him.

The manager managed to mask his surprise behind a forced smile which threatened to shatter his dour features. 'Would you care to come to the reception desk, sir? I'll have one of our receptionists call Mr Ravallo's suite to let him know you're here. May I have your name, sir?'

'Sam McIndoe.'

The manager led the way to the desk where the call was made. 'Mr Ravallo has asked that you go straight up to his suite. Room 300. Third floor.'

McIndoe rode the lift to the third floor. When he alighted he got his bearings from the direction board in the corridor. Why had Ravallo chosen to make contact with him again after nine years? He'd considered all the options and still not come up with a satisfactory answer. To gloat over his treachery? No, that wasn't his style. Whatever else Nicky Ravallo was, he wasn't petty-minded. Revenge? That seemed a more obvious choice. But how? If he was as wealthy as he maintained, he could just as easily have dispatched . . . what were they called in the gangster films? – a 'gunsel' to do his dirty work for him. That was just too fantastic. He'd been watching too many Humphrey Bogart films. Why risk publicly dredging up the past? As before, he didn't have the answers. Only Ravallo did. Taking a deep breath, McIndoe rapped on the door.

The door swung open. Nicky Ravallo hadn't changed much in nine years. Dressed in his elegant tuxedo he still gave the appearance of a suave, debonair Hollywood film star. Ravallo reached out a hand of greeting towards McIndoe, his white teeth shining in a great grin of welcome. 'Damn, but it's good to see you again, Mac.'

'Meaning you'd lost all hope of ever catching up with me?' McIndoe said coldly. He made no move to take Ravallo's outstretched hand. The smile faltered on Ravallo's face as he stepped to one side and used his extended hand to gesture McIndoe into the room. McIndoe found himself in a plush lounge. Looking around, he noticed a set of sliding doors which he assumed led into the master bedroom. He waited until Ravallo had closed the door into the corridor before speaking again. 'How did you come by my address?'

'Contacts,' was all Ravallo would venture.

'Well, here I am. What do you want?'

'A little civility wouldn't go amiss for a start,' Ravallo said as he crossed to the drinks cabinet.

'That's rich coming from you,' McIndoe replied disdainfully.

'If you're so sure I betrayed you, then why did you come all the way down here to see me?' Ravallo asked softly. 'Why didn't you just tear up my telegram and be done with it?'

'I've been asking myself the same question ever since I boarded the train this morning. I guess I need to know the truth to finally set my mind at rest. If you're man enough to admit it, that is?'

Ravallo's hand froze as he was about to retrieve two crystal tumblers from the ledge underneath the drinks cabinet. Then he smiled to himself and picked up the tumblers which he placed on the lowered flap. 'I won't insult by offering you a Jack Daniels. How about a Johnnie Walker?'

'No, thank you,' came the cold reply. 'Just tell me why you asked me down here tonight so that we can go our separate ways again. I don't want to be in the same room as you any longer than is absolutely necessary.'

'I'm still the condemned man, I see,' Ravallo said, pouring out a generous measure of bourbon into a tumbler.

'You always will be, as far as I'm concerned,' McIndoe said, taking a packet of cigarettes from his jacket pocket. He lit one. 'Your treachery cost the lives of five good men on that operation. But what I still find so hard to comprehend

440

is the way you sent Stella ashore that night, knowing she was going to a certain death.'

'Is that what you believe?' Ravallo said as he sat down on the sofa.

'She was shot by the Germans and you know it,' McIndoe said angrily.

'Is that what you heard?'

There was something about the tone of Ravallo's voice, the look in his eyes, which for a brief moment had McIndoe questioning the very convictions he'd held so close to his heart for the past nine years. Then he cursed himself silently for allowing himself to be deceived so easily by the old Ravallo charm. Yet, as his eyes lingered on Ravallo, a sense of uncertainty slowly washed over him. And it angered him because he knew he had no reason to feel that way. He wasn't wrong about Ravallo. Ravallo was a traitor. A Nazi spy. So why was he finding it increasingly difficult to keep convincing himself of that?

'If I am the condemned man, at least grant me a last favour,' Ravallo said. 'It is my privilege, after all.'

'I'm listening?' McIndoe said tersely, but his choler was now directed more towards himself.

'You don't even have to do that,' Ravallo said, then took a sheet of paper from the folder which lay on the sofa beside him and held it out towards McIndoe. 'Read that.'

'What is it?' McIndoe asked, standing his ground defiantly.

'Read it,' Ravallo pressed.

McIndoe plucked the sheet from Ravallo's hand. It was a copy of a classified document which was dated the day following the ill-fated operation. It had been sent by Vice-Admiral Starr to the head of US Military Intelligence in Washington.

Dear General,
   I would firstly like to take this opportunity to express my sincere gratitude to you on behalf of the Special Operations

441

Executive for your moral support in this, a most grave matter of national security, which we discussed over the telephone yesterday. In view of the successful outcome to the operation, I am pleased to inform you that I am now in a position to furnish you with a more detailed account of why this most regrettable decision had to be taken as a matter of such urgency to sacrifice four of our operatives in order that we would be certain of terminating the Germans' pipeline into the Italian Section of our organization.

I have known for the past eight months there was a German collaborator at work inside the Italian Section, whose treachery on at least four different occasions has resulted in the deaths of three of our operatives, as well as compromising dozens of brave Partisans who have been interrogated and subsequently executed by the Gestapo. I carried out a thorough internal investigation over a five-month period but was unable to identify the traitor. I was, however, able to narrow it down to three possible suspects: Bruce Hillyard, Neville Johnson and the Frenchman, Georges Passiere. The traitor has, however, proved to be exceptionally devious, only passing on information to the Germans when the three of them worked together as part of a team, thus shielding himself from any possible retribution. I have always tried, wherever possible, to place these three individuals in different teams but, as you will appreciate, we only have a limited number of operatives working in the Mediterranean, and it has not always been possible to achieve this end.

I had serious reservations about bringing them together for this operation, but they were the only operatives available at the time and, as you know, this was a situation where we had to act quickly if we were to have any chance of success. My worst fears were soon realized when Lieutenant McIndoe's reports appeared to confirm that the traitor was once more engaged in his nefarious work. We knew we were no closer to identifying him, and it was decided at the highest level of His Majesty's Government that, if necessary, dras-

tic steps would have to be taken to ensure the continued safety of our other operatives in the Mediterranean.

It was with this in mind that I came up with the plan which was implemented last night. I realized that to make it appear authentic, I had to ensure that both Major Ravallo and Lieutenant di Mauro were involved as well. They, as you rightly pointed out over the telephone, had to be protected at all costs, which was why I arranged for them to go ashore as soon as they reached the rendezvous.

My only concern was for Lieutenant McIndoe, whom I regard as the finest operative we have working in Italy, but I realized I could not let sentiment rule my head and that, if necessary, he would have to be sacrificed along with the other innocent members of the team. I made sure the Germans were able to intercept the coordinates by having them broadcast over an open channel. Knowing my operatives would never allow themselves to be taken alive, it would leave the Germans with no option but to destroy the boat. That way not only would the Germans be doing our dirty work for us, but it would also ensure we could satisfactorily close this unwholesome chapter without having damaged the credibility of the Special Operations Executive.

I look forward to continuing the excellent relationship which already exists between the Special Operations Executive and the United States Military Intelligence.

Yours very sincerely

Vice-Admiral Sir Edmund Starr, GCB.

McIndoe sat down slowly on the nearest armchair, still struggling to come to terms with what he'd read. A rush of emotions seemed to surge through him all at once. Helplessness. Disbelief. Resentment. Anguish. Anger. Then, almost as if in a daze, he reached out and placed the document on the glass table in the centre of the room.

'I think you could do with that whisky, after all,' Ravallo said softly, then went to the drinks cabinet and poured out a shot for McIndoe. He crouched down beside the chair and pressed the glass into McIndoe's hand.

'Were you in on this from the start?' McIndoe asked in a hollow voice.

'That's the first I knew about it,' Ravallo replied, gesturing to the document on the table. 'And, believe me, I was as shocked as you are when I discovered the truth. Starr had your colleagues killed to cover up for his own incompetence at not being able to root out the traitor in your organization. I bet you wouldn't mind a few minutes alone with him right now. Just to set the record straight.'

'That would be pretty difficult,' McIndoe said as he stared absently at the opposite wall. 'He's dead.'

'I didn't know that.'

'In 1944. Heart attack. Died at his desk. Having read that, though, I can't say I'm surprised. You carry that much guilt around inside you, sooner or later something has to give,' McIndoe said. He drank down the whisky in one gulp.

'You want another?' Ravallo asked, taking the tumbler from McIndoe's hand.

'I'd drink the whole damn bottle if I thought it would help,' McIndoe replied, then shook his head at Ravallo. 'No, thanks.' He got to his feet and crossed to the window where he looked out across the dark, swirling waters of the Thames River. His eyes lingered on a lone barge, the bearded skipper visible on the dimly lit bridge, as it slipped surreptitiously under Waterloo Bridge before disappearing from sight.

He thought of Charlie Higgins, cutting a dashing figure as he stood on the bridge of the MTB. Windswept hair. Cheery smile. And little Emma, the daughter he'd so adored. Not so little now, though. She would be sixteen or seventeen. A young lady. But she would always be little Emma to him. He thought of Bruce Hillyard, quick to pass judgement and never shy to speak his mind. They'd had their differences, but he'd still regarded Hillyard as a fine soldier. Another one with a young daughter who'd been forced to grow up without her father. He thought of Neville Johnson. Dour Neville, the Nottingham schoolteacher. Polite but removed. The quiet one. He thought of Taffy Evans and a sad smile touched his lips. The nimble-fingered peterman who'd spent much of his adult life in a succession of His Majesty's jails before finally turning his skills to building up a very successful explosives firm in Swansea. He owed Taffy so much but, above all else, he'd cherished his loyalty and friendship. The smile broadened when he thought of Georges Passiere. Frenchy. The likeable rogue. Dishevelled hair. Unshaven face. The wise guy, but still the consummate professional when the need arose. And, of course, Stella. Beautiful Stella with the sultry, mysterious eyes. He'd loved her once. Foolishly perhaps, but he had. Hers was a face he'd certainly never forget. Never . . .

Now all gone. It was then the smile faltered. Had Starr been justified in destroying the whole barrel for the sake of one bad apple? Was Nicky right, had Starr resorted to such drastic measures in a last, desperate attempt to cover up for his own incompetence? So many questions. No answers. Nor was there an answer to the most vexing question of all: which of the three was the traitor?

'Do you know who the traitor is?' he asked Ravallo without looking round at him.

'No. It's possible the British may have found out later, I don't know, but if they did they didn't pass on their findings to Military Intelligence. That's the only document there is in the archives of Military Intelligence relating to the Sicilian operation.'

'You know you could be prosecuted for having that document in your possession?' McIndoe said. 'That's classified information. How did you get your hands on it?'

'Contacts.'

'Here we go with the "contacts" again,' McIndoe said as he sat down.

'Because that's what they are. In my line of business, you have to have them. It's the only way to keep one step ahead of the competition. They don't come cheap, either. And neither did that document. But when it became available, I was prepared to pay over the odds to get my hands on it.'

'Why, when you knew all along you had nothing to hide?' McIndoe asked.

'You didn't think so when we last parted company, and that's what's been eating away inside me for the past nine years. Not a day's gone by when I haven't thought about it. We'd only known each other for a few days back in '42, but in that time I came to regard you as a good friend. And friendship means more to me than anything else in this whole goddamn world. Strange as it may seem, I don't have many friends. Sure, I'm an extrovert and I love being centre stage, but when it comes down to it, I regard most of the people around me as little more than acquaintances. That's why I went to the lengths I did to procure the document. I needed something to prove to you that I wasn't the monster you thought I was. And there it is.'

'You did all this for my benefit? I . . . I don't know what to say,' McIndoe stammered, a sudden and overwhelming sense of guilt striking him like a self-administered dagger through his heart.

'You don't have to say anything,' Ravallo told him. 'You know the truth now. That's all that matters.'

McIndoe took the cigarettes from his pocket again and held them up to Ravallo. 'Have you managed to kick the habit yet?'

'I'm still working on it,' Ravallo replied with a rueful grin as he took a cigarette from the packet. 'One day, perhaps.'

McIndoe tossed the packet on to the table and turned his cigarette around in his fingers as he struggled to marshal his confused thoughts into some kind of order. It took him some time before he felt comfortable enough to say anything. When he did, it didn't come out the way he had hoped. 'Nicky . . . I realize that . . . well, that I've misjudged you all this time, and, well . . . you know . . .'

'I know,' Ravallo said when McIndoe trailed off with an uncomfortable shrug. 'And before you go blaming yourself for thinking I was the traitor, just remember that you didn't have the benefit of Starr's letter to guide your reasoning. I'm the first to admit I made some chronically bad mistakes on that operation. In fact, with hindsight I reckon you had every right to suspect me. Of course I didn't see it like that at the time, but I've since come to realize that some of those incidents could have been misconstrued as being beneficial to the Germans. But as I said to you at the time, it was naïvety, not treason.' He smiled to himself. 'Is it any wonder they kept me behind a desk for the rest of the war? I guess I'm just one of those people who are better at delegating than doing. That's why I've been so successful in the oil business. I just sit in an office all day and send out orders over the phone.'

McIndoe sat forward in his chair. 'Nicky, do you still think about Stella?'

'He'd better,' came the reply from behind McIndoe's chair. The voice was soft and feminine and husky with emotion. And so very familiar.

For that fleeting moment the world stopped turning for Sam McIndoe. Time stood still. He sat motionless, as if suddenly turned to stone. His mind was the first to react. First came the total and utter disbelief, then came the unadulterated and unashamed joy. Finally his limbs seemed to unlock from their colligated state and he was on his feet, pirouetting nimbly on his toes in one graceful movement which would have impressed the great Nijinsky. Stella stood there, even more beautiful than the last time he'd seen her. She was smiling and crying at the same time. He pulled her to him and, as they embraced, he felt tears of his own running down his cheeks. He didn't know how long he held her before she finally eased herself gently from his arms. 'I knew

447

this was going to happen,' she said as she wiped the tears from her cheeks with her fingertips. 'That's why I didn't put on any mascara before I came out of the bedroom. It would just have been ruined.'

'But you're alive,' McIndoe blurted out, and cursed himself silently. What kind of a stupid remark was that to make at such an intense moment?

'I certainly hope so,' she said with a grin, then she took his hands in hers and squeezed them tightly. 'God, it's good to finally see you again. Nine long years. It seems like an eternity. And you've hardly changed.'

'This has,' McIndoe said, disengaging a hand to pat his thinning pate.

'It makes you look distinguished,' she replied.

'It makes me look bald,' he said, then grabbed her hand again.

'What happened that night? Starr said you'd been killed by the Germans while trying to evade capture.'

'That was the official story put out by Military Intelligence,' she said. 'I made it to the rendezvous all right. I was met by two Partisans, but we'd only travelled a few hundred yards when we were ambushed by a German patrol. One of the Partisans was killed. I was shot in the shoulder. The two of us managed to escape and I was taken to a local doctor who patched me up. I spent the next couple of days at a Partisan hideout near Gela, then I was picked up by a British sub and taken back to Gibraltar. That's when I learnt that my cover had been blown. My future as a field operative was over. So Military Intelligence decided to put out the story that I was dead. They seemed to think it would help to tie up any loose ends back in Sicily. As you know, our own version of the SOE, the OSS – the Organization of Strategic Services – was established in 1943. I was posted there as an instructor shortly after it came into existence. It wasn't the same, though. I missed being out in the field. I stayed on until the end of the war, then I threw in the towel. I'd had enough.'

'How did you get off Sicily?' McIndoe asked Ravallo.

'Fortunately, I was intercepted by a Partisan patrol shortly after the boat was blown up,' Ravallo told him. 'I was holed up in a safe house for a while, then transferred to a sub and taken back to Gibraltar.'

'Nicky told me about the boat when we met up again in Gibraltar. At the time we didn't know you'd survived. We assumed everyone had died. I cried.' Her eyes went to Ravallo. 'Didn't I, Nicky? I cried all night. So much for being a tough field operative. Pretty second-rate really.'

'Not from what I saw of your work,' McIndoe assured her.

'Thanks,' she said softly. 'How did you survive the explosion? Nicky saw the boat go up. He said it just disintegrated before his eyes.'

'The devil looks after his own, Stella,' Ravallo said with a half-smile in McIndoe's direction. 'Not so, Mac?'

'He does at that,' McIndoe agreed, then balanced Stella's left hand on the palm of his hand and pointed to the wedding ring on her finger. 'I see you two finally tied the knot after you got back to the States.'

'So you saw through our little secret, did you?' Ravallo said.

'I worked it out eventually,' McIndoe replied with a knowing look in Stella's direction.

'You wouldn't have if you hadn't tried to get me to go out on a date with you,' she said with a smile as she wagged a finger of mock-admonishment at him.

'Yeah, I heard about this,' Ravallo said, folding his arms across his chest. 'Trying to chat up my wife, eh, Mac?'

'She wasn't at the time, though,' McIndoe said.

'But she was,' Ravallo corrected him, and saw the look of astonishment on McIndoe's face. 'We got married shortly after I was posted to Gibraltar. You can understand why we kept it a secret, though. I didn't even tell my parents. Nobody knew. Can you imagine what would have happened if our superiors at Military Intelligence had found out we were married? We'd have been sent to opposite sides of the world. We only made it public at the end of the war.'

'You must have been worried sick about each other's safety every time a shot was fired when we were in Sicily,' McIndoe said.

'We wouldn't have chosen to work together, but fate played its hand and there was nothing we could do about it,' Stella said.

'It wasn't easy, but we managed to pull through. And now I'm stuck with her,' Ravallo said mischievously, but he wasn't quick enough to dodge her playful slap which caught him on the arm.

'Not just me,' she reminded him.

'I thought we'd wait and tell Mac about that over dinner,' Ravallo said, then gave a quick shrug. 'Oh, what the hell? Go on, you tell him.'

'I found out last week that I'm pregnant,' she said with a broad grin.

'That's wonderful news,' McIndoe said and kissed her. 'Congratulations. I'm so pleased for you both.'

Ravallo shook McIndoe's hand. 'Thanks, Mac. We've been trying for a couple of years now. We were beginning to think that it wasn't going to happen for us.'

'Then let's hope it's the first of many,' McIndoe said.

'Not so quick,' Ravallo said, raising a hand towards McIndoe as if to ward off the well-intentioned sentiment. 'We may both be from Italian stock. And we all know the Italians are notorious for having big families. But we'd be quite happy with just the one child. It seems appropriate after all the tears we've shed trying to conceive a baby.'

'Mine, mostly,' Stella said as she laid her head against Ravallo's shoulder. 'Nicky's been a rock these last two years. If it hadn't been for him . . . I don't think I could have coped with the constant disappointment.'

'You'd better go and finish putting on your face, Stella,' Ravallo said, then turned to McIndoe. 'I took the liberty of reserving a table for three at the restaurant tonight. The food's excellent.'

'I'm hardly dressed for the occasion,' McIndoe was quick to point out as he gestured to his crumpled suit. 'Everybody's in a tuxedo around here.'

'You're fine like that, Mac,' Ravallo assured him. 'Now, how about another drink?'

When Stella emerged from the bedroom some minutes later, she found the two men on the sofa, deep in conversation. 'Well, are you two going to sit there all night gossiping, or are you going to take me to dinner? I'm starving.'

'And so the dreaded transformation into motherhood begins,' Ravallo whispered to McIndoe in his best Boris Karloff voice.

'You're incorrigible, do you know that?' McIndoe said, chuckling to himself as they crossed to the door. He held out the crook of his arm towards Stella. 'May I?'

'I'd be delighted,' Stella said, looping her hand under his arm. 'We've got so much catching up to do. I want to know everything you've been doing since we last saw you. And don't you dare leave anything out.'

Ravallo opened the door and smiled to himself as he watched them chatting amiably together as they headed towards the lift. A special friendship had been renewed. That felt good. He closed the door behind him and went after them.

EPILOGUE

James McIndoe brought the car to a halt in the driveway. Switching off the engine, he climbed out and went round to open the passenger door. His wife, Heather, got out and smoothed down a crease on the front of her black dress. 'I see the rest of the family are already back from the cemetery,' she said, indicating to where the secondhand Mazda they'd recently bought for their daughter, Isobel, was parked in the street.

'Hopefully Isobel will have put on the kettle by now,' McIndoe said as he rubbed his hands together. 'It's absolutely freezing. I could certainly do with a nice hot cup of tea to warm me up.'

'This is our daughter you're talking about here, isn't it?' Heather said with a gentle smile. 'When have you ever known Isobel to put on the kettle without first having to be asked a dozen times?'

'That's true. It must be a lot colder out here than I thought. The chill's obviously affecting my brain.'

'I'll make a pot of tea. You see to our guest,' Heather said, looking across at the car which had pulled up on the opposite side of the road.

McIndoe met the German at the gate. 'I'm sorry about the awful weather but it's been like this for the last week now. God knows when it's ever going to get any better.'

'This is paradise compared to being bogged down in the trenches on the Eastern Front in the middle of winter,' the German told him.

'I can well imagine, judging from what I've read about the campaign,' McIndoe said as they walked towards the house.

'No, I do not think you can begin to imagine the horror of the Eastern Front. Nobody can, unless they were there. Even now I rarely talk about it. Not after what I saw.'

McIndoe sensed a tone of hostility in the German's voice and let the subject lapse. He ushered him into the house, then closed the front door behind them. 'May I take your hat and coat for you?' He hung them up in the hall, then led him into the lounge where he gestured to the elderly couple who were seated on the sofa. 'I'd like you to meet my father's closest friends. We've always regarded them as a part of the family. They flew in yesterday from America for the funeral. Nicky and Stella Ravallo.' He indicated the German beside him. 'This is Herr Hans Riedler.'

Ravallo reached for the walking stick he'd been forced to adopt under great protest ever since the stroke he'd suffered some years earlier. He brushed off Stella's hand when she tried to help him and hauled himself to his feet.

'You will not know me by name, but we have met before, albeit briefly, during the war,' Riedler said as Ravallo crossed the room towards him. 'The Grand Hotel. Palermo. 1942. Only then you were dressed as a Gestapo officer.'

'Major Hans Riedler of the German Third Parachute Regiment. Later of the Special Forces in North Africa. One of the most decorated German officers of the Second World War. Oh yes, I know you by name,' Ravallo said disdainfully, then levelled a trembling finger at Riedler. 'How dare you come here? And today of all days. Or are you here to gloat over Mac's death, just as you must have gloated over the deaths of his colleagues when you blew up their boat in 42? You disgust me.'

'Nicky, that's quite enough!' Stella said sharply as she got to her feet.

'You're lucky this is my godson's house, otherwise I'd already have thrown you out on to the street,' Ravallo hissed. 'It's where you and your Nazi kind belong. In the gutter.'

'Uncle Nicky, please,' McIndoe pleaded. He never really understood why he still insisted on calling his godfather 'Uncle'. Respect? Endearment? He couldn't say – it just seemed appropriate. He'd long since dropped the 'Aunt' when he addressed Stella. But it would always be 'Uncle Nicky' and consequently the rest of the family called him that as well, despite all Ravallo's attempts to get them to drop the prefix which infuriated him so much.

'Nicky, I think we should leave James and Mr Riedler alone,' Stella said, taking her husband's arm.

'Don't worry, I'm leaving,' Ravallo said, pulling his arm free of her light grip. He moved to the door, then turned back to his godson. 'And I'm not your goddamn uncle. So stop calling me that.'

'I'm so very sorry,' Stella said to Riedler with an embarrassed smile before going after her husband who'd already left the room.

'I can only apologize for Uncle Nicky's behaviour, Mr Riedler. He's never been the same since he lost his son four years ago. He was killed by friendly fire during the Gulf War. Uncle Nicky was devastated. He suffered a stroke within days of his son's death which changed his whole personality. He used to be a warm, generous man who lived life to the full. Now he's just a shadow of his former self. You get the feeling now he's all but given up on life. It's so sad.'

'He is lucky to have a wife who is prepared to stand by him during these dark hours,' Riedler said.

'Stella would never leave him, no matter how bad things got. Her determination reminds me so much of my own mother. I guess that explains why they were such close friends for over thirty years.'

'This is your mother?' Riedler asked, picking up a framed photograph on the mantelpiece.

'Yes, that's my parent's wedding photograph.'

'A very beautiful woman,' Riedler said, replacing it on the mantelpiece.

'In every way. She passed away twelve years ago.'

Heather entered the room carrying a tray. 'Please, won't you sit down, Mr Riedler? Would you care for some tea? Or a coffee perhaps?'

Riedler eased himself down into the nearest armchair. 'A coffee would be most welcome, thank you.'

'What part of Germany are you from?' Heather asked as she poured out a cup of coffee for him.

'My wife and I lived in Berlin for much of our married life, but two years ago we retired to my home town of Koblenz. You have heard of it?'

'I've heard of it, but don't ask me to place it on a map,' Heather said, handing him his coffee. 'I'm afraid geography was never my strong point.'

'It is in the Rheinland, south of Cologne. We have a small vineyard there.'

'Sounds lovely,' she replied.

Stella appeared in the doorway and shrugged dejectedly when McIndoe looked at her. 'He's in one of his moods. It's best just to leave him to it. The funeral's affected him a lot more than I thought it would. Perhaps with hindsight it wasn't such a good idea taking him on to the cemetery after the memorial service at the church.' Her eyes went to Riedler. 'I can only apologize for my husband's behaviour. It was quite unacceptable.'

'There is no need to apologize,' Riedler said, getting to his feet to address her. 'Mr McIndoe has already explained the situation to me. I am very sorry to hear of your loss.'

'Thank you,' Stella said to Riedler as she took a cup of tea from Heather. She'd been hooked on Earl Grey tea ever since she and Nicky had first visited Glasgow forty years earlier.

Riedler waited until she'd sat down before resuming his seat. 'I do not wish to intrude on your grief any more than is necessary, Mr McIndoe. Perhaps I could explain why I am here?'

'By all means,' McIndoe told him.

'I do not know whether your father ever told you, but he first contacted me back in the early Fifties when I was working for the BND, the West German Intelligence Service, to ask if I could find out the identity of the Gestapo's agent in the Italian Section of the SOE.'

'I don't remember him ever mentioning your name,' McIndoe replied, 'but then my father contacted so many people over the years in his on-going search for the truth that names became irrelevant after a while.'

'It is perhaps not surprising that you do not remember my name. I made several enquiries for him, but without success. We lost contact shortly after that, and it was not until last week while I was doing some research for an article I was preparing for *Der Spiegel* that I happened, quite by accident, to come across a file relating to the SOE operation in Sicily. It was then I remembered your father and his request all those years ago. When I rang him at his home he told me that he had recently suffered a heart attack and could not travel to Berlin to meet with me so I offered to bring the document to him here. We had agreed to meet at his house today, but when I went there a neighbour told me what had happened. I thought that having come all this way, I should at least pay my last respects to him. I did not want to intrude, so I remained in the background during the service. That is when you saw me.'

'I'm very glad you came,' McIndoe said. 'I know my father would have appreciated it.'

Riedler removed an envelope from his pocket and handed it to McIndoe. 'There are two documents, both relating to the identity of the Gestapo agent. I am afraid they are in German.'

'Then you'd better read them, Stella,' McIndoe said, handing the envelope to her.

'My German must be pretty rusty by now,' she said, removing her glasses from her handbag. Although both she and her husband had always listened dutifully to Sam McIndoe over the years when he'd recounted the latest developments in his endless quest for the truth, neither of them had ever become actively involved. It had never affected them in the same way. It hadn't been one of their colleagues who'd betrayed them. In effect, it was a very British affair, and they regarded it as such. Yet her hands were now trembling with excitement as she slit open the envelope. Then, slipping on her glasses, she removed the two sheets of paper and unfolded them in her lap. Both documents had been seized from Gestapo headquarters in the Piazza Bologni after Sicily had been overrun by the Allies in 1943. The first referred to a decapitated body which had been washed up on the shore three days after the MTB had been destroyed. A secret lining had been discovered in the flap of the corpse's belt-pouch. Inside was an oilskin envelope with a list of thirty transmitting and receiving station wavelengths. Six of them were positively identified as German, and one of those was for a secret transmitter at Gestapo headquarters in Palermo.

She turned her attention to the second document. Her eyes went no further than the first line and the name of the Gestapo's agent.

'Well, who was it?' McIndoe asked, desperate for the truth.

She looked up slowly at him. 'The Frenchman. Georges Passiere.'

'Passiere?' McIndoe replied incredulously. 'I don't believe it. Dad always said that, of the three, Passiere was the one he least suspected. He always thought the traitor was Bruce Hillyard.'

'So did Nicky,' Stella said. 'I had my own suspicions about Passiere until the incident when he claimed to have been attacked in the radio room. He was very convincing at the time. It certainly threw me.'

'Obviously a self-inflicted wound to deflect any suspicion away from himself after he'd radioed through to the Gestapo to give them the boat's coordinates,' McIndoe concluded. 'Very clever.'

'But why did the Gestapo kill him?' Heather asked. 'Surely he'd have been more useful to them alive.'

'I can answer that,' Riedler announced. 'The Gestapo suspected his cover was in danger of being blown. They could not take the chance of him being interrogated by the British.'

'The Gestapo certainly knew how to repay loyalty,' Heather said.

'It also explains why the Gestapo did not receive any information from him after you and your colleagues went ashore on your first mission,' Riedler said, addressing Stella. 'Your boat was anchored inside a cave, not so? The radio would have been useless in there. Too much interference.'

'So Charlie Higgins saved our lives out there,' Stella said thoughtfully. 'If he'd chosen to anchor in a sheltered inlet instead of the cave, Passiere would have been able to keep in touch with the Gestapo.'

'Does it say how he was recruited?' McIndoe asked, gesturing to the document in Stella's hand.

'Let's see,' she replied, scanning the page. 'Recruited while an active member of the Free French in December, 1940. Now this is interesting . . .' she said, nodding her head to herself.

'What is?' McIndoe asked in exasperation when she fell silent.

'Hmm?' she asked, looking up at him. 'Oh, sorry. Have you ever heard about the deplorable incident which occurred at Oran in 1940?'

'No, I can't say I have,' McIndoe replied.

'I'm not surprised. It's not something the British should be particularly proud of. After the French surrendered to

458

Germany in 1940, Churchill demanded that the French scuttle their four remaining ships – two battleships and two battle-cruisers – to prevent them from falling into German hands. The French refused and the four vessels took refuge in the Algerian port of Oran. Churchill despatched a heavily armed convoy to Oran where the French were again ordered to scuttle their ships. Again they refused and when they tried to break out of the harbour the British convoy was ordered to open fire on them. Of the four vessels, only the *Strasbourg* managed to escape. The other battleship was sunk and the two battle-cruisers were crippled. Over thirteen hundred French seamen perished. Passiere's best friend was amongst those drowned when the *Bretagne* capsized in shallow waters. That's what turned Passiere into a traitor. Not money or ideology. Revenge.'

'Surely the SOE would have learnt about Passiere's friend before they recruited him?' Heather said in surprise.

'How often did Dad say that the SOE's recruitment programme, especially in the early years of the war, was appallingly lax? The Dutch Section was infiltrated from the outset by the *Abwehr*. I'm certainly not surprised that Passiere was able to infiltrate the SOE with such ease. After all, he had the *Croix de Guerre*. That alone would have got him one foot in the door.' McIndoe turned to Riedler. 'What I don't understand is why Passiere's duplicity has only come to light now? If that information was available before, my father would have found it. Believe me, he would have found it.'

'Those documents were kept under lock and key in Germany at the behest of the British government. They were only released six months ago.'

'But why?' McIndoe asked.

'Did you know that Georges Passiere had a brother?' Riedler asked.

'I remember him mentioning it,' Stella replied. 'He was a senior officer with the Free French, wasn't he?'

'That is right,' Riedler said. 'Jacques Passiere. After the war he was appointed the deputy-director of the *Service de Reseignements* – the French Military Intelligence. He was promoted to director after three years and later brought into the de Gaulle government, where he held the powerful defence portfolio for several years. Only Jacques Passiere had been recruited by British Intelligence in 1946. The British knew he would be ruined if his brother's duplicity were ever made public. With Germany in financial ruin after the war, it would not have been difficult for the British to ensure that, in return for some or other favour, Georges Passiere's treachery was kept a secret until after his brother died. He died earlier this year. That is when the documents were made public.'

'How did you know Passiere's brother was an agent for British Intelligence?' Stella asked suspiciously.

'You get to find out these things as senior officer in the BND,' Riedler replied with an uninterested shrug, as if it were unimportant. 'It also explains why my queries were blocked when I tried to discover the identity of the Gestapo agent back in the Fifties.'

'If only Dad were here now,' McIndoe said wistfully, and smiled sadly at Heather when she squeezed his hand. 'You know as well as I do just how much this would have meant to him. To have finally known the truth.'

'Your father knew the truth before he died,' Riedler said. 'When I rang him last week he demanded that I read out both documents to him over the telephone. He told me he had waited fifty years for that moment and that he was not prepared to wait a minute longer. I was only coming out here to give him a copy of the documents and to reminisce over old times. After all, we never actually met. And that is something I will always regret.'

'I'm sure he felt the same,' Heather said as she cast a side-long glance at her husband. 'Don't you agree, James?'

James McIndoe just smiled. A contented smile. He knew now his father was finally at rest.